odyssey

odyssey

jack mcDevitt

ace books, new york

THE BERKLEY PUBLISHING GROUP
Published by the Penguin Group
Penguin Group (USA) Inc.
375 Hudson Street, New York, New York 10014, USA
Penguin Group (Canada), 90 Eglinton Avenue East, Suite 700, Toronto, Ontario M4P 2Y3, Canada
(a division of Pearson Penguin Canada Inc.)
Penguin Books Ltd., 80 Strand, London WC2R 0RL, England
Penguin Group Ireland, 25 St. Stephen's Green, Dublin 2, Ireland (a division of Penguin Books Ltd.)
Penguin Group (Australia), 250 Camberwell Road, Camberwell, Victoria 3124, Australia
(a division of Pearson Australia Group Pty. Ltd.)
Penguin Books India Pvt. Ltd., 11 Community Centre, Panchsheel Park, New Delhi—110 017, India
Penguin Group (NZ), Cnr. Airborne and Rosedale Roads, Albany, Auckland 1310, New Zealand
(a division of Pearson New Zealand Ltd.)
Penguin Books (South Africa) (Pty.) Ltd., 24 Sturdee Avenue, Rosebank, Johannesburg 2196,
South Africa

Penguin Books Ltd., Registered Offices: 80 Strand, London WC2R 0RL, England

This book is an original publication of The Berkley Publishing Group.

Text design by Kristin del Rosario.

First edition: November 2006

Library of Congress Cataloging-in-Publication Data

McDevitt, Jack.
Odyssey / Jack McDevitt.—1st ed.
p. cm.
ISBN 0-441-01433-X
1. Space ships—Fiction. I. Title.

PS3563.C3556O39 2006
813'.54—dc22

2006019259

PRINTED IN THE UNITED STATES OF AMERICA

10 9 8 7 6 5 4 3 2 1

Acknowledgments

I'm indebted to Michael Shara of the American Museum of Natural History, to David DeGraff of Alfred University, and to Athena Andreadis, author of *To Seek Out New Life* (Three Rivers Press, 1998), for technical assistance. To Howard Bloom, for his excellent *The Lucifer Principle* (Atlantic Monthly Press, 1995). To Ginjer Buchanan, for editorial support. To Ralph Vicinanza, for his continuing encouragement. Special appreciation to Walter Cuirle for the Origins Project. Thanks to Sara and Bob Schwager. And, as always, to my wife and in-house editor, Maureen.

Dedication

For Robert Dyke
The ultimate time traveler

prologue

ORDINARILY, JERRY CAVANAUGH would have been asleep in his cabin while the AI took the ship closer to the Sungrazer, the gas giant at Beta Comae Berenices. A world on fire, as the public relations people referred to it. And there was no denying it was a spectacular sight. This flight marked his eighty-eighth visit, and he never tired of looking at it.

The Sungrazer was a Jovian, four times more massive than Jupiter, with a tight orbit that took it literally through the solar atmosphere, where it burned and flared like a meteor. He marveled that the thing didn't explode, didn't turn to a cinder, but every time he came back it was still there, still plowing through the solar hell, still intact. The ultimate survivor.

It orbited its sun in three days, seven hours. When you got the angle of approach right, got black sky behind it, it became even more spectacular. Of course, the view on the ship's screens didn't reflect the view from the ship. In order to get the kind of perspective management wanted, that gave Orion Tours its reputation, the *Ranger* would have had to approach much closer to the sun than was safe. Instead, when the dramatic hour arrived, he would put the Sungrazer chip into the reader and people would look through the viewports and see images taken from the satellite. It was breathtaking stuff, and if it was a trifle deceptive, who really cared? Orion did not keep the method secret. Occasionally someone asked, and Jerry always told them, yes, the view they were getting was not really what it looked like from the bridge or through the ship's scopes. Too dangerous. This is what you would see if we could get in sufficiently close. But of course you wouldn't want that.

Of course not, they always replied.

That would not happen, of course, until tomorrow morning, when they made their closest approach. The tour was timed so that the visual changeover happened during the night, when the passengers were—usually—asleep in their cabins. At around seven or so, when they began getting up, the first thing they saw would be the Sungrazer, and it was probably the most dramatic moment of the entire flight.

He had thirty-six passengers, a full load, including three sets of honeymooners, seven kids fourteen or under, one clergyman who had saved for a lifetime to make the trip, one contest winner, and two physicians. The contest winner was a young woman from Istanbul who had never before been outside her native country. He wasn't clear on the precise nature of the contest, and his language skills did not allow explication. But she sat wide-eyed near the main display all during the approach.

JERRY HAD BEEN enduring sleepless nights on recent flights. He'd resisted going to see someone about it, but the condition had worsened this time out. On this last night before starting home, he hadn't been able to sleep at all, so he'd dressed and come up to the bridge, where he sat, paging listlessly through the library. The AI was silent. The navigation screens gave him views at several magnifications of the sun and the gas giant.

He heard muffled voices in one of the compartments. Then the ship was quiet again, save for the vents and the electronics.

This would be his last flight before retirement. The kids were grown and gone now, so he and Mara had thought about taking off somewhere alone, an extended vacation to Hawaii, but in the end they'd decided it would be nice to stay home. Jerry had lost whatever passion he'd had for travel. He'd settle for going down to the bridge club, and maybe eating dinner at the Gallop—

The AI's voice broke in: *"Jerry, we have activity at one eight zero."*

Jerry looked up at the screen carrying the feed from the after scope. The sky was brilliant, the Milky Way trailing into infinity.

"Sensor reading," said the AI. *"Objects approaching."*

"On-screen."

"They are *on-screen. If you look closely, you can see them."*

Dark objects moving against the stars.

"What are they, Rob?"

"Unknown."

"Asteroids?"

"They are artificial."

"Are you saying they're not ours?"

"I am merely saying I am not familiar with vehicles of this type."

"Moonriders."

"Are there such things?"

"Right now I'd say yes. They aren't on a collision vector, are they?"

"No. But they'll come close. Within twenty kilometers."

That was enough to scrape the paint. What the hell were those things?

"Range is twenty-two hundred kilometers and closing."

He counted eight of them. No, nine. Flying in formation like a flock of birds. Coming up his tailpipe.

Flying in formation. What natural objects fly in formation?

"They'll pass on the port side," said the AI.

"Anybody else supposed to be out here, Rob?"

"Negative. No other traffic scheduled."

"How fast are they coming?"

"Fifteen kilometers per second. They will reach us in two and a half minutes."

"Nothing on the circuit?"

"Not a sound."

"Okay. Let me know if anything changes. Meantime, let's get a close-up. I'd like to see what they look like."

The AI focused on the lead object. The others vanished off-screen. It was a sphere. Not much reflectivity. That was odd so close to the sun. *"Do we wish to alert the passengers?"* asked Rob.

There was no reason to believe the objects were dangerous. But he didn't like things he couldn't explain. He woke Mysha, his flight attendant, and told her what was coming. Then he flicked on the allcom. "Ladies and gentlemen," he said, "I'm sorry to disturb you, but we may have to maneuver. Please secure your harnesses."

The objects were in precise formation and, as he watched, all nine began to turn to starboard. Jerry delivered a string of expletives. "They're on a collision course."

"Not quite," said the AI. *"If they maintain present heading, they will still pass to port. The closest of them will approach to within two hundred meters."*

He thought about easing away. But it was probably not a good idea. The first law of successful navigation was that when somebody else was close by, make no surprise moves. "Hold steady," he told Rob.

"They are ninety seconds away."

He'd flicked on the bank of harness status lamps. Two of his passengers were still not belted down. "Rob?" he said.

"I will see to it."

Moonriders. He'd never taken their existence seriously. But there they were. "Rob, give me a channel."

"Jerry, I have been trying to contact them."

"Let me try."

"Channel is open."

The last two warning lamps winked off. Other lights came on. Some of his passengers wanted to talk to him.

Jerry took a deep breath. "This is the *Ranger*," he said. "Is anybody there? Please acknowledge."

He waited. But heard only static.

"They're slowing," said Rob.

BLACK GLOBES. HE could make out devices on the hulls, antennas, other equipment that might have been sensors, or weapons. They reformed themselves into a straight line running parallel to the course he was traveling. Still to port.

"Distance between units is four kilometers."

The first one passed.

"Antennas are pointed in our direction," said Rob.

And the second. They blinked quickly past, one every couple seconds. Then, as quickly as it had begun, it was over, and the line pulled well ahead of him. He watched them settle back into their vee.

"Phenomena of this type," said Rob, *"have been reported here and in several other locations over the past two years."*

"We have everything on the record?"

"Yes, Jerry."

Ahead, the globes were becoming hard to see. He got on the allcom. "Anyone on the port side will have seen unidentified vehicles passing. I don't know what they were, but they are gone now. However, I'd like you to stay belted in for the moment."

Moonriders. So named because they'd first been reported as dark shadows moving among the moons of Pollux IV. That had been forty years ago.

They were gone now. Like the tour ship, they seemed headed toward the Sungrazer. Sightseers from somewhere else?

PART ONE

macallister

chapter 1

> Wherever it is dark, there will always be strange lights. In primitive times, the luminescences were fairies. Then they became departing souls headed for paradise. Then UFOs. Now they're moonriders. It doesn't seem as if we ever grow up. Those imaginative souls reporting alien vessels circling the Pleiades cannot bring themselves to believe the anomaly might be anything so prosaic as a reflection. Or perhaps not enough ice in the Scotch.
>
> —Gregory MacAllister, "Slippery Slope"

Wolfgang Esterhaus squinted at the man at the bar, compared him with the picture in his notebook, and approached him. "Mr. Cavanaugh?"

The man was huddled over a beer. The glass was almost empty. He threw Esterhaus a surprised look, which quickly morphed into hostility. "Yeah? Who are you?"

"Name's Wolfie. Can I spring for another round?"

"Sure. Go ahead, Wolfie." His voice had an edge. "What did you want?"

"I'm with *The National*."

"Ah." The irritation intensified. "And what would *The National* want with me?"

"Just talk a bit." He signaled for two fresh glasses. "You work for Orion Tours, right?"

Cavanaugh considered the question, as if the answer required serious thought. "That's correct," he said. "But if you want to ask me about the moonriders, do it. Don't stand there and screw around."

"Okay." Wolfie was too professional to get annoyed. "I'm sorry. I guess you get hassled a lot these days."

"You could say that."

"So tell me about the moonriders."

"I doubt I can add anything to what you've already read. Or seen."

"Tell me anyhow."

"Okay. There were nine of them. They were round. Black globes."

"They weren't carrying lights of any kind?"

"Didn't you see the pictures?"

"I saw them."

"What did *you* see?"

"Not much." Wolfie hunched over the bar and looked at his own image in the mirror. He looked like a guy who could use some time off. "And they were in formation."

"Went past us one after the other, then lined up into a vee."

"You didn't see them again?"

"No." Cavanaugh was on the small side. Black hair, dark skin, carefully maintained mustache. Dark eyes that concentrated on the beer.

"How did the passengers react?"

"Only a couple of them saw anything. At the time it was happening, I don't think they thought anything about it. Only afterward, when I told them what it was."

"They didn't get scared?"

"Afterward, maybe. A little bit."

"How about *you*?"

"If I scared that easily, I'd find another line of work."

Esterhaus had always assumed that people who saw moonriders were lunatics. That the visual records they came back with were faked. But Cavanaugh looked solid, unimaginative, honest. Utterly believable.

Still, it was hard to account for the images on the record. Dark globes in formation. Furthermore, they'd been seen since by others.

Reginald Cottman, on October 3, while hauling cargo out to the Origins Project, halfway between 61 Cygni and 36 Ophiuchi. And Tanya Nakamoto, on another Orion Tours cruise, had seen them at Vega. A construction crew, four or five people, had reported a sighting a couple weeks ago at Alpha Cephei.

Physicists had been trying to explain them away without invoking extraterrestrials. The general public was excited, though of course it doesn't take much to do that. It was why *The National* was interested. Gregory MacAllister, his editor, didn't believe a word of it, but it was a hot story at the moment. And a chance to cast ridicule, which was what *The National* did best.

The reality was that this was a bad time for interstellar flight. Several bills were pending before Congress that would reduce funding for the Academy and other deep-space programs. The World Council was also talking about cutting back.

Meantime, the number of moonrider sightings was increasing. MacAllister suspected Orion Tours had tricked the passengers on Cavanaugh's ship, had put together an illusion, and he'd hired an ex-pilot to demonstrate how it could be done. It was, after all, only a matter of running some images past a scheduled flight. How hard could it be?

"Could it have been rigged?" Wolfie asked.

Cavanaugh finished his beer. "No. I was there. It happened just like I said."

"Jerry, how long have you been working for Orion?"

He looked at the empty glass, and Wolfie ordered more. "Sixteen years this November."

"Just between us, what do you think of management?"

He grinned. "They're the finest, most upstanding people I've ever known."

"I'm serious, Jerry. It won't go any further."

"They'd stab one another for the corner office. And they don't give a damn for the help."

"Would they cheat?"

"You mean would they pull off something like the moonriders if they could?"

"Yes."

He laughed. "Sure. If they thought it would help business, and they could get away with it." The beers came. Cavanaugh picked his up, said thanks, and drank deep. "But there's no way they could have made it happen."

"Without your help."

"That's exactly right."

LIBRARY ENTRY

. . . Yet there is palpable evidence for the existence of moonriders. There are visual records available to anyone who wants to look. It might be time to get serious and make an effort to find out what these objects are.

—*The Washington Post*, Monday, February 16, 2235

chapter 2

We have spent a half century now poking around the local stars. What we have found is a sprinkling of barbarians, one technological civilization that has never gotten past their equivalent of 1918, and the Goompahs, of whom the less said the better. Mostly what we have discovered is that the Orion Arm of the Milky Way is very big, and apparently very empty.

We have spent trillions in the effort. For what purpose, no one seems able to explain.

The primary benefit we've gotten from all this has been the establishment of two colonies: one for political wackos, and the other for religious hardcases. It may be that the benefits derived simply from that justify the cost of the superluminal program.

But I doubt it. Jails or islands would be cheaper. Education would be smarter.

Today, as we consider pouring more of the planet's limited wealth into this financial black hole, maybe we should pause to ask what we hope to gain from this vast investment. Knowledge? Scientists say there are no privileged places in the universe. If that is so, we are now in position to calculate, as the fanatics like to say, what's out there.

What's out there is primarily hydrogen. Lots of nitrogen. Rocks. A few spear-carrying cultures. And empty space.

It's time to call a halt. Put the money into schools. Rational ones that train young minds to *think*, to demand that persons in authority show the evidence for the ideas they push. Do that, and we won't need to provide a world for the Sacred Brethren who, given the opportunity, would run everyone else off the planet.

—Gregory MacAllister,
interviewed on the Black Cat Network,
Tuesday, February 17

It's a long way to Betelgeuse. One hundred ninety light-years, give or take. Almost three weeks in jump status. Plus a day or so at the far end to make an approach.

Abdul al Mardoum, captain of the *Patrick Heffernan*, usually had no objection to long flights. He read history and poetry and played chess with Bill, the AI, or with his passengers, if they were so disposed. And he put time aside for contemplation. The great void through which the Academy's superluminals traveled tended to overwhelm a lot of people, even some of the pilots. It was big and empty and pitiless, so they tried not to think about it but instead filled their days with talk of whatever projects lay ahead and diverted their evenings with VR. Anything to get away from the reality of what lay on the other side of the hull. But Abdul was an exception to the general rule. He loved to contemplate the cosmic vastness.

They were, at the moment, in transdimensional space, which was another matter. The void was gone, replaced by eerie banks of mist and an absolute darkness illuminated only by whatever light the ship might cast. All ships necessarily moved through the cloudscape at a leisurely pace. It was a physical law that Abdul didn't quite understand. The *Heffernan* might have been a sailboat adrift on the Persian Gulf. To Abdul, it was daunting, yet he accepted it as more evidence of the subtlety and providence of the Creator, of His care to leave pathways through a universe so vast that without their existence the human race would have been confined to its home sun.

It was the second week of the mission. Their destination was Betelgeuse IV, one of the oldest known living worlds. Intelligence had never developed there, at least not the sort of intelligence that uses tools and devises political arrangements. Because the biosystem was so ancient, it was of intense interest to researchers, who had established an orbiting station and were forever scrabbling about on the surface of the world, collecting samples to be taken to the orbiter and examined with relentless enthusiasm. The local life-forms did not use DNA, a fact of great interest to the biologists, though Abdul never understood that, either.

This flight, he realized, was going to be long. Usually he enjoyed these missions, took a kind of perverse pleasure in the solitude, looked forward to the conversations that the environment invariably stimulated. But this would be different.

The *Heffernan* was carrying four passengers, all specialists in varying biological fields. The senior man was James Randall Carroll, *Professor* Carroll, no casual intimacy, thank you very much. He was tall and a trifle bent. He was forever brushing his thin white hair out of his eyes. He smiled a lot, but you never got the sense he meant it. Despite his inclination toward formality, he wanted very much to impress his colleagues and Abdul. He did that by going on endlessly about the differences between terrestrial reptiles and their closest cousins on Betelgeuse IV.

There were, he would point out as though it really mattered, fascinating similarities in eye development, despite the differences in the local spectrum. Here, let me show you. And twenty minutes later they were into the feeding habits of warm-water reptiles. Or mating procedures. Or the curious and as-yet-unexplained diversity of propulsion methods by certain inhabitants of one of the southern swamp areas. Particularly annoying was his habit of periodically asking Abdul whether he understood, whether he grasped what the change in refraction really implied. The professor even followed him onto the bridge when he tried to retreat. (He'd made the mistake of inviting the four passengers to come forward anytime they liked, to see how the ship operated. It was a tradition, an offer he'd been making for years. But no more.)

Betelgeuse was approaching supernova stage. It would happen sometime during the next hundred thousand years or so, and Abdul found himself wishing it would happen while Carroll was in the vicinity. He'd like to see his reaction if the world, the swamps, and all its lizards, were blown to hell.

Abdul had been piloting Academy ships most of his career. He loved the job, loved carrying researchers to faraway places, loved watching their reactions when they saw the pale shrunken suns, or the supergiants, or the ring systems. He had no family, could not have had one and kept his career. It was the sacrifice he'd made. But it was well worth it. He treasured every mission. But Carroll was going to take this one from him.

"Abdul." It was Bill, the AI. *"We're getting fluctuations from the 25s."*

The 25s were the jump engines. They controlled action across the interface, in and out, and provided initial momentum after insertion. But once the *Heffernan* was under way through the clouds, they went into maintenance mode. There should not have been any fluctuations. "Can you see a problem, Bill?"

He blinked on. In his gray eminence persona. That meant he was trying to reassure Abdul everything was under control. Which scared the devil out of him. *"Don't know. I'm getting contradictory signals. Mixer's not running properly, but it appears the entire system is misfiring. Power levels are dropping."*

Abdul opened a channel to Union, the space station. "Ops immediate," he said. "This is the *Heffernan*. We are having engine problems. May have to abort flight." He closed the channel while he thought what else he wanted to say. "I've been with this outfit my entire life," he told the AI. "It's always been smooth riding. I'd like not to blow an engine now."

"Maybe you're due."

"Maybe." He opened the channel again but was startled to see the Academy logo blink on. And then an ops officer.

Odd coincidence. From out here, at a range of fourteen light-years, a transmission should take about eighteen minutes to reach Earth. So they couldn't have a reply already.

"Acknowledge your last," the ops officer said. Abdul stared, unbelieving, at his image. *"Leave the channel open. We'll stand by to assist."* The screen blanked. The lights on the hyperlink flashed and went off. *"The system's down,"* said Bill. *"Power surge."*

"Can you restore it?"

"Negative."

"How's the radio?"

"Radio's okay." Not that that would help if they were stranded out here. *"We are getting a prejump warning, Abdul. Four minutes."*

How did the reply come back so quickly? What was going on?

The jump engines were designed, in the event of a major problem, to terminate operations and return the ship to normal space. That was what the warning was about. Jump in four minutes. Nobody wanted to break down in hyperspace. If you did, no help could reach you. If the engines blew, you couldn't get out. Ever. He didn't know whether it had actually happened to anyone. Two ships *had* vanished during the seventy years or so that the superluminals had been in operation.

"Bill," said Abdul, hesitantly, "are we capable of making the jump safely?"

"I am optimistic."

Abdul opened the allcom so he could speak to his passengers. They were gathered in the common room, where Carroll was going on about predators in saltwater marshes. "Everybody buckle in," he said. "We have a minor engine difficulty, and we're going to jump back into normal space until we can get it resolved."

That got their attention. *"How big a problem?"* one of them asked.

"Not serious. Strictly nuisance value." He didn't really know that was true. There was, for example, an outside chance the engines could explode. And there was a somewhat better possibility that the jump would fail. That power levels were not sufficient to move the ship between dimensions. "We should be fine," he added, knowing before he'd finished the remark that it was the wrong thing to say.

"Can you fix it?" asked the youngest of his passengers, Mike Dougherty, who was just out of Bernadine. Nice kid. Of the four, Abdul suspected he was the one who'd really be missed if things went wrong.

"No. It has to go back to the shop, Mike." He heard them moving to the couches, heard the harnesses taking hold. "Sorry about the short notice. These things are automatic, so I've no control over them. But we'll be out the other side in a couple of minutes. Just sit tight." He activated his own harness. Bill's image disappeared. "Bill."

"Yes?"

"Are we by any chance not where we think we are?"

"It would seem to be the only explanation for the response from ops. We've apparently traveled a much shorter distance than we should have."

"Damn. What the hell's happening?"

"I suspect we haven't left the solar system."

Okay. Whatever. Under the circumstances, that might be a good thing. But the priority at the moment was to make a safe exit. He went through the check-off list with Bill, the readings on both sets of engines, fuel levels, pile temperature, probable entry vector, external mass indicator. If necessary, he could abort the jump. But everything was within the guidelines.

"One minute," Abdul told his passengers. "Everybody belted in? Please let me hear it." He did not have the warning lamps of the tour ships.

One by one, they replied. All set. But their voices betrayed a degree of nervousness. "How far out are we?" asked Carroll.

"We should be a bit over eighty light-years." Except that the response from ops had come back too quickly.

"Will they be able to find us?" asked Mike.

"Sure," he said. No reason why not. Abdul left the channel open. Heard Carroll comment that jump engines could be dangerous. *"My uncle was on a flight once—"*

"Ten seconds," said Abdul. He thought his voice sounded relaxed. Professional. Utterly confident.

LIBRARY ENTRY

There is no safer method of transport than superluminal. Since the passage of the Kern-Warburton Act, almost thirty years ago, there has not been a single documented case of catastrophic loss due to malfunction.

—*The Engineering Annual*, XXVII, p. 619

chapter 3

. . . So we have progressed to the point where we can move politicians around faster than light. I'm not sure I see the advantage.

—Gregory MacAllister, *Notes from Babylon*

They woke Priscilla Hutchins before dawn with word that the *Heffernan* was missing. Lost. We don't know where it is.

"How do you mean *lost*? It's in hyperflight."

"Something went wrong. They jumped out."

She was talking to the watch officer at the Academy. "Who's on duty at Union?"

"I got the news from Peter." That would be Peter Arnold, the watch supervisor.

"Patch me through." Hutch was already on her way down to her living room, pulling on a stylish satin robe that she kept specifically for these occasions.

"Hello, Hutch," Peter said, as she descended the stairs. *"We have no idea where they are."*

"That's Abdul's mission, isn't it?"

"Yes, ma'am."

"What happened?"

"We got a message from him about fifteen minutes ago. He said there was an engine problem. They were going to exit back into normal space."

"And you haven't heard from him since?"

"No, ma'am."

"Okay. Get me an estimate of his probable location, and let's start looking to see who else is in the area."

"Already working on it, Hutch."

She descended into her living room and switched to visual. Peter was a big, easygoing guy who had been an interior lineman during his college days. But at the moment he looked worried. "Where are they now? How far out?"

"About ninety light-years."

"Okay. I take it there's been no follow-up transmission?"

"No, ma'am, that's why I'm worried." His forehead was creased. *"The engines may have exploded. During the jump. Otherwise, we should have heard from him by now."*

"He may not have been able to get a message off right away. He has passengers to worry about. There's also a possibility the hypercomm failed."

"At the same time as the engines? I doubt it."

"The *Heffernan*'s a Colby class, Peter. The systems are interrelated. They could have gone down together. If so, they're adrift out there somewhere. Waiting for help to arrive."

"My God. If that's the case, it's not going to be easy to find them."

"You know precisely when communication stopped. If they made the jump successfully, that will tell you approximately where they are. More or less."

"Yes, ma'am."

"Scramble anything you can find. And, Peter—"

"Yes, Hutch?"

"Try not to let it get out. Keep me informed and let me know if you need anything."

SHE ALERTED MICHAEL Asquith, the Academy's commissioner. He listened patiently, commented that these things never seem to happen during business hours, and asked how serious she thought it was.

"They're probably okay," she said. "The ship's old, but the drive system is well designed. It's *possible* they got stranded in hyperspace, and it's possible the engines could have exploded. But either of those eventualities is unlikely. They're almost certainly adrift somewhere. But without communications."

"They have radio?"

"Probably."

"But the search area's too big for radio?"

"It won't be easy if that's all they have."

"Okay," he said. *"Stay on top of it. And keep me informed."* He signed off. At the moment, there was nothing more to do, so she went back to bed. But she didn't sleep.

She gave up eventually and headed for the shower. She was covered with soap when Peter called back. They'd worked out the search area. It was *big,* but that was inevitable because of the vagaries associated with hyperflight, and the fact they didn't have the precise moment when the *Heffernan* made its jump. *"But we caught a break,"* said Peter. *"The* Wildside *is in the immediate area. They can be on the scene early Tuesday morning. We couldn't have planned it better.*

"The al-Jahani *is also in the neighborhood, so I've diverted them as well."* The *al-Jahani* was an Academy ship, on its way back from Quraqua. It had passengers on board, but there'd be room for the *Heffernan* people if a pickup was necessary. As seemed likely.

She updated Asquith. Got him out of bed to do it. He listened, frowned, nodded, shook his head. *"Let's keep the lid on this,"* he said, *"until we know what's happening."*

"I've cautioned our people, Michael. But we're not going to be able to sit on it long. The story's too big."

"Do what you can."

"You might want to think about holding a press conference later this morning. Tell the media what we know. Control things a bit. It's just a matter of time before it gets out."

"Okay," he said. *"See to it."*

"Michael," she said, making no effort to hide her annoyance, "Eric works for *you*."

He nodded. *"Coordinate with him. Make sure he has everything he needs."*

* * *

THERE WAS STILL no word from the *Heffernan* when she got to the office an hour later. Not a good sign. She turned on her desk lamp, said hello to Marla, her AI, and collapsed into a chair.

If Abdul's hypercomm was down, they had a serious problem. They could not precisely compute the ship's position in hyperspace. Where transdimensional space was concerned, there was always a fudge factor. Academy pilots were trained, in the event they had to exit, to send a message immediately before they took the action. His failure to do so left them operating from guesswork.

Vehicles moving through hyperspace traveled at an equivalent rate of approximately 1.1 billion kilometers per second. Not knowing precisely when Abdul made his jump meant they could be anywhere along a track billions of kilometers long. Abdul and his people might be pretty hungry by the time help arrived.

She listened to the original message, in which Abdul said he was having engine trouble, and they were going to make their jump. And she decided she was worrying unnecessarily. The guy was a veteran, and he was telling them he was seconds away from pulling the trigger. The *Wildside* should have no trouble finding them.

Nothing more she could do. Outside it was still dark. She let her head drift back and closed her eyes.

"Hutch," said Marla. *"Sorry to interrupt. You've a call from Eric."*

Eric Samuels was the Academy's public relations director. He held the job primarily because he had an engaging smile and a reassuring manner. Everybody liked Eric. When he was in front of an audience, you knew things were going to be okay. He was about average size, black hair, blessed with the ability to sound utterly sincere no matter what he was saying. Curiously, his private manner was at contrast with the public persona. He was a worrier, his gaze tended to drift around the room, and you always got the feeling the situation was headed downhill. His subordinates didn't dislike *him*, but they didn't like working for him. Too nervous. Too excitable. *"Do you really think it blew up?"* he asked.

"I hope not, Eric. We just don't know yet."

"Have we started notifying the families?"

That was the problem, wasn't it? The families would assume the worst no matter what they were told. "No," she said. "When do you plan to talk to the media?"

"At ten. We can't wait any longer than that. I understand the story's already gotten out."

Moments later she had another call. *"Cy Tursi,"* Marla said. Tursi did the science beat for the *Washington Post. "Wants you to get right back to him. And hold on, there's another one coming in. Hendrick, looks like."*

Hendrick was *Newsletter East.* "Refer them to Eric, Marla. And get me the commissioner."

"He's not in his office yet."

"Get him anyway. And I need to see the passenger manifest for the *Heffernan.* And a next-of-kin list for them and for Abdul."

Asquith's voice broke in on her: *"What is it, Priscilla?"* He always used her given name when he was annoyed with her.

"The story's getting out. We need to notify the families."

"I know. I'd appreciate it if you'd take care of it. Personally. Tell them all we know is we lost contact. No reason for alarm."

"I'd be alarmed."

"I'm not worried about you. Anything else?"

"Yes. I assume you've talked to Eric."

"Not within the last hour."

"Okay. The press conference is scheduled for ten."

"Good. I'm going to want Eric to keep it short. Just read them a statement and maybe take no questions. What do you think?"

"Michael, we can't get away with that. Not in this kind of situation." She pointed to the coffeemaker, and the AI turned it on.

"Okay. Maybe you're right. I hope he's careful out there. I'm not sure you shouldn't do it."

"If you change the routine, you just ratchet things up. Eric'll be fine."

"Okay."

"Michael."

"Yes?" He was wishing the situation would go away.

"After I talk with the families, I'll want some time with you. Are you on your way in?"

He sighed. *"I'll be there."*

Hutch was in her sixth year as director of operations. She'd had to make these sorts of calls after the losses at Lookout, and when the *Stockholm* had bumped into the dock at the Origins Project and killed a technician. In past years, talking to families had been a duty assumed by the commissioner, but Michael had delegated it to her, and it was just as well. She squirmed at the prospect of wives and kids getting bad news from him. He was a decent enough guy, but he was always at his worst when he was trying to be sincere.

SHE CALLED PETER first, but he still hadn't heard anything. So she started making the calls. Get it done before the press conference begins.

It was painful. In all five cases, as soon as she identified herself, they *knew*. Two were in the NAU, where it was still an ungodly hour, and that alone screamed bad news. The others were across the Atlantic. They took one look at her and eyes widened. Fearful glances were exchanged with whoever else was present. Voices changed timbre.

In the case of one of the researchers, the wife had come out of a classroom, where she was conducting a seminar of some sort. She came close to cardiac arrest as Hutch explained, as gently as she could, then had to connect with the front office to get help for her.

Among the four passengers, three had never before been in Academy ships. One near-adult child told her that he *knew* something like this would happen, that he'd pleaded with his father to stay home.

When at last it was over, she sat exhausted.

THE SUN WAS well over the horizon when she cornered Asquith in his office. "Do we have any news yet, Priscilla?" he asked.

"Not a word."

He took a deep breath. "Not good." Asquith was a middle-aged guy who was always battling his weight, and whose primary objective in running the Academy was to stay out of trouble. Keep the politicians happy and continue to collect his paycheck. His doctorate was in political science, although he never disabused people of the notion he was a physicist or a mathematician.

The first thing Abdul should have done after the jump would have been to send a message. Let everybody know he was okay. And where he was. The silence, as the saying goes, was deafening.

Asquith was behind his desk, keeping it between them. "The

Colby-class ships," she said, "are no longer safe. We need to scrap them."

He reacted as if she'd suggested they walk on the ceiling. "Priscilla," he said, "we've had this conversation before. We can't do that. You're talking about half the operational fleet."

"Do it or cut the missions. One or the other."

"Look. We're under a lot of pressure right now. Can we talk about this later?"

"Later might get somebody killed. Look, Michael, we don't really have a third alternative. We either have to scale things back or replace the ships."

"Neither of those is an option."

"Sure they are." She stared at him across the wide expanse of his desk. "Michael, I'm not sending anybody else out on the Colbys."

"Priscilla, I'll expect you to do what the missions require."

"You'll have to find someone else to do it."

His face hardened. "Don't force me to take action we'll both regret."

"Look, Michael." She was usually even-tempered, but she kept thinking about Abdul and his passengers when the alarms went off. "I knew before the *Heffernan* went out that it wasn't safe."

He looked shocked. "You didn't tell me that."

"Sure I did. You just don't listen unless I beat on the table. The whole Colby line is unsafe. We're taking people's lives in our hands. You and me. It's time to go talk to your friends on Capitol Hill."

"All right," he said. "Okay. Keep calm. Take a look at what you think we have to do. Give me a plan, and we'll go from there. I'll do what I can."

MOST OF THE reporters were scattered around the world in remote locations, but twenty or so showed up physically for the briefing, which was being held on the first floor of the conference center. Hutch watched from her office.

Eric, who pretended to believe Michael Asquith was a leader of uncommon ability, made a brief opening statement, reiterating what the journalists had by then already learned, that the *Heffernan*, while in hyperspace, had apparently developed a problem with her engines, and was currently unaccounted for. *"The* Wildside *is on its way, and will be on-site within twenty-four hours. The* al-Jahani *is also close by. We're optimistic everything will be okay."*

The first question, the one they all knew was coming, was asked by the *New York Times*: *"Eric, there've been reports of breakdowns throughout the Academy fleet recently. Just how safe are the starships? Would you put your family in one?"*

Eric managed to look surprised that anyone would ask. *"Of course,"* he said. *"People are safer in Academy vessels than they are crossing the street in front of their homes."*

The *Roman Interface* inquired whether the Academy fleet might be getting old.

"The ships are tried and proven." Eric smiled, as if the question was foolish. No reason for concern. *"If we thought any of our ships had become untrustworthy, we'd pull them out of service. It's as simple as that. Robert?"*

Robert Gall, of Independent News: *"What actually happened out there? Why'd the engines fail?"*

"It's too soon to say. We'll conduct an investigation as soon as we're able. And the results will be made public." He signaled a young brunette in the front row.

Her name was Janet and she worked for the *Sidney Mirror*: *"Is there any truth to the story that funding cuts are responsible for the recent spate of accidents?"*

"Janet, a few cases of mechanical malfunction do not constitute a spate of accidents. No, we have everything we need to perform our mission."

"And how do you perceive your mission, Eric?" This came from Karl Menchik, who represented one of the Russian outlets and who, Hutch suspected, was a plant, accredited to ask softball questions and get Eric off the hook.

"To take the human race to the stars," he said. *"To set out across the infinite sea, to land on distant shores, and to report what's out there."*

It could have come right off one of the monuments.

LIBRARY ENTRY

Interstellar flight has run its course. It has been a harmless diversion for the better part of a century, but it is time to move on. Sea levels are rising, famine is common in many parts of the globe, thousands of people die every day from a range of diseases for which cures exist but for various reasons are not available, and population continues to outrun resources. A quarter of the global population is illiterate.

It is time to rearrange priorities. We should begin by recalling the superluminals, which contribute nothing toward creating a better life for the planet's inhabitants. Let's put the exploration effort aside for the present. Let's concentrate on solving our problems at home before we go wandering off to other worlds whose existence have no impact on anyone other than a few academics.

—*Venice Times*, lead editorial, Monday, February 16

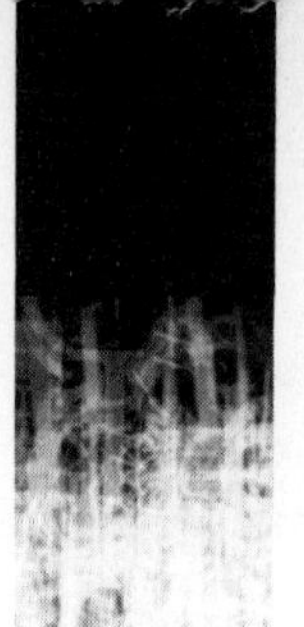

chapter 4

We're a population of dunces. Consider the level of entertainment available to the home. The single most valuable skill in showbiz seems to be the ability to fall, with panache, on one's face.

—Gregory MacAllister, *Life and Times*

"I believe him."

MacAllister stared down out of the taxi at the network of bridges and islands that was modern Tampa. "No question in your mind, Wolfie?"

"Well, you know how it is, Mac. I wouldn't bet the house, but yeah, I'd have a hard time believing it didn't happen exactly the way he said it did."

Below him, the city was a complex network of canals. Beautiful from the air. A prime example of the human capability to make art out of bad news. But the oceans were still rising, and they'd have to redesign the place yet again when the ice cap went into the water or the next big hurricane came along.

Homo imbecilus.

"So are we going to do the story?"

"Hell, Wolfie, what's the story? What do we have to say? That somebody's out there riding around in black ships?"

"That's what it's beginning to look like."

"Wolfie, you have any idea how that sounds?"

"Yeah, I do. Doesn't mean there isn't something to it."

"It's bogus. You have a combination of slick corporate types who want the government to put more money into space, and a general population that will believe anything. But go ahead. Run with it. See what you can come up with."

IT FIT WITH an idea for a new book, a history of human gullibility. In eighty-six volumes. How people make things up, and other people buy in. Organized religions. Notions of national or racial superiority. Political parties. Economic boobery. Whole armies, for example, who thought they could earn indulgences by killing Arabs. Or the seventeenth-century Brits who concluded they were intended by God to carry His truth to the benighted. Or the lunatic Jihadists of the twentieth and twenty-first centuries. People still believed in astrology. And in cures that medical science didn't want you to know about.

He was on a book tour, promoting *Guts, Glory, and Chicken Soup*, a collection of his essays. It had been a profitable trip so far. Readers had lined up in fourteen cities across the North American Union to buy his book and tell him they shared his views on politicians, college professors, bishops, the media, school boards, corporate service centers, professional athletes, and the voters. Well, some of them did. Others came to yell at him, to call him a rabble-rouser and an atheist and a threat to the welfare of the nation. In Orlando the previous evening he'd been told his mother must be ashamed (which, curiously enough, was true), and that no decent person would read his books. One woman offered to pray for him.

But they were buying *Guts and Glory*. It was jumping off the shelves. *I wouldn't read it myself, but I have a deranged brother.* Sometimes they brought pies or whipped cream, hoping to get a clear shot at him, but the dealers knew feelings ran high when he was in town, so they disarmed everyone coming in the door.

In Houston, the mayor, anticipating his arrival, had given an interview saying no person was so disreputable that he wasn't welcome in that fine city. The *Boston Herald* advised readers planning to attend the signing at Pergamo's to keep their children home. In Toronto, a church group paraded outside the bookstore with signs telling him he was welcome at service if he wanted to save his soul.

He was used to it. Enjoyed it, in fact.

The taxi started down. MacAllister realized he was hungry. It was getting on to midmorning, and he hadn't had anything other than toast and orange juice. He was scheduled to appear as a guest on Marge Dowling's *Up Front* before going over to Arrowsmith's later that afternoon for the signing. The show was at ten.

It was a bright, pleasant day. In February, Florida was always bright and pleasant. He hated pleasant weather. A little of it was all right, but he liked storms and snow, heavy winds, downpours. He didn't understand why its residents didn't move north.

The taxi settled onto the roof of Cee Square Broadcasting. MacAllister paid up and climbed out. One of the staff appeared in a doorway and hurried over to greet him. Good to see you, Mr. MacAllister. How was your flight from Orlando? We've been looking forward to having you on the show.

The guy couldn't even pretend to be sincere. He was scared of MacAllister, and his voice was squeaking. MacAllister could have put him at ease, but he resisted the temptation.

Marge waited downstairs. She delivered the standard embrace that was not quite an embrace. Nothing touched him but fingertips and one cheek. She was tall, with dark hair and dark eyes, carried away by her self-importance. The sort of woman who'd have been okay had she stayed home and baked cookies. Everything with her was an act. Her enthusiasm at seeing him, her pretenses at modesty ("So good of you to spend some time with us, Mac"), even her accent. She'd been born and reared in Minnesota, but she sounded like someone who'd be going home after work to the plantation. "Mac," she said, "it's been a long time."

Not long enough. But her show provided a perfect format for him. There'd be a second guest, someone who would be expected to provide contrasting views to his own. In past years, the guests had been local champions of social uplift, whom he'd dismembered at leisure. The primary topic for that day's show was to be interstellar expansion, and his opponent would be an Academy pilot. A woman, no less. When he'd first heard, he'd thought it might be Hutch, but it wasn't. And he was relieved. He wouldn't feel right sticking barbs into an old friend in front of a large audience.

She got him fresh coffee and turned him over to the makeup people. "See you in a few minutes, Mac." In his case, makeup was a joke. He had a commanding presence, always looked good, and had no need of cosmetics. But the producers insisted.

Right. MacAllister sat down, and a young woman who should have had better things to do with her life tried to take the shine off his nose. When she was done, a guide took him to the green room, where he sat down, exposed to *The Morning Show*, a network offering with two people going on about a kidnapping in Montana. Then the guide came back for him and led him through a side corridor into a studio. Three leather chairs were placed around a table. The walls were paneled. When the picture was transmitted, they would appear to be filled with leather volumes. One would have a fireplace. If the fireplace didn't alert the viewer it was all a scam, MacAllister couldn't imagine what would.

A kid producer sat in one of the chairs, studying a script. He jumped up when he saw MacAllister and shook hands a bit too enthusiastically. "It's a pleasure to have you back, Mr. MacAllister," he said.

"Thank you."

The kid looked at his notes. "You're going to try to explain why we shouldn't be spending tax money to support the Academy? Am I right?"

"I can do that," said MacAllister. He didn't like to think of it quite that way. And he considered informing the producer there might be a middle ground somewhere. But in the larger scale of things, his opinion didn't count anyhow. The politicians made the decisions, and the voters paid no attention.

Marge came in, carrying a copy of *Guts, Glory, and Chicken Soup*. She had changed clothes and was smartly set out in shades of brown and blue, white collar, gold bracelet. "They told you we were going national?" she said.

"No. Why? What happened?"

"The *Heffernan*. It's become a big story."

"And *I've* become an expert?"

"Oh, Mac, it's not you. Valentina is an Academy pilot." She glanced at a clock. "Our segment will be twenty-two minutes plus break time."

"I assume Valentina is the other guest?"

"Yes. It turns out to be nice timing."

"I assume they haven't heard anything yet? About the *Heffernan*?"

"Not a word. Our sources tell us things are a bit rattled at the Academy. This may not have a happy ending."

MacAllister tried to remember the details. "Five on the ship. Was that what I heard?"

"Yes. It's one of the research missions."

"Pity. I'm sorry to hear it."

She looked down at the book. "My people tell me this is hell on wheels," she said. She'd probably read it, but she was sending MacAllister a message. You don't intimidate me, big fella. "How's the tour been going?"

"Okay." He pulled out a chair and sat. "How's life in showbiz?"

"Same as always." She was all warmth and charm. "I suspect you'll be glad to get home, Mac. Are you free for lunch today?"

MacAllister thought about it. Actually he'd prefer to eat alone, but it was to his benefit to keep Margie happy. "Sure," he said, "that would be nice. I know you're very popular here, though." A little stroking never hurt. "Can we find a place where the peasants won't recognize you?"

"No problem," she said. "We'll go over to Carmen's."

WITH ABOUT THREE minutes to go, the kid producer came in and rearranged the seating. "You're here," he told MacAllister, moving him to his right. "It gives you the library backdrop. You'll look very literary. Exactly the effect we want." He checked his notes. "Just relax."

Irritating little squeak.

Marge seated herself in the center, asked what the next book would be, but pressed her finger over her earpiece before he could answer. "Valentina's here," she said. "She'll be right in."

"What's her last name?"

"Kouros. She says her friends call her 'Valya.' She's Greek."

"Okay."

"You'll like her."

"I'm sure I will." MacAllister couldn't imagine why anyone would want to spend most of her waking hours sitting in a tin can traveling between Tampa Bay and Arcturus. Priscilla Hutchins had spent years doing that. As women went, Hutch was no dummy, but she couldn't have been all that smart.

He heard voices in the adjoining room. A woman appeared at the door, talking to someone he couldn't see. She was a striking creature, tall and athletic. The sort of woman who had probably starred on her college soccer team. She finished her conversation, nodded, and came in. A hand closed the door behind her.

Valentina had red hair, intense blue eyes, sculpted cheeks, and she looked at MacAllister as if she thought there was something vaguely comical about him.

Marge did a quick set of introductions. Valentina spoke with a mild accent. She said she was pleased to meet him, but she didn't seem to know who he was. Poor woman needed to keep up. The producer, now sealed in the control room, was whispering into a mike.

Marge signaled they should leave the studio. "We want to make an entrance," she said, leading them off to the right. "What we'll do," she said, "is talk about the Academy's mission, whether starflight is safe, what we're getting from it, and so forth." She smiled at them both. "Try not to agree with one another any more than you have to."

Somebody was doing the weather. While they waited, they did some small talk. Valentina had been piloting for the Academy twelve years; she was originally from the Peloponnesus; and she had the impression MacAllister might once have flown with her.

"Not me," he said. "I've only been off the planet once."

"You've missed quite a lot," she said.

Red lights flashed, the show's theme music came up, he heard a voice telling viewers they were watching the 282nd edition of *Up Front* with Marge Dowling. Fingers pointed their way, and Marge returned to the set while a virtual audience applauded enthusiastically. She welcomed the greater Tampa Bay area, and the nation at large, and summoned first Valya, then MacAllister. They took their assigned seats while she reviewed the latest update, which was that the *Heffernan* was still missing. She went on to provide some background on the mission, why they were going to Betelgeuse, how big the star was, and so on. MacAllister's eyes started to glaze over. What he was willing to go through to sell a few books.

* * *

THE FIRST QUESTION went to Valentina: "We've had starflight now for more than two generations. The common wisdom is that superluminals are a safe form of transportation. Is that true?"

"Yes," she said. "I know how this sounds in light of the event you just reported. But nevertheless, considering the distances traveled, there is no safer mode of transportation in existence."

MacAllister rolled his eyes. "What is it, Mac?" Marge asked.

"Look out for statistics," he said. "At the beginning of the space age, the first space age back in the twentieth century, they used to measure transportation safety by the number of fatalities per passenger-mile. Using that method, the safest form of travel in 1972 was the Saturn moon rocket. We don't really want to measure distance. If you simply count fatalities against the number of flights, the superluminals don't look quite so good."

Valentina sighed. "You're right, Gregory," she said, putting a slight stress on the name, informing him he was out of his league here. "You can prove pretty much anything statistically. I've been riding the Academy's missions all my adult life, and I never have a qualm." She smiled. "And I've never lost anybody. Nor has anyone I know lost anybody."

Her adult life probably consisted of about fifteen years, but he let it go.

"What's your best guess?" Marge asked. "How serious is this *Heffernan* thing? How's it going to turn out?"

"I think we'll find them," she said. "It's just a matter of getting to the area where they were lost and picking up a radio signal. Of course you never really know, but it shouldn't be a problem."

"I hope not," said MacAllister. "But the real issue here is, why do we bother to go out there at all? What's the point?"

Marge tossed the question to Valentina.

"This is our backyard," she said. "We'd be remiss not to look around. To see what's there."

"Our backyard," said MacAllister, "by your reckoning is pretty big. And I can tell you what's there: rock and hydrogen. And empty space. And that's it. We've spent billions on starflight, and we have nothing to show for it. Zero."

Valentina looked as if he were being irrational. He drew a condescending smile from her. "A year ago," she said, "we intercepted an omega cloud that would eventually have destroyed the planet. I know Mr. MacAllister thinks that is of no real consequence, but I'm sure your viewers would have their own opinions.

"We also rescued the Goompahs. You've probably forgotten that, Gregory." Again that offbeat stress on his name. Poor Gregory. He's not too bright.

"Saving the planet is good," MacAllister said with a straight face. "But it's done. I'm obviously glad we were able to do it. That doesn't mean we should stay out there indefinitely, at an escalating cost to the taxpayer. Look: There are millions of people in undeveloped countries who never get a decent meal. Every time we wipe out one plague, we get another. Meantime, the oceans continue to rise. They're talking about a collapse of the Antarctic ice shelf within the next ten years. If that goes, folks in Pennsylvania are going to get their feet wet. Right now, we charge back and forth between Sirius and the Dog Star—"

"Sirius *is* the Dog Star," said Valentina.

"And what do we have to show for it? We get a physical description of another place nobody cares about."

"You want to save us from the greenhouse problem—?"

"Of course."

"And from famine?"

"That would seem to be a good idea."

"Solving either problem will require technology. We can learn a great deal more about planetary maintenance by studying what goes on elsewhere. We have to do more now than simply raise the cities another three or four meters. We have to find a way to get control of the climate. That means experimentation. But I don't think we want to be conducting experiments of that nature at home."

"I think, Valentina, that may be a little over the top."

"Maybe. But if you're right, and nobody really cares what's out there, I wonder whether we're even worth saving."

MACALLISTER FOUND HIMSELF thinking of Hutchins sitting in her office at the Academy. She wouldn't be watching this live, but she'd hear about it, would probably see it that evening. So he tried to go easy. But it wasn't in his nature. Pouring big money into starflight at a time like this was unconscionable. And dumb.

"Dumb?" said Valentina. "You remind me of the guys in the Spanish court who said something like that about Columbus."

"In those days," he said, "you could breathe the air in America. It makes a difference. I say, if people want to go to the Big Dipper, let them buy their own canoe."

"You're talking as if only a few of us have gone to the stars. In fact thousands of people have experienced superluminal flight. And anyhow it's not really individuals who've gone to Arcturus, it's the species. We've *all* gone."

"Tell that to the people on East Fifty-third in the Bronx."

"Gregory, we're wired to go. You and I can sit here and talk all we like, but that won't change anything. There's a destiny involved. We could no more *not* go than you could sit through a conversation like this and not say a word."

He sighed. "When people start talking about destiny, it means their argument has hit the wall. What we should do is get the people who are always going on about the stars, pile them onto a few ships, and let them go colonize Alpha Boobus III. With the single proviso that they stay there."

IT'S MORE OR less traditional after these on-air debates to shake hands after the show. MacAllister had even gone for drinks occasionally with people with whom he'd conducted blistering debates. This one had been innocuous enough, but Valentina wasn't a professional. She took everything personally, and when Marge congratulated them on a good performance, the Academy pilot glanced at him as if he were not worth her time, said *good day* in a voice an octave lower than the one she'd used during the show, and stalked out of the studio.

Normally, MacAllister was proof against beautiful women. They were okay for ordinary males, but they could prove a major distraction for somebody who operated at his level. Still, he liked to be admired by the fair sex, enjoyed the occasional come-hither glance, and was inevitably willing to follow up on the invitation so long as he could see no downside. But when Valentina strode out in that uncivil manner, his feelings were hurt.

And there again was evidence of the damage women could do. Had she been a male, he wouldn't have given a damn. As it was, riding back to the hotel in his cab, he sat uncomfortably holding up his end of a conversation with the publisher's rep, wishing Valentina had been a better sport about things.

Female star pilot.

He owed his life to one of those. And he resented that, too.

He wondered what Hutch was going to think about his performance.

Damn.

MACALLISTER'S DIARY

I can't imagine why the peasants are so upset about enhancement. It doesn't work. Anybody who looks could see that. A recent study showed that approximately 8 percent of people who are products of the technique failed to graduate high school. Fifteen percent can still find time on a regular basis to watch talk shows. And almost half describe themselves as sports fans. If people want smart kids, they might try reading to them.

The reality is, we don't want our kids to be smart. We want them to be like us. Only more so.

—Monday, February 16

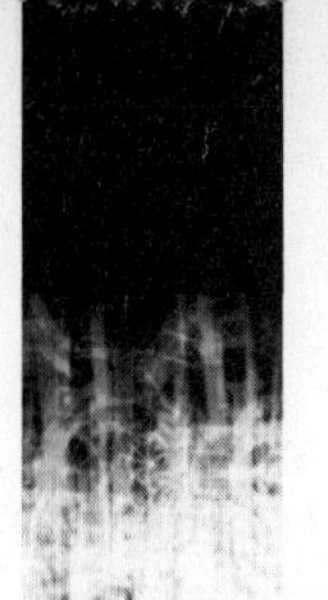

chapter 5

> Most government and corporate leaders would have trouble getting people to follow them out of a burning building. One way you can tell the worst of them is that they talk about leadership a lot. I doubt Winston Churchill ever used the word. Or, for that matter, Attila the Hun.
>
> —Gregory MacAllister, "First Man Out of Town"

"Hutch, I keep thinking about the *Heffernan*. We'll have to get rid of Louie Alvarez." Asquith sucked in air, a gesture designed to indicate firing Louie was a painful necessity.

"Why?" she asked.

"It's a maintenance failure." He shook his head. Pity. "But there's no way around it."

"It's not his fault."

"How do you know? You haven't looked into it yet."

"Nor have you. Louie's warned us repeatedly that something like this was inevitable. When it turns out that he can't work miracles, that four of those ships have slipped past their termination dates, then we'll have to find another excuse."

"Is that true? Four of them?"

"Yes. You have several memos on the subject."

"Is the *Heffernan* among them?"

"No. Not yet. Give it a few months."

"Then we're off the hook." He came around the desk, vastly relieved. Everything's going to be all right. "Hutch, you and I have been through a few problems over the last year or so. Let's calm down. Keep cool about this."

"People's lives are involved, Michael."

"I know that. And I'm not suggesting we put anyone at risk. Let's just not get excited. What we need to do is concentrate more on maintenance." He patted his stomach and let his gaze wander over the various plaques and trophies on display. It was the way he reassured himself of his capabilities. "Look, let's get the *Heffernan* back. Then we'll figure out where we go from here."

She got up, started for the door, but stopped short of the sensor area. Didn't want the door open yet. Asquith had already gone on to something else, was looking down at a stack of folders, signaling that the interview was over. He was not an impressive figure. Barely taller than Hutch. His thin brown hair was combed carefully over his scalp. He'd just been through a messy public divorce, one of those ugly things with his wife claiming adultery and demanding a huge settlement while he maintained she was deranged. Everything had been played out in the media amid rumors that there was pressure on him to resign. Hutch wouldn't have been unhappy to see him go, but she knew what political appointments usually were, and she'd prefer dealing with Asquith, who was at least open to argument.

He knew she was standing there, and his eyes rose to meet her. "Something else?" he asked.

There was a silent plea in the way he asked the question. Please don't make waves. "Louie stays where he is. And I'm starting the administrative procedure to take the Colbys out of service. You'll have to sign off on some of it."

He shook his head. "No. I told you we can't do that. Not possible. Look, call them in if you want, check them as each one reports. Make sure they're okay."

"We already do, Michael. It's the routine."

When he got frustrated, he literally threw up his hands. He did that now. "We need to make sense," he said. "We don't have enough ships as it is to carry out the missions."

She stood her ground. "Then do what you said you would. Put

some pressure on the politicians. They want the programs, they have to be willing to fund them."

"I'm *doing* that, Priscilla. What do you think I do up here?"

She wasn't sure, but she knew it had nothing to do with pressuring people above him. "Talk's not enough," she said. "We need to cut back. We can reduce survey operations. Maybe stop them altogether until somebody comes up with some money."

"Or they call our bluff."

"Don't make it a bluff, Michael." That was the problem with him. Even if he did threaten, nobody would take him seriously. "We have to mean it. We can also stop hauling research and support personnel around. And shut down the Nok mission. We don't need it. What are we learning from those idiots anyhow?" The Noks were eternally shooting at one another while humans mostly hid and took notes. "And I'll tell you something we could cut that would make the point. Stop our support for the Origins Project." Origins was a largely European effort, a hypercollider under construction out on the other side of 36 Ophiuchi.

He rubbed the back of his hand against his mouth. "I'm not sure I'd want to go that far." Origins had the potential to confirm or reject various long-held speculations about the nature of the universe. Unfortunately, none of them held promise for showing a monetary profit. Because they were blue-sky operations, the most that could be said was that *maybe* there would be a practical benefit. Unfortunately, that sort of talk carried no weight with Congress or the World Council. "Priscilla, do you have any idea what the political price would be if we did that?"

"I don't much care about the politics."

"You damned well better. Check your job description."

"Michael," she said, "do what you want. You'll have my resignation this afternoon."

He looked pained. "I don't want your resignation. I want you to help me get past this. This is a bad time for all of us. I know you too well to believe you'd walk out."

There was nothing more pathetic than watching Asquith when he was genuinely scared. He had reason to be. A resignation by the director of operations at a time like this would point a finger directly at him. "It's your call, Michael."

He sat, staring up at her. "All right," he said finally. "Let me think about what we can do, okay? I'll get back to you."

Hutch moved within range of the sensor, and the door opened. "The next Colby flight is the *Kira*, next week."

"Okay. Sit tight for a bit. Let me figure out what we want to do." His eyes settled on a note written on his calendar. "By the way, keep your schedule clear this afternoon. Senator Taylor will be here later, and he wants to see you."

"He wants to see *me*?"

"He'll have his daughter with him. She's a big fan of yours, apparently." His tone suggested he was puzzled why that might be.

"Things are pretty crowded today, Michael."

He waved the problem away. "Make yourself available. He specifically wants his daughter to say hello to you."

"Okay."

"I think her name is Amy. She wants to be a pilot. And you might keep in mind that Taylor will have a lot to say about whether we get decent funding next year."

SHE WAS IN conference with a couple of her department heads when the call came. *"The commissioner says Senator Taylor's on the grounds. Please go up to his office."*

"Okay," she said. "I'm on my way." She made her apologies and reset the meeting for four o'clock. It was a cool day, and the heating system didn't seem to be functioning. She grabbed a jacket out of her closet and headed up to the second floor. Asquith kept her waiting about ten minutes in his outer office, then rolled out, straightening his collar and giving directions to his AI, Don't call me, I'll be back in half an hour. Take care of the place.

He signaled her to follow, and they hurried down to the ground level and out of the building.

"Where are we meeting them?" she asked, as they descended the front steps and turned north on one of the walkways.

"In the courtyard." Taylor was a Greenie senator from Georgia, a guy who had no time for the Academy, star travel, or the sciences generally. He had gone to Congress on one issue only: a promise to do whatever was necessary to get the greenhouse under control. He had grown up on St. Simons Island, off the Georgia coast. A resort back in the twentieth and twenty-first centuries, it wasn't much more than a sandbar now. "He wants to talk about the future of the Academy."

"I thought this was a social thing."

"With politicians, Hutch, social things are always business." He used the word *politician* with contempt, as he always did. You would never have thought he was one himself.

Ahead, a flyer descended into the parking area beside the courtyard. Two people got out, and the vehicle lifted away. She recognized Taylor. The girl with him looked about fifteen. She was pretty, as kids of that age invariably are. She glanced around at the administration building while her father spotted Hutch and Asquith and started in their direction, leaving her in the rear.

"The kid admires you," said Asquith. "She thinks you're a hero." He smiled at the absurdity of the notion.

"Okay."

"She wants to see the lander." The lander from the *Shanghai* was on display at the far end of the courtyard. It gleamed in the sunlight.

AMY HAD BROWN hair combed into bangs and wide brown eyes and restless energy and a smile that was both charming and unsteady. Hutch felt sorry for her. Growing up with the senator would not be easy. What she knew of him suggested he wasn't flexible enough for parenting, and the wife had taken off years ago with somebody. Another political figure, but she didn't recall whom.

"Good to see you guys," Taylor said, with a hearty handshake. Quick smile in Hutch's direction, but his eyes leveled on Asquith. "Pretty scary with the *Heffernan*, Mike. What's the latest?"

"We haven't heard anything yet, Senator. We'll have a couple of ships arriving in the area tomorrow to look for them."

"But you really don't know where they are?"

"Not for certain, no."

"How'd it happen?"

"We don't know that either. Yet. But we're on top of it. I'll keep you informed."

"Old ships," said Hutch, as Amy joined them.

Taylor turned a quizzical look in her direction. "You're telling me they're a hazard?"

"The commissioner has ordered them grounded," she said. Asquith studied the tops of the trees.

"When were you going to tell me, Mike?" he asked.

The commissioner smiled. One of those smiles you get from a guy who's just fallen off his cycle and is telling you he's okay, it's not as bad as it looks. "Senator, it's one of the reasons I was glad you decided to come by today."

Taylor let them see he was surprised that they might have defective ships. Then he shrugged. It was of no consequence. "Priscilla," he said, "this is my daughter Amy. Amy is quite an admirer of yours."

The child blushed and squirmed. "It's nice to meet you, Ms. Hutchins. I've read all about you."

Hutch took her hand. "It's nice to meet *you*, Amy. And my friends call me *Hutch*."

Amy's smile widened. "I was reading Janet Allegri's book about you."

"*The Engines of God.*"

"Yes."

"That's not really about *me*, Amy. It's about the omegas."

"And Quraqua. I'd like to go there someday."

It was a world of ruins. She recalled how they'd looked in the moonlight. She'd been young then, only a few years older than Amy. Most of the ruins were gone, swallowed by the terraforming effort, begun and later abandoned when it got too expensive, and things went wrong. "How much do you know about Quraqua, Amy?"

"I've seen the holos. But it would be different *actually* to go there. To *touch* some of those places." She took a deep breath. "I'm going to be a pilot."

"She doesn't really want to do that," the senator said, talking as if Amy had gone for a walk. "It's too dangerous. And there's no future in it."

"It's not dangerous, Dad."

"Tell that to the people on the—what is it?—the *Bannerman*?"

"The *Heffernan*, sir," said Asquith.

"Whatever. Anyhow, Amy, you're young yet. We'll see how things go." He patted her on the shoulder. His expression suggested she was basically a good kid. Just a bit slow. "We're planning law school for her."

Taylor's first name was Hiram. He was tall and aristocratic. He didn't so much have a Southern accent as a distinct Southern flavor emanating from an education at Yale or Harvard. His hair was darker than Amy's, as was his smile. It lasted longer, though. In fact, it never really went away. It was as if the world always contained something that Taylor thought mildly amusing.

Amy asked when Hutch had begun her piloting career, asked to see the lander, wanted to know what it felt like to walk on another world.

Hutch saw a signal pass between the senator and Asquith. The commissioner relayed it to her and glanced toward the lander. A few tourists stood in a short line, waiting to go inside. "Come on, Amy," Hutch said. "Let's go take a look."

The girl led the way. They got into the line, and Hutch did not look back, but she knew they'd be talking seriously, or rather Taylor would and Asquith would be listening. It wasn't hard to guess the way it was going, either. If you have to take the ships off-line, do it. We don't want any more of these *Heffernan* things. The work's just not that important.

The Academy wasn't high on the list of things the public was worried about. Taylor had presidential ambitions, and he was laying groundwork for the future. The environmental damage done over the past two centuries had been the major issue in the past several presidential campaigns. If you thought rising water was okay, that warm winters were temporary, and a wheat belt that kept heading north would correct itself, you could forget about the White House. Those days were long over. If you advocated spending money on frivolous causes, like the interstellar missions that never seemed to produce anything, you could be made to look irresponsible.

The controls were roped off. Tourists were able to look into the cabin, try the seats, even bring the harness down to secure themselves. Hutch would have liked to bypass the lines, put the child in the pilot's seat, let her *touch* the yoke, maybe even activate the AI so she could talk with it, but with people waiting it wouldn't set a very good precedent.

Maybe another time.

* * *

WHEN SHE RETURNED Amy to her father, he looked pleased. The commissioner was nodding, a man in the process of accepting something he didn't like. He was saying okay, we'll do what we have to.

The conversation stopped dead on their arrival. Hutch waited a moment, but no one spoke. Time to lighten the mood. "Senator," she said, "if you'd like to bring Amy over sometime when things aren't so rushed, I could take her on a personal tour. Better yet, if you like, I could even arrange to take her up to Union."

"That's very kind of you, Hutch, but it's really not necessary."

"I'd be happy to," she said.

He studied her, the smile still playing about his lips, pointless, as if he'd forgotten it was there. "Would you like to go to the space station, Amy?"

Would she? Does the sun rise in the east? "Yes, Dad. Please. I'd love to go up there again." And back to Hutch: "Would you really do that?"

"Tell you what," Hutch said. "I have a daughter, too. She's a bit younger than you. But if you'll help me keep an eye on her, we'll all go. Okay?"

Taylor thanked her. His flyer reappeared and descended onto the tarp. They climbed in while Amy waved. Hutch and the commissioner waved back, the door closed, and the vehicle lifted into the late-afternoon sun and circled out over the Potomac.

"I think you've made a friend," said Asquith.

"Maybe a new pilot." They started back. "How bad was it?"

A shadow settled on his face. "It was pretty much what I expected. He's not going to support us."

"No increase at all?"

"Another cut. He says they need the money elsewhere."

"They waste enough on construction projects and military bases and naval vessels. When's the last time anybody tried to threaten the NAU?"

"I know, Hutch. You're preaching to the choir." He jammed his hands into his pockets. "He says we may be near the end of the interstellar program. Suggested I get my résumé ready."

The basic problem, she knew, was that the corporate effort intended to carry space exploration through the century had never happened. The corporations were there, but the only profits to be made came from government contracts. The sole exceptions were a couple of transport companies and Orion Tours.

"You know," he said, "none of this is going the way we thought it would forty years ago. Before your time, Hutch. Once the drive became available, we thought we were opening up the stars. That there'd be no stopping us."

It was a time when people assumed everyone would want to go out and look at the Big Show, but transportation, even with Hazeltine technology, simply took too long. It wasn't like a cruise to the Bahamas, where you could wander across the deck at night and enjoy the sounds of the ocean. Tourists were locked inside steel hulls. Shipboard VR was okay, but it was still VR, and they could do that at home. Everybody's favorite was the Goompahs, the race we'd saved at Lookout. But Lookout was a couple thousand light-years away, and it took almost nine months to get there. It was three months to Rigel. Even nearby Betelgeuse, the destination of the *Heffernan*, was close to three weeks away.

There was considerable interest in black holes. But none was known that could be reached inside a year. And these were all one-way numbers.

There was a lot of talk about developing a better drive. Periodically, somebody announced a breakthrough, but it never seemed to lead anywhere. "You might want to start looking around for a new career yourself, Hutch," Asquith said. "Maybe write your memoirs."

They started up the steps to the main entrance. She expected him to complain that she'd taken the initiative with the senator, but he said nothing about it. Maybe he'd had enough confrontation for one day.

He stopped in front of the entrance. "Listen, Hutch, I appreciate what you tried to do back there. But it's going to take a lot more than that."

"What I tried to do?" He was obviously not talking about grounding the fleet. "You mean Amy?"

He nodded. "You were pretty good with her."

"For the record, Michael, it had nothing to do with politics."

LIBRARY ENTRY

The current effort to reduce Academy funding can only accelerate with the *Heffernan* incident. Insiders have been reporting for years that the Academy's ships are not safe. A decision will have to be made whether the interstellar program is to continue or be abandoned. We hope the Congress and the World Council will have the foresight to recognize that the human future lies in the stars, that they will not give in to those who want to spend the money on their own projects. We've seen only a very small piece of what Ory Kimonides calls *The Far Shore*. To conclude there's nothing significant left to find, as some so-called experts are suggesting, would be terribly remiss.

–*Yokohama Calling*, Monday, February 16

chapter 6

> Idiots are not responsible for what they do. The real guilt falls on rational people who sit on their hands while the morons run wild. You can opt out if you want to. Play it safe. But if you do, don't complain when the roof comes down.
>
> —Gregory MacAllister,
> "Ten Rules for a Happy Senility"

Hutch stayed late in her office, ate almost nothing, thought about going home, finally called Tor and asked whether everything was all right. "Can you take care of Maureen tonight?"

"*Sure,*" he said. "*You're not going to stay there all night, are you?*"

"The *Wildside* is due to hit the search area at about 0200. I want to be here when it does."

"*You haven't heard anything from them yet? From the* Heffernan*?*"

"No."

"*That pretty much means they're dead, doesn't it?*"

"No. What it means is they don't have a working hypercomm. That wouldn't be a surprise if they'd lost their drive. But they should still be able to use the radio."

"*What happens if you don't hear a radio signal?*"

She didn't want to think about it. "To be honest, Tor, I don't expect to. At least not right away. The search area's too big. I'm hoping we'll get lucky."

"And if you don't?"

"We'll keep looking until we do."

He took a deep breath. *"You okay?"*

"Ask me after we find them." There wasn't really anything she could do here that she couldn't do equally well from home. But this was where she should be.

"Let me know if I can do anything, Love."

She kept him on for a while, to have someone to talk to. But eventually he had to get to Maureen, and Hutch was alone.

She tried doing some work, then tried reading. She checked in with Peter to let him know where she was. He was putting in overtime, too. She switched on the VR and watched three people arguing politics.

At around eleven she dimmed the lights and sank onto the couch. She'd just closed her eyes when she was startled by footsteps in the corridor. And a knock at the door. "You in there, Hutch?"

It was Eric. She opened up, and he came in. With a box of brownies. "I saw the light and thought you could use some company."

"What are you doing here at this hour?"

"Same as you, I guess. Waiting for news." He sat down opposite her, opened the box, and held it out to her. "They're good."

She took one.

"What are we hearing?"

"So far, not a thing."

"I've written two statements for the pool," he said.

"Press conference tomorrow?"

"At nine."

"*Two* statements? One if we find them; one if we don't?"

"Yes."

"It may take a while before we have anything definite."

"I know." He hesitated. "Hutch, I heard you're going to close down some of the flights. Is that true?"

"Yes."

"Which ones?"

She told him. "But I'd appreciate it if you'd keep it quiet until I give you the all clear. I want to talk to the people who will be affected before they hear about it over their VRs."

He questioned her about the search pattern, shook his head while she described it. "Doesn't sound hopeful," he said.

"It depends on whether Abdul was able to do what he was supposed to do."

He nodded. It would be the first question he'd face in the morning.

After a while he commented that she looked sleepy, that he was tired himself, and he got up and headed for the door. "When you hear something," he said, "I'll be upstairs." Then he was gone, and the silence closed in.

TWO O'CLOCK CAME and went. She knew not to expect immediate information. But when the clock struck four, and there was still no word, she started thinking about calling Peter. She was about to when Marla told her he was on the circuit.

"Hutch," he said, "the Wildside *has exited hyperspace. So far, though, no signal."*

Damn.

"Okay." Moonlight filtered through the curtains. Maybe the *al-Jahani* would hear something.

"They're three hours out. Hutch . . . "

"Yes, Peter?"

"I'm not optimistic."

She called Eric and passed the word. He grumbled something about bad luck. But you can't expect to find them right away. As if he knew something about it. She kept him on the circuit, talking about nothing of consequence. She just wanted the company. Probably they both did, and her respect for him, which had never been very high, went up.

She opened a window and looked out at a moonless sky. She debated calling Tor, but he had an exhibition in the morning. Better to let him sleep. So she went back to the sofa and lay in the dark, listening to the hum of insects, wondering why she insisted on putting herself through this. Maybe, when it was over, it would be time to move on.

She dozed off. But it was a fitful rest, and she was awake again as the sky began to brighten. Time to get some air. She showered, toweled off, and paused momentarily in front of her mirror. Still look good, babe. She had a son on the way, but no one would have known.

She selected fresh clothes from her wardrobe. It was one of her guiding principles that she never allowed people to see she was under pressure. Stay relaxed. Dress well. Always look as if the situation is under control.

She was on her way out the door when Peter called again. *"The* al-Jahani *has made its exit. Approximately four minutes farther down the track. Still no signal."* It would coordinate a search pattern with the *Wildside*. Meantime, she would have to get more ships out there.

The area was simply too big. Even if they scrambled everything they had, finding the *Heffernan* was not going to be easy.

She had no appetite but decided to go to breakfast anyhow. She needed to get some people around her. The only nearby place open that early, though, was Stud's. Not her favorite. She crossed the Academy grounds, strolled past the Retreat, dodged traffic on the Parkway, and went into the Academy Mall. It always irritated her that the hucksters had stolen their name.

She walked into Stud's. There were maybe a dozen people inside, a couple from the Academy, most from local businesses. She ordered a bagel and coffee and smeared a ton of jelly on the bagel.

Living dangerously.

BACK IN HER office, Marla greeted her with a cheery good morning, as if Hutch hadn't been there all night. Sometimes Marla didn't seem to function properly. *"Today is Tuesday, February 17,"* she said. *"Staff meeting is scheduled at eight thirty."*

"Thanks, Marla."

"You have several calls. Priority is low, so I did not think you'd want to be disturbed."

"Queue them. I'll get to them later this morning."

She sat down in the armchair and let her head drift back. Within minutes she was asleep.

ASQUITH, WHO—LIKE pretty much everyone else—didn't understand the distances involved, assured her everything was going to be okay.

"They'll find them," he said. He was convincing because he believed it. The commissioner did not think in terms of light-minutes or billions of kilometers. To him a flight to Capella took about four days. Four days was not a long time, ergo the distance covered couldn't be all that far.

"Maybe. But we need more ships."

"We can't do that. We don't have more ships available."

"I can get some corporate help. We should also freeze everything we're doing until we get this thing settled."

"And how long do you think that might take?"

"Weeks. Maybe a month or more."

"My God. Really?"

"Yes. Really."

"Do they have enough food and water on board? To survive that long?"

"Yes. They have plenty of rations."

His eyes narrowed. "Hutch, we don't even believe they're alive, do we?"

"We don't know."

"Yes or no, Hutch. Do you believe they're still alive?"

"They may be in a place where we can't reach them. But that's not the point."

"Let's give the *Wildside* and the *al-Jahani* a little time before we scramble everybody's schedule. Okay? Let's just hang on a bit. We don't want to panic." He closed his eyes and made a noise deep in his throat. Thank God he was on-site to keep his crazy staff in check. "What else have we got?"

It was hard to think about anything else. "I've begun putting together what we have to do as we take the Colbys out of service. I have the recommendations on mission cutbacks and cancellations for you. I meant to get them to you yesterday, but I got sidetracked."

He had a tendency, when you opposed him, to look at you as if you were being unreasonable. As if we'd been all through this before, and now you were starting again. "It's not possible, Hutch. I would if I could. You know that."

"Michael, we still need a decision on the *Kira*."

"Where's it headed?"

"Nok. Next week. It's scheduled to carry eight passengers."

"Hutch, we have to let it go."

"I'm *canceling* it. I'm going to notify everybody today."

"I wish you wouldn't."

"I will not sign off on the flight. You want the mission, get somebody else to do it."

His jaw muscles worked. "Who's on the goddam thing?"

"A team from the University of Berlin and the Lisbon Field Unit. The sooner they're informed, the less flak there'll be."

"Yeah. Right. You know, this is easy enough for *you* to do. *I'm* the one who takes all the heat." He looked wounded. Betrayed. "Okay," he said. "Do what you have to. But let them know we'll find a way to get them out there. That it's only temporary."

BY LATE MORNING, the *Wildside* had made a second jump. Still nothing.

She put in calls to eight of the corporate entities at the station. To Nova Industries and MirrorCorp, to Thor Transport and Maracaibo, to Hawkins and MicroTech and Orion Tours and WhiteStar. The message was the same to each: Can you contribute a ship to the *Heffernan* search?

They could. Hawkins thought they could get one off later in the day. WhiteStar could send one by the end of the week. The others fell somewhere in between. "Okay," she said. "Stand by. Don't send anything out until I tell you. But be ready to go."

Hiram Taylor called just before noon to ask whether she'd meant what she said about taking Amy to the space station. He was in a custom gray satin suit. Amy would love to go, he said, especially with her. *"I'm not all that excited about the idea,"* he added, *"but I'm willing to go along with it. So if you really want to—"*

"I'd enjoy it," said Hutch. "It would give me a chance to do something different."

"What would be a good day?"

"She has to go to school; I have to work. How about Saturday?"

"Saturday will be fine."

"I'll pick her up at seven."

"You're sure it's no trouble?"

"No. Of course not. It'll be a pleasure to have her. I'll take Maureen as well. Make it a family outing."

"Hutch, thank you."

"It's my pleasure."

"You understand I'm not worried about safety. I just don't like playing to these crazy ideas of hers."

"You could do worse, Senator."

"I don't want to encourage her."

"Of course not." He hesitated, embarrassed. "Listen, don't worry. She'll be fine." Hutch resisted the impulse to tell him he was a jerk.

"Hutch," he said, *"I'm grateful for what you're doing, but you understand it won't influence the way I vote on Academy funding."*

"I wouldn't have it any other way, Senator."

NEXT CAME THE flight cancellations. It was early evening in western Europe. She called her contacts at the University of Berlin and at the field unit and left messages. Flight to Nok indefinitely postponed. Regret the inconvenience. We are looking at alternatives.

Another mission two weeks beyond that would have to be shut down as well. That was the *Bill Jenkins,* bound for the Origins Project. When she canceled that one, which she would do the next day, the howls would go all the way to the Congress.

In the middle of that, Peter called to inform her the *al-Jahani* had made its second jump. Also with no results.

She called the corporate entities that had volunteered to help and asked them to send whatever they could as quickly as possible.

COVERAGE ON THE newsnets was heavy. The Black Cat had an expert pointing out that the Colby class, to which the *Heffernan* belonged, was obsolete. *"Would you ride one?"* asked correspondent Rose Beetem of their superluminal expert.

"No way, Rose. Nada. Not a chance."

Worldwide was doing a piece attacking the World Council for failure to fund the Academy. InterAct was running comments by someone described as a science analyst: *"There's simply no point to spending taxpayers' money so the idle rich can run around in space, or so the world's malcontents have somewhere else to go. It's silly."*

ERIC CALLED. *"YOUR buddy was on yesterday."*

"Who are we talking about?"

"MacAllister. He was on a show with one of our pilots. Talking about us."

Uh-oh. Mac rarely said anything good about anybody. "How'd it go?"

"I don't want to prejudice you. But you should take a look."

Hutch sighed. "Who was the pilot?"

"Valya," he said.

She told Marla to find it and put it up. Moments later, the office darkened, and Marge Dowling did the introduction for her show. Then she brought out Valya. Then MacAllister swaggered into view. Somehow he always contrived to make an entrance. She didn't like any of her people going up against MacAllister. At least Valya would have been about as strong an advocate as the Academy could have produced out of its pilot corps. But MacAllister was a professional assassin. Arguing with him always left you running downhill in front of an avalanche.

Dowling started by reviewing the *Heffernan* situation. Hutch fast-forwarded through it until she saw the discussion begin with a question to Valya. How safe were the starships?

Absolutely safe, Valya insisted, while Mac contrived to look as if she wanted everyone to believe in fairies. *"We've done the important stuff,"* Mac said a few minutes later. *"We've taken a good look at the neighborhood we live in, we got rid of the cloud that was headed our way, and we've allowed our academics to fill their computers with data nobody will ever use. It costs a lot of money to run back and forth to Orion's belt—"*

"We haven't gotten that far yet—" said Valya.

"Wherever. It's time to come home and fix the problems we have here. It's time to grow up." She froze the picture. MacAllister sat there, mouth open, index finger pointing at the ceiling, a model of rectitude and conviction, going on about spending billions and getting nothing back. She picked up a paperweight, a brass model of the *Wildside,* and tossed it at him. It passed through his left shoulder.

TWENTY MINUTES LATER Marla informed her she had a visitor. Nobody was scheduled until two thirty, when she was supposed to sit down with representatives from two laboratories who'd gotten into a battle over scheduling priorities. "Who is it?" she asked.

"Harry Everett."

Everett was a Native American, the pilot with whom she'd made her qualifying flight at the beginning of her career. The guy who'd told her she had a responsibility to do more than deliver researchers to their target sites. She'd never forgotten his comment, made while they orbited Terranova out at 36 Ophiuchi, the first world discovered to have multicellular life-forms. "If they're going groundside," he'd told her, looking down at the planet's lush green continents, "you need to stay with them, mentally, and maybe physically as well. They will have a tendency to forget how dangerous some of these places can be."

"I've got it, Marla." She strode through the door into the outer office. Everett was standing in his dark blue uniform, looking a bit older than the last time she'd seen him. But still pretty good.

He wasn't smiling.

She put out her hand. "Glad to see you, Harry," she said. "It's been a long time."

He looked at the hand. Looked at her. "I used to get a hug," he said.

Forgot. Directors don't go around hugging the help. "Got out of the habit, I guess." She embraced him, but he didn't cooperate much. "What's wrong, Harry?"

"You have a minute?"

"For you? Sure. Always." She led him back into the office and closed the door. "How's Annie?" His daughter, product of a marriage long gone south.

"She's good," he said. "She's married now. I'm a grandfather."

"Congratulations." She got coffee for them, and they sat down. "I take it this isn't social."

"No."

Okay. She could guess the rest. "The *Heffernan*."

He nodded. "How could you let that happen?"

Everett was a head taller than Hutch. More than a head. There was something in his dark eyes that let her know that she might be the director of operations, but to him she was still a twenty-two-year-old neophyte pilot. "Harry," she said, "there's a problem with money. We're doing everything we can."

The eyes never left her. "You've got a whole squadron of unsafe ships out there."

"I know."

"You were running on pure luck. What's happening right now was inevitable. What the hell's the point of your getting this kind of office"—he glanced around—"this kind of authority, if you don't step in to help your people?"

Hutch could hear voices outside somewhere. Kids. In the park. And a dog barking.

Everett sat without moving.

"The only alternative we have right now," she said, finally, "would be to shut down a sizable piece of the program. How would the pilots respond if the workload was cut by a third?"

"There's another option."

"And what would that be?"

He looked puzzled, as if she'd said something completely off the wall. "What in hell's happened to you, Hutch? Do I really have to explain it? You've been sitting quietly while the Academy hangs us out there. You're not getting the funding? What about making some noise? How about putting up a fight? Or have you forgotten how?"

LIBRARY ENTRY

We've satisfied our curiosity about the local stellar neighborhood. What is perhaps more important, we now know that the mere attainment of technological achievement does not guarantee species survival, and may indeed contribute to our eventual termination.

The lesson to be taken from our experience so far is that we need to wake up, to recognize that we are at risk, not only from cosmic forces over which we have limited control at best, like the omega clouds, but also from the unfettered development of science. Unfortunately, technology brings with it enormous risks that, until recently, we've been reluctant to face. The runaway greenhouse explosion comes immediately to mind. There are other hazards, which we would do well to take seriously.

—*Paris Today*, Tuesday, February 17

chapter 7

> Freedom sounds good. Freedom of religion. The right to privacy. The right to protest when you don't like the way things are going. Unfortunately, all these benevolences assume a mature, rational population, because they can be powerful weapons when misused. Freedom and idiots make a volatile mix. And the sad truth is that the idiocy quotient in the general population is alarmingly high.
>
> —Gregory MacAllister, *Editor-at-Large*

MacAllister rapped his baton several times on the lectern, exactly as he'd seen it done by the conductor of the Geneva Philharmonic. The vast concert hall fell silent. He glanced around at the hunched figures arranged across the stage, illuminated only by the pivot lamps on their music stands. Behind him, the audience waited. Someone coughed.

He felt the tension of the moment, as one always does during those last seconds before the performance begins. He gazed over at the violins and signaled them to start.

The opening strains of Kornikov's *Charge of the Cossacks* stirred, as if something in the night were just awakening. MacAllister summoned it forth, listened to it gather strength, felt it flow past the dimmed lights out into the audience. He knew its power, knew also that he controlled it, that it reacted to his baton, and to his fingertips.

He signaled the oboes, and the wind began to pick up. It blew mournfully across the steppe, gradually resolving itself into the sound of approaching cavalry. They came, the hoofbeats rising to a crescendo that at last shook the sky. MacAllister leaped onto his gray steed, Alyosha, his companion in a thousand battles, and joined them. He was draped in fur, an ammunition belt slung over one shoulder, a musket strapped to the animal's flank. They moved through the night while the moonlight glittered against their weapons, and the viols sang.

He brought in the brass with a clamor, and they erupted in full gallop toward a hidden enemy. Toward women and children held captive. Toward invaders of the mother country.

Born to be a Cossack.

APPLAUSE ROLLED THROUGH the night. MacAllister generously pointed his baton toward the orchestra, and the noise went up a few decibels. He bowed and looked up to the boxes on his left. To *Jenny's* box. He hadn't programmed her in, *never* programmed her in, but it didn't matter. She was there, and he saw her, gazing down at him, wearing one of the dark blue gowns she always wore on formal occasions. Then the curtain dropped and Tilly put the table lamp on and he was back in his living room.

"Very good, sir," Tilly said, in his deep baritone. *"An outstanding performance."* There was a hint of mockery in the AI's comment, but that was okay. Tilly knew it was more or less expected.

He would have liked to reopen the curtain. To invite Jenny down to join him. And in fact it was possible. He could have her stroll across the stage and draw up a chair and sit and talk with him in her New England accent. He could send the rest of the audience home while they reminisced about the old days. He'd married late. He'd never expected to meet a woman to be taken seriously until Jenny erupted into his life.

Irreplaceable.

He'd always owned a reputation as something of a chauvinist. It wasn't really true, of course. It was simply that he was a realist. He understood that women were, for the most part, not talented. Rule out the intersection of their anatomical attributes and his hormones, and they had little to offer. But he also understood that the great bulk of the male population were also vapid, easily led, dreary creatures. If Hutch got her wish, and we did one day encounter truly intelligent aliens, whom would we send to speak with them? To impress them with our capabilities? A politician? A college professor? Best, probably, would be a plumber. Someone lacking too high an opinion of himself.

Jenny had been a graduate student from Boston University, doing a research paper on him. She'd shown up out of the blue to watch him do a presentation at Colonial Hall in Boston. His subject had been "Your Future and Welcome to It." She'd sat up front, but, incredibly, he hadn't noticed her until she'd come to him afterward, patiently waiting while others presented books for his signature, shook his hand, and tried to ingratiate themselves. And then she'd been standing there, dark eyes, dark hair, shy smile. And the rest, as they say, was history.

They'd had three years.

MacAllister had lived, on the whole, a happy life. He'd accomplished, and in fact far exceeded, his childhood ambitions. He'd become a celebrated figure and a renowned editor. He'd won every major nonfiction literary and journalistic prize. He was accorded VIP status wherever he went, and he was proud of his enemies, who were the self-righteous, the arrogant, the uplifters who wanted to direct the way everybody else did things. During the course of those early years, he'd maintained that love was an illusion generated by chemistry and biological processes. That a man was far better off to resist the urge to mate. And then he'd met Jenny.

He'd been living in Baltimore then. They'd married within a few months, and she'd moved into his house on Eastern Avenue. And for three years they'd lived a gloriously happy existence. They went everywhere together, attending concerts and VR immersions and ball games. She'd joined him at presentations, had participated in Married to the Mafia panels at press luncheons, had been there when he delivered his graduation remarks at Western Maryland University, a performance that had sounded the clarion call against President Thompson and his corrupt crowd while nearly landing MacAllister in jail. And most of all, there'd been the pleasant evenings on their porch, alternately reminiscing about their own lives together and then debating the influence of Montaigne on Flaubert.

He lost her suddenly, and unexpectedly, to a disease named for a German researcher, something almost no one ever came down with. Something that twenty-third-century medicine, with all its advances, was helpless to halt. And he'd watched her waste away. The dark eyes had stayed bright until the end. Her mind had remained clear. But her body had shriveled and withered.

She'd died at home, declining the option that would have kept her alive but left her helpless.

MacAllister closed his eyes and let his head sink back. He could have re-created the front porch, had he wished. Could have re-created *her*. Put her beside him where they could watch the lights of passing traffic and talk as they had in the old days.

A lot of people did that. But it was the way to despair. Furthermore, it would have dishonored her memory. She would have told him to move on. Remember me but move on. So he resisted the temptation, and let her rest in peace.

"Tilly," he said, "have you the news wraps?"

"Whenever you're ready, Mr. MacAllister."

He got up, while Jenny and the Cossacks slipped away, and got himself a beer. "Let's go, then."

He was always looking for stories that could be explored in *The National*. These, preferably, were tales of abuse by political and corporate authorities, academic malfeasance, wrongdoing in high places, hypocrisy by guardians of the nation's moral fiber, and, his particular target, school boards that opted for indoctrination rather than literacy and math.

Last year, at the behest of the English Department of Rogan High School in Berwyck, Georgia, he'd appeared at a board meeting to fight an effort to ban from the schools any book containing any profane expression whatever. Good-bye, *Gone With the Wind*. Farewell, *Moby Dick*.

Attacked as a purveyor of foul language—someone had counted the number of *damns* in one of his essays—MacAllister had erupted. "When I go to a sporting event," he'd told the board, "I no more want to sit behind a sewer mouth than any of you. But if it happens, I can assure you the perpetrator will not have learned it from Salinger or Munson or me."

It was, he'd discovered, not easy to embarrass a school board.

It had been an interesting news week. The *Heffernan*, of course, was the lead story. Oklahoma was in the process of becoming the first state of the original fifty to ban firearms. This after three kids ranging from ten to twelve years old had wandered through a downtown shopping mall in Muskogee, killed seventeen people, and wounded forty-five more. The voters had apparently had enough of watching politicians get bullied by the arms industry and its surrogates.

In Philadelphia, distraught teenage lovers had climbed out onto a twelfth-floor balcony and jumped. Both families had opposed the match because of political differences. It was believed to be the first time a Greenie and a Republican had leaped together out of a building in Pennsylvania history.

In London, Philip Cage, a physicist known primarily for making artificial gravity possible during spaceflight, continued to claim he had *not* been enhanced by his parents, despite evidence to the contrary. The entire affair was in doubt because the records had been destroyed in a fire, and a lot of people thought nobody could be that smart without help.

From Derby, North Carolina, came the story that caught his attention, and that would make the next edition of *The National*: A tax auditor had been jailed for assault. The assaultee had been the Reverend Michael Pullman, of the Universal Church of the Creator. The tax auditor, one Henry Beemer, had approached the Reverend Pullman and, with no apparent provocation, struck the preacher with a book he was carrying and knocked him down. The book was *A Connecticut Yankee in King Arthur's Court.*

The motive? Henry Beemer claimed psychological damage resulting from a church-operated school run by Pullman. "Starting when I was seven," he was quoted as saying, "they talked all the time about hellfire. How hot it was. How you burned forever. How easy it was to go there. I'm forty-two, and I've never been able to get it out of my mind."

That would be an irresistible story for *The National*. MacAllister assigned one of his reporters to look into it, and decided to go a step further. "Tilly," he said, "see if you can get this guy Beemer on the circuit for me."

* * *

HENRY BEEMER DID not look like the sort of man who would assault somebody in a bookstore. He appeared to be about average size. He was thin, with thin lips and thin hair and brooding gray eyes, a man, perhaps, who did not get enough sun. You would have known immediately that he worked in an office, in a subordinate position.

"What can I do for you, Mr. MacAllister?" he asked. He was seated on a cheap imitation-leather sofa. A wall full of books rose behind him.

"I'm from *The National*, Henry."

"I know who you are."

"We might be interested in doing your story. Would you be willing to cooperate?"

"I don't think so, sir," he said. *"I'd just like this to be over."*

"I understand. Do you have a lawyer?"

"Yes. Mr. Pontis."

MacAllister hesitated. Then: "Tell me why you did it."

"Look," he said, *"I've already talked to the reporters."*

"Talk to me, please. I'll only take a minute."

"I can't really explain it in any way that makes sense."

"Try me."

He scowled. *"I was annoyed at what he'd done. What they're still doing."*

"What had he done?"

"He runs the church school." He cleared his throat. Swallowed. *"I mean, I don't even believe in hell."*

"If you did, you wouldn't have attacked him."

He laughed. It wasn't the halfhearted chuckle MacAllister might have anticipated, but a genuine cackle. Then he settled down. *"They're going to fire me."*

"Who is?"

"Jackson Brothers. My employers. We're an accounting firm."

"I'm sorry to hear it."

"My own dumb fault."

"Tell me what happened, Henry."

Beemer thought about it. *"You ever been to a church school, Mr. MacAllister?"*

"As a matter of fact, I have."

"Did they talk much about hell?"

"Yes, they did."

"For minor things. Miss church, you go to hell. Kiss a girl, you go to hell."

"I remember the routine."

"I started when I was seven. I hated it. I used to wish I'd been born into some jungle tribe where everybody was a heathen. Thinking that way was a sin they hadn't thought of, so I thought I was safe.

"In the history class they talked about freedom of religion. And I used to think how that was for other people, but not for me. I had no freedom to choose how I might worship. If I left the Universals—"

"The Universal Church of the Creator?"

"Yes. If I left them, I was damned. And they described in graphic detail how it would be. Imagine putting your hand on a hot skillet and holding it there. For a full minute. Then imagine you can never pull it away. And that is nothing compared to—"

"I get the idea."

"I was pretty innocent, as kids went. But they made it sound almost inevitable. Slip once—"

"I went through the same thing, Henry. You must have thrown it off at some point."

"I did. More or less." His eyes slid shut. *"But I've never been able to convince myself that they might not have it right. That when I die, a final judgment will be waiting for me."*

"All right, Henry. What do you plan to do in court?"

"Plead guilty. Take what they give me."

"You know," said MacAllister, "there are millions of kids across the country now going through exactly what you went through. Why not confront the church for what they did?"

"Confront the church?"

"Yes."

"No." He shook his head. *"I couldn't do that."*

"Why not?"

"Nobody would buy it, that's why. People around here are pretty religious. I'd have to move."

"You've already shown that you'd like to hit back. Why not do it in a way that wouldn't get you jailed? That might raise the consciousness of some of these people?"

He sat for a long minute, staring at MacAllister. *"How would I go about doing that?"*

"Decide right now that you're willing to put up a fight. Do that, and I'll get you one of the best lawyers in the country."

* * *

MACALLISTER HAD NOT exaggerated when he'd described his schooling background. He'd come from a religious family. His parents had been conservative, and there'd been a time when his father had hoped young Gregory would become a preacher. Which showed how out of touch the old man had been. The earliest religious feeling MacAllister could recall was being annoyed at Adam, because it was his fault that girls subsequently had to wear clothes. In later years, as his lack of faith became increasingly apparent, he'd driven his mother to tears and his father to distraction. His mother had once told him at a church service that he was an embarrassment to the family. This was a family that had never done anything notable, other than stay out of jail.

The evening of his conversation with Henry Beemer, MacAllister recruited Jason Glock, who had a long history of fighting unpopular causes, to offer his services to the defendant. *Pro bono*.

THERE WAS SOMETHING else of interest. Buried in the routine accounts of rioting in the Middle East, celebrities in trouble, and corrupt politics, was another moonriders sighting. A distant one this time. Out at Capella. Wherever that was. There had been a flurry of sightings recently, and the odd part was that they were being captured by sensors and telescopes. Visuals could be faked easily enough, but it was hard to understand professional pilots going to the trouble. Especially when they knew they were going to be laughed at by skeptics.

He'd been gathering material for years on a history of self-delusion. The book, with the working title *Dark Mirror*, would contain chapters on religion, communism, the Shakers (those magnificent celibates who had gone inevitably out of existence), various political movements, the back-to-nature fantasies of the mid twenty-second century, and a host of others. He was coming to realize he should incorporate a section on alien visitors. Yet this didn't feel like quite the same thing. "Tilly," he said, "see if you can get through to Priscilla Hutchins for me."

He started leafing through the report from the marketing division, looking first at the bottom line, which was okay. MacAllister always started with the bottom line. In all things. Had anyone asked, he would have said it was the secret of success. He was still analyzing numbers and projections when Tilly told him the connection had been made, and the woman herself materialized in front of him.

"Hutch." He put down the papers. "Good to see you."

"And you, Mac. It's been a while." Despite the leisurely tone, she seemed cool. *"What can I do for you?"* She always looked good. Dark hair, penetrating eyes, an elfin quality that never quite went away.

He wondered whether she'd seen, or heard about, the Tampa broadcast. "How've you been?"

"We're good. You?"

"On the run." He wanted to lighten things a bit, but wasn't sure how. He asked about Tor and Maureen, and whether there was any news yet on the *Heffernan.*

"Nothing yet," she said. *"We have two ships in the search area. It may take a while."*

"What are their prospects?" The Academy spokesman had said only that they were "hopeful."

Her demeanor darkened. *"Not for release."*

"Of course not."

"Chances are slim. They probably didn't make it out of hyper."

"I'm sorry," he said. "I hope you're wrong."

"So do I."

"There's something else I'd like to ask about."

"Go ahead."

"What do we know about the moonriders?"

She grinned. *"You're talking about the* Ranger *story."*

"I'm talking in general. Is there anything to it? Do we have visitors?"

"There's something going on, Mac. But we don't have a clue what it is."

"Are they artificial? The objects people keep seeing?"

"Don't know."

"Is there any alternative explanation that makes sense to you?"

"We have some speculations that might cover some of the sightings. A lot of them, in fact. But there are a few that are difficult to explain away."

"Did the *Lassiter* find anything?" The *Lassiter* had gone out a year ago looking for them, had toured a half dozen or so systems where the objects had been seen.

"You've seen the report." There it was again. She was annoyed with him.

chapter 8

> The secret to a successful career in virtually any field is good public relations. Forget results. Forget the facts. Perception is all that matters.
>
> —Gregory MacAllister, "Downhill All the Way"

Wednesday, February 18.

Michael Asquith had not been a child of privilege. He'd grown up on a North Dakota farm. His father had belatedly discovered a talent for oratory and for telling people what they wanted to hear, and had gone all the way from raising corn and tomatoes—the crops had been moving north—to the Senate. He'd made a lot of money along the way. By the time full-blown success had arrived, Michael, the youngest of three sons, was flunking out of medical school at the University of Minnesota. Later he flunked out of business school. He ascribed these early misadventures to his being a restless, independent spirit. No respecter of authority, he was fond of saying. But it didn't matter. Eventually he collected a doctorate in political science. Meanwhile Dad had gotten him a post with the North Dakota elections commission, and later he connected with a rising young politician from Fargo. Asquith discovered a talent for directing campaigns,

"Hutch," he said, "I'm sorry if the broadcast shook things up. I didn't mean to create a problem."

"What broadcast?" The temperature dropped another five degrees.

"What do you expect me to do? I'm a journalist. They ask me questions, I tell them what I think."

"I wish you weren't so good at it."

Hutch was a relatively diminutive woman, but she had a lot of presence. He wished she could loosen up a bit, though. "There's been speculation that the *Lassiter* might have found something but that the Academy is keeping it quiet."

"Don't tell me you've become a conspiracy wacko, Mac."

"If they *had* found something, would you have made it public?"

"Yes. Look, Mac, it would have been in our interest if they'd found something."

"Something unearthly."

"I guess you could put it that way. Sure. The public is bored with interstellar exploration. So we've become a target for politicians. And opportunistic media types."

He let it pass. "Okay. Thanks."

"You're welcome." She was about to disconnect.

"May I ask one more question?"

"Ask away."

"What's *your* opinion? What do you think the moonriders are?"

"Mac," she said, *"I don't do opinions. When we have some conclusions, I'll let you know."*

MACALLISTER'S DIARY

Sometimes the cost of integrity is the loss of a friend.

—Tuesday, February 17

and he and the young politician had gone together to Bismarck, and eventually to Washington.

In time he'd made friends, gained influence, and when the top job at the Academy came open, Asquith had walked into it. His major goal was eventually to run a presidential campaign. Hutch hoped it wouldn't happen. The prospect of his being close to the seat of power was unsettling. It wasn't that he was irresponsible. Or ruthless. It was that he was essentially hollow. Believed in nothing save his own advancement. (Although he didn't realize that. Asquith thought of himself as a shrewd, progressive leader. The nation would be better off were he at the levers of power.) He lived strictly on the surface. Liked symbols. Mistook metaphors for reality. Enjoyed being photographed outside churches, but had no clue what the New Testament was really about. Even now, after several years at the Academy, he could not get excited about a new discovery, whatever it might be. His first thought was inevitably how the discovery might affect the Academy's political standing, or its funding. To be honest, though, that was his job.

Wednesday morning, while Hutch continued to wait anxiously for word of the *Heffernan*, he called her up to his office. She expected questions on the status of the search. He surprised her. "You see this thing MacAllister did the other day?"

"The show?" she said.

"Yes. I thought he was supposed to be a friend of yours."

"He is."

"We don't need any more friends like him." She could see a vein pulsing in his forehead. "Did you know ahead of time he was going to do this?"

"No. I had no idea."

"Stop me if I'm wrong, but didn't you save his sorry ass a few years back?"

"Pretty much," she said.

"It's not the first time he's done this to us."

"No."

"When you get a chance, would you *talk* to him? Explain that he owes us something. At least if he can't help, he should shut up."

"I don't think he'd be receptive."

"Wonderful. No good deed goes unpunished. He doesn't give a goddam what happens to us, does he?"

"It's not that," she said. "He tends to say what he thinks."

"Well," Asquith said, "one of these days I'm going to find a way to take him down."

"He *is* a little cranky," she admitted. "But if I got into trouble, he'd be the first guy I'd want at my side."

"Yeah. Sure." If he got the point, he didn't react. "I'm getting too old for this, Priscilla."

That was her cue to reassure him, but she was in no mood to comply. "Anything else?" she asked.

"What's the latest on the *Heffernan*?"

"We still haven't heard anything."

"Hutch." His eyes grew troubled. "Are we going to find them?"

She took a few seconds to answer. "Probably not."

The energy drained out of him. He brushed back his hair, massaged his temples, clamped his teeth. "Goddam. This is turning into a public relations nightmare."

"We're probably going to lose a few people, too."

"I know, Hutch." His voice softened. "I know. It's terrible. And it's getting worse."

"How do you mean?"

"The science committee is going to be looking at our situation."

"That's the one Taylor sits on, isn't it?"

He nodded. "Hiram tells me they're going to hold hearings, then they'll recommend the reduction in our funding. He says they have no choice. Can't throw good money after bad, he says."

She felt helpless. "The funding cuts over the last few years are the reason we're having the problem."

"*You* know that. And *I* know it. For that matter, Taylor knows it, too. But they feel they have to cut *somewhere*."

"You might point out to them that we're a quarter of a percent of the federal budget."

"I will. Have no fear."

"If they do it, we'll have to eliminate another round of missions. But we should arrange things to hit them where it hurts. We have to get the people who count on us to understand there's a problem. If they don't go after the Senate, Taylor and the rest of that crew will put us out of business."

"I understand that. But, Hutch, we've never canceled missions before. We've built a reputation for reliability." He looked seriously worried. "I really hate the way this is going."

"Michael, we canceled a mission yesterday. And we'll cancel five more by the end of the week."

He stiffened, as if this was something he hadn't heard before. "Most of those missions won't happen for a while. Why not delay the decisions?"

"Because the people who are depending on us should get as much advance notice as possible."

He mumbled something about a headache. Then: "I mean—" He stopped, not sure what he meant. "We can't go on like this."

"We don't have any choice. Until the politicians provide some resources, they're going to have to face the consequences."

"I know how you feel, Hutch. But somehow we have to maintain the service."

"Like hell, Michael. We're not a military organization. We don't risk people's lives. At least not deliberately."

SHE WAS TEMPTED to catch a flight up to Union and follow the search from the operations center. It would look good when the inevitable investigation started to assess blame for the loss of the *Heffernan*. But there was really nothing she could add to the effort, so she resisted. The last thing Peter and his people needed was to have the boss looking over their shoulders.

Heavy clouds moved in from the west at midafternoon, and a violent lightning storm rolled across the capital. By five, the sky had cleared. Asquith called again, asking whether there was any news, whether there was anything more they could do. Some corporate ships were on the way. "It'll take them a while to get there," she said.

She sent out for pizza, called Tor to tell him she was going to stay at the office again, until she had word one way or the other. She talked to Maureen for a few minutes. "*I miss you, Mommy,*" her daughter said. "*Where have you been?*"

"I miss you, too, Sweetheart. Mommy's had to work."

"*Why?*"

As Maureen grew older, Hutch was feeling an increasing sense of unease over the amount of time she spent away from her daughter. The child was changing before her eyes, growing up, and the truth was that Hutch knew she would one day look back on these years and regret the lost time. That she'd wish she had done things differently.

Maybe it *was* time to step down. Let somebody else deal with Asquith and monetary shortfalls and outraged academics. Not for the first time, she asked herself what she really wanted out of her life.

EXPERTS AND CONSULTANTS were showing up across the media, unanimously predicting the *Heffernan* would not be found. Peter called to say that an independent commercial vessel, the *Macarias,* had arrived on the scene and joined the hunt. Hutch was second-guessing herself by then. Harry Everett had been right. She should have taken a stand when it first became evident that the fleet was deteriorating. There had been a string of incidents, and then the *al-Jahani* had driven the point home by blowing an engine during the Lookout rescue operation. The Academy's stock had skyrocketed when its ships rescued the Goompahs, and a few weeks later took out the Earth-bound omega cloud. Riding a wave of Academy popularity, the administration had promised ten new ships, *Flambeau* models, top-of-the-line. But the economy had gone south and the president discovered that starflight was suddenly not a big item with the voters after all.

Hutch knew about the early days of spaceflight, when the Americans went to the moon and then took the better part of the next half century off. And the second burst, which had featured a few manned missions to Mars and points beyond. But there had seemed nothing particularly interesting in the solar system. At least not to politicians and ordinary voters. Who cared whether microbes might be found on the fourth planet or in Europa's ocean? (As it happened, they weren't.)

There was a good chance the cycle was about to repeat. Eventually, she knew, the human race would spread out around the Orion Arm. But it wasn't going to happen quickly.

As for her, well, she imagined herself selling real estate or maybe running a physical fitness center somewhere. Hutch's Gym.

She was wrapping up her work, getting ready to go home, when Peter called again. *"We've got them."* He sounded as if the issue had never been in doubt. *"They're okay."*

"Thank God." She uncharacteristically raised a jubilant fist over her head. "Who found them? Where were they?"

"Nobody. We got a radio signal from them. Here. *At Union."*

"At Union? You're telling me they never got out of the solar system?"

"That's right."

"How do you mean? What happened?"

"They're well out past Sedna's orbit." The outermost known body in the sun's family. *"Seventy billion kilometers. Apparently, the drive never fully engaged. Or something."*

"That's not supposed to be possible."

"Well, there you are."

"So, they bounced out and sent a radio signal."

"Yes, ma'am."

SHE CANCELED THE remaining corporate flights. Then she called Asquith at home.

"Well, I'm glad to hear they're all safe," he said without enthusiasm.

She'd expected him to be delighted. "So what's wrong?"

"You say it was still in the solar system?"

"More or less. It was out near the orbit of Sedna."

"Which is where?"

"About ten times as far as Pluto."

"Incredible." She wasn't getting a picture, which meant he was sitting there in his pajamas. *"So all along, we were looking in the wrong place."*

"That's correct. Where they were, we'd never have found them. They radioed in."

"It took two days for the radio transmission to get here?"

"Something like that."

"You know, Hutch, from a public relations standpoint, this is almost as bad as losing the ship would have been."

"What are we talking about, Michael? They're alive. They all get to come home—"

"But they were in the solar system. *And we didn't know it. Think how that makes us look."*

"That's because something went wrong with the drive."

"You and I understand that. But we have the whole world watching,

every news organization on the planet following this thing, and it turns out nobody was ever in danger."

"Michael, nothing like this has ever happened before. What we understood about Armstrong space was that you could only travel through it at a fixed rate. It was always the same. You were in there one day, and you covered a little over ten light-years. You were there one second, and you did a billion klicks. That was it. No more, no less."

"We were wrong."

"The *physicists* were wrong. *Armstrong* was wrong."

"Unfortunately, we're the ones in the crosshairs. The only thing the public knows, and Hiram Taylor and his crowd, is that the thing was in our backyard, and we had no idea. We look dumb. What about the other ships you were sending out?"

"I've canceled them."

"Next time, I hope you'll show a little more patience." He shook his head, a great man rising above ordinary mortals once again.

LIBRARY ENTRY

If we conclude that the drive to explore the stars is *not* fueled by a desire to communicate with otherworldly beings, as has always been supposed, what then does it represent? I think an argument can be made that it is the same characteristic that brought us out of Africa, that sent men in wooden boats around the globe, that gave us the arts and ultimately the sciences: an insatiable need to know, to understand, to penetrate the dark places of our environment and throw light on them. It does not matter that there may be no one out there waiting for us, or that, if there is, they may turn out to be mundane. What does matter is that there are vast emptinesses, places we have not been, worlds we have not seen. If they are sterile, or if they have shining cities afloat on their seas, it is of no consequence. What *does* matter is that we will have been there, mapped the place, and moved on. And that so long as there is ground on which we have not walked, we will be unable to sit quietly in our living rooms.

—A. J. Klein, *The Cosmic Dance*, 2216

chapter 9

> When things go wrong, the standard management strategy is to decide who takes the blame. This should be an underling, as far down the chain as possible, but preferably with some visibility so people know management means business.
>
> –Gregory MacAllister,
> interview with *The Washington Post*

It should have been a night for celebrating. Hutch got a voice message from Abdul, thanking her for organizing the rescue. She really hadn't done much other than sit and watch, but it was one of the perks of the job that she got credit when good things happened. At least, inside the organization. Still, she was dismayed by the level of sarcasm aimed at the Academy. *"Right here in the solar system the whole time,"* said the Black Cat's Rose Beetem. A headline in *The Baltimore Sun* read: UNDER THEIR NOSES. One late-night comic observed that he now understood why we couldn't find intelligent life elsewhere: *"We can't find it at home."* A guest analyst on Worldwide endorsed the notion of a congressional investigation; another said it was time to shut the Academy down: *"Costs too much. And what do we have to show for more than forty years of massive expenditures? Where's the payoff?"*

She slept fitfully through the night, and woke shortly after dawn to Franz Liszt. One of the Hungarian Rhapsodies.

THE MORNING WAS warm and damp. Heating up already. Flocks of geese filled the sky, headed north. She called Mission Ops and Union Control and left messages of appreciation for all who had participated in the search. She relayed similar messages to the three ships that had conducted the hunt and to the two that had launched from Union only to be called back.

She also sent a reply to Abdul and his passengers: "Good to have you back. Next round is on us."

When she got to the office, she took time to express her appreciation to the people who'd secured corporate help. They were glad it had ended the way it had, and they told her anytime. But she detected a sense of distance in their voices. As if she worked for a minor-league outfit.

Later, Asquith sent for her. *"There's someone here I want you to meet."*

The visitor rose as she went in. He was middle-aged, well dressed, handsome in a sedentary sort of way. His hair was just beginning to gray. His eyes were blue, set close together. He had a long, narrow nose, and an expression that projected a general camaraderie. We're all in it together. The commissioner, seated with his back to the door, was commenting that "we need to find a way to shut down the irresponsible criticism." He might have been talking about Mac, but at the moment the entire planet was firing salvos at them. He looked toward her and pretended to be surprised to see her. "Priscilla," he said. "Didn't hear you come in. This is Charles Dryden."

Dryden almost looked impressed. "Priscilla Hutchins? I'm delighted to meet you. Please call me Charlie. I've heard a lot about you."

"Charlie works over at Orion Tours," Asquith said, signaling her to take a seat. "Something odd has been happening. Something we wanted your opinion about."

She looked from one to the other. "And that would be?"

A bot brought coffee. "You probably know," Dryden said, "we're in the process of building a hotel."

"I've heard," said Hutch. It was to be called the Galactic, and would be located in the Capella system, in orbit around the third world.

"Yes," he said. "When it's finished, it'll be gorgeous. There'll be easy transport to the ground. The planet itself has magnificent peaks near one of the oceans. Great beaches. Warm water."

"But no life."

"That's right. None whatever. That's another reason why we like it. We can put entertainment facilities anywhere we want. We'll be able to ferry people around, put them up in oceanside villas, or take them on VR hunts, and we don't need to worry about anybody getting gobbled. No predators. No bugs. No concerns about allergies. The skiing's good, and the vistas are breathtaking. The kind of place *you'd* like, Hutch."

Hutch resented the familiarity. But she let it pass. "Yes," she said, "I'm sure I would." And, in the same leisurely tone: "Is there a connection of some sort between the Galactic and the Academy?"

"Not directly." He rearranged himself in his chair. Big news coming. "Two weeks ago, at Beta Comae Berenices, one of our flights encountered some moonriders."

"I saw that," said Hutch.

"We've been seeing them on a regular basis. The day before yesterday, a flight of the things buzzed the construction site. The Galactic. Eleven of them."

"Charlie," she said, "we've never gotten anything solid about these things. They're probably a natural phenomenon—"

"Natural phenomena don't operate in formations."

"Sure they do. Bode's Law. Trojan-point and Lagrange-point orbits. Rings around gas giants. Braids in the rings. Rocks on a seashore. Lines of tornadoes. Northern lights. Sand dunes—"

"Okay. I get the point. What I'm trying to say is that moonriders have been around a long time. They go all the way back to the Bible."

"What are you suggesting, Charlie?"

"I think the Academy has a duty to find out what they are. If they're natural, as you argue, fine. But they may not be. I have to tell you, Hutch, I think you're closing your mind to this."

In fact she had not rejected the possibility that the moonriders were indeed visitors. But she was getting maneuvered somehow.

"Charlie thinks," said Asquith, "we should mount a campaign. Get some answers. Settle the issue."

"We'd help however we could," he said.

She looked at Dryden. "I'd think Orion would prefer not to have an explanation for the moonriders. If we come up with one, and it turns out to be, say, some sort of quantum thing that becomes visible in certain types of radiation, all the romance goes out of it. I can't see how that would benefit the tours at all."

She saw the silent exchange between the two. Conspirators caught in the act. Asquith managed a weak smile. "Can't fool you," he said.

"Actually," she said, "you don't give a damn about the moonriders. You want the publicity. You'd like us to put together a mission. The media would make a lot of noise about it. There'd be leaks, and somebody would notice how the moonriders are seen all over the tour routes. And Orion won't have enough flights to accommodate its customers. Am I right?"

"I told Charlie we'd have to level with you," said Asquith. "It all goes back to the funding issue, Hutch."

"And your problem," said Dryden, "is our problem."

That much at least was true. Orion's long-range tour operation was heavily dependent on the Academy's bases for replenishment, and also as ports that allowed their passengers to get out of the confines of the ships for a day or two. Orion and the Academy were joined at the hip. "If the Academy went under, Orion would have to establish and maintain its own stations, or stick strictly to its tours of the local neighborhood."

"We can't afford to let that happen," Dryden said. "And we don't intend to." He pressed his fingertips together. Man in charge. Everything was going to be all right. "Hiram Taylor's leading the effort in the Senate to cut you folks off at the knees. We need to make it politically uncomfortable for him to do that." Back in the good old days, Dryden would simply have bought Taylor. Or tried to. There would have been big campaign contributions. But that sort of thing had gone out two centuries earlier. The country had been taken over briefly by a corporate autocracy and hopelessly corrupt politicians. Money bought access. But the Second American Revolution had happened, people began taking the Constitution seriously again, and the practice of renting and buying congressmen had been stopped by the simple expedient of getting money out of the campaigns. Contributions of all types became illegal. Campaigns were funded by the voters. You gave money to a politician, it constituted bribery, and you could go to jail.

The world had changed. Politicians had come dangerously close to developing integrity. But as MacAllister would have said, they were no more competent than ever.

"We need to find a purpose for the Academy," Dryden said.

She was getting annoyed. "I was under the impression we had a purpose."

"You do. You do." He became apologetic. "You're talking about science. But science doesn't fly with the voters. Did you know that, among the major nations, nobody is more scientifically illiterate than we are?"

"I've heard that," she said.

"Go after the moonriders. If you solve the riddle, you advance the cause of science. Even if you don't, you stand a good chance of getting the voters excited about you again."

"They'll laugh at us," she said.

"That's probably true. Some will. But they'll also be interested. Involved. Get this thing up and running, and you might be able to head off Taylor and his cronies."

She looked at Asquith, secure behind his desk. "Where would you get the ships? We're already canceling missions."

"For the moment, we'd only need one," he said. "Just enough to engage the public interest. And Charlie has offered to make an Orion ship available."

"It wouldn't work if we use an Orion ship," she said.

"You're right," said Dryden. "Our ship would replace one of yours. It could take a mission out to Sirius or wherever, and free up one of your carriers."

"What it would do," said Asquith, "is visit some of the local systems where these things have been seen. It leaves a monitor in each, something specifically designed to watch for, and do a spectrographic analysis of, the objects. If any of them show up."

"These sightings are rare," said Hutch. "We'll make a big thing of this, plant the monitors, and see nothing. In the end, we just look silly again."

Warmth and goodwill literally radiated from Dryden. "We've

been seeing a lot of them along the Blue route, Hutch. Management has been trying to keep it quiet."

"The Blue route."

"It's our tour of the local area. Capella, Alpha Cephei, Arcturus, places like that."

"Why would Orion management want to do that? Keep it quiet?"

"They're afraid it'll scare away the trade."

They couldn't possibly be that dumb. "I doubt they need worry about it. If anything, people would line up to get a good look at moonriders."

"That's what I've been trying to tell them. But our management is a bit less"—he paused, searching for the right word—"creative, than yours."

Absolutely, she thought. They don't get any more creative than Michael. "I'm not excited about the idea."

Asquith held up his hands. Not your call. "We're going to do this, Priscilla. I mean, what can we lose? If we don't take some action, we'll be closing this place down in a few more years. You want to preside over that?"

"We've seen a lot of them," Dryden continued. "I don't think it would take very long before you started getting hits. Hutch, I know you're not excited about this. But please give it a chance. Give the *Academy* a chance."

"A mission to look for moonriders," she said.

Asquith cleared his throat. "I'll need you to set it up, Priscilla. Have it ready to go within six weeks."

"What about the monitors?"

"I've already talked to Mike." The Academy's chief engineer. "They'll be ready."

"Okay," she said. "Whatever you want."

Dumb. Orion had nothing to lose, but the Academy's credentials were about to go into the tank.

LIBRARY ENTRY

When one considers the state of the global environment, and of the global economy, the notion of spending enormous sums of money on star travel seems bizarre. There might be more stupid ways to throw money away, but it's hard to think of one.

—Marie Culverson (G-ME),
The Congressional Daily, February 18

BEEMER OUT ON BAIL
Preacher Will Press Charges

chapter 10

Talking with most people usually involves a search for truth. Talking with congressmen is strictly special effects.

—Gregory MacAllister, "I've Got Mine"

Hutch caught a break. The *Ron Peifer* was coming in Saturday morning with Abdul and his passengers. It meant she could make the dawn flight out of Reagan and be on hand to join the party. That had meant rearranging things with Amy. But the girl didn't mind. *"You're going to pick me up at four thirty? I'll be ready."*

"Glad you'll be there," Asquith told her. "We should have someone on hand when they come in."

She invited Tor to go along. But he was still involved in his exhibition. So it happened that Hutch, accompanied by her four-year-old, Maureen, collected Amy Saturday before dawn at the senator's Virginia home and headed for Reagan. There they caught the shuttle up to Union. Maureen had never been off-world before, and she sat in her harness straining to see out the cabin windows as the vehicle rose through a rainstorm and plunged into a sea of clouds.

It was fun. Hutch felt seventeen again, and they laughed and told jokes and had a good time. Amy took charge of Maureen, and the girls became fast friends. "You said you've been up there before," said Hutch.

"Yes. Years ago with my folks. It had something to do with work, and Mom and I went with Dad and we spent a few days there. We stayed in the Starview." The hotel. "And I was also there last year with my class."

"Why do you want to be a pilot?"

"It's what I've always wanted. Don't ask why. I can't give you a reason. My father's not happy about it, but"—she shrugged—"it's what I want."

"You'll enjoy it," said Hutch.

"How did *your* parents feel about it? When you told them *you* were going to be a pilot?"

That was a long time ago. "My father was dead by then, Amy. I think he expected me to become a librarian. Or maybe an accountant."

"Why?"

"He used to tell me I wasn't active enough. I guess I was something of a homebody. 'You need to go out and get some sun, Prissy.' That was what they called me. 'Prissy.' "

Amy giggled.

"I wouldn't answer to 'Prissy.' The other kids started using my last name. Which got shortened pretty quickly."

"How about your mother?"

"She was there when I got my license. She'd resisted it the whole time. Wanted me to find a good man and settle down. But I could see she was proud."

"Good."

"She never liked the idea of my being far away. She got rattled once when we went on a class trip to Lexington, Massachusetts. There was no way she was going to be happy about my heading off to Alpha Centauri."

They slipped into orbit, and the sky turned dark. The attendants served eggs and biscuits.

"But you did get married," Amy said. She smiled down at Maureen, who was waving a toy shuttle around. "So everything had a happy ending."

"Yes. I'd say so. But it kept my mom nervous for a long time."

Amy grinned. The thought of making the senator nervous must have appealed to her.

There were times that Hutch missed piloting. She had loved taking researchers out, especially ones who'd never been in space before, to see the objects they'd spent a lifetime studying. She'd been with Berghoff, the lifelong brown dwarf specialist, the first time he'd actually seen one. And with Dupré, who'd go on to do groundbreaking work on radio pulsars, when he got his first look at JO108-1431.

But she was happily married now, and if Tor wasn't always as exciting as, say, a flight to Procyon, it was okay. She wanted her life to be a bit dull. Dull was good.

"You don't really believe that," said Amy.

Hutch laughed. "I didn't mean for you."

THEY NEEDED TWO hours to overtake the station. When they did, Maureen clapped while Amy commented how beautiful it was. The senator was going to have trouble keeping her on the ground, Hutch thought.

They slipped under Union's flaring approach modules and banged clumsily into the dock. Harnesses lifted, and Hutch led her charges out through the airlock, along the ramp, and into the concourse. A press shuttle had arrived just moments earlier, and the boarding area was filled with journalists. She got past without being recognized. Minutes later they stopped at one of the viewports to get a look at the Earth. The ground was invisible through a solid layer of clouds, but they could see patches of ocean to the east.

The *Peifer* was due in a bit less than an hour. She checked in with Peter and let him know she'd be there when it arrived.

"Is the commissioner coming?" he asked.

"No," she said. "He had work to do." It was another thing she disliked about the job, covering for him.

After Peter signed off, she turned to the girls. "Okay, what do we do first?"

The concourse was filled with shops—buy a souvenir cap, enjoy a pizza, get a space station jacket, pick up a better piece of luggage. "Could we look at one of the ships?" asked Amy. "Maybe go on one?"

"Sure," said Hutch. "We'll go on board the *Peifer* when it arrives.

Meantime, how about some snacks?" They strolled along the concourse. The girls looked out the viewports at the blue planet beneath them, at the moon and stars. They stopped for cinnamon buns and saw a supply ship leave for somewhere. Amy insisted on watching it until its lights dwindled to a rapidly dimming star.

WHEN THE TIME drew near, they went down to the lower levels and turned onto one of the loading ramps. Hutch watched the girls react as they walked through a connecting tube giving them a view of the entire maintenance area. One of the ships, Maracaibo's *Alice Bergen,* cast off as they passed and started out. They stopped to gawk.

"It's beautiful," Amy said.

Hutch wasn't given to nostalgia. She'd learned early the importance of being able to cut ties and move on. Still, while she stood watching the long, gray shape slide through the doors, her heart skipped a beat. She wondered, not for the first time, if she'd made a mistake pulling the plug on her career so early. She had no passion for assembling flight schedules and assigning priorities to missions. She had done it not because she wanted to move up in the bureaucracy, but because she wanted to secure a stable home life. Because she wanted Tor and Maureen.

It had been a long time since she'd felt the emotions associated with making an approach to a previously unvisited world, or with standing in front of a temple built thousands of years ago by alien hands.

Peter broke in to warn her the *Peifer* was only minutes away. She didn't take the girls directly to the boarding area because visibility was limited. Instead, she slipped into Peter's communications section, where they could see the dim star that was the approaching vessel. It was coming in over the rim of the moon, growing progressively brighter, and they watched it blossom into a cluster of individual lights. At last they could see the outline of the ship itself, the sleek prow, groups of thrusters, the line of lighted windows marking the bridge. It was even possible, as it drew nearer, to see people inside. They watched it brake and finally disappear beneath the line of the viewport.

Hutch took them below so they could see the ship ease into its dock. "It's so *big,*" Amy said.

It was an electric moment. One Hutch suspected Amy would remember.

A boarding tube snaked out and connected with the airlock. The reception area was crowded with Academy technicians, journalists, family members, and probably others who just happened to be at Union and had come down to watch the excitement. They heard voices in the tube, everyone pressed forward, and the passengers began to come out. Four were the biologists who had been on the *Heffernan*; the others were passengers on the *Peifer*.

There were cheers and embraces. Then Abdul appeared. And finally the *Peifer*'s captain, tall and resplendent, the hero of the hour. His name was Koballah, and he had, until then, enjoyed a relatively quiet career.

The media crowded in, asking questions, getting pictures. "How did it feel?" they demanded of the biologists. "Were you scared at any time?" And, "Are you glad to be home?" Several backed Abdul into a corner.

A couple of the journalists, including a woman from *The National*, tried to raise the level of conversation, asking about the nature of the project in which the *Heffernan* had been engaged, and whether, in view of recent cancellations, there were any plans to reschedule the mission. In response to one of the questions, Abdul looked toward Hutch, and the press spotted her.

They left him and hurried in her direction, firing questions. What kind of condition were the Academy's ships in? Could she guarantee there wouldn't be more incidents? What exactly had happened? "I don't have any answers yet," she said. "You can see I have my hands full." She glanced down at the girls and got a laugh. "For now," she concluded, "we're just glad everybody got home safely. We'll let you know what happened as soon as we know the answer ourselves."

"Why," asked *The Washington Post*, "were you looking for the *Heffernan* in the wrong place?"

"We just didn't know where it was, Frank. It's pretty big out there."

She congratulated Abdul and his people on their safe return and took time to express her appreciation to the *Peifer*'s original passengers for their patience. She shook Koballah's hand and thanked him for bringing everybody home. Then she took the girls in tow and edged toward the tube. "Would you guys like to go on board the *Peifer* now?"

Amy said yes, could they look at the bridge? That was enough to engage Maureen's enthusiasm.

"Absolutely," said Hutch. She got Koballah's okay, and started up the boarding tube, which was transparent from the interior. Maureen looked out at the ship.

"It's pretty, Mommy," she said.

ON AN ADJOINING dock, the Academy's *Edward Barringer* was undergoing an engine overhaul. The rear of the ship was laid open, and three or four people, all in e-suits, were clambering across the hull. The *Barringer* was a Lakschmi class. It was of more recent vintage than the Colby, but by no means new.

Hutch used her link to ask Bobby Watson, the maintenance team chief, what was happening.

"It should be junked," he said, *"if you don't mind my saying so, ma'am."* Watson had been there since before Hutch started her career. He was near retirement, gray-haired, bearded, not inclined to put up with nonsense. *"There's no one single problem, Hutch. As far as we can see, it's okay. It'll probably get where it's supposed to go. It's just"*—he shrugged—*"these things have a lot of parts. They reach a point after a while where you don't trust them."*

"That bad?"

He looked across at her and glanced at the girls. *"You wouldn't want to take those two out on this one."*

"Bobby," she said, "give me a copy of the report. Okay?"

Amy led the way through the hatch into the *Peifer*. The engine room had already been sealed off by a maintenance unit, but Hutch showed them the living compartments, the VR tank, the workout area, the common room, and, finally, the bridge.

Amy beamed as she slipped into the pilot's seat and ran her fingers across the controls, dreaming what it would be like to direct the power of a superluminal. "I don't suppose we could go somewhere now?" she asked.

Hutch smiled. "I don't think the mechs would approve." She activated the status screen. It blinked on, turned red, and flashed NEG. "Needs fuel and a recharge."

"Do you think I could go out in one of these, Hutch? Not today, maybe, but when you have a chance?"

"I'll see what I can do."

She grew thoughtful. "This is the one you piloted, isn't it?"

"Yes. This was one of them."

"Why would you ever stop?" she asked. "Now you work in an office."

"Yes, I do. It's complicated, Amy." She looked around the bridge. "Bill, are you there?"

The ship's AI responded. *"Hello, Hutch. Welcome to the* Peifer. *Are these your daughters?"* Amy lit up. Daughter of a star pilot. She liked that. Hutch introduced them. Bill said hello to the girls and commented that Maureen looked like her mother. *"Hutch,"* he added, *"I've missed you."*

"I've missed you, too, Bill." The girls were looking through the viewports. All they saw, of course, were spotlights, cables, docks, and bulkheads. "I wish I *could* take you out," she told them. "You'd like riding with Bill." She could have arranged a virtual ride, but they'd know. Amy would, anyhow. And it wouldn't be the same.

Hutch looked at Maureen, wondering what *she* would see during her lifetime. Maybe, if Amy's father had his way, she'd watch the government shut down the interstellar effort. He was right, of course, to worry about the home world. But it didn't have to be a choice between staving off the greenhouse or continuing deep-space expansion.

FTL was not pork. Maybe it was time for the Academy to adopt a new motto.

"Bathroom, Mommy," said Maureen.

LATER THEY TOURED the station's maintenance section and looked at engines. But Amy wasn't all that interested, so they went back up to the main concourse while the senator's daughter talked about where she'd go if she had command of the *Peifer*. "Out to Betelgeuse," she said. "And to a black hole." She grinned. "I'd love to see a black hole."

"There aren't any close enough to reach," said Hutch, wondering if you really could *see* a black hole. That was a flight she'd like to make herself.

"And I'd love to see some of the monuments."

At first Hutch didn't put it together. Then she realized Amy was talking about the enigmatic creations left scattered around the local stars thousands of years ago by the inhabitants of Beta Pac III. The Monument-Makers. "There's one on Iapetus," she said.

Amy was holding Maureen's hand. "I know."

Maureen's attention had gone elsewhere. "Over there, Mommy," she said, pointing at Big Bang Burgers.

Hutch looked at Amy. "Hungry?"

"I could eat," she said.

They started across, but had to give way while a pair of preoccupied middle-aged types, a man and a woman, hurried past. They were shaking their heads, both talking at once. Hutch tried to listen, but the only phrase she caught was "—How this could happen—"

They disappeared around the curve of the mall. She took the girls into the Big Bang and both ordered more than they could eat. Shortly after the food arrived, hamburgers, salads, and french fries, Hutch saw John Carter hurry past. Carter had gone through life listening to jokes about his name. At the moment, he was carrying on an animated conversation with his commlink, and he looked tense. Carter worked with the station operations group, which was responsible for scheduling departures and arrivals. They were not connected with the Academy team, which coordinated and tracked missions.

"What's wrong, Hutch?" asked Amy. There was a tremor in her voice.

"Nothing, Amy," she said. "Why do you ask?"

"You look worried."

The tables in Big Bang Burgers were almost filled. Through one of the viewports, the Milky Way was visible, far brighter than it ever appeared from the ground. Hutch's mother claimed never to have seen it. Too much glare. Hutch herself rarely noticed it in the sky over Washington.

Somebody else charged past. Two of them. Going the other way. What was happening? She opened her link to Mission Ops. One of the watch officers, a woman, replied. "*Mason.*"

"This is Hutchins," she said. "What's going on?"

Mason sounded relieved. "*If you'd called a couple minutes ago, ma'am, I'd have told you maybe the end of the world.*"

* * *

THE ACADEMY'S OPERATIONS center was located down one level from the main concourse. Peter Arnold was on duty. Three or four technicians were grouped around him. They were staring at one another. Nobody was saying anything. "How big was the asteroid?" Hutch asked.

Peter looked simultaneously relieved, embarrassed, grateful. Like a man who'd just walked out of a building and seen it explode behind him. "I *do* think," he said, "somebody's looking out for us."

"Big," said one of the technicians.

"Where?"

"Just passed us. Came within two thousand klicks."

Maureen didn't understand what he was saying, of course, but she caught the tone and squeezed against her mother. "Are you serious, Peter?"

"Do I look as if I'm kidding?"

"We never saw it coming?"

"Somebody in McCusker's looked out and saw it as it passed." McCusker's was one of the dining areas. Peter took a deep breath. "I heard you were here." Then he noticed Maureen and Amy and managed a smile. "Yours?"

"The little one."

He said hello, and Amy asked whether they had any pictures of the asteroid.

"Let me play it for you." He spoke to the AI and one of the monitors came on. The asteroid was a flattened, potato-shaped object, tumbling slowly, end over end. The long blue arc of the Earth merged into the picture.

"How big?" Hutch asked.

"Four kilometers. Over four. They're telling us it would have been lights out for everybody. If it had gone down." The object was growing smaller. The Earth dropped gradually away. "That's taken from one of the imagers here, on the station."

"I can't believe we never saw it coming," said Amy. She looked at Hutch for an explanation.

Had it hit, Hutch knew, it would have thrown substantial amounts of debris into the atmosphere. Winter would have set in. Frigid, desperate, permanent. Unending. An infant born that day, and enduring for a normal span of years, would not have lived long enough to see the freeze end.

She opened a channel to station operations. "This is Priscilla Hutchins. May I speak with François, please?" That was François Deshaies, the director.

"Wait one, Ms. Hutchins."

She turned back to Peter. "Let the commissioner know."

"Okay."

She heard François's voice. *"Hutch. I assume you're calling about the rock."*

"Yes. Any more out there? Sometimes these things travel in packs."

"We've been looking. Don't see anything."

"Okay. François, how much warning did we have?"

"We didn't see it until the last minute." He sounded uncomfortable. *"We didn't know whether it was going to hit or not until it had passed.* C'est embarrassant."

"Could have been worse."

"Priscilla, I must go. We are getting traffic."

Peter was whispering into his link, watching her, and saying yes to somebody. Finally, he signaled her. "He wants to talk to you."

She switched over. "Hello, Michael."

"It's getting a lot of play," he said.

"I'm not surprised."

"How come we didn't know about it before time?"

She wanted to say he should ask his buddy Senator Taylor. "The old Skywatch program was shut down years ago."

"Skywatch? What the hell's that?"

"It was a few dozen independent astronomers who tracked Earth-crossers. But the Congress cut off their funds, so now they're down to a handful of volunteers."

"Hell, I don't care about that. What about our operations people?"

"It's not the Academy's responsibility, Michael. It's not what we do. Technically, it's up to the station."

"That's not going to sound like a very good answer when the questions start coming. Which I'm waiting for now."

"Michael, we don't even have sensing equipment. We ride along on the gear that Union uses. And now that I think of it, it's not their job either. They track flights. In and out. And that's all they do."

"Well," he said, *"there's going to be hell to pay. Asquith out."*

She smiled at that last one. Asquith out. As if he'd ever been *in*.

AS ARRANGED, SENATOR Taylor, with two security types, was waiting for them at Reagan, in the reception area. He collected his daughter and asked whether she'd enjoyed herself.

"Yes, Dad," she said. "We were on board the *Peifer*."

"Good." He looked at Hutch with an expression that suggested weariness. "You had an exciting day up there."

"You mean with the asteroid?"

"Yes."

"It was a near thing," she said.

"It's ridiculous, Hutch. All the money we spend and look what happens."

"We need to spend it a little more intelligently, Senator. Fund the Earth-crosser program. It's nickels and dimes."

"We have telescopes all over the world. And satellites. You name it. And nobody sees this thing coming?"

"You need something specifically dedicated to the task. A lot of—"

He put up a hand. "It's okay. I hear you." He told Maureen how pretty she looked. Looked at the child while he spoke to Hutch. "Thanks," he said. "I appreciate your doing this."

"You're welcome. It was a pleasure to have Amy along."

Amy looked from Hutch to her father. She seemed hesitant. "If you and Maureen go up again sometime," she said, "I'd love to go with you."

"You're on," said Hutch.

One of Taylor's security people took Amy in tow, and they headed for the exit.

LIBRARY ENTRY

The world narrowly averted a cataclysm today when a giant asteroid passed within less than a thousand kilometers. It is the closest known approach in historic times. Those who are expert in such things tell us the result, had it crashed, would have been global catastrophe.

The aspect of this event that is most troubling is that, given a reasonable advance warning, turning it aside would have been quite simple. But for reasons that are as yet unclear, the people manning the sensors and telescopes at Union never even saw it coming. The word is that they noticed the killer rock only moments before it would have impacted.

How close did it come?

It skimmed across the atmosphere. It could not have been closer. It was rather like having a bullet part our hair.

So who's responsible? You can bet there'll be an investigation. And somebody needs very much to be hung out to dry. The only real question at the moment: Who?

—Moises Kawoila,
Los Angeles Keep, Saturday, February 21

BEEMER SHOULD GET MAXIMUM

The unprovoked attack on a local clergyman should be dealt with severely. Violent crime has been on the rise during recent years. It is time to get serious with these thugs. The Henry Beemer incident is particularly outrageous. Beemer doesn't even have the justification that the assault occurred during a robbery. In this case, it was simply a mindless act, intended to inflict harm on an innocent man of the cloth. Nothing less than the maximum sentence is called for.

—Derby (North Carolina) Star

chapter 11

> The term *congressional hearing* is an oxymoron. No congressional hearing is ever called to gather information. Rather, it is an exercise designed strictly for posturing, by people who have already made up their minds, looking for ammunition to support their positions.
>
> —Gregory MacAllister, "I've Got Mine"

It was never possible to determine who first saw the asteroid. The guy in the restaurant had been first to report it to the operations center. But he said a young boy pointed it out to him. Two technicians working on a solar observatory in high Earth orbit at about the same time called their supervisor when they noticed a star moving through the sky. A group participating in an outdoor prayer service in Lisbon claimed to have seen the object and watched it for two minutes before it disappeared over the horizon.

Several calls were made to the Central Observation Group, and within seconds tracking devices in orbit and telescopes in northern Spain and the Caucasus broke off their current schedules and swung toward the object.

Word flashed around the world. The ultimate near miss. Close enough, in the words of the director of the Anglo-Australian Observatory at Epping, "to leave a few singed tail feathers."

By the end of the day, scientists were being interviewed on all the talk shows. While they disagreed on the level of risk posed by Earth-crossers, they were unanimous in predicting that eventually one of the rocks would hit. There was a lot of talk about dinosaurs. The headline on *The Guardian* summed it up:

IT'S JUST A MATTER OF TIME

Experts explained that there was really no need to be concerned about such objects because we had the capability to divert or destroy them. "But somebody," said the CEO of Quality Systems, Inc., "needs to let us know it's coming."

"So why didn't we see it?" Tor asked Hutch that evening, as they sat in their living room while Maureen played with a toy train.

"The Newhouse administration eliminated funding for the Skywatch program almost twenty years ago," she said. "Attempts to revive it keep getting scuttled, most recently with help from our good friend Senator Taylor. We've had a tracking program, off and on, using volunteers and private funding. But we need a more substantive effort. The odds against getting hit in any one president's administration are so astronomical"—she said it with a straight face—"that nobody takes it seriously. It's frustrating. All they have to do is pay a few people to watch the damned things. It would cost pocket change. But they can't be bothered."

Tor was a big guy, even-tempered, quiet, easygoing. When Hutch got frustrated and came home in a rage—as she periodically did—because of bureaucratic shortsightedness and mismanagement, he was always there, suggesting they head out to dinner, get a couple of drinks at Barbie's, and maybe spend the night at the theater. (There was a local repertory company that was quite good. Tor frequently talked about trying out for a part, but he wouldn't do it unless she agreed to audition also. Hutch, though, was inclined to stage fright. "I'll do it," she said, "if I can play a corpse. Or carry a flag, or something. I don't want any speaking parts.")

The frustration came with the territory, she told herself. She'd accepted the directorate and all that went with it. Still, when someone like Harry Everett came in and told her she was betraying her old comrades, the people who made the Academy work, it hurt. She hadn't told Tor about that conversation. Wasn't sure why. It might have been there was some truth to the charges.

"So what are you going to do?" he asked.

An image of the asteroid floated in the center of the room. It was part of a newscast, but they'd turned the sound down. "Maybe we got a piece of luck," she said.

He followed her gaze. "The asteroid?"

"It should remind people why they have to have an off-Earth capability. There are other big rocks out there."

"Maybe you should get Samuels to call a press conference Monday. Talk about it a little bit." Maureen pulled her train through the room and out onto the porch. It was supposed to be a glide train, but it only rose off the ground when you put it on the magnetic track. That was too much trouble.

SHE SPENT SUNDAY with Maureen and Tor, but had a hard time thinking about anything other than the asteroid. Monday morning, as she flew toward the Academy in her taxi, she looked down at the Virginia forests and thought of the vast distances she had traveled and how sterile the universe was. So few places could function as home to a tree. Humans took vegetation, and the biosystem as a whole, for granted. A forest seemed like the most natural thing in the world. Provide a patch of earth, some sunlight and water, and voilà, you got trees. But you needed other things that weren't so readily apparent. A regular orbit. A stable sun. Lots of distance between you and other celestial objects. It was not the sort of thing that would occur to you if you didn't get much beyond Virginia.

But anyone who'd gone out on the superluminals had a different mind-set. Robert Heinlein, back in the twentieth century, had gotten it right: the cool, green hills of Earth. What a treasure they are. Once you got off-world, the nearest forest was on Terranova, orbiting 36 Ophiuchi. Nineteen light-years away. How long would it take her taxi, cruising lazily through the gray early-morning mist, to cover nineteen light-years?

It dropped her at the rooftop terminal, and she strolled down to her office on the main floor, happy that the world was still intact, sobered by the thought of what might have happened. The *Heffernan* passengers were safe, the asteroid had missed, and all was well.

Or so it seemed until Marla wished her good morning in the voice she reserved to indicate something was happening.

"What?" asked Hutch.

"The commissioner wants you to keep your schedule clear this morning. He's going to want to see you."

"Did he say *when*?"

"No. 'Later.'"

"Did he say what about?"

"No, ma'am."

A smarter executive than Asquith would be summoning her to bestow congratulations on the recovery of the *Heffernan*, well done, join me later for lunch, I'm buying. But generally you only heard from Michael when there was a problem.

She poured herself a cup of coffee and switched on the newsnets. There were Abdul and his partners being welcomed at Union, handshakes and smiles all around. There, in the middle of her office, was the *Heffernan*, gray and black, its eagle markings illuminated by its rescuer's navigation lights. It was a satisfying moment. There was more heat to come, of course, but she could tolerate that. What she wouldn't have been able to handle was the knowledge someone had died because she hadn't stood her ground.

"It's hard to believe, Gordon," said a female voice-over, *"that the* Heffernan *was right here in the solar system and they never realized it."*

The solar system is a big place, lady.

"I suspect," said Gordon, *"there are some red faces over at the Academy. Which brings us to the near miss we had yesterday. How could they not notice a rock that big? Four kilometers long."* The asteroid appeared to Gordon's right, rotating slowly. It was nickel-iron, he reported, a relic from the formation of the solar system. Billions of years old.

"Nickel-iron," said the woman, *"means it would have made a bigger splash when it hit than simply a rock asteroid."*

She switched over to Worldwide, which had climatologist Joachim Miller talking about the Antarctic ice pack. *"It's melting fast, and it could slide into the sea at any time,"* he said. *"If it does, look for the ocean levels around the world to rise a hundred-seventy feet."*

"A hundred-seventy feet?" asked the show's moderator, visibly

shocked. Hutch wondered whether they'd rehearsed. *"That much?"*

"If we're lucky."

"Over the next few centuries?"

"If it happened today, I'd say by Wednesday."

IT WAS A pretty good argument for moving to Mars. Or establishing a colony somewhere. There was a lot of talk about doing just that, and in fact two colonies had been founded, one by political malcontents, the other by religious fanatics. Both were now on life support. It was just as well. The last thing the species needed was to provide a pristine world for lunatics, of whatever stripe. Do that, she suspected, and it would eventually come back to haunt us.

Even off-world habitats had not prospered. There were plans to construct two in the Earth-moon region, but the contractors had run short of funds, and promised subsidies had never materialized.

The asteroid had been named, prosaically, RM411. The Black Cat had tried to tag it the Armageddon Special, but their own consultants laughed at them, so they dropped the attempt after the first feeble efforts. *"Legislative bodies around the world,"* Detroit News Online was saying, *"are promising investigations of how it could have happened. An unnamed source with the World Council said there'll be a substantive review, and that they intend to determine who's responsible."*

Science & Technology predicted that *"somebody's head will roll. Why are we giving the Academy all that money?"*

It's not our job, you idiot. Just because something is off-Earth doesn't automatically make it our responsibility.

She switched over to Capitol News, which was interviewing Hiram Taylor. Live from the Senate building. He looked angry and righteous, and his black hair kept falling into his eyes. They were by heaven going to straighten things out. The American people deserved better than this. *"It's only by the grace of God that it missed us. No thanks to the people in place who are supposed to protect us from these things."* He didn't name the Academy, presumably because he knew better. But he left it out there, knowing full well the conclusions his audience would draw.

Hutch wondered what the going rate was for a hit man. The Senate's Science Advisory Committee, to which Taylor belonged, did not, of course, control funding for the Academy, but the House panel that decided such things would listen closely to what they said.

She called the commissioner. Not in yet. She went to Eric. "They're blaming us," she said.

"I know." Eric threw up his hands. *"I have a press conference scheduled later this morning. We've put out statements, I sent Ernie down to do an interview, and I'm taking a couple of the media guys out to lunch."* Ernie was Eric's staff assistant.

The other newsnets were all taking a similar approach. They were questioning scientists around the globe. Burnhoffer of Heidelberg admitted he didn't know who had been assigned the responsibility for the Earth-crossers, but that someone was clearly remiss. Burnhoffer had ridden the Academy's ships to Procyon and Sirius and had briefly held the Odysseus trophy as the human being who had gone farthest from the sun. That had been presented after a mission to Canopus. (Those making the award considered only the senior person on the mission, and of course never the pilots.) She'd liked Burnhoffer, but here was an object lesson in keeping your mouth shut when you didn't know what you were talking about.

It was pretty much the same with every politician and academic type in sight. The Academy was at fault.

Shortly after ten A.M., Asquith called her to his office. "I'm heading over to the Hill."

"For the committee?"

"Yes."

"The asteroid?"

"That. And probably the *Heffernan*." He cleared his throat. "You've got the fort." And before she could respond, he was gone.

SHE WATCHED ON Worldwide. There were about three hundred people present in the hearing room. Six senators were distributed around the table, backed by a phalanx of aides. Seated before them, looking supremely uncomfortable, was Asquith. She felt sorry for him. The secret of his success had always been that he knew just enough to get by, stayed out of confrontations, and made friends in the right places. He also had a talent for not getting singed when fires broke out. But not this time.

Opening remarks came from the committee chairman, Elizabeth

Callan, expressing her gratitude for his taking time to come down and speak with them. Throughout her comments, Hiram Taylor smiled benignly while alternately scribbling notes and nodding to a staff aide.

The Green Party was currently in the majority, so the Academy was already in difficulty. The Republicans had no interest in attacking the interstellar program. It had been around a long time, so they were for it. But the Greens were a different matter. Money that could be put to good use at home was going into space.

Callan recognized Ames Abernathy, a Republican from Iowa, but one who thought scientific advance was dangerous. Abernathy started by noting the Academy's many accomplishments over the years. He extended his congratulations to Asquith for "superb leadership." *"We're all indebted to you and to the brave men and women who risk their lives out among the stars."* Et cetera. Finally, he got to business: *"I assume, Dr. Asquith, this has been a difficult week at the Academy."*

"Not really, Senator. Actually, we're doing well, thank you. We continue to push out into unknown systems. To explore—"

"Yes, yes. Of course. But we know your time is valuable, so let's go directly to the point. You lost one of your ships last week. For about three days."

"That was actually closer to two days, Senator."

"Yes, very good. I appreciate the correction. What we'd all like to know, and I think I can speak safely on this point for my colleagues, how could that ship, the Heffernan, *have been right here in the solar system all that time, and your people not know about it? Doesn't that suggest somebody's not doing his job over at the Academy?"*

"Not at all, Senator. You have to understand the solar system is a big place."

"I think we're all aware of the size of the solar system, Dr. Asquith. What we're wondering, though, is how it's possible to lose a starship in it for two days?"

"We didn't exactly lose the ship."

"You didn't know where it was, did you?"

"No. Not precisely."

"Not precisely. I seem to recall hearing ninety light-years *bandied around. Would that be correct? Is that how far you thought it had traveled?"*

"Yes. But there's a reason for that."

"I'm sure there is, Doctor. But in fact it was out around Pluto."

"Actually it was considerably farther than Pluto—"

"Be that as it may, Doctor, you had no idea where it was. Am I correct?"

"Yes, Senator. But there's a reason—"

"And I'm sure we'd all like to hear it. After all, it's like looking on the other side of the Mississippi for something you misplaced in the cloakroom."

It went on like that for a while, the others taking their turns pummeling the director. Eventually, Taylor got a chance. His first few questions were softballs, what sort of long-range plans did the Academy have, where should we go from here, and so on. But he couldn't resist going after the organization, and eventually he zeroed in on the asteroid. *"We never saw it coming, did we?"*

"No, Senator. But you should be aware it's not our responsibility—"

"You have all that equipment at Union. You watch ships come in, and oversee their departures. How can it possibly happen that an asteroid several miles wide could sail in and not be noticed?"

"We weren't looking for it, Senator."

"That seems to be the case. Would you have been able to see it, had you been *looking?"*

At no time was it a fair fight, and when it ended, three hours later, Asquith got up from his table and walked out, a beaten man.

LIBRARY ENTRY

There is a tendency to denigrate the Congress. No one will argue that the congressional wars, over the years, have had any trace of nobility about them. Yet, despite everything, we have the consolation of knowing that we leave the great national issues in the hands of men and women who, if they are not always evenhanded, are nonetheless invariably competent and well-informed, and who place the welfare of their fellow citizens above all other considerations. *(Audience laughter)*

—Milly Thompson,
The Comedy Hour, March 12, 2141

DATE SET FOR "HELLFIRE" TRIAL
Henry Beemer Goes to Court April 22

chapter 12

> Faith is conviction without evidence, and sometimes even in the face of contrary evidence. In some quarters, this quality is perceived as a virtue.
>
> —Gregory MacAllister, *Life and Times*

The light from the fireplace flickered against the heavy wooden altar. His Majesty staggered forward, supporting himself against the gray stone wall. He stopped by the portal, gazed wearily out at the night sky, and listened to the wind moving among the battlements. Then he turned back to the altar and fell to his knees.

MacAllister stood unseen in the doorway. Only a few steps away. He drew his sword. *Now might I do it pat,* he thought, *now he is praying. And now I'll do't.* He stepped out into the uncertain light. And paused. *And so he goes to heaven: and so am I revenged. That would be scann'd; a villain kills my father; and for that, I, his sole son, do this same villain send to heaven.*

The king bowed his head. He was praying audibly, but MacAllister could not make out the words.

He took my father grossly, full of bread, with all his crimes broad blown, as flush as May; and how his audit stands, who knows save heaven? But in our circumstance and course of thought, 'tis heavy with him: and am I then revenged, to take him in the purging of his soul, when he is fit and season'd for his passage?

No. Up, sword, and know thou a more horrid bent: when he is drunk, asleep, or in his rage, or in the incestuous pleasure of his bed . . .

Across the room, a red light winked on. Responses to the Beemer package were in. Another time, then. He stood several moments, then withdrew from the chamber, leaving the king deep in prayer.

ADVANCE COPIES OF the Henry Beemer hellfire story, which would appear in the upcoming issue of *The National,* had been sent to a number of media preachers for comment. He preferred media preachers to those who simply worked in churches because they were far more likely to overreact. And indeed, as he looked through their responses, he saw that he had exactly what he wanted. They called him an atheist and a godless sinner. He was all that was wrong with the country. He and his satanic publication should be banned. *Burned.*

To get some balance, he'd also sent copies to less fiery clerics. Their replies were also predictable: We don't push damnation much, they said. We tend to believe hell is reserved only for special cases. That was reasonable, but MacAllister wasn't looking for *reasonable.* He wanted the true believers.

While he read through the stack, selecting the most raucous for the letters column, he switched on Worldwide and was surprised to discover Michael Asquith appearing before the Senate Science Committee.

It was a mugging. The commissioner was being taken down by a gang of politicians. What did that say for the level of leadership at the Academy? He wondered how Hutch could tolerate working for the guy.

Meantime, it was Monday, his busiest day, the day he put *The National* together. But he was running ahead for a change. The layouts were done, the stories in place, all except the cover story, which he wasn't satisfied with. The letters column and the lead editorial still needed to be assembled. But he had a draft of the editorial, which addressed the unavailability of jobs across the nation for any but highly trained specialists with advanced degrees. There was always a need for physicians. But roofers, carpenters, waiters, stock boys: All were effectively things of the past. The result was a chasm between the well-off and everybody else. As an example, *The National* had no use for a copy editor. Everything was done by an AI. Reporters, yes. There was a staff of eleven full-time correspondents, and a substantial number of occasional contributors, but there were no other employees. Meantime, the welfare rolls swelled, and crime grew exponentially. If you wanted to be sure of a career, become a physician or a lawyer. Everything else was, at best, pizza delivery.

He'd assigned his most linguistically abrasive associate to get the Beemer interview and do the research. The result, "Hellbound by Lunchtime," would ruffle some feathers. Already had. The cover depicted Beemer, looking tired and forlorn, surrounded by a group of ten-year-olds, all staring at flames that looked as diabolical as Tilly had been able to produce. The subtitle ran across the bottom: EDUCATION OR INDOCTRINATION?

The National, like most publications, was interactive. You could read an interview, you could watch it, and, to a degree, you could participate in it. A lot of his readers thought they were talking with the editor. They were, of course, getting Tilly. Tilly was named for Attila, a figure who was, in many ways, admirable.

On-screen, the committee had finished with Asquith, were filing out, or standing around talking to each other while the commissioner disconsolately made his way out of the room.

THE NATIONAL WAS devoted to commentary on science, politics, and the world at large. It ran book reviews, a letters section, three editorials, political cartoons, a logic puzzle, and a section on the state of the language. MacAllister had never lost his affection for a well-composed sentence, and nothing drew his disgust quite as effectively as overwritten pieces, prose that wandered about without ever getting to the point. He didn't think well of adjectives, despised adverbs, and insisted his correspondents rely on nouns and verbs. *They do the heavy lifting,* he'd said numerous times while handing back copy with large chunks carved out of it.

The staff meeting for each issue was held Monday afternoon after the current issue had been put to bed. So what was on the horizon for next week that we want to cover?

All eleven correspondents were present, two physically, the others via hookup. The lead story, they decided, would be on the danger posed by the possibility of the southern ice cap giving way. How serious is it? he asked the reporter who'd been assigned to do the background work.

"Worse than the Council's letting on," she said. *"It could let go with virtually no warning. If the whole thing goes down, as they expect it will, there'll be hundreds of thousands dead along the coastlines."*

"What are the odds?" asked Chao-Pang, in Madagascar. *"We've been talking about it for two centuries."*

"They're still doing computations. But they look scared."

Okay. That would be the cover. Let's take a serious look at this thing. How likely is it to occur in, say, the next year? How prepared are we? Has the administration taken serious steps, or are they hoping nothing will happen until they're out of office? (He already knew the answer to that one.)

Next up was a developing political scandal, a prominent House leader taking money and other benefits from lobbyists.

"Guilty?" asked MacAllister.

"Absolutely."

"Will he step down?"

"Not voluntarily. But it looks as if he'll wind up in jail."

Then there was the artificial sperm issue, which would make it possible to dispense with males in the reproductive process. Not desirable, of course, but possible. And that was enough to bring out the legions who feared for the moral fabric and claimed we were playing God.

Who's your daddy? The phrase would take on a whole new meaning.

"How's it going to go?" asked MacAllister.

The response came from Hugh Jankiewicz, who covered the House. *"There'll be a fight, the ban will fail, then there'll be a reaction and a bigger fight. Eventually everybody will get used to it. I suspect nobody will be able to show any harm done, and we'll move on to something else."*

"Where's the advantage?" asked MacAllister.

"Purely political," said Jankiewicz. *"It will enable some women to claim men have become irrelevant."*

* * *

WHEN THE LINE cleared, a call was waiting.

"Mr. MacAllister? My name's Charles Dryden." MacAllister immediately decided he didn't like the speaker. He smiled too easily. It was okay for young women, but in men, especially older men, it was a giveaway. He was dressed in the kind of clothes one wore in the executive suite.

"Yes, Mr. Dryden," he said. "What can I do for you?"

"Mr. MacAllister— May I call you Gregory?"

"If you like."

"Gregory, I represent Orion Tours. We're putting together a major advertising campaign. We've been looking at the reading audience of The National. *By and large, they fit the profile of the sort of people who use our service. They are intelligent, well educated, and they do not lack for resources."*

MacAllister roundly disliked people who couldn't flatter and sound as if they meant it. "Thank you for the compliment."

"We'd like to make your publication one of the core engines of the campaign."

He wasn't certain what a core engine was, but he wasn't going to quibble. "Excellent, Mr. Dryden," he said. "I'm sure you'll find *The National* a profitable investment."

"Yes, indeed. I have no doubt it would be advantageous to both our organizations. By the way, please call me Charlie."

"Okay, Charlie. It's a pleasure to meet you. How about if I transfer you to our marketing director and you can let him know precisely what you want." The marketing director, of course, was Tilly.

"Before you do, Gregory, there is one thing we'd need to clarify. You, personally, are on record as being opposed to the effort to promote starflight."

"Well, that's not quite accurate. I think interstellar exploration is fine. I'm just not sure it should be a high priority for taxpayer funds at the moment."

"Yes." He glanced at something far away. The smile looked a bit pained. *"I understand the distinction, of course. Unfortunately, we have some people on our board who perceive you,* you, *not the magazine, as an active opponent to the effort to take humanity to the stars."*

"I'm sorry to hear that, Charlie."

"What we'd like you to do is soften your stand somewhat."

"What would you suggest?"

"Oh. Nothing major. Just maybe an editorial pointing out that you do *favor the expansion of the human spirit into deep space. Something to that effect."*

"You know, Charlie, you're right. That's exactly how I feel. I'm not entirely sure what it means, but I'm for it."

There was a moment of confusion while Dryden considered what MacAllister was saying. Then the smile came back. *"Excellent. Then there's no problem."*

"—But I won't write the editorial."

"Well, a simple statement on one of the interview shows would probably be sufficient."

"I'm sorry, Charlie. It's not on my list of priorities at the moment. Orion is welcome to take advertising space with *The National,* or not, as it pleases. But you don't get to dictate editorial policy. I enjoyed talking with you."

HE SPENT THE evening reading a new novel by Judah Winslow, a young man who had a magnificent career in front of him. He'd just finished the book and was about to call it a night when Tilly let another caller through. *"Anthony DiLorenzo,"* the caller said. *"I'm a physicist. University of Cairo."*

"What can I do for you, Dr. DiLorenzo?"

He looked like the Ancient of Days. Lined face, white whiskers, full jowls, watery eyes. *"I saw the show you did last week.* Up Front."

"Okay."

"I'm in full agreement. But you've missed the real boondoggle."

"Which is what?"

"The Origins Project. It costs tens of billions."

"I'm aware of what it costs, Doctor. At the moment we're fighting one battle at a time. Anyhow, the bulk of the funding for it comes from the Europeans."

"It doesn't matter. I suggest you fight this one and forget the Academy."

"Why?"

"How much do you know about Origins?"

"Just that it's expensive."

"Did you know there's a chance it could blow up?"

"Sure. That's why they moved it out to 36 Ophiuchi."

"Mr. MacAllister, actually it's located several light-years the other side of 36 Ophiuchi."

"What are you trying to tell me, Doctor?"

"It might not be far enough."

That got his attention. "What do you mean? What kind of explosion are they expecting?"

"They aren't expecting *one, but they are concerned about the possibility."*

"Could you explain, please?"

"Several kinds of miscarriages are possible. But, since they are where they are, we need only concern ourselves with one."

"Okay."

"Worst-case scenario: It's possible an event at Origins could destroy the Earth."

"Doctor, they are *light-years* away."

"The Origins Project is a hypercollider, Mr. MacAllister. Nothing remotely like it has ever been built before. And it's probably perfectly safe."

"Probably."

"There's an outside chance that the thing could tear a hole in the fabric of space."

"A hole in space? What does that mean, exactly?"

"If it happens, the end of everything." He began trying to explain, citing equations and theorems that meant nothing to MacAllister.

"Wait a minute," MacAllister said, finally. "What's *everything*? You mean the entire project might blow up?"

"The entire universe, sir. Everything."

"You can't be serious."

"The chance that it would happen is remote. But there is *a chance."*

"Give me a number."

"Maybe one in a million. It's hard to say."

"One in a million they could blow up the universe."

"That's not precisely what would happen. But the effect would be the same."

"Do the people in charge agree with your assessment?"

"Some think the odds are longer. Some that there is no chance at all. It's possible the odds are very low. We simply do not know."

"What's the point of the research?"

"To learn how the Big Bang was generated." His eyes bored into MacAllister. *"You have influence in high places. Get it stopped."*

MACALLISTER'S DIARY

"Give me the children until they are seven and anyone may have them afterward." Francis Xavier's comment. A child's mind is open to learn, and it is a cruel and heartless thing to fill it with myth disguised as history, to impose upon it a bogus lifelong perspective, and close it up again, leaving it proof against common sense and all argument. Surely, if there is a hell, people who do this are the ones who will get their tickets punched.

A judgment by the God who devised the quantum system should be considerably different from the one the Reverend Koestler envisions. I gave you a sky full of stars, and you never raised your eyes. I gave you a brain, and you never used it.

—Monday, February 23

MOTHER APOLOGIZES FOR
SON'S ATTACK ON PREACHER
"Always a Difficult Child"

chapter 13

> An optimist is somebody who thinks our various political and social systems, schools and churches, support groups and Boy Scout troops, jury trials and congressional committees, are on the up-and-up. That they are intended for the benefit of the members. The reality is that they are designed to keep everyone in line.
>
> —Gregory MacAllister, "Red Flags"

When Asquith arrived at his office in the morning, several of his staff surrounded him, telling him how good he'd been, how he'd struck exactly the right note, how he couldn't have done more for the Academy. Hutch was in the lobby a half hour later when he came out of one of the conference rooms. She saw that the happy talk had had no effect. The commissioner *knew*. He flicked a pained smile at her and shook his head. Then he was gone, down the corridor that led to his office.

She felt sorry for him. He wasn't really a bad guy. Had he not gotten into politics, he would probably have been okay.

She returned to her own suite and went back to work on the rescheduling. She was bringing the Colbys back to Union, one by one, and arranging to have them removed from service. That meant telling people who thought they'd arranged transportation a year or so ago that their projects were delayed or canceled.

Four of the eight Colbys were engaged in survey work, which consisted of visiting and mapping star systems along the frontier. She had done a lot of that in her time. It was easily the most exciting assignment a pilot could get because you never really knew what you might find. The researchers had always maintained they were interested primarily in their specialties, gas giant climatology, ring system formation, volcanic influences on the origin of life, and so on. But they were just like the pilots: They lived for the day when they'd blunder onto an advanced society. When they entered a system and somebody said hello.

It had never really happened. Not in the sense that we found our technological equals.

Nor, of course, had we found the possibility that really gripped the imagination: a million-year-old civilization. The evidence so far indicated that societies rose, flourished for a brief period, and declined. Or fell precipitously. It was still too early in the game to draw general conclusions, but Hutch was beginning to suspect no long-term civilizations existed.

She reluctantly drew red lines through four scheduled flights. She rearranged things to keep imminent operations on track and give those who were being canceled at least two months' warning. That meant moving everybody around a bit. She knew sometimes the programs couldn't be carried out if the timing was thrown off, but she did it anyhow. When she was satisfied she could do no more, she called Asquith.

"I'm going to notify these people today," she said. "I'm sure you'll be hearing from them. They are not going to be happy."

His eyes slid shut. It was hard, being persecuted by a shortsighted world. *"Hutch, I wish you would rethink this."*

"I got the report on the *Heffernan* this morning." She explained to him how the pressure generated in the jump engines weakens the entire system over time. "Nobody was killed on this flight, but it need not have happened that way. It could have blown up in their faces. There are other problems as well, and they can't all be fixed. Michael, we do not want to continue with things as they are."

"I think we need to avoid going off half-cocked, Priscilla."

She sent him a document. "This is a copy of the maintenance report on the *Barringer.* It's Lakschmi class."

He stared at it. Squinted. *"It's a bit technical. What's it say? Plain English."*

"Unsafe."

He stared at her for a long moment. *"That's a ninth ship."*

"It's going to require extensive work. Costs more money in the long run than replacing it."

"Okay."

"Is that *okay,* make the schedule changes, or *okay* we'll buy a new ship?"

"Make the changes, Hutch. Maybe it's just as well. Maybe it'll put some pressure in the right places."

IT WAS TIME. She'd been stalling on the later cancellations, hoping some divine intervention would occur and she wouldn't have to go through with them. But there was no way that could happen.

She could have simply sent notifications to everybody who was involved. They would have responded by calling Asquith and yelling at him. Which he profoundly deserved. But she couldn't bring herself to do it.

She'd canceled sixteen missions that would have gone out over the next six months, and rescheduled twenty-seven others. Altogether twenty-three organizations were involved. "Let's start with the cancellations," she told Marla. Get the really ugly ones out of the way first.

"Paris Gravity Labs," said Marla. *"Connecting with René Dufresne."*

Dufresne was her liaison. When he appeared, she explained the situation. Some of our ships are old. Don't trust them. Terribly sorry. Have to cancel the April mission.

"Cancel?" said Dufresne. He was tall, not young, unfailingly polite. That made giving him bad news even more difficult. "Don't you mean *postpone*?"

"Unfortunately not, René. At the moment we have no way to compensate. Gravity Labs has three missions scheduled, with four more in the queue. Something's got to go. We can't just back everything up."

He was seated in an armchair, a sheaf of papers open on his lap. *"The director won't be happy, Priscilla."*

"None of us is happy, René. But the director would be much more upset if we took some of his people out and got them killed."

"Well," he said, *"can't you even give us a choice on which projects get canceled?"*

"Within limits," she said. "Give me your preferences, and I'll try to accommodate. Unfortunately, I can't promise."

It made for a long morning. Most of the others were more excitable than Dufresne. A few threatened her, informed her they'd go over her head to the commissioner, insisted they'd have her job. At Morokai-Benton, the liaison was also the chief of the research team. He all but broke down and sobbed.

ASQUITH INVITED HER to lunch. That was a rarity, usually only done when he wanted something. He took her to his club, at the Rensellaer, which was a place of leather, filtered sunlight, soft music, and hushed voices. "Thought you'd like a break," he said. "My treat."

They talked about trivialities, personnel problems, upcoming visits. She avoided politics. He asked how she was coming on setting up the moonrider tour.

"Okay," she said. "We'll be ready to go."

"Good." He was looking for a chance to introduce whatever it was he had on his mind. "It would be nice if the mission actually showed some results."

"Yes, it would." She ordered a burgundy and a steak salad. Asquith went with tuna and a Scotch and soda.

"We'll get some benefit out of it," he said, "if it does no more than call attention to the moonriders."

"Let's hope."

"You still don't believe there's any rationale for this mission, do you, Hutch?"

"If we had resources, I'd say sure. But we're tight."

"We're always tight. Even when the funds are flowing, there are too many projects. As long as I've been here, it's never been any different." He adjusted himself, and she knew they were about to get to the point. "The mission would get a lot more attention if the right person went along."

"Who's the right person?"

"Your buddy MacAllister." The drinks came. Asquith watched her try hers, asked how it was, and wondered aloud if the editor would be open to an invitation.

"To go out hunting moonriders?" Hutch couldn't resist a laugh. "I can't see *that* happening."

"If he were on board, it would guarantee a lot of attention."

"It would make us look that much more foolish when we don't find anything."

"Hutch, we're not expecting to find anything. All we're doing is distributing monitors. This sort of thing takes a while. That's simple enough. People have to have patience." He bent over the Scotch and lowered his voice. "Look, what I'd really like to do is expose him to what we do, and how we operate. Up close, you know what I mean? Get him out of his office, let him see what's out there. Maybe we could win him over."

"I doubt it."

"You're so negative, Hutch. What can we lose?"

She sighed. "All right. I'll do what I can. But if you want him, we shouldn't make an announcement yet about the flight."

"Not make an announcement? But the whole point—"

"Trust me. Keep it quiet for the moment. And tell Charlie not to say anything, either."

"Okay." He checked the time. Man in a hurry. "Do we have a pilot yet?"

"I'm working on that, too. I'll let you know in a day or so."

"Who did you have in mind?"

"Gillet."

"I was talking with Valentina yesterday. I mentioned it to her. She said she'd like to go."

"Michael, I think Gillet—"

His shoulders sagged. "Hutch, why is everything with you an argument? Valentina's a better bet."

"She's more photogenic."

"Bingo."

SHE WOULD USE the *Maria Salvator* for the moonrider mission.

Orion was providing a ship to carry out the flight for which the

Salvator had originally been scheduled. So she didn't have to cancel anything. But the operation was going to be an embarrassment anyhow. When word got around they were out hunting spooks while simultaneously grounding scientific operations, there'd be a second wave of screams.

Asquith had sent down a stringent budget for the moonriders. She called him, and they bickered back and forth until she'd gotten a little more. Then the cost of the monitors became an issue. It had turned out that the commissioner wasn't entirely serious, and had shown that lack of seriousness to Mike Cranmer, who'd been charged with putting together the design specs. Hutch talked with Cranmer, and with a few others, and got a sense what the monitors should be able to do.

Mike suggested an upgrade for the sensors. It was also possible to get better analytical gear. Hutch would have liked units capable of giving chase if they spotted something, rather than just sitting there passively. But a serious drive unit would send the cost over the horizon.

She called Asquith and told him the changes they were making, including the drive unit, which she knew would never pass muster. It was a bargaining chip, though, and she ultimately conceded it for the other upgrades.

Then there was the issue of programming the monitor AI. If the moonriders responded to the scan, if they asked the monitor how it was doing, what sort of answer did we want to give? Please hang around; we're on our way? Where are you from? What's going on?

Eric put his head in. "You doing anything, Hutch?"

"Other than flushing my career? No. How about you?"

He took his accustomed seat. "I'm good," he said. "I spent the morning putting together a press release."

"On what?"

"The orbital configuration at Toraglia."

The *Britton* had reported an incredible tangle of eighteen worlds, with accompanying moons, and two companion stars, orbiting the red giant. Three more planets orbited one of the companions. Six of the worlds were thought to have been captured from a passing star. None possessed a biosystem, of course. So the public would likely pay no attention.

Eric talked about his job, that he was getting bored, that he wished Asquith took public relations more seriously, that he was beginning to realize he'd hit his head on the ceiling and was thinking about putting in his résumé elsewhere. Finally, he got to the point: "The moonrider mission."

"Yes."

"It's still scheduled to go out in April?"

"Beginning of the month."

"When are we going to make a public announcement?"

"In a few days."

"May I ask why we're keeping it quiet?"

"I'm trying to bait a hook."

"You want the story leaked?"

"Yes."

That got a smile. "Okay. You want me to do it?"

"Do you know any of *The National* reporters?"

"Sure. Wolfie Esterhaus usually covers us for them."

"Okay. Good. Leak it to Esterhaus."

"When?"

"Today would be good."

"All right. I'll take care of it. Now I have a favor I want from *you*."

"Sure, Eric. What do you need?"

"How long do you anticipate the mission will be out?"

"A month or so."

"Who's going?"

"Valentina."

"Who else?"

"Don't know yet." She wasn't inclined to invite anyone. No researcher with a reputation to protect would want to go anywhere near it.

"I was wondering if I could make the flight."

He looked serious. "Why, Eric?"

"I'd just like to get away for a while. Do something different."

"I have no problem with it. Can you get an okay from the boss?"

"I've already talked to him. Told him I was considering it. I suggested it would be a good PR move if I went."

"Okay. Sure. I don't see any reason why not."

"Good. Then it's settled."

"It's settled."

"Thanks, Hutch."

"My pleasure." She hesitated, and they sat watching each other like a pair of boxers. "You want to tell me why you *really* want to go?"

"You wouldn't understand."

"Try me."

"People here take you seriously, Hutch." His eyes drifted away. "Me, I'm just a guy who came in from an ad agency."

"The media know you represent the commissioner."

"I'm not talking about the media. Though they're part of it. I'm really talking about the people here. Inside the building. I get tolerated. That's all."

"Eric, that's not true."

"Sure it is. Even by you. When you talk to me, I can see it in your eyes." He tried to push it away. "Look, I'm sorry. I didn't mean anything by it. But I've been here almost twelve years now. You know I've never been off-world?"

She didn't. Although she wasn't surprised.

"I've never even been up to Union."

"Eric, I hear what you're saying. But this mission . . ." She almost said it was just PR. "I don't think we're serious about it."

"You know, Hutch," he said, "there *is* something out there."

"And you want to be part of the flight that finds it."

"I'm not dumb enough that I think it'll find anything. But it'll lay down the monitors. And there's a good chance the monitors will eventually pick something up." He tried to look upbeat. "Even if it doesn't, at least I'll be able to say I've been out in the fleet."

NEWS DESK

THREE KILLED IN ANTIGRAVITY SHAFT

Power Failure Causes Mishap

Fall Seventeen Floors

Everett-Glasko Insists Systems Are Safe

POPULATION CRUNCH WORSENS

Global Count to Hit 7 Billion This Summer

Catholic Church Will Not Change Contraceptive Ban

Can Anybody at the Vatican Count?
(Comment by Josh Tyler)

"VIOLENCE" GENE CAN BE REMOVED
Ultimate Anger Management May Be
Available for Next Generation
But Do We Want People Who Won't Get Angry?

POLL: PUBLIC IN THE AIR
ABOUT INTERSTELLAR TRAVEL
39% Oppose, 30% in Favor, 31% Undecided or Don't Know
Recreation for the Rich? Yes and No, Say Americans
Many Admit to Conflicted Views

EVANGELICALS AGREE: MAKE FOR THE STARS
"Closer to God," Says Massey

FUNDAMENTALIST GROUPS
OPPOSE REFORESTATION BILL
Baker: "No Need to Worry about Environment;
End Times Are Near"

HOLLAND TUNNEL MUSEUM TO CLOSE
Maintenance Expenses Force Shutdown
Roadway Converted to Museum in 2179
Mayor to Make Final Trip Through

ACCIDENT AT MOONBASE: TWO DEAD
Both Victims Members of Construction Team
Water-Extraction Module Had Just Passed Safety Inspection

FLU OUTBREAK KILLS THOUSANDS IN EAST AFRICA
Medical Teams on the Ground Too Late
Where Were the Vaccines?

STUDENT SHOOTS SIX IN JERSEY HIGH SCHOOL
Uses Antique Rifle
Sheriff's Son Charged; Described as Loner

RUSSIANS, CANADIAN-AMERICANS
BECOME MAJOR AGRI-POWERS
Corn and Wheat Belts Moving North

MOONRIDERS ARE NOT ALIENS: TALVANOWSKI
"Probably Quantum Jets"

MACALLISTER WILL PAY FOR
DEFENSE IN HELLFIRE TRIAL
National *Editor Stirs Pot*

chapter 14

> There are few professions whose primary objective is to advance the cause of humanity rather than simply to make money or accrue power. Among this limited group of humanitarians I would number teachers, nurses, bookstore owners, and bartenders.
>
> —Gregory MacAllister, "Icons"

The Virginia Education Association met annually in Richmond during the third week in February to name the recipients of its Teachers of the Year awards. These were granted to a plethora of elementary and high school instructors. Various civic groups joined in. The Thomas Jefferson Freedom Guild granted special recognition to the winner of the political science award. The Jump Start Reading League provided plaques to several of the elementary teachers. The Academy gave its Distinguished Contribution to Science Education Award to the VEA's science teacher of the year.

The National also presented a trophy for auspicious public service, known among the correspondents as the Courage Under Fire Award. The recipient would be a science teacher from a West Virginia high school who had defied demands by his school board and a small posse of parents that human enhancement be targeted as not proven, not safe, and socially unacceptable.

Usually, MacAllister assigned the presentation to one of his reporters. But this year, he had decided to do the honors personally. The reason was that he wanted to take advantage of the occasion to have a few words with its guest of honor, the prize-winning physicist, Ellen Backus.

He enjoyed the social advantages that came with celebrity. He drifted through the hotel meeting room, shaking hands with visiting dignitaries, pretending to the precise level of humility that he associated with greatness.

Shortly before seven thirty, the guests began filing into the banquet room. MacAllister found his place at the head table, shook hands with the emcee, introduced himself to Backus, and sat down. Moments later salads and rolls arrived.

He was still in the process of telling Backus that he was impressed with her work when his commlink vibrated. He excused himself and wandered to the side of the room. It was Wolfie.

"Yes," he said.

"Mac, I was talking with an Academy source."

"Okay."

"They're putting together a moonrider mission. Going out looking for the things."

"Are you serious?"

"Yes. And apparently it's not just a stunt."

"How do you mean?"

"How else can I say it? They are serious."

"Explain that to me."

"I don't know if I can. I get the impression there've been more sightings than anyone's been admitting. Apparently, they've been seeing them all over the place."

"You trust your source?"

"He's always been on the money before, and he has no reason to lie to me."

AFTER THE CEREMONY MacAllister took Backus aside. "I've a question for you, Professor."

She looked barely out of high school. Smooth face, honey-blond hair, soft hazel eyes. "Of course, Mr. MacAllister. Fire away."

"Do you have any connection with the Origins Project?"

"You mean, have I ever been out there?"

"No. I mean, are you aware of the details?"

"It's not my specialty, Mr. MacAllister—"

"Call me Mac."

"Mac. But I know a little about it."

"Are there hazards?"

"How do you mean?"

"Are the experiments dangerous in any way?"

The eyes locked on him. "I don't think there are any undue hazards. You start crashing atoms together at the kind of velocities they're using, and there's always going to be a degree of risk. That's why they built it out where they have."

Mac tried her first name. "Ellen—"

She smiled. "You're talking about where the universe goes down a black hole."

"Something like that. I had a call from Anthony DiLorenzo. Do you know him?"

"Not personally. I know of his work."

"Would you mind giving me your opinion of him? It'll go no further."

"As I say, Mac, I don't know him. He has an outstanding reputation."

"He says there's a chance that when they turn on the hypercollider it will"—he consulted his notes—"rip the fabric of space. End everything."

She nodded. Looked as if someone had just belched in the middle of dinner. "Yeah. I've heard that. I don't think the possibility is very likely."

"Then it *is* possible."

"Oh, sure. You get into an area like this, where we still don't know very much, and *anything* is possible. But I don't think it's worth worrying about."

"You're telling me the Origins Project could conceivably destroy the universe, but it's not worth worrying about?"

She looked amused. "Mac, I had no idea you were given to panic."

"How would you state the odds?"

"Astronomical."

"For or against?" She laughed, but she was beginning to look around. It would be just moments before she realized she had to be somewhere else. "Doesn't it seem to you," MacAllister continued, "that if there's a potential for a catastrophe on that scale, we should stay clear of the experiment, no matter what?"

"Mac." She looked up at him. "Don't lose any sleep over it."

HE CALLED HUTCH, but her AI told him she was in conference. She got back to him an hour or so later. He was home by then, working on a review of a new book by Zacarias Toomas. Toomas had done a series of brilliant introspective novels, analyzing the assorted misconceptions and hypocrisies of suburban life in modern America, but this latest one, *Parlor Games,* was a disaster. Despite his reputation, MacAllister took no pleasure in assaulting good people. He didn't mind taking out after the assorted blockheads who consistently got themselves into the public eye. But somebody like Toomas . . . He was a MacAllister discovery. And a friend.

Ah well.

Then Hutch was sitting in front of him. *"What can I do for you, Mac?"*

She was cool and businesslike. He tried to soften the moment, commenting that he'd watched Asquith testify.

"We'll survive it," she said. *"Eventually we survive everything."* He read the implication: *Even our friends.*

He refused to get annoyed. "I understand you have an April mission going out."

"We have a couple missions in April. Which one were you referring to?"

"The moonrider flight."

"Ah. Yes. I'm surprised you heard about that. We haven't released the information yet."

"Then it's true?"

"Oh, it's no big deal. We're just going to take a look around."

"When's it leaving?"

"I'm not supposed to say anything."

"Hutch." His fatherly voice. "Between us. It'll go no further." When she hesitated: "I have a reason for asking."

"I'm sure you do. We'll be launching at the beginning of the month."

"Why hasn't there been an announcement?"

She hesitated. Lowered her voice. *"I know how the moonriders play, Mac. I didn't want people laughing at us."*

"You think they're really spaceships?"

"No." She tried to laugh it away.

"Then why are you running the mission at all?"

She took a deep breath. *"Because there's a chance, Mac."*

"It must be more than that, Hutch. What aren't you telling me?"

"There's been a wave of sightings. We can't just dismiss them all." She sat back and crossed her arms. *"How'd you find out?"*

He switched to his east European accent. "Ah, my dear, I have my methods."

"I'm sure. Is there anything else you needed?"

She looked as if she were about to terminate the conversation. "How long will the mission run?" he asked.

"About a month. Maybe a bit longer." She looked off to one side. *"Mac, I have to go. I'm awfully busy right now."*

"Okay. Just give me a minute more, and I'll get out of your way. Are they going to find something?"

"That's not the purpose of the mission. They're just going to be distributing monitors."

"These recent encounters, the ones that haven't been made public, can you describe some of them for me?"

"I'm just not free to do that, Mac."

"You're not a good liar, Hutch." She stood quietly watching him, not reacting. And he knew exactly what she was up to. "If I were to ask to go along, you'd make room for me, wouldn't you?"

"Reluctantly."

"*Reluctantly*, hell. You want me to make the flight. That's what this is all about, isn't it?"

She sighed. *"You got me."*

"Why?"

"Mac, we're hoping to use the flight to create some public interest. Get people excited about the work we do."

"I see. And you thought if I went along—"

"The story would get bigger."

"Why didn't you just ask?"

"I didn't think you'd do it."

"Try me."

She softened. Smiled. *"Mac, it's not as much fun that way."*

"You wanted to fox me, didn't you?"

"I thought you'd have enjoyed the flight. You get a cabin to yourself and a tour of some of the loveliest places in the area."

In fact, the mission might provide some material for *Dark Mirror*. At the very least, he saw no problem with giving the Academy space in *The National*. He expected, though, that she wouldn't care for the result. "You still haven't asked if I would go."

"Mac, would you go? Do it for me?"

"Sure," he said. "Wouldn't miss it."

LIBRARY ENTRY

Press Release: Kingston Foundation

The Martha Kingston Foundation, which donates millions every year for scientific research in a wide range of fields, today announced that Charles Dryden, an executive with Orion Tours, will receive this year's coveted Kingston Prize, awarded annually to their most successful fund-raiser.

Mr. Dryden is a product of the University of Kansas. He started his career as a political aide. . . .

BEEMER ON MEDICATIONS

Henry Beemer, charged with attacking a preacher in a bookstore last week, has been increasingly depressed and quarrelsome, according to coworkers and friends. . . .

—*Derby (North Carolina) Star*, Tuesday, February 24

chapter 15

There was a time when you could retreat from the mass of humanity simply by moving into the forest, or heading for an island. Then it became the back side of the moon. With the development of FTL, nowhere is safe. If history is a guide, we will not stop until every green patch in the Milky Way has a squatter.

—Gregory MacAllister,
"Slower Than Light Is Fast Enough for Me"

Hutch's exchange with MacAllister left her in a glorious mood. She had never thought of simply coming out and asking. Well, she had, but it would have seemed too much like an imposition, so she'd not seriously considered it.

She had not been exaggerating when she'd told him she was busy. A stack of documents a foot high waited on her desk, and a group of Israeli astrophysicists was due in the building at any moment.

"Hutch," said the AI, *"Amy Taylor is trying to reach you."*

Amy? "Put her through, Marla."

The teenager wore khaki shorts and a University of Virginia pullover. She flashed a smile that was at once innocent, shy, and calculating. *"Hi, Hutch,"* she said. *"I hope I'm not disturbing you."*

"Not at all, Amy. I'm a little rushed at the moment. But what can I do for you?"

"I just wanted to know if I could come over sometime and you could maybe show me around the Academy? If it's not too much trouble."

"Sure. When did you want to come?"

She was trying to say something else. Hutch waited while she found the words. *"Hutch, the truth is, I'd love to go on an Academy mission. Go somewhere nobody's ever been before."*

"Amy, those flights tend to be long ones. You'd be away a few months. I'm not sure that would work."

Amy nodded. *"You don't have anything close by? I know we haven't gone everywhere around here."*

"There are a lot of places that are only a couple of days out that we haven't bothered with, Amy. But usually there's a reason."

"Okay." She shrugged. *"I just thought I'd ask."*

"There are tours."

"I don't think it would be the same. Anyhow, my father wouldn't approve."

"If he wouldn't approve of a tour flight, why would you think he'd go along with something more exotic?"

"A flight in an Academy ship? How often does that come along? He might see a political advantage to it."

The girl's explanation sounded reasonable. "I'll take a look around, Amy. See if we have anything."

SHE WAS NEVER sure when the possibility first occurred to her to offer Amy a berth on the *Salvator*. Later, recalling the sequence of events, she thought she'd been toying with the idea before the call came in. The more she thought about it, the more promising it seemed. She'd only be gone a few weeks. There would be, for a teenager, a certain cachet about the mission. The ship's AI could handle her schooling. She'd be in good company, and the trip would be something she'd remember for a lifetime.

She put through a call to the senator. He got back to her late that afternoon from his office. *"Hello, Hutch,"* he said. *"It's good to hear from you."*

"Senator, we have a flight going out in early April—"

"The moonrider flight—"

"I don't guess we've had much luck keeping it quiet."

"The commissioner mentioned it to me." He shook his head. *"These are crazy times we live in."*

"Yes, they are."

"I hope you find something. It would be nice to know whether there's anything to these stories."

"I doubt there is," she said.

"I take it this is Michael's idea."

"Pretty much."

His standard smile widened. Became genuine. *"He claimed you were behind it."*

"Ah," she said. "He likes to give credit to the help."

"Yes, I'm sure." He held up a hand to stall the conversation, exchanged comments with someone at the other end, then turned back to her. *"Sorry, Hutch. Now, what can I do for you?"*

"Senator, I was thinking we might do something nice for Amy."

"That's very generous." He looked wary. *"What did you have in mind?"*

"She's mentioned that she'd enjoy making an Academy flight. Most of the missions go too far. They're out too long. But the *Salvator,* which is doing the moonrider flight, is just going to be making a tour of local star systems. Anyhow, we have space if you'd approve, and I thought it would be something she'd enjoy."

Taylor looked reluctant. "I don't know," he said.

"She'd get to see the Origins Project. And the Galactic Hotel at Capella, and the Hightower Museum. And Terranova, and—"

"Hold on, Hutch. That sounds good. But I'm not comfortable having her away from school that long."

"Once-in-a-lifetime experience, Senator."

"Also, I'm not sure I can accept this kind of favor."

"That's a call you'd have to make, sir."

"Yes. Hutch, let me get back to you."

It took less than twenty-four hours. Hutch got a call from an excited Amy the next morning minutes after she'd arrived in her office. *"Hutch,"* she said, *"thank you."*

* * *

CLEARY'S WAS A small, posh coffee shop overlooking the Retreat, the alien habitat that had been disassembled and transported from the Twins and reconstructed on the banks of the Potomac in Pentagon Park. It was midmorning, and Hutch was sitting at a corner table snacking on coffee and bagels when Valya walked in.

The Greek pilot scanned the interior, spotted her, and came over. "Hi," Valya said. "Sorry I'm late. I lost track of the time." She was wearing a flowery yellow blouse and gray plaid slacks. "What's up?"

The moonrider flight was a mission to nowhere. Oddly, though, Hutch was beginning to regret she wouldn't be on the bridge. "Not much. We're losing missions left and right."

"So I hear." Valya had soloed with Hutch. It had been her qualifying flight. "The bagels look good." She collected one from the counter and sat down. Fresh coffee came. She smeared grape jelly on the bagel and took a bite. "Well," she said, "I hear we're going out looking for gremlins."

"Moonriders," Hutch corrected gently. "The mission's scheduled to leave April 2."

"Sounds intriguing."

"I understand you'd like the assignment."

"Yes, I'd be interested in doing it." She tried the coffee. "Truth is, with what's happening to the missions, I was afraid I'd be grounded for a while."

"If there are any other flights that interest you—"

"Yes?"

"Talk to me first. Don't go over my head again."

"Hutch," she said, "that's not the way it was—"

"However it was, don't do it again."

"Okay." She lowered the cup slowly onto the table. "I'm sorry. I didn't mean to create a problem." For a long moment neither spoke. Then: "What's going to happen? Are they going to shut down the Academy?"

"I don't think they're that dumb."

"You don't sound hopeful."

Hutch shrugged. "I just don't know." Valya shared her passion for the Academy. She recalled their brief time together on the *Catherine Perth* with a sense of pride. It was a time when the Academy was sending missions in all directions, when people still talked about finding what they called a sister civilization. Someone we could talk to. Compare experiences with. The term had fallen into disuse in recent years. And the hunt for the sister civilization had by and large been replaced by teams that went out to inspect stars, to measure their characteristics, and to place them in categories. Necessary work, she supposed, from the point of view of astrophysicists, but boring to the general public. The imagination and the electricity had gone out of starflight, had drained away like a receding tide. And now the Academy wondered why Congress was talking about cutting its subsidy once again. Maybe Michael was right. Maybe the only real course they had was to take a chance, go with a shot in the dark, and hope the *Salvator* found something. Hope the ship turned out to be appropriately named.

It would be uniquely satisfying if, after all the probing hundreds of light-years away, we found that the sister civilization had come to visit *us*.

"I think the Academy will survive," Hutch said, "but we're in for some rough times in the short run."

Valya sat back. Hutch had to concede that Michael had picked the right pilot for a PR flight. She had lovely features, luminous eyes, congenial personality. And she was quick on her feet. "I hope you're right," she said.

"Valya, have you ever seen any of these things?"

"No. I haven't."

"That's probably a good thing."

"I thought so, too. So you want me to place the monitors. Do you know precisely where, in each system?"

"Bill knows." The AI.

"Okay. Now, let me ask the next question."

"Go ahead."

"Suppose we were actually to spot one of these things—"

"That's unlikely."

"But if we do, do you want me to try to contact it? To give chase? What?"

"That's simple enough. Try to find out what they are. Record everything you can. Get an explanation. Sure, if you get a chance to pull alongside and say hello, do so."

"Absolutely. Maybe we'll bring them home for dinner."

"That would be nice."

"Who's going to be on the team?"

"There *is* no team. You're it. Eric Samuels will be on board."

"The public affairs guy?"

"Yes."

"Why?"

"He wants to go. Give him a chance, Valya. He's a good man."

"Okay. Anybody else? Don't I get a specialist?"

"There are no moonrider specialists. At least none we want to be associated with. But there *are* two other passengers. One's a friend of yours."

"Really? Who's that?"

"The guy you did the show with last week. Gregory MacAllister."

She stiffened. "You're kidding."

"I thought you did a good job, by the way. Held your own against a pretty tough character."

"What on earth is MacAllister doing on this flight? He's a windbag."

"Actually, he's one of the more influential people in the country."

"He's still a windbag, Hutch. You're not really going to lock me up with him, are you? He's out to sink the Academy."

"You're right that he doesn't think what we do is very important. That's one of the reasons he's going. He hasn't traveled much off-world. In fact I think this is only his second flight, and the other time out he damn near got killed. He's offered to go along and take a look around. You'll be showing him some of the more spectacular local sights. It's a chance to win him over. If you could manage that, you'd be doing us all a major good turn."

"Hutch, I've seen this guy up close. I don't think his mind is open."

LIBRARY ENTRY

The Case for a Navy

The sightings in recent years of strange vehicles in faraway systems, and in some cases over Arizona, are probably attributable to drifting gas, to overwrought imaginations, to people seeing what they want to see. Is anyone other than ourselves really out there flying starships? The answer to that however is most certainly *yes*. Just within a hundred light-years or so, we have several technological civilizations, or their artifacts. And an additional handful of places with recognizably intelligent creatures. The old notion that the universe was essentially ours to do with as we please was never tenable.

If the moonriders are illusory, just reflections in the vastness of space, then so be it. But we owe it to common sense to determine whether that is so. In the meantime, we would be prudent to consider what our position would be if we encounter others, and they turn out to be hostile. Most experts maintain that any civilization smart enough to cross the stars will have long since dispensed with warfare. But we've already seen that idea trashed by the omega clouds. Who knows what else awaits us?

It's only common sense that we begin to construct a fleet of warships. It would be costly, but not nearly as costly as finding ourselves trying to head off extraterrestrial creatures who think we would look good on a menu.

—*Crossover*, Thursday, February 26

PART TWO

amy

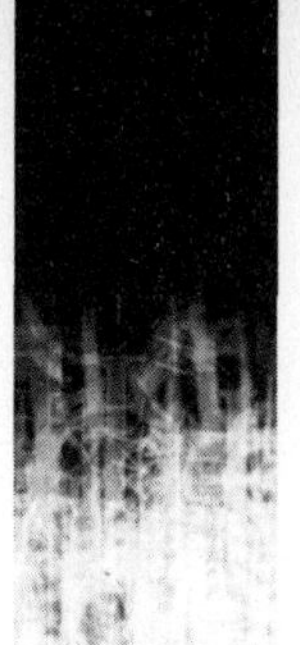

chapter 16

> Certain types of decisions can be safely ignored. Some issues will go away with the passage of time, others will be so slow developing that the decision-makers will depart before the results of their neglect become manifest. Which brings us to the environment.
>
> —Gregory MacAllister, "No Rain Again Tomorrow"

MacAllister told Wolfie to take over while he was gone on what he called his "grand tour." His last official act before leaving was to write an editorial arguing that the Origins Project be shut down. Primarily he cited the cost. In addition, he noted, we are not going to get a better can opener from it. He tried to work in the danger that lay in the project, but no matter how he phrased things, the notion that a facility nineteen light-years away could be a hazard to people living in South Jersey just didn't make the cut for serious commentary.

He'd made a few calls to physicists with whom he'd come in contact over the years, but they all took the same tack Ellen Backus had. There was just enough of an admission to raise the hair on the back of his neck. But nobody was willing to speak for the record. The idea was just too far-out.

So he'd let the editorial go without bringing in the Armageddon feature. If it turned out he was right, and everything blew up, he wouldn't be able to take much satisfaction in it anyhow.

Several major stories were developing. A best-selling novel, it appeared, had been written by an AI. A group of fanatics claimed to have found an ark halfway up Ararat. MacAllister had been having a good time all his life at the expense of the pious; but if indeed there was only one universe, and all the parameters had been set exactly right to permit the birth and development of living things, then it was hard to see how else it could have happened save by deliberate intent. He wondered whether he would spend his twilight years in a monastery.

The president was caught in an influence scandal that was sapping his ability to govern, and the American Catholic Church was talking about reuniting with the Vatican. Another cloning bill had surfaced. (The technology had gone worldwide, but was still banned in the North American Union.) Almost 75 percent of kids grew up missing at least one parent. Crime rates were down, but violent crime—murder, rape, and assault—was up sharply. It had been climbing for almost ten years. Why was that?

As the date for departure neared, he grew less enthusiastic about the project. For one thing, he'd discovered the pilot would be the overbearing Greek he'd had to deal with on *Up Front*. For another, he began to feel he'd been carried away by the emotion of the moment. He tried to persuade himself he'd enjoy the tour, would get to places he'd never see otherwise, but he was going to be sealed up alone with Valentina Whoever; Eric Samuels, who was an idiot; and a fifteen-year-old girl. He'd committed to it, so there was no getting out. But after this, he and Hutch were even.

Other than delivering a few snickers, the media had paid no immediate attention to the announcement that the Academy was undertaking a mission to look for moonriders. It was "simply an assessment of the situation," according to the Academy's press handout. "An effort to determine whether there's a factual basis for reported sightings." Magnificently noncommittal. The fact that he would be on board was leaked later, suggesting there was more to the story than the Academy was prepared to admit. As a result, a few barbs had come his way. The *Hartford Courant* considered itself surprised that any serious journalist would be party to a moonrider hunt. *Moscow Forever* wondered whether he'd "finally gone over the horizon."

The deviousness left MacAllister feeling compromised. He'd complained to Hutch, who'd assured him everything would be fine, and advised that he "just ride it out." "You're bulletproof," she'd added later, when the media began suspecting the government was keeping some sort of terrible secret and MacAllister was in on it.

He'd responded by issuing a statement that the media were right, that there was something MacAllister knew that the world was not yet ready to hear. "We've been analyzing moonrider activities," he said. "It looks as if the aliens are every bit as dumb as we are." He took to calling them UCMs. Unidentified Cruising Morons.

There was a popular fantasy series at the time, *Quantum Street,* which had a distinctive musical theme, and people began warbling it in his presence. The two women he was seeing socially couldn't resist knowing smiles. And he even started getting requests for interviews on the subject, all of which he turned down.

MACALLISTER WAS PROUD of his reputation as a major-league crank. People who didn't know him assumed he was the same way socially, cantankerous with friends, and generally hard to get along with. None of that was true. Susan Landry, who was the closest thing to a romantic interest in his life, was fond of describing him to friends as a pussycat. He knew Hutch thought him a soft touch.

The lesson to be gleaned from all this was that he needed to start behaving seriously like the crank whose image he so assiduously cultivated.

A small group of friends threw a party for him the night before departure. During the course of the evening, they smiled and drank to the moonriders and wished him luck. It was almost as if he were going on a one-way mission. He understood the implication: Make a flight like this and expect never to be taken seriously again. At least not as a journalist.

Susan assured him she'd love him no matter what.

One of his reporters gave him a complete bound Shakespeare and talked as if MacAllister was not coming back. Another observed how good it had been to work with him all these years, and that he would never forget him. The guy was actually close to tears.

When it was finally over—thank God—they stumbled out into an unseasonably chilly night, shaking his hand as they went. Geli Goldman gave him a wet kiss. Geli had tried once to get him into her bedroom. She was forty years younger than he was, just becoming an adult at the time, and it would have been unspeakable to take advantage of her. Especially in light of the fact she was a talented writer who would undoubtedly have recalled the incident in some future memoir. He kept reminding himself of that possibility. It was the linchpin of his virtue.

SHORTLY BEFORE DAWN, he took a last look around the apartment, went up to the roof, and climbed into a taxi. It was warm and muggy, with no stars. Occasional flashes of lightning played along the western horizon. But the ride was smooth and quick.

At Reagan he checked his bags, had breakfast, paged through the *Post,* and, just after six, boarded the shuttle.

The vehicle, which had a capacity for twenty-eight, was half-empty. Among the other passengers he saw two families, both with kids, obviously heading for a vacation. He checked to see whether one of the big cruise liners was scheduled out. But there was nothing currently in port. So they were probably just treating the kids to the space station. See what the world looks like from orbit. Well, in that way, at least, there was profit to be had. Nobody could look down at the planet, green and blue, with no borders in evidence and no sign of human habitation, and not get his perspective forever altered.

Twelve years earlier, MacAllister had walked the ground of Maleiva III, a world as large as the Earth, during the last few days before it plunged into the clouds of a gas giant. Aside from the fact that the experience had terrified him, his perception of planetary stability had changed radically. He'd returned home with a heightened awareness of how delicate the seemingly indestructible Earth really was. It had made him a dedicated Greenie. Now he had only contempt for people who thought the world was forever and it was all cyclical and human beings were too puny to cause any lasting damage.

An hour and a half after his departure from Reagan, the shuttle docked at the orbiter, and his harness released. MacAllister was off-world for the second time. He told himself to straighten up, that he'd enjoy the flight and catch up on his reading if nothing else. In fact he needed a break. This would be his first vacation in nearly nine years. (He prided himself on telling people he *hated* vacations.) But it would be good to get away from the routine for a while. He let the other passengers get off before he rose and headed casually for the exit.

As he emerged from the boarding tube, he was surprised to find Hutch waiting. As always, she looked good. Crisp white blouse, dark blue slacks. There was a teenage girl with her. That would be Amy. "Good to see you, Mac," she said. "Hope you had a good flight."

"Yes, indeed," he said. "I've been looking forward to this."

"Good. I suspect you'll enjoy yourself. Amy, this is Mr. MacAllister."

The girl was almost as tall as Hutch. She looked bright enough, but he could see a resemblance to her father. That was a problem since he didn't like her father. Taylor's politics were sensible; but he made too many speeches and clearly thought well of himself.

Despite the resemblance, she was pretty. She extended her hand, and bracelets jingled while she told him she'd read *The Quotable MacAllister*. "I enjoyed it," she said. "You have a marvelous sense of humor."

The book had been put together by a pair of maverick journalists. MacAllister hadn't gotten a cent out of it. "Thank you, Amy," he said. He was impressed. The girl obviously had a brain.

"You'll be leaving in four hours," Hutch said. "I've arranged to have your bags delivered directly to the *Salvator*. I hope you don't mind."

Hutch never seemed to change physically. But she'd become more subdued over the past two or three years. The devil-may-care attitude he remembered from the Deepsix rescue was gone. Maybe it was motherhood; more likely it was watching the decline of the Academy. He wished there were something he could do to ease that particular trauma.

They stopped at a place called All-Night Charlie's for coffee. "They've been servicing the ship," she said. "But it should be ready for boarding in an hour or so."

"Wish you were coming?" he asked.

"Part of me does." She glanced at Amy, who was hanging on the answer. "One day, when the kids are on their own, I'd like to take one of the ships out and go deep again."

" 'When the kids are on their own.' You have another one coming?"

"Yes," she said. "A boy."

"When's it due?"

"September." She looked radiant.

"Congratulations."

Amy squeezed her hand. "When it happens," she said, "I'd like to be your pilot." Hutch smiled.

"You know," said MacAllister, "you sound as if you don't really expect it to happen. The flight. The deep one."

Hutch considered it. "Tor's not like you, Mac. He's not much of an adventurer." That was her little joke, but she didn't crack a smile. "He's been off-world just enough to know he prefers life in Virginia."

"You don't think he'd go?"

"He might. To keep me happy. But he wouldn't enjoy himself. And that would pretty much take the pleasure out of it."

The coffee came. They had a good view of the moon through one of the ports. MacAllister marveled at the mountains and craters. They were spectacularly bleak.

VALENTINA WAS WAITING on the ship, seated in the cramped cockpit they call the bridge. She was busy talking to the AI, raised a hand to say hello, but never really broke off the conversation. She'd apparently already met Amy, who had spent the night on the station. MacAllister backed away, mildly irritated, and retreated to a larger room just off the bridge. This was, Amy explained, the common room. "It's where everybody hangs out," she said.

Moments later, Valentina joined them. Her eyes fastened on MacAllister, and she broke into a smile that was almost mischievous. "Sorry," she said, "I was in the middle of something. Hutch, the monitors are loaded and ready to go."

"Okay." Hutch was visibly amused at the interplay between the pilot and her passenger. "I guess you're all set then."

She nodded. "How've you been, Mr. MacAllister?"

"Good," he said. "Done any more shows?"

The smile widened. "No. I'm not much of a debater."

"On the contrary, you can be quite argumentative. By the way, since we're going to be in pretty close quarters for a while, you might want to call me Gregory. Or Mac."

"I think I prefer Mac." She offered her hand. "I'm Valya."

He shook it and turned to Hutch. "Is the mission purely hit-or-miss? Are we really just going out there and hoping for the best?"

"Pretty much," she said. "All you're doing is planting monitors. Think of it as time off. Read, relax, and enjoy yourself."

"Okay."

"For what it's worth, there's been another sighting along Orion's Blue Tour, at 61 Cygni. It's your first stop, so who knows? You might get lucky and come home with the story of the century."

"I'm sure."

"Valya says," said Amy, "that even if we see some moonriders, we might not be fast enough to catch them."

MacAllister smiled at her enthusiasm. In fact, it hadn't occurred to him he might become part of a pursuit. "I assume," he said, "if we were to see something, we'd try to talk to them."

"If you can," said Hutch.

"Well, we'll see what happens."

Someone else was coming on board.

"It's getting close to time," said Valya.

Eric Samuels strolled through the airlock. "Hello, all," he said, with that phony cheerfulness he always exuded in public. "Are we ready to go hunting for moonriders?"

It was going to be a long trip.

THE *SALVATOR* WASN'T exactly the *Evening Star*. It was cramped, uncomfortable, everything squeezed together. Its carrying capacity was a pilot and seven passengers. The walls were paneled, there was a carpet, and pseudoleather furniture. MacAllister chose a compartment toward the forward part of the vehicle. He'd read somewhere that the farther you were from the power plant, the safer you were. The compartment would be big enough provided he didn't try to stand up. It contained a basin, but other facilities were located in twin washrooms. Only a contortionist, he saw, would be able to manage the toilet.

Samuels took a compartment in the middle of the ship, and Amy picked one at the rear. Their luggage arrived. They hauled everything inside and got settled.

Hutch got up to go. Good luck, everybody. Happy hunting. "We'll try to bring something back," Valya said.

"It would be nice," said Hutch. "You guys have everything you need?"

MacAllister knew it would turn out he'd forgotten something. He always did. But he ran a quick mental check of the essentials. Unsure what the ship's library would hold, he'd brought a generous supply of novels in his notebook. "I'm all set," he said.

So were the others. "I've talked with Union Ops," said Valya. "We've got launch in twenty."

"Then I'm out of here, folks. See you when you get back." Hutch shook their hands, embraced Amy, pressed her lips to MacAllister's cheek, and strode out through the main hatch.

Valya closed it behind her. "We'll be accelerating during the first thirty minutes or so," she said, "which means we'll all be locked down. You guys have anything you need to do, this would be a good time."

NEWSDESK

ROBOT RUNS LOOSE; TERRORIZES TASMANIA
2 Dead, 7 Injured after Rampage

IS THERE AN UPPER LIMIT TO INTELLIGENCE?
Study Suggests Few Meet Their Potential
Social Conditions Get in Way
Beliefs Block Mental Processes
Trick Is to Keep Open Mind, According to Experts

PATENT GRANTED TO ARTIFICIAL INTELLIGENCE
"Bob White" Gets Groundbreaking Authorization
MIT Project Develops New Sensing System
Next: Are AIs Sentient?
James Watson Parker: "They Have No Souls"

LONGEVITY BREAKTHROUGH IMMINENT?
Today's Infants May Get Indefinite Life Span
World Council Debates "Talis" Research
"Where Will We Put Everybody?"

MIDDLE EAST TURMOIL UNLIKELY TO END SOON

DODGERS TRADE FOR BAXTER

HURRICANE SEASON WILL START
EARLIER THIS YEAR, LAST LONGER
Storm Intensity Likely to Continue to Grow
Atmosphere Seeding Helps, "But Probably Too Little Too Late"

STOCKS MOVE TO RECORD HIGHS

LITERACY RATE IN NAU CONTINUES TO DROP
AI Might Write New War and Peace, *But Will Anybody Read It?*

BEEMER CLAIMS HARM FROM RELIGIOUS TEACHING
Anti-Christ Loose in North Carolina?

chapter 17

Intelligence is like pornography. I can't define it, but I know it when I see it.

—Gregory MacAllister, "Keeper of the Keys"

One of the things MacAllister disliked about the *Salvator* was that, unless you were on the bridge, you had no windows. On the *Evening Star*, the walls of the dining area had been transparent, and even his compartment had provided a view of the stars. The *Salvator* was oppressive. The outside world was limited to what you could see on a set of display screens. It wasn't at all the same thing.

Hutch had explained to him once that windows, viewports in the vernacular, needed special reinforcement because they didn't withstand air pressure well, and it was simply safer not to have them, to use monitors instead. Nevertheless, he didn't like it very much. He wondered what the Orion tour ships were like.

They were seated in the common room. The ship was still accelerating away from Earth, preparing to make its jump into the foggy morass they called hyperspace. Amy couldn't take her eyes off the displays, and he could hear Valya on the bridge talking to the AI again. MacAllister was trying to manage a conversation with Eric. But the guy's enthusiasm for the flight was almost beyond bearing.

"Something I've wanted to do all my life, Mac," he said. "I can hardly believe I'm here." And: "Look at that moon. Isn't that incredible?" And: "A lot of people don't like to admit it, but in the end this is the way we'll define ourselves. Make the stars our own, or sit home." He'd attempted a piercing look, in case MacAllister missed the implied criticism. The guy was as subtle as an avalanche.

Amy Taylor was also awed by the experience. But she was fifteen, so it was tolerable. She'd opened a book, Norma Rollins's *The Nearby Stars,* but she was too absorbed in the receding Earth-moon system to pay much attention to it. She told MacAllister she knew about his exploits on Deepsix and asked him to describe the experience. That was the way she'd put it. Exploits. In fact all he'd done was try to stay alive for a few days while Hutch figured out a way to save all their asses.

Amy seemed to have done surprisingly well for herself, considering she was growing up under the care of a full-time politician. The mother had run off years before with the senator's campaign manager, abandoning both her husband and Amy. That must have been hard to take, and he wondered whether her desire to follow in Hutch's footsteps didn't really mask a desire to get away from her life at home.

Eventually the acceleration eased off, and Valya came back to join them. She inquired whether everybody was feeling all right, then told them they'd be jumping in about six hours.

"We're headed *where* first?" asked MacAllister. "Something-or-other Cygnus?"

"61 Cygni," she said. "It's eleven light-years out. Takes about a day to get there." She was wearing a white jumpsuit. Her red hair, cut shorter than it had been in Tampa, looked more military.

The furniture wasn't especially comfortable. MacAllister grumbled at the prospect of having to deal with it for the next few weeks. "How long have you been doing this?" he asked Valya. "Piloting Academy ships?"

"Almost fifteen years," she said.

"You don't get bored?"

"Never."

He recalled Hutch's talking about how tiresome it could get, how pilots often made the same flights back and forth. How it could go on for months. Or the long flights. The mission to Lookout had taken the better part of a year one way. He tried to imagine being cooped up inside these bulkheads until next January.

"I wouldn't want that either," said Amy. "But you can get pretty cooped up groundside, too." She'd come aboard prepared to talk like a pilot. Groundside. Bulkheads. I'm going aft for a minute when she was talking about the washroom. The kid was right at home. But talk was cheap. MacAllister was prepared to give her a couple days before the idealism came crashing down. "If my father had his way," she continued, "I'd be stuck the rest of my life in courtrooms and offices."

"And on beaches and at parties," said MacAllister. "You won't find many of those out here." As a rule, he didn't approve of adolescents. They were rarely smart enough to understand the depths of their inexperience. To be aware they really didn't know anything. The few he encountered invariably behaved as if their opinions were as valid as his. Amy was no exception. But there was a degree of shyness about the child and an intellectual openness that engaged his sympathy. She thought the world a friendly and well-lighted place, where people really cared about each other, and all the stories had happy endings.

"Mac," she said, "I was surprised when I heard you were coming."

"Why was that?"

"You don't like the Academy."

MacAllister tried to explain his position. It was hard to do with Eric sitting there casting disapproving glances his way and Valya rolling her eyes.

When he'd finished, she looked at him a long time. Finally, she said quietly, "It's wrong, Mac. We went over the greenhouse thing in school. It's not just a matter of money. Ms. Harkin says it's people's attitudes that have to change."

"Ms. Harkin's your teacher?"

"In Current Events, yes."

"She's right. But that doesn't justify wasting money somewhere else."

Amy's eyes got very round. "It's not a waste, Mac."

Valya smiled. "As long as we have people like you, Amy, we'll be okay."

"They'll never shut it down," said Eric, his eyes locked on the receding moon. "They could no more do that than the Europeans could have turned their backs on America after Columbus."

"Or we could have gone to the moon," said MacAllister, "then forgotten how to do it."

Eric was one of those people who would spend his life reaching for something better than he had because he wasn't smart enough to realize what really mattered. MacAllister thought how much better the world would be if there were fewer people like Eric and more like himself. Pragmatists. People who kept open minds. Who were content to live their lives, enjoy the sunrise, make the moment count.

THEY HAD AN uneasy dinner. MacAllister understood he was the cause of that. Eric and Amy both wanted to talk about where they were going, how exciting it all was, but he loomed over the general enthusiasm like a dark cloud. He couldn't help it. Couldn't pretend to get excited because they were going somewhere to look at a star up close. You've seen one burning gasbag, you've seen them all. But he tried. While they dined on roast beef he made occasional comments about how he'd never been to 61 Cygni, or 63 Cygni, or whatever it was, and wasn't that where the alien monument was? He knew damned well it was, but it sounded self-effacing. Even if he wasn't a good enough actor to ask the question as if he really cared.

They finished dinner in a gloomy mood, while the other three united against him. No one said anything, and everybody was unfailingly polite, but there it was. He was odd man out. After years of playing the VIP everywhere he went, it was annoying to be excluded.

Twenty minutes after they'd cleared the dishes they belted down, the Hazeltines took over, and the *Salvator* adjusted course for 61 Cygni and slipped between the dimensions. MacAllister was aware of the brief change in lighting when the moment came. When the jump was complete, Amy and Eric congratulated each other.

Valya returned from the bridge, announced they were on their way, and proposed a toast. Poor Amy, who was underage, got grape juice. "Here's to us," Valya said.

WHEN HE'D BEEN on the *Evening Star*, the passengers had spent their time at parties scattered throughout six or seven decks. You could stand before the see-through bulkheads and look out at the void, or at the quiescent mists of hyperspace. But despite its proximity, the world outside had seemed far away. Distant. Something seen but not really experienced. You were inside a warm, comfortable cocoon composed of soft bunks, dining areas, game rooms, and dance floors.

It was different on the *Salvator*, where the vast outside could only be seen directly from the bridge, where it pressed against the hull. Where his heart beat slightly faster, and he could *feel* the empty light-years stretching away in all directions. It became even more unsettling after the jump, because hyperspace theoretically had no boundary, and no physical features of any kind except the mist.

It intrigued Amy. "What would we do," she asked, "if lights appeared out there?"

Valya looked up at the screen. "If we see lights out there," she said, "we'd clear out in a hurry."

They laughed at the idea. Eric said the notion gave him a chill, and MacAllister, pretending to be buried in a manuscript, was inclined to agree.

Amy and Valya challenged each other to a role-playing game. Eric watched for a while, but finally declared it had been a long day and drifted off to his compartment. MacAllister tried to look interested. It had something to do with a quest in a medieval land. There were wizards and dragons and elves and magical artifacts that had gotten lost and other such nonsense. Had he been alone, MacAllister might have run the old Bogart vehicle *Casablanca* with himself as Rick. He'd done it at home any number of times and never grew tired. Play it, Sam.

Eventually, Valya also retired for the evening. Amy, left to herself, wandered over and asked what he was reading. It was *Bleak Angel*, by Wendy Moran. A classic from the previous century. Amy looked bored when she heard the title. Like most kids, she automatically ruled out anything older than she was. "It's about things that get lost," he said. "Things we care about."

She nodded, smiled, excused herself, and headed for the bridge.

He wondered briefly if she could get into trouble up there, then dismissed the idea. Or tried to. She didn't come back, and eventually he left *Bleak Angel* and brought up a proof copy of a first novel. The editor had sent it to him hoping he'd review it, or possibly find something kind to say about it. He paged through and quickly concluded the writer had talent but insufficient discipline. There were too many adjectives and adverbs. Plotting, characterization, conflict, everything worked, but you couldn't get the guy to write a simple sentence.

When Amy came back, her eyes were shining. "I love being here," she said.

IT FELT GOOD to climb into the bunk, turn out the lights, and slide down into the sheets. There was no sense whatever of movement. In the darkness, MacAllister could hear the murmur of power in the walls and the occasional whisper of a fan. Once, he heard bare feet in the corridor and, probably, the sound of a washroom door. He remembered nothing else before he awoke and looked at the time. It was almost seven o'clock.

He climbed into his robe and looked out into the corridor. The lights had come up, and the others were having breakfast.

Amy called out a hello, and he padded down to the common room. "Good morning," he said.

Eric raised his orange juice, and Valya inquired whether he'd slept okay. "Sometimes the first night aboard can be difficult," she said. Bill, the ship's AI, asked what he'd like for breakfast.

He showered, dressed, and returned to a plate of pancakes and bacon.

AMY AND ERIC played a game that involved corporate empire building. Valya found things to do on the bridge. MacAllister went back to *Bleak Angel* for a while, but eventually put it down and joined her. She invited him to take the right-hand seat. "How'd you manage to get invited on Margie's show?" he asked.

She smiled. "It *was* fun, wasn't it?"

"You can be a tough cookie."

"I'd been on a couple of their science programs before. I guess the arrangement whereby you showed up was more or less a last-minute thing—"

"It was—"

"So they called the first person they could think of. And I thought, holy cats, I get to go up against Gregory MacAllister himself."

"That's odd," he said.

"What is?"

"I had the impression you had no idea who I was."

"Really?"

"Yes."

She looked amused. "I guess you caught me. I looked you up before I went down there."

"Oh."

"You have a major-league reputation. *The Insider Report* described you as 'not the biggest curmudgeon of the age, but among the top five.' "

"I thought you held up your end of things pretty well."

"You were actually far more polite than I'd expected you to be."

"I'm sorry I was a disappointment."

She laughed. "Mac," she said, "I doubt you're capable of disappointing anybody."

He understood she was trying to reel him in, but that was okay. He couldn't resist being pleased with the compliment. "We'll be leaving monitors at each site," she said. "Would you be interested in taking a look at them?"

He could hardly have cared less what the monitors looked like, but she seemed interested in showing them off. "Sure," he said.

"Good." She seemed almost surprised at his answer. Had she expected him to grumble and pass? She got up and led the way to the rear. "We have eight units altogether. Four of them are secured outside to the hull. The others are in cargo." They went down the zero-gee tube to the lower deck.

He was disappointed to see they were simply black boxes. Big ones, big enough to pack an armchair inside. But there was no sign of an antenna or a telescope.

"Everything pops up once it's been activated," she said. "They have sensors and a scope. And a collector, so it'll continue to draw power from the sun as long as it's on-station. And it has a hypercomm system." MacAllister understood that meant it was capable of sending and receiving FTL transmissions. "We'll be leaving one close to the Origins Project. There's no sun there, so they've added a dark-energy unit. That one cost three times what the others did."

"Do we think the moonriders are likely to show up near Origins?"

"They've been seen in the area."

The casings were covered with spindles, brackets, jacks, and coils.

She pointed at a slot. "This is the reader, where it gets its instructions." She produced a chip.

"Does it have a thruster? Can it move on its own?"

"You mean, if it sees a moonrider, can it take off and follow it?"

"Yes."

"No. Once we put it in orbit, it'll stay there. It'll report to us and to Mission Operations. After that, I guess if there's any chasing to be done, we'd do it."

LATER HE FOUND himself with Eric while Valya read and Amy grabbed a nap. "I'll admit to you," Eric said, "I was a bit nervous about this flight."

"Why's that?"

"First time off-world. It's kind of scary." He flashed a nervous smile. "I'll tell you the truth, Mac: I haven't been sleeping well the last few nights."

This was not a guy you'd want on board if things went wrong. "I'd never have known."

"Thanks."

"Are you here under orders, Eric?"

"No."

"Then why—?"

He looked past MacAllister as if he could see something in the distance. "You're not going to believe this, but I haven't done much with my life."

MacAllister fought hard not to smile. Oh, yes. It was hard to believe.

Eric walked over to the viewport and looked out. The navigation lights were off. There was no point running them in hyperspace. But the illumination from the bridge reflected against the mists. "I have a brother and a sister who envy me. They see me live doing the press conferences. So in their eyes, I'm famous. And they think I make big money. And I suppose, in a way they're right. I'm doing a lot better than most of the people I grew up with. Better than I ever expected. But the truth is I haven't really ever accomplished anything."

"You seem to be doing pretty well. You're the face of the Academy."

"Mac, you're a famous man. Everybody knows you. Everybody

knows Hutch. *She's* the big hero at the Academy. People are always asking me about her. What's she like in person? Has it all gone to her head? They want to know whether they can meet her. I have a nephew who was heartbroken when Hutch got married." His eyes came back to MacAllister. "You know what it's like to work with somebody like that?"

"It can't be that bad. She seems okay."

"It's bad, believe me. I mean, nothing against her. It isn't her fault. But I'd like to be able to say I've done something, too. To *know* I've done something."

"You're not married, Eric, are you?"

"No. How'd you know?"

"Just a feeling."

He looked momentarily wistful. "It shows, huh?"

"Not really." MacAllister smiled. "And that's why you're coming? To try to do something more with your life?"

"That's why. You know, you're lucky. You were part of the Deepsix rescue—"

"I was one of the people who needed rescuing—"

"It doesn't matter. You were there." He sighed. "I wish I'd been there."

"You wouldn't have enjoyed it."

"Maybe not. But it would have been nice to be able to tell *that* story. Anyhow, now at least I'll have something."

MACALLISTER HAD PROMISED himself he would actually convert the flight into a vacation. Catch up on his reading, relax, watch some shows. And, of course, take in the sights. But by noon on the second day he was already thinking about future stories for *The National*. A new challenge to institutional marriage had risen: Men and women were getting involved in virtual affairs with avatars who represented their spouses at a younger age. Was it infidelity to spend a romantic evening with your wife as she had looked and behaved at twenty-two?

Then there was the Origins Project. Major breakthroughs coming. "Mac," said Valya, "did you know it's not fully operational yet?"

"It won't be for years, apparently," he said.

"I don't know whether you actually want to stop at Origins or not. They're not expecting us. We should probably just put our monitor over the side and keep going."

"That might not be a bad idea. It's nothing more than a giant physics lab." He shook his head. "Never could stand physics."

They'd caught Amy's ear. "Valya," she said, "Origins is the most exciting place on the flight. Let's stop and take a look. Please."

LIBRARY ENTRY

SOMETHING IS WATCHING US

The space agencies have done what they can to sweep moonrider reports under the table. Various astrophysical phenomena have been advanced to explain the sightings. But lights moving in formation and throwing sharp turns do not lend themselves to credible natural explanations. Last week's reports from the *Serenity* orbiter are especially startling, because the observers were not only ordinary travelers but also included a group of physicists.

If in fact there is even a reasonable possibility that we are being observed by alien intelligences, then the current notion that we should disband the interstellar program is both shortsighted and dangerous.

—*The London Observer*, Thursday, April 2

chapter 18

> 61 Cygni is a binary system located approximately eleven light-years from Earth. It is in the constellation Cygnus, the Swan. Both stars are visible in the terrestrial sky, but they are quite dim. They orbit each other at a range between 50 and 120 AUs. (The distance to Pluto is about 40 AUs.)
>
> —*The Star Register*

As soon as the jump was complete, they all crowded onto the bridge to look out through the viewport. Nobody was happier than MacAllister to see the mists go away. The transdimensional fogscape reminded him that the real world was far stranger than anything humans had dreamed up, with its quantum effects, time running at different rates depending on whether you're standing on the roof or in the basement, objects that aren't there unless someone looks at them. Hamlet had been right.

It was good to see the stars again. And there was an orange-red sun. It looked far away. Or very small. It was difficult to know which. "That's Cygni A," said Valya. "It's a main sequence dwarf. Weighs in at about seven-tenths solar mass, but it's only about ten percent as bright as the sun."

"Why?" asked Amy.

Valya passed the question to Bill who, surprisingly, didn't know. *"It just says here,"* he said, *"that it's dimmer."*

"Where's *our* sun?" asked Eric, who could barely restrain himself.

Valya glanced around the sky. "Can't see it from this angle," she said. She told Bill to put it on the display. "This is zero mag, and *there's* Sol." One of the stars momentarily brightened.

"That doesn't look very bright either," said Eric.

Amy was more interested in Cygni A. "It has six planets," she said.

"Where's the other star?" asked MacAllister, recalling that 61 Cygni was a binary.

Valya referred that question also to Bill, who did better this time. He highlighted Cygni B off to one side. It might have been nothing more than a bright star.

Amy obviously had been doing her homework. "They orbit around each other every 720 years."

MacAllister simply stared. "The last time they were in their current positions respective to each other," he said, "Columbus was poking around in the Americas."

"That is correct," said Bill, who seemed delighted to have passengers who cared about such things. *"Cygni A, by the way,"* he continued, *"is a fairly old star. Considerably older than the sun."*

"Is there a green world in the system?" asked Eric. "In either system? I assume both suns have planets."

"B has four," said Amy. "But there's no life anywhere."

"Not in either system," said Bill. *"A is so cool that a planet would have to be right on top of it to have liquid water."*

"How close would that be?" asked MacAllister.

"Closer than Mercury is to the sun," said Amy.

MacAllister loved listening to a know-it-all kid trying to outdo a know-it-all AI. He resisted saying anything, contenting himself with looking out at Cygni A. And at the firmament of stars surrounding it. "Where's the monument?" he asked.

SITTING ON THEIR front porch in Baltimore, he and Jenny had contemplated how exhilarating it would be to do an interstellar tour. Jenny had talked of seeing the four stars at Capella. (Was that right, she'd asked? Was it four? Or five?) And she'd wanted to see a living world. The nearest was at 36 Ophiuchi. But she'd had something more dramatic in mind. She wanted Quraqua, where a civilization had once thrived. She'd talked about visiting the ruins. But there was no easy way to get there. The tour services didn't exist then. Even now nobody went out that far.

Most of all she'd wanted to see the monuments, those magnificent works of art scattered through the Orion Arm ten thousand years ago by a race that had since gone out of existence, leaving only a few savage descendants who possessed no technology and had no memory of their great days.

The first monument had been found in the solar system, on Iapetus. It was a statue, a self-portrait of its creator. A lone female standing on that bleak moonscape, its eyes turned toward Saturn, which remained permanently fixed above a nearby ridge. It was, in fact, the discovery of the Iapetus statue at a time much like the present one, during which the space effort was losing momentum, that had led to the suspicion that *somebody* had FTL, that it was possible to build an interstellar drive.

He'd promised Jenny they would go to Iapetus. And they'd eventually visit two or three of the other monuments. (That was a time when there seemed no limit to what they could do together.) But the illness had struck shortly after, and they never got beyond Baltimore.

"The Cygni monument," said Amy, apparently in answer to a question, "was discovered in 2195 by Shia Kanana."

"*It was a follow-up mission,*" said Bill.

"The first mission missed it?" asked Eric.

"Passed right by it and never noticed." Amy seemed delighted that adults could be such buffoons.

"Of course," said Eric, "there was no Academy then." MacAllister's eyelids sagged. The guy was breathtakingly loyal. "The way they were operating in those days," he continued, "everything was hit-or-miss. And the truth is, despite what they said, they were really only looking for two things: habitable worlds and aliens."

"There's something I never really understood," said MacAllister.

"What? Habitable worlds? For settlement."

"Right. I understand that. What I don't understand is why? You know the damned places won't be comfortable. What sort of idiot wants to live on a frontier? Would you, Amy?"

"Not really," she said. "I just want to ride around out here."

Eric smiled benignly. "There are a lot of people who'd like to get away from the cities," he said. "Away from all the fuss at home."

"Well, my God, Eric, move to the country."

"You're so narrow-minded, Mac. You know, eventually we'll terraform a lot of these places, turn them into garden worlds."

"That's something else that could cost an arm and a leg. And it's typical. We tried to terraform Quraqua, and all we did was destroy an archeological treasure house."

"Mac, you're a cynical cuss."

"You can't really deny that it's true." MacAllister sighed. "So where's the monument?" he asked.

Bill responded: *"The second planet. It's just a large piece of ice and rock. There's a moon, about a third the size of Luna. The monument's in orbit around the moon."*

"The monuments were usually put in orbit," said Amy.

Bill had the last word: "There are only four on the ground."

TWO OF THE seventeen known monuments were images of their makers. Five others were depictions of creatures that might have been either biological or mythical. (One was known definitely to be mythical.) The rest were geometric designs.

The one at 61 Cygni fell into the latter category.

Valya was feeding images from the ship's telescopes to the two displays mounted in the common room. One was centered on the sun; the other gave them a picture of the target world, Alpha II, and its moon. Alpha II constituted as sorry-looking a piece of real estate as MacAllister had ever seen. He knew there'd be no green areas. There were also no seas, no deserts, nothing but a gray-black mantle of what appeared to be solid rock. In some areas there'd been eruptions and lava flows. But the surface was, for the most part, smooth and featureless. No craters, no ridges, no mountains, no river valleys. It was as if the planet were simply one oversized boulder.

Its moon was a pale crescent, and lay at a considerable distance, half again as far as Luna was from Earth. It, too, seemed composed of the same featureless rock.

"They've seen moonriders out here?" asked Eric.

Valya nodded. "Three tour flights have reported them in the last month."

"Where were they?" asked Amy. "Were they here? Near the monument?"

Valya needed a moment to consult her screen. "Yes," she said. "This is the area."

"Maybe," Amy continued, "they were just sightseeing. I mean, they've been at all the places along the tour route, right?"

"It could also mean," said MacAllister, "that they're only seen close to the tour sights because that's where the ships are. They could have an entire invasion fleet sitting over at the other star. What's its name again?"

"Cygni B," said Amy.

"Beta. Okay. There could be a fleet there, and we'd never know it because nobody ever goes there."

Amy looked at him, not sure whether to laugh. "An invasion fleet? I've seen that in sims."

MacAllister chuckled and did his best private eye impersonation. "Just kidding, Sweetheart. No, I don't think we need to worry about invaders."

"Why not, Mac?" she persisted. "Just for the sake of argument, how would we know? It's possible." He got the impression she would welcome an invasion.

"Sure it's possible, Amy. Anything's possible. But ask yourself why anybody would bother."

"How do you mean?"

"We don't have anything that anybody would want."

"How about real estate?" asked Eric.

MacAllister shrugged. "Plenty of places out here if anybody wants one. Truth is, I think the one thing we can be sure of is that the moonriders, whatever they are, do not pose a threat." He looked over at Valya. "By the way, are we watching out for them? Just in case?"

"Bill's doing a complete sweep in all directions. He'll give us a yell if he sees something."

THE CYGNI MONUMENT was the largest known. It reminded MacAllister, from a distance, of a temple, complete with Doric columns. It stood (if that was the correct term for an object in orbit) atop a platform, and was accessible on all sides by stone steps. It was polished and graceful, unmarked by fluting, or sculpture, or triglyphs. It did not look like a structure that had been assembled so much as one that had been *poured*. It possessed a power and majesty that was stunning.

It was believed to be about eleven thousand years old, making it slightly older than the self-portrait on Iapetus. It had picked up a couple of dents where it had been hit by pieces of debris.

Temples all seemed to be alike, regardless of the culture from which they sprang, regardless of the sweep of the roof, or the general design of molding rings and parapets. Whether a temple was from one of the various terrestrial eras, or whether it had been built by Noks, or by the long-gone inhabitants of Quraqua, or by the Monument-Makers themselves: They were always large and spacious with high overheads, everything oversized to ensure that the visitor understood at the deepest levels how insignificant and utterly inconsequential he was, except that the powers that ran the universe gave him meaning by allowing him into their sanctuary.

Everybody's psychology is going to turn out to be the same.

The monument was thirty-one and a half meters wide at the entrance, 126 meters front to rear. A factor of four. The same proportion could be found throughout. The columns were four times as high as they were wide. The roof was four times as thick as the base. (Ratios of one kind or another were found in almost all the monuments.)

There was a contradistinction of good order in the presence of those steps, out where there was no gravitational pull. He looked beyond them into the great gulf, toward the stars, and it seemed as if they were awaiting a visitor. That they'd been placed for a specific purpose. He wondered if anyone had ever walked on them.

Some people read the general design of the monument as a statement of defiance against a hostile and chaotic universe. Others saw it as a symbol of harmony, forever absorbed in the dance of worlds around 61 Cygni, and permanently afloat in the moonlight.

MacAllister had sat in his Baltimore apartment and taken the virtual tour, had ridden his armchair onto the platform. But this was different.

The *Salvator* was making its approach. Valya got on the link. *"Everybody belt down."*

MacAllister punched a button and the harness slid over his shoulders. He checked to make sure Amy was secure. Found her doing the same for him.

Braking rockets fired. He was pushed forward against the harness.

The monument was on both displays. He watched it grow larger. Watched it move into the sunlight.

"Beautiful," said Amy.

MacAllister agreed. If the race that put it there had never done anything else, it was sufficient.

"Okay," said Valya. *"We're in business."* She shut the engines down.

"Valya," he asked, "any chance of getting out onto it? Of going inside?"

"Sorry," she said. *"It's illegal."*

Nobody would ever know. But it was just as well. He hadn't really meant it. But it seemed like the thing he was supposed to say. He'd have liked very much to climb those steps, to go into the temple. But the prospect of exiting the ship out here was a little scary. Still, it was nice to have everybody—especially Valya—think he would do it if he could.

"If you folks would like to come forward and look out the viewport, you might find it worthwhile."

Amy led the way. "Oh, yes," she said, squeezing Valya's shoulder. "I've never seen anything like it." Her voice was up a few decibels.

The temple floated in the night sky, bright with reflected light. MacAllister had been impressed by the architecture at Rheims and Chartres and Notre Dame, but here was a true seat for a deity.

"It was carved from an asteroid," said Amy.

The moon, desolate and airless, lay below. The nearby planet, Alpha II, was a narrow gleaming crescent near the horizon. Valya saw him looking in its direction. "From here," he said, "it looks magnificient."

"Where do we put the monitor?" asked Amy.

"Our instructions are to leave it right where we are now. In orbit around the moon."

"That's sacrilege," said MacAllister.

She allowed herself to look shocked. "That has an odd sound coming from you, Mac."

"Kidding aside," he said, "this place should be left exactly as it is. Why don't we just nail it to the monument?"

"This is where the sightings have been concentrated," said Eric. "I think we should follow the plan."

MacAllister ran his hand through his hair. "The sightings have been concentrated here because this is where the tours come." Idiot.

"If we have aliens," said Valya, "this is likely to be one of the places they'd want to visit. It's the logical place to put the thing."

"Put it somewhere else," said MacAllister.

Eric was unhappy. "You're asking her," he said, "to put her job at risk. She can't just disobey the director's instructions."

MacAllister waved all concerns away. "I'll take responsibility for it."

Valya turned an amused glance in his direction. "Okay," she said. "But first I need to know where you fit in the chain of command, Mac."

"Hutchins is a close friend."

"Well, I'm sure that'll cover things."

Eric laughed. "I suggest we just follow the instructions." He produced a cup of coffee and took a long sip. "I wonder if anyone's ever thought about bringing this one home? Think how nice it would look in Jersey."

MacAllister needed a moment to realize he was joking.

"Okay," said Valya. "If everybody's seen enough, let's go do what we came for."

VALYA CHANGED COURSE. Amy stayed up front so she could watch through the viewport, or maybe simply to be close to the pilot. It was hard to know which. MacAllister liked the child, but her enthusiasm was wearing on him. It was a pity, really. She believed that people were intrinsically good, and that most knew what they were doing. He wondered what she'd be like after another twenty years. It had been his experience that the worst cynics all started out as idealists.

After a few minutes, the sense of acceleration went away.

MacAllister couldn't remember a time of innocence in his own life. He'd always known civilization for what it was: an illusion. There was never a day he didn't understand that institutions were out primarily to take care of themselves, and that only individuals were ever worthy of trust. And damned few of those.

He closed his eyes and drifted off to sleep. Bill's voice woke him. *"Launch in two minutes,"* he said.

He checked the time, was surprised to discover he'd been out more than an hour.

Eric made a crack about his sleeping through the day and added that he wished time machines were possible. "I'd love to have been able to come here when the Monument-Makers were putting that thing in place."

"You'd probably have found," MacAllister said, "they were a lot like us."

"How do you mean?"

"Unsure of themselves."

"How can you say that, Mac? Honestly? They had an advanced civilization. They had FTL, for God's sake. You don't get that from people who are unsure of themselves."

"Of course not. They had an occasional genius to show the way. Just like us. But they were trying to make a mark here. What is this other than something to let us know they were here. Admire us, it says. Remember us."

"One minute," said Bill.

The monument was on one display; the other provided a close-up of one of the monitors mounted on the hull. Presumably the one scheduled for launch.

MacAllister looked beyond the monitor and the monument, half expecting to see moving lights in the sky. There were countless stars, and like everybody else he wanted to believe that somewhere out there civilization lived and prospered. Civilization as it should be. With the day-to-day necessities taken care of, and intelligent creatures sitting around discussing philosophy. Or attending ball games.

"Thirty seconds."

Then Valya's voice, from the bridge. *"When I tell you, Amy, press this."*

MacAllister sat up straight so he could get a better look at the display.

"Now," said Valya.

Good for you, Valentina. But I hope we stop short of having the kid pilot the ship.

The monitor detached itself and began to drift away.

"Now this one, Amy."

And a masculine voice: "Salvator One *fully functional.*"

Moments later Amy came into the common room and looked sternly at MacAllister. "If she gets in trouble for this, Mac," she said, "it's your fault."

"*My* fault? For what?"

Valya appeared behind her. "We did a compromise positioning. The monitor will be orbiting Alpha II instead of the moon."

How about that? The woman's got something going for her after all.

ERIC ENVIED VALENTINA. The mere fact that she was a pilot earned his respect. Amy was delighted to be helping her. Even MacAllister took her seriously. He, on the other hand, did public relations. It was one of those professions that people always made jokes about and instinctively distrusted. And why would they not? His job, after all, had nothing to do with truth; it emphasized instead an ability to put the best possible face on things. Presumably on mediocrity.

The truth about Eric, the reality that he kept hidden even from himself, was that he had never committed a courageous act in his life. He'd never needed to. Nobody had ever challenged him, other than in the ordinary give-and-take relations with the media. He'd grown up sheltered and protected. Was given the best education. Got his start through his father's influence. And coasted. When he entered a room, no one noticed. When he spoke, people's eyes glazed over. (This in spite of the fact that he handled the spoken word quite well. Had in fact mastered the techniques of persuasion.)

But it was he himself, the *person,* who commanded no respect.

He saw how MacAllister was treated when he came to the Academy, how people's voices changed in his presence, how they stood straighter. Literally came to attention when he walked in. The same was true with the pilots. And with Hutchins. She'd been a bureaucrat for a couple of years now, one of the most contemptible professions, but people still remembered who she was. Eric, though, was another Asquith. But without the authority.

Though they never said anything to him, he sensed how Valya and MacAllister felt. He was just extra baggage. A friend of Hutch's, to be taken care of. But of no real consequence on his own merit.

LIBRARY ENTRY

To date we have not found a world with a high-tech functioning society. We have however seen remnants of nine technological civilizations. At least one of these, the so-called Monument-Makers, achieved interstellar flight. There is evidence of one other such species, the creatures who helped evacuate Maleiva III when it fell into a brutal ice age several thousand years ago. But we don't know where they came from, or where they went.

The overall picture for long-range survival by a civilization is, therefore, historically, not bright.

Our most recent evidence indicates that many societies experience an industrial revolution, followed by exponential technological development, followed by rapid growth, followed by a general collapse. None that we know of, other than the Monument-Makers, seem to have lasted more than three hundred years beyond the development of the computer.

This is not to say there is a cause and effect relationship between technology and extinction. But Colm Manchester, in his monumental *Study of Civilization*, points out that societies with limited technology tend to be more durable and far harder to destabilize.

It is now more than three and a half centuries since we started using computers. Let us hope the trend does not apply to us.

–*Tokyo Daily*, Saturday, April 4

RHINE: HELLFIRE SERMONS AFFLICT MANY
"Constitute Child Abuse"

STUDY: RELIGIOUS EDUCATION MAY CLOSE MIND
"Hell Invented by Dante"

chapter 19

> There's not much to be said for sightseeing. You go somewhere that has a waterfall. You have a beer, watch the water go over the edge, and move on. Tours are all the same. In the end, the only thing that matters is the beer.
>
> –Gregory MacAllister, "Endgame"

The monument needed a name. Something other than the Cygni Temple, which was how it was commonly known. When it had first been discovered, decades before, religious organizations had pointed to it proudly as proof that even alien societies recognized the Creator. It might have been true, but the reality was that nobody had any idea what the structure had meant to the creatures who'd put it into its lonely orbit.

MacAllister had begun to realize that, even if he did not get close to the moonriders, there was decent potential on this flight for a good story. He put aside his notes on *Dark Mirror* and was thinking instead that he might, in visiting these various sites, record his own insights and reactions. It was easy to wax philosophical about places like the temple. So he began a journal.

Before leaving the system, they took pictures. Of the captain and passengers gathered on the bridge, of Amy with the monument behind her, of Eric studying the monument while taking notes. Valya transposed images, so they had shots of Eric leaning against one of the columns, and Amy standing at the foot of the steps, inches from infinity. Even MacAllister allowed her a degree of latitude, and she superimposed his features over the monument, as if *he* were the resident deity.

"You're sending me a message," he said.

They were alone in the common room. "Not at all." She had a smile that could penetrate his own inner darkness, and she used it, showing him, yes, of course it reflects you, the *real* you, the guy who thinks he knows everything. But she softened it somehow.

At home, MacAllister was a constant target for attack. Usually it was just people hitting back after he'd delivered a well-deserved criticism. He routinely accepted the reactions as part of the job. Fleabites from persons of no consequence. But when he saw reproach in Valya's eyes, and for reasons he did not understand, it hurt. He wanted to explain to her that he wished the Academy well, wished *her* well. That he wasn't the jerk she so plainly thought he was.

"Did you volunteer for this?" he asked.

"In a manner of speaking. I could have refused."

"But you didn't."

"Is there a reason I should have?"

"I thought you might have preferred not to have me aboard."

"To be honest," she said, "I was reluctant when Hutch first told me you were coming. Look, Mac, since you ask, you're not exactly one of my favorite people. It's not personal; it's political. But it's okay. We can make it work while we're out here."

"I'm sorry if I've offended you."

She shrugged. "I know. But you're on the other side. It's not easy to be friendly with the enemy."

"I'm not an enemy, Valya."

"Sure you are." She lowered her voice. "You and Amy's father. And four or five other nitwits on the committee. No. Let me finish. I understand about the seas and the duck problem and all the rest of it. But you're behaving as if this is an either-or situation. If *we* close down, if the Academy goes away, we won't get serious starflight up and running again probably during my lifetime.

"And I know what you're going to say. This isn't about one person. And to be honest I'm not sure about that. Maybe it *is* me. I like to be out here, and if the day comes they shut us down, shut *everybody* down, Orion and Kosmik and everybody else, then my life is over. And if you think the human race is doing just fine sitting on its front porch, as long as the evenings are cool, then I think you need to ask yourself what goddam good we'll be to ourselves or anybody else."

Had she just called him a nitwit? "Valya, I never said we should shut down the Academy."

"Sure you did. Not verbatim, maybe. But you're aiding and abetting. Look, I can understand you don't want to support us. But you owe Hutchins a lot. If it weren't for her, you wouldn't be walking around. The least you could do is stay out of the fight. Just don't say anything."

"I can't do that, Valya. I'm an editor. *The National* has an obligation to its readers."

"Do your readers agree with you? About the Academy?"

"Some do." He hesitated. "Most do. We've taken a reasonable position. Head off the imminent danger first. *Then* put money into starflight. Anything else would be irresponsible."

She changed the subject. Talked about 36 Ophiuchi, and the Origins Project beyond.

TIME TO GO.

When the warning came to buckle up, MacAllister was ready. So was Amy, who'd lost interest in the monument and was doing a history assignment with Bill. But as they were pressed back into their seats, and the temple began to recede, she took a last look and smiled at MacAllister. "I'll be back," she said.

Acceleration continued several minutes, then went away. The green lights came on. It was okay to release the restraints and walk around. The lights were intended for those so feebleminded they couldn't tell when it was possible to stand up without getting thrown against the aft bulkhead.

Valya asked MacAllister to come up front.

"No problems, I hope," he said as he slid into the right-hand seat.

"We're fine, Mac." She released her own harness and rotated her shoulders. "I wanted to ask a favor."

"Sure," he said. "What do you need?"

"While we're out here, I'd like to take Amy to see the supernova."

The statement puzzled him. "How do you take somebody to see a supernova?" He looked at the quiet sky. "Where is it?"

"I'm talking about the supernova of 2216."

That was nineteen years ago. A monster event. It had brightened the night sky for days. "How are you going to do that? We have a time machine?"

"Yes," she said. "We can pass the light, then turn around and look at it."

Yes. He knew that. Just hadn't stopped to think. "Why would you want to do that?"

"Mac, it was before Amy's time. We all got to see it, but Amy wasn't born yet. I think she'd enjoy it, and we don't really have to go out of our way. It'll cost a day or so, but that's all."

"I keep forgetting we can do this stuff."

"So what do you say? Is it okay? It's on the way to our next site."

"Sure," he said. "No moonriders associated with it?"

"No. It's part of the Blue Tour, but no lights have been seen near it."

MacAllister shifted his position. "Did you ask Eric?"

"He's all for it."

"Okay," he said. "Sure. I'd enjoy seeing it again."

THEY CAME BACK together and Valya put the question to Amy. "Would you like to take a ride into the past?"

"Into the past?" she said. "How do you mean?"

"Do you know about the supernova of 2216?"

"Sure."

"Would you like to see it?"

The child, apparently brighter than MacAllister, lit up. "Would you really do that for me?"

"If you want."

"Sure. Thanks."

They made the jump into the mists that evening. When it was done, MacAllister announced he'd had enough excitement for one day and headed for his compartment. Amy was doing homework, and Eric had hunched down in front of his notebook, reading.

He was glad to hit the rack, to get by himself for a few hours. That was another problem with the *Salvator*. Everybody needed time alone, MacAllister more than most. But he knew he couldn't take to hanging out in his compartment for long stretches without exciting comment and resentment. You go on a trip like this, you have to be willing to socialize. So it felt especially good when night came and the ship's lights dimmed, as they did at ten P.M., and he could justify retreating.

He settled in with Ferguson's latest, *Breakout*, a history of the first twenty years of interstellar flight. But it turned out to be dreary stuff. The most rousing piece of writing in the entire book was the title. The author had done substantial research, and he wanted the reader to be impressed. Consequently he loaded every page with irrelevant dialogue and descriptions of engine thrust, even to the point of listing the supply inventories for several early flights. Nobody went to the washroom without Ferguson's recording it.

MacAllister made a few notes and decided it deserved to be reviewed. It was his duty to warn an unsuspecting public.

AT MIDAFTERNOON THEY transited out of the mist and glided back under the stars.

"We're about six light-years beyond 61 Cygni," said Valya, "moving in the general direction of the galactic core. Out here, it's not easy to be precise about distances. Can't be sure exactly where we are."

"Which one is it?" asked Amy, looking at the stars on the displays. "The one that's going to explode?"

"It's not visible to the naked eye," said Valya. She used a marker to indicate its location. "It's right here. Thirteen hundred light-years the other side of Sol. Out toward the rim. They figure it exploded in A.D. 946."

The light from the event reached Earth in 2216. "I was at Princeton," said Eric.

MacAllister had been in the second year of his marriage. He was with the *Sun* then, and Jenny had been teaching American history at a local high school.

The supernova had happened on a warm Tuesday evening, just after sunset. MacAllister was clearing away the dishes from dinner. Jenny had been outside talking with neighbors, and suddenly she was at the kitchen door, urging him to come out. *Look at this, Mac.*

He'd gone outside, expecting to discover that a flight of ducks had landed or some such thing—Jenny was forever feeding stray animals, and they came in swarms—but he was surprised to see her and his next-door neighbors staring at the sky.

Directly overhead, a star had appeared.

The sky was still much too light for stars.

The "star" got brighter as they watched.

He wondered whether it might be a comet. But there'd been no announcement to that effect.

"What is it, Mac?" she asked.

He checked with the *Sun* office. Nothing was happening that they knew of.

And it kept getting brighter.

The sky darkened, and other stars appeared, but none burned with the sheer intensity of whatever it was hanging over Eastern Avenue. People were coming out of their houses and standing on their lawns and in the street.

Eventually, he went back inside and made more calls. Air Transport said it was not in the atmosphere. The Wilkins Observatory seemed surprised to hear there was an anomaly. They told him they'd get back to him, but never did. He was about to call the Deep Space Lab in Kensington when the city editor at the *Sun* contacted him: They think it's a nova.

By then the entire neighborhood was outside looking up. It was the only time in his entire life he'd seen something like that. Even the passing of Halley's Comet, a couple of years earlier, had played to only a few people.

Eventually, the experts would decide it was a *super*nova.

EVEN AMY GOT bored while they waited. Valya showed them where the sun was; pointed out 61 Cygni, where they had been yesterday; and 36 Ophiuchi, where they would be tomorrow. Both were dim, even at close range.

They watched *The London Follies* that evening, leaving Bill to keep an eye open for the supernova. It came in the middle of the second act.

"It's beginning," he said.

Amy led the charge out of the common room onto the bridge. Valya had turned the *Salvator* around so it was facing back toward

Cygni, toward Earth, and they could see everything through the viewport.

Valya had Bill rerun the event from the beginning. A star appeared where none had been before, and within moments it became the brightest object in the sky.

"It's a rare sight," said Valya. "Whole generations live and die without seeing one of those."

He went up front and took his turn at the viewport. It chilled him to realize how far from Baltimore he was at that moment. "It was like that for three nights," he said.

She nodded. "Seventy-nine hours before it began to fade."

"I seem to recall they sent a mission."

"The *Perth*. That was the Long Mission."

Eric nodded. "At that time, it was the farthest we'd been from home. And the record stood a lot of years."

"Wasn't there something about aliens?" asked MacAllister.

"There was a theory," said Eric, "that the supernova would attract anyone who could see it and who had an FTL capability. Just as it had drawn the *Perth*. So when they got to the system, they watched for a few weeks. Before they started back, they inserted a couple of monitors to say hello in case anyone showed up."

"But nobody ever did," said MacAllister.

Valya grinned. "Give it time. It's early yet."

"It's been thirteen hundred years since the event. I suspect if anybody intended to go, they'd have been there by now."

"But it's only nineteen years since we left the satellites. There might have been visitors long before we got there. And most of the galaxy hasn't seen the light yet. Doesn't even know about the event."

AMY HAD HEARD her father describe the night it had happened, how he and her mother had been on a flight somewhere, and they'd thought a meteor had exploded overhead. He'd told her how the sky had filled with light, and they'd all held their breath until the pilot got on the comm system and told them there was nothing wrong with the aircraft, that they were looking at some sort of astronomical phenomenon. *"He didn't have a clue what it was, any more than we did,"* her father had explained. She'd heard him tell the story a hundred times. But until tonight she hadn't really understood.

Her father still believed that she was destined for a life like his. Maybe put in some years as a prosecutor somewhere. Eventually go into politics. Her fascination with the cosmos was a phase, a childish inclination that would go away with the onset of adulthood, of maturity. She loved him, and she wished he could see the world as she did. But she'd make him proud, in time.

She thought how, one day, ten light-years closer to the galactic center, she'd park another ship in front of the wave and show her passengers this same supernova. In a way, it suggested that the future Amy Taylor already existed.

Bill broke into her thoughts: *"On average, the Milky Way experiences two supernovas per century."*

"Were there any living worlds out there?" she asked. "Where the star exploded?"

"We don't know," said Bill. *"The system was so thoroughly wrecked it was impossible to be sure."*

"I can't imagine what it would be like," she said, "to be in a place like that."

"Where the sun was going to explode?" MacAllister shook his head. "It would raise hell with real estate values."

Eric had seen so many reports of sterile systems that it had never really occurred to him there might have been anyone out there.

"What about our sun?" MacAllister asked. "It's stable, right?"

Valya smiled at him. Amy thought the pilot liked him, although she never said anything. It was obvious that Valentina wanted to tell him no, the sun could blow up at any time, and *you* want to sink the space program. She could never bring herself to forget MacAllister's opposition to the Academy. You could see it in the attitude of the two toward each other. It was a pity. They'd have made an interesting couple, though they were both kind of old. "It's fine," Valya said. "Good for a few billion years yet."

"*How* many?" asked Amy, trying to sound worried.

"A few billion."

"That's a relief," she said, wondering if anyone there had heard the old joke. "For a minute I thought you said *million.*"

MacAllister laughed and went on: "Just for argument, if the sun were going to go supernova, we'd know about it, right? Well in advance?"

Valya passed the question to Bill. *"As I understand it,"* he said, *"the sun's not sufficiently massive to go supernova. And I don't think it can go nova either. But I'm not sure."*

"In either case, it blows up?" said MacAllister.

"Yes. But the explosion is much less violent."

"I can see," said Amy, "where that would make a difference."

"Have no fear," Eric said. "The sun's in good shape."

MACALLISTER'S DIARY

I don't know how to record this. I watched that star erupt, watched it become the brightest thing in the sky. And all I could think of was the first time I saw it, nineteen years ago, with Jenny. And I would have liked to have been able to see the Earth again, to see Baltimore on that night, just off Eastern Avenue. To see Jenny again. Alive and well.

—Sunday, April 5

chapter 20

> 36 Ophiuchi is a multiple star system. It's located slightly less than twenty light-years from Earth, in the constellation Ophiuchus, the Serpent Tamer. The system is composed of three stars, all orange-red dwarfs. Ophiuchi A and B orbit each other in a highly irregular pattern, approaching within a range of 7 AUs, retreating to 170 AUs. A complete orbit requires 574 years. Ophiuchi C orbits the inner pair at an average range of about 5000 AUs. It is a variable star.
>
> —*The Star Register*

"This is what everybody comes to see," said Valya, as they approached a blue-green world. It was orbiting Ophiuchi A at a distance of seventy-five million kilometers, placing it squarely in the biozone.

"Terranova," said Amy. The new Earth.

It was the second world on which life had been found, the first whose living creatures had been visible to the naked eye. That was eighty-five years ago. It was an unlikely system in which to find a planet with a stable orbit, let alone a living world. But there it was.

In an odd bit of serendipity, Terranova numbered among its occupants the largest known land animal. That was the unhappily named groper, which maybe should not qualify because there was still an ongoing argument whether it was animal or plant or a hybrid. It spent most of its life squatting over nutrient sources. It fed on a variety of slugs, bugs, and grasses. And periodically, when it had exhausted the output in one location, it climbed onto about two hundred legs and rumbled elsewhere. It used photosynthesis as a secondary energy source. Seen in motion, the creature resembled nothing so much as a giant green slug.

Also growing on Terranova were the largest known trees, the titans.

"Can we go down and take a look?" asked Amy.

"If you want." Valya glanced toward MacAllister and Eric to see if anyone wanted to join them. "It wouldn't take long."

"Be careful," said MacAllister, who remembered his flight on the lander at Maleiva III.

"You don't want to come, Mac?"

"Thanks. I'll guard the fort."

"How about you, Eric?"

Eric looked uncertain. "Okay," he said, finally. "Yes. Sure. Why not?"

"Good." Valya looked back at Amy. "You understand nobody leaves the lander."

"No, no, that's fine," said Amy. There was, of course, no danger that Eric would want to get out and go for a stroll.

"Just as a precaution," said MacAllister, "what do I do if something goes wrong?"

Valya looked amused. "What could go wrong?"

"You and the lander could get grabbed by a pterodactyl."

That got a laugh from Amy. "Mac," the girl said, "there aren't any pterodactyls here. You're always fooling around."

Valya raised her voice a notch: "Bill."

"Yes, Valya."

"If you lose contact with me, you will take instruction from Mac."

"Yes, ma'am."

She looked serenely at MacAllister. "Eric already functions as a backup, in case something were to happen to me. But since he'll be with us in the lander, you're in charge. It's not likely there'll be a problem. If there is, and for some reason we can't get back to the ship, and can't communicate with you, tell Bill to relay the situation to Mission Ops. They'll send help."

"Okay."

"We're at a substantial range, so it would take a few hours before you'd get an answer. But all you'd have to do is sit tight."

"All right." MacAllister didn't like the idea of their going down, but he didn't want to be a spoiler. Let the girl get a look at the walking slug, if that was what she wanted. She might not get another chance.

He accompanied them to the launch bay, which also doubled as a cargo hold. Valya broke out e-suits—electronic pressure suits—and gave them a quick course in their use. "We won't be using them," she said, "but we never go into hostile country without them. Just in case."

"Air's not breathable?" asked MacAllister.

"It has a bit too much methane," she said. She opened the hatch and watched her charges climb in. "We'll be back for dinner, Mac."

THE SHIP SEEMED bigger with everyone gone. MacAllister tried reading, tried to sleep, tried doing some work. Valya had left the lander's link active so he could listen to the conversation on the ground. Bill aimed the ship's telescopes at the surface and picked up visuals, which he put on-screen. MacAllister saw continents and oceans and an enormous inland sea. Terranova had ice caps and mountain ranges and island groups. It was an odd experience, looking at a place so Earthlike, but with unfamiliar landmasses. With one exception: A continent sprawled across the equator *did* vaguely resemble Australia.

He asked Bill for close-ups and saw something that looked like a water spider charging across the ocean surface. Watched a pair of jaws seize one of its hind legs and drag it under. Saw hordes of animals that *looked* big, although he couldn't be sure. And long-necked creatures with wings that did in fact resemble pterodactyls. He wondered what he'd say to Hiram Taylor if his daughter got snatched by something, and he went home alone. That would be an ugly scene.

A lot of the animals had armor. A few predators were up on their hind feet. He watched a plant—at least it looked like a plant—seize a four-legged creature that might have been a zebra with a long snout.

While MacAllister was admiring his good sense in staying behind, the lander settled onto a beach. There were huge shells in the surf, and a lot of birds.

"Valya," said Amy, *"could we get out and look? Just for a minute? I'll be careful."*

The beach was rimmed by hills and wetland. MacAllister wanted to tell her *no,* stay where you are, you shouldn't even be on the ground.

Something that was almost a blur swept across the sand, angling toward them and then away. It was a blue-green streak, moving so quickly he couldn't even tell whether it was airborne.

"No," said Valya. *"Stay put."*

He asked Bill if he could replay the sequence and freeze the image. Bill complied. The thing looked like a giant eight-legged mantis. Big jaws. Sharp mandibles. Scary eyes.

He opened a channel to the lander. "Valya," he told her, "be careful. You've got monsters in the neighborhood."

"I know, Mac," she said. *"I saw it."*

Yeah, he thought. Great place for a stroll.

THEY WERE BACK three hours later, flushed and excited.

"I'd have loved to be there when they found this place," said Eric. "They went through almost a hundred worlds that were in biozones before they found Genesis." Genesis, of course, was the breakthrough world, the place where life had finally been found. It had been strictly unicellular, but nevertheless there it was. Those who'd been arguing that life on Earth was unique, that it took a combination of exceedingly unlikely conditions to get it started, or even a divine decree, had begun to look prescient. Then a sample of water from Alpha Cephei III, quickly named Genesis, had revealed cellular life. "You know," he said, "they were getting ready to shut the program down then, too. People said it cost too much. And what was the point?"

"It's still a fair question," said MacAllister.

Valya interceded to head off a debate. Amy told MacAllister she liked him, and she hoped he wouldn't take offense, but this was a good example why they should have an amendment barring old people from becoming president. "Not that you're old," she added, embarrassed by the slip.

MacAllister began to realize that, of his three fellow passengers, Amy might be the most formidable. She was a believer, and she wasn't going to be swayed by economic arguments. In the end, of course, it was all a matter of what you cared about.

That evening, Valya took them into a higher orbit and released the monitor. "Moonriders have been seen close to Terranova," she said. "We'll see whether they show up again."

MacAllister watched the black box drift away. "We still don't really know how life got started, do we?"

"I think they have a pretty good idea," she said. "But I don't believe anybody can prove anything yet. There's a world out in Majoris somewhere, a proto-Earth, that they're studying. They think they've got the beginning of the chemical process. But who knows?"

Eric asked Bill to put the titan trees on the display. "Biggest living things in existence," he said.

"Known so far," added Amy.

So the biggest land animal and the biggest tree were both located on the same world. "Anybody know why?" asked MacAllister.

Nobody did. Even Bill didn't know whether there was a theory to account for it.

Amy was staring at the titans. Bill superimposed a sequoia. It was about half as tall. "You know what I don't understand," she said. "What's the point of being a tree? I mean, root system and chlorophyll and all the rest of it, what's the point of being alive if you're a tree?"

Mouths of babes, thought MacAllister. "What's next?" he asked.

"Origins," said Valya.

STATE OF THE PLANET DIGEST
(April 2235)

CONTENTS

Baseball Moving North: Toronto, Montreal, Winnipeg Get Teams from South 28
Climatic Instability Confuses Migration Patterns 31
Still No Snow in Moscow: Seventh Straight Year 35

EVANGELICALS PREPARE FOR "HELLFIRE" TRIAL

Derby Police Chief Warns Demonstrators to Stay Away

chapter 21

The rationale for the Origins Project is that we will be able to push the creation event back a few more microseconds. To do this, we have spent vast sums, and will spend considerably more. We are talking here about blue-sky science. The search for knowledge that doesn't necessarily do anyone any practical good but allows us to sit back and feel smug. I suppose there's something to be said for that. On the other hand, a few billion would also make me feel pretty smug.

—Gregory MacAllister, "Science on the Couch"

Beyond 36 Ophiuchi lies a void, a vast dark gulf roughly sixteen light-years across. It is as empty of dust and particles as can be found within reasonable range of Earth. It is empty in the truest sense of the word, a place where the distance between occasional passing atoms is measured in hundreds of kilometers. It is the home of the Origins Project.

The facility housing the project was designed to be as stationary as possible. Billed as "an exploration of the universe before there was light," it would, when completed, constitute by several orders of magnitude the largest engineering effort in history. It would be approximately six hundred thousand kilometers long. Positioned as it was in a starless gulf, it consisted of a tube constructed primarily of wire strands, connecting two terminals, the East and West Towers. Only the towers were readily visible. These were platforms, two enormous spheres, housing staff, equipment, supplies, and operating personnel.

Origins was, of course, a collider. A device for smashing particles together. The tube used a series of artificial gravity rings, installed at intervals of 150 kilometers, to drive the acceleration. The rings were dipoles. One side attracted, while the other side repelled. Forces were always equal and opposite at equal distances on either side of the ring. The effect, of course, fell off with distance.

It was by far the largest device of any kind to use artificial gravity technology, and the only accelerator above the class of training prototypes. Because it used shaped gravitational rather than electric or magnetic fields, it could accelerate anything: charged particles, neutral beams, pebbles, anything at all with mass.

Construction had begun fourteen years earlier. The project was still in its early stages. When the *Salvator* arrived in its neighborhood, it was barely ten thousand kilometers long. But the platforms were moving apart by ten kilometers daily, using spools of wire brought in by a fleet of automated government-owned haulers. An additional ring was installed every two weeks.

The labs containing the beam sources were nestled in the towers, centered in large spinnerets. The target area, located midway in the tube, was necessarily an ultraclean environment. Only spike-powered (antigravity) vehicles, specially scrubbed to prevent outgassing, were allowed near it. These vehicles had no maneuvering jets. Instead, they operated with clutched gyros or, in an emergency, with mass-driver reaction motors that launched trackable missiles the size of tennis balls. (It was considered a disgrace to get into a situation in which it was necessary to use the mass drivers. That was muddying the waters. Flights from the tower to scoop up expended missiles—the mud—were invariably accompanied by a wave of laughter.)

As with other legendary projects, Stonehenge, the Great Pyramid, the Golden Gate, the Apollo missions, the level of technology at the outset was not quite adequate to the task. We were learning as we went.

* * *

THEY RELEASED THEIR monitor millions of kilometers away, then Valya got clearance, locked in her course, fired the engines, then shut them down for the duration of the flight. Nobody was permitted to use engines anywhere in the vicinity of the accelerator. Hours later, when they drew sufficiently close to the facility, their approach and docking would be managed by Origins and its directed-gravity fields.

It was dark in the middle of the gulf. They were almost on top of the tower before they saw it. Lighting was sparse; there was little more than a gossamer glow. But as they drew near, they saw the outline of a massive sphere. A shaft emerged from it and extended into the night. MacAllister focused on the shaft. It appeared to be made of wire, glittering in a woven cross pattern. *"The design,"* Bill explained, *"minimizes eddy currents."*

"Why?" asked Amy.

"Eddy currents would defocus a beam of charged particles."

The response seemed to make sense to her.

A small ship, little more than an open cockpit with a cargo platform and thrusters, moved along the shaft, outward bound from the tower. Carrying construction materials, apparently.

MacAllister was able to read lettering on the sphere. He needed a minute as they passed to make out INTERNATIONAL SCIENCE AGENCY.

"This is the East Tower," said Valya.

Amy was glued to the portal. "East of what?" she asked.

"Your imagination, kid," said MacAllister.

"Funny," she said. Then: "I wish we could see a bit better."

"By the way," said MacAllister, "this place costs several times what they're paying to keep the Academy running."

Valya sighed and let it go.

EVEN THOUGH ORIGINS was operated by the European Deep Space Commission, the Academy was involved in transporting supplies and personnel. Consequently, questions about the program had frequently surfaced during the press conferences, and Eric considered it his special field of expertise. Except he couldn't answer the big question: What actually might they find out? Nobody knew. But it was asked regularly anyhow, and when it was Eric kicked it around as best he could.

It would be enormously helpful, when he got back, to be able to throw in comments like, "When I was out there last year, I asked precisely that question. What they had to say . . ."

This was something he should have done ages ago. Talked his way on board one of the mission flights. He'd been a staff assistant when Hutch had gone out with the Contact Society to investigate odd radio transmissions and they'd found that automated alien vessel. That had been his opportunity. He could have arranged to go along, but he'd been too placid. Too uninvolved. Too *something*.

He had since allowed friends and associates to believe that he *had* tried to get passage but that his boss denied permission. His boss probably *would* have denied permission. So it wasn't really such a stretch.

But there was another reason it was good to be here. You didn't really feel the enormity of the effort, what we were really doing, sitting in an office back in Arlington. When people talked about a structure that was currently ten thousand kilometers long, getting longer every day, it sounded big, but not that big.

When he looked out through Valya's viewport and *saw* the thing, saw the sphere that formed what they called the East Tower, saw the gulf that was its home, and knew that the connecting tube between East and West started over there where the sphere was and extended into the night seemingly forever, he was able to grasp the magnitude of the project. No wonder it generated such passion. It wasn't simply about elucidating the Big Bang. It was also a demonstration of what we could do.

AS FAR AS MacAllister was concerned, Origins was another oversized boondoggle. It had gotten its start as part of a global deal to get a trade package approved. Originally, it was to have been of modest proportions and reasonable cost. Then the concept had caught fire, and now they were looking at a massively expensive project. The Europeans, always a bit on the ethereal side, were delighted. So it had gone through with the usual high-level machinations and justifications delivered by NAU politicians who wouldn't have known a quark from an aardvark. And there it was, a black hole for taxpayers, sitting out in the middle of nowhere, producing answers to questions nobody sensible would ever think to ask.

You weren't permitted to run engines within several million kilometers of the facility. That had meant a low-velocity approach that went on for the better part of a day. As they closed in, Valya had everyone strap down. "They're going to use gravity fields to bring us in," Valya said. "It's a bit unnerving if you haven't done it before. Just try to relax." Then, after a few moments: "Okay, here we go."

The deck beneath him began to tilt. The rear of the ship started to tilt *down*. MacAllister gripped the arms of his chair.

Amy squealed with delight.

It felt as if the *Salvator* was turning over. The bridge moved steadily *up* until it was almost directly overhead.

"Don't worry," said Valya. "It's a directed-gravity field. They're slowing us down."

THERE WAS A mild jar as they completed the docking maneuver. Then *down* was once again in the direction of the deck. "Okay, everybody," said Valya. "They have quarters set aside for us. We'll sleep in the tower and come back to the ship tomorrow."

The outer hatch opened. A cheerful male voice said, "Hello. Welcome to Origins."

He was middle-aged, with a high forehead and receding black hair, convivial green eyes, a thick mustache, and a casual manner. He wore a mud-colored sweater and a silver bracelet-style commlink. "This is a pleasant surprise," he said, extending a hand to help Amy with her bag. "My name's Lou Cassell. I'm on the director's staff."

Lou was amiable and sincere. The sort of individual who inevitably tried MacAllister's patience. It was easy to picture him leading a church choir. He shook hands enthusiastically. Good to have you aboard. "Unfortunately, Dr. Stein will not be able to meet with you. He wanted me to convey his disappointment, but to ensure that you got everything you need." He introduced them to a few other staff members, asked whether they needed anything, and escorted them to their quarters, which were, to MacAllister's surprise, smaller and more spartan than those on the *Salvator*.

They took a few minutes to get organized. Then Lou suggested they might want something to eat.

It was early morning for Valya and her passengers, but the occupants of the tower, which ran on Greenwich Mean Time, were just settling in for lunch. They followed him into a large, crowded dining area. "How many people do you have here?" asked MacAllister.

Lou looked around, as if he needed to do a count. "I think we have seventy-seven on board at the moment," he said. "And another ninety or so in the West Tower." He passed the question to the AI, who confirmed the number at seventy-nine. "Plus yourselves, of course."

Of course.

"You mentioned a director? Stein? Does he run the entire operation?"

"You mean the entire facility?"

"Yes."

"More or less. He sets overall policy and whatnot. But the day-to-day operations in the West Tower are handled by his deputy."

MacAllister was surprised there were so many people. "I understood Origins wouldn't become operational for years."

"*Fully* operational. We've been up and running for eighteen months. We don't have anything like the capacity the system will have when it's completely put together. But it's still far and away the world's best collider.

"It takes a lot of people to make this place go, Mac. It's okay if I call you that? Good. About a third of them are engineering and construction types. Another third do technical support and administration. You know, supply, general maintenance, life support, and so on. The rest are scientific staff. The researchers. They rotate. They come on board in groups by project. And they compete for instrument time from the first day they get here."

"What would they be doing on the instruments?" asked Amy, who couldn't keep the excitement out of her voice.

MacAllister thought about her father trying to send her to law school and couldn't suppress a smile.

"They'll want one more run on the beam, or more time on the computers, or a little more bandwidth on the comm channels. We can't possibly keep everybody happy."

MacAllister was still thinking about DiLorenzo. "Is the place safe?" he asked.

"Absolutely. You couldn't be in a safer place."

"You're not going to blow up this part of the galaxy?"

"I've heard those stories, too. I wouldn't take them too seriously, Mac." Lou allowed himself a polite smile. Didn't want to offend anybody, but it was a dumb question.

Lou did a lot of introductions, including some to people whose names he had trouble remembering. Hardly any of them recognized MacAllister's name.

He wasn't used to people smiling, shaking hands, and turning away.

WHEN THEY'D FINISHED, Lou announced it was showtime, and led the way out into a corridor. "If you'll allow me," he said, "I'd like you to see what we're about."

They crossed into a dark room, and the lights came on.

It was a circular VR chamber. They took seats around the wall, and Lou brought up an image of a long narrow line, which stretched wire-thin from one side of the chamber to the other. "This is our basic structure as it is now constituted," he said. "The East Terminal is on your right; the West to the left. Between, of course, is the tube." He put up a silhouette of North America, and laid it over the line. Origins extended from Savannah, Georgia, to Los Angeles and out into the Pacific almost to the Hawaiian Islands.

"All one structure?" said Amy.

"All one. When it's finished, it will be considerably larger." The line lifted off the map. Hawaii and the Pacific and the NAU shrank and were seen to be on a curved surface. Then the Earth was dropping away. The line extended off-world, well past the moon.

And finally stopped.

"I know the wire's thin," said MacAllister, "but that's still a lot of the stuff. Where's it come from?"

"We mine it. Iron asteroids in the Ophiuchi system. We do everything over there, extract it, smelt it, whatever, put it on spools, and bring the spools here."

"It's *enormous*," said Eric. "I don't think I ever realized how big this place is. How big it will *be*."

"In fact," said Lou, "the collider, when it's finished, will be too short."

MacAllister stared at the line projecting out past the moon. "You're not serious."

"Oh, yes. Eventually we'll have to build another one. When we have the resources."

"And when you know more," said MacAllister.

"That, too."

The image rotated and gave them a close-up of the East Tower. "Accelerator beams are generated here," he said. "And at the other end, of course." The sphere opened up, and they were inside, looking at a round, polished disk. Lou launched into a standard lecture. Here was how the beam was aimed, here's what the robots did, there's how they kept even a few stray particles from getting into the tube.

MacAllister started getting bored. "Lou," he said, breaking in, "what's it for? What do you expect to learn?"

Lou inhaled. Looked simultaneously proud and cornered. "The easy answer," he said, "is that we will be collecting accurate data that can't be had any other way. The true reason, though, the one that gets to the heart of things, is that we don't know what we might learn. *Won't* know until we see it. It's fair to say we're looking for ultimate answers. Why is there a universe instead of nothing? Are there other universes? You might even say we're looking for the right questions to ask."

"Such as?"

He fumbled that one. "Nobody else would want to be quoted saying this, but there are a lot of people here who think the same way I do about this." He paused. "It would be nice to know whether our existence has any meaning beyond the moment."

That was a bit too spiritual for MacAllister. The taxpayers were spending enormous sums so Lou Cassel and his crowd could look for answers to questions that, by their nature, had no answers.

Lou finished finally, and the lights came on. "If you like," he said, "we can walk over and take a look at the generators."

But Valya had her link clasped to her ear. When she'd finished, MacAllister moved next to her. "What's going on?"

"It's Bill. The probe we left at Ophiuchi—"

"Yes?"

"Has reported moonriders."

ARCHIVE

Origins isn't about physics. It's not even *mostly* about physics, or anthropology, or art, or history. Or, God help us, engineering. It's about bigger issues. It's about faith as opposed to religion. Understanding rather than belief. The project will be a place where we are invited to ask any question. The only requirement will be a willingness to accept the answer. Even though we may not like it.

We can create the appearance of knowledge, the illusion of knowing how to grapple with a problem. Far too many educational systems have done exactly that. The result is generations of mouthpieces who can pour forth approved responses to programmed stimuli that contribute nothing to rational discussion. Dogma is for those who wish only to be comfortable. Catechisms are for cowards; commandments, for control freaks who have so little respect for their species that they are driven to appeal to a higher power to keep everyone in line.

If indeed we have a Maker, I suspect He is proudest of us when we ask the hard questions. And listen for the answers.

—Filippo Montreone, commenting on the proposal to build the hypercollider, 2193

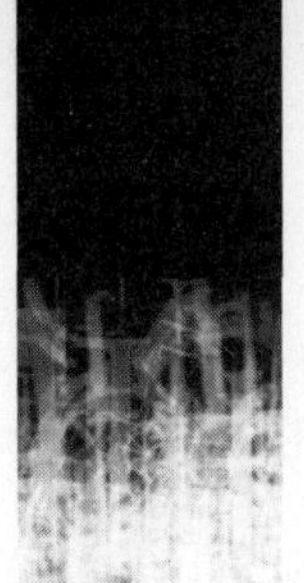

chapter 22

We're not enamored of truth. It is too often painful, discouraging, and it tends to undermine our self-image. We prefer comfort. Reassurance. Well-being. Good cheer. Naked optimism. Nobody wants to hear the facts when they clash with a happily imagined reality. It is, after all, a terrible thing to be the only person in town who can see what's really happening. But I've gotten used to it.

—Gregory MacAllister, "Gone to Glory"

"Lou," said Valya, "can we borrow one of your projectors?"

Lou was one of these people who seemed to enjoy bestowing favors. "Sure," he said. "Did I hear something about moonriders?"

"At Ophiuchi."

He lit up. "Are you serious?"

"Of course. There's apparently something there."

"Projectors." He thought about it. "Follow me." He led the way into a corridor, passed a few doors, and entered another VR chamber. "A few of our people have seen them."

"So we heard."

"You've got the feed?"

"Yes."

"Mind if I watch?"

"Not at all." They grabbed seats while Valya tied into the system. "Go ahead, Bill," she said. "Let's see what we have."

Bill adopted his professorial tone. *"First images arrived three minutes ago,"* he said. The room went dark, and the Ophiuchi sky appeared. A red star, a sensor image, was moving. Left to right, across the front of the chamber. It brightened as they watched.

Coming closer.

"It's not responding to radio calls," said Bill.

"Comet," suggested MacAllister.

"It's under power."

"Is it one of ours?" asked Valya.

"Negative."

MacAllister wasn't buying it. "How do you know, Bill?" he asked.

"The electronic signature doesn't match anything we have." The object grew bigger. *"Switching to the monitor's onboard telescope."* The red glow went away, and they were looking at a black globe. *"Mag two hundred,"* said Bill.

The crosswise movement had stopped. But it continued to get larger. "It looks as if it's coming right at us," said Amy.

Valya nodded. "It's closing on the monitor."

"If that thing doesn't belong to us," demanded Lou, "what the hell is it?"

Question of the hour.

There had to be a rational explanation. "Can we try talking to it through the monitor?" MacAllister asked.

"The onboard AI's been trying to say hello. Not getting an answer."

"How about if *we* try it?" he persisted.

"Too much of a time lapse," said Valya.

The object drifted in virtually nose to nose with the monitor. And stopped.

"Diameter of the globe," said Bill, *"is 61.7 meters. The monitor reports it is being probed."*

"I wish we could react to it in some way," said Eric. "Wave a flag, do something."

Amy was delighted. Overwhelmed. She raised both fists. "It's scary."

For a long time, no one else said anything. It felt almost as if the moonrider was in the chamber with them.

"So what do we do?" asked Eric. "Do we go back to Ophiuchi?"

Valya looked uncertain. "I doubt it would still be there when we showed up."

"Still," said Amy, "it's why we're out here. Shouldn't we at least try?"

Eric nodded. Yes. Let's go. Valya looked at Mac. "What do you think?"

"Let me ask a question first: If it's still there when we arrive, would we be able to run it down?"

"Don't know," she said. "We don't have a read on their acceleration capability. In any case, we don't know that it would run from us."

Or *after* us. There was a sobering thought. "Okay," he said. "Let's see if we can find out what the damned thing is."

Lou wished them good luck and said he was sorry to see them leave so soon. He reminded Valya that she was not permitted to start her engines until the facility gave her an all clear.

He escorted them back to the boarding area. Minutes later, while they strapped in for another gravity launch, the moonrider began to withdraw from the monitor. By the time they were ready to go, it had almost vanished.

The departure was more harrowing than the docking procedure had been, because the forward area went *down,* and the chair MacAllister was using faced the bridge, which rotated until it was straight down and he was hanging by the harness.

Gradually, the effect went away, and they were able to move around again. But it was a long, slow flight out to the point at which they received permission to ignite their engines.

VALYA INFORMED UNION Operations that the *Salvator* was on its way back to Ophiuchi. Five hours later she had a response from the watch officer: *"Exercise caution. Keep us informed."*

The monitor passed along its analytical data, such as it was: Moonrider drive unit unknown. Light source unknown. Attitude thrusters detected. And sensing devices. Unintelligible symbols on the hull. *"It appears to move by casting and manipulating gravitational fields."*

"That sounds a little bit like what we were doing," said MacAllister.

Valya agreed. "Except we wouldn't be able to do it from inside the ship. At least not if we wanted to pick up any velocity."

Finally, they made their jump and began the long cruise through the fogbanks. Meantime the monitor stayed silent.

Previously, they had passed their time more or less as individuals. Eric enjoyed reading mysteries, and he'd already gone through three. Amy alternated between homework and games. MacAllister worked on his notes or read. Valya disappeared onto the bridge for long periods, during which they could hear the soft beat of Greek music.

There was an inclination now, perhaps in the presence of the moonrider, to draw together. They played a four-handed game of snatchem, talked about what they would do when they got home, broke for a meal, and decided to do a musical.

They let Amy make the call, and she chose *Manhattan*, the story of the fabled alcoholic song writer Jose Veblen, and his alternately inspirational and destructive romance with the singer Jeri Costikan. They apportioned the roles, with Eric playing Veblen and Valya as Jeri. Amy played Jeri's best friend (and better self), while MacAllister portrayed Veblen's long-suffering agent.

During the showstopper at the end of the first act, which featured Amy's and Valya's characters, accompanied by the cast at large, singing and dancing their way through "Y' Gotta Let Go," the monitor reported a second sighting at Ophiuchi.

Valya killed the show, and Bill provided a picture. *"It's moving across the monitor's field of vision,"* Bill said. *"Range is eight hundred kilometers."*

"There's nowhere to go in that system," said Eric. "What's the point? Are they just riding around?"

MacAllister laughed. "You'd think, if they were really intelligent aliens, they'd have something more important to do than hang around out there all day."

"Apparently not," said Valya. She looked at Amy. "What's so funny?"

"Maybe they're kids."

"It's braking," said Bill.

MacAllister leaned forward and propped his chin on his hands. "Maybe it's coming back to have another look at the monitor?"

"I don't think so," said Valya. "It's not going in the right direction."

Amy was completely oblivious to anything but the screen. She got in front of MacAllister and momentarily blocked his view. "There's another one out there," she said. "See? Beside it."

There was indeed a second moving object. But it was starlike.

"That is odd," said Bill. *"If it's another moonrider, the monitor hasn't reported it as such."*

"It's something *else,"* said Valya.

The monitor's telescope belatedly focused on it.

"Asteroid," said Amy.

Eric nodded. "No question about it."

Bill appeared in the entry to the bridge. He reminded MacAllister of a physics professor, gray beard, rumpled jacket, distracted eyes. *"The moonrider is shedding velocity,"* he said.

Valya was seated beside MacAllister. She put a hand on his forearm. "It's going to land on the thing."

The monitor's onboard AI apparently drew the same conclusion, and ratcheted up the magnification. The asteroid was misshapen, nondescript, doing a slow tumble. *"It's nickel-iron,"* said Bill. At first the globe looked bigger than the rock, but as it moved closer it began to shrink until it was in fact minuscule in contrast. *"The asteroid is approximately two kilometers in diameter."*

The moonrider settled like a dark insect onto the surface.

There was a series of ridges near one pole, and something had sliced a deep crevice through them. "What could it possibly want with that thing?" asked Amy.

Valya shook her head. Wait and see.

It snuggled into the crevice. And became imperceptible. Then it reddened, glowed, and faded. And again. Like a heartbeat. "This is where it would be helpful," said MacAllister, "if the monitor had a drive unit of some sort."

"Costs too much," said Valya.

They waited for something to happen.

And waited.

The asteroid continued its slow tumble. The moonrider brightened and dimmed. The picture was becoming smaller, as the asteroid, with its cargo, moved farther from the monitor's telescope.

MacAllister's imagination ran wild. Maybe the asteroid was a base? The moonrider might be attached to a boarding tube.

"What would they be doing with a base in a godforsaken place like that?" said Eric.

MacAllister hadn't realized he was thinking aloud.

"Maybe they use it for refueling," Amy said. "Or recharging." She turned to Valya. "Is that possible?"

"Anything's possible," she said. "We just don't know enough yet."

"Valya." Bill sounded surprised. *"The asteroid's changing course."*

"How do you mean?"

"It's being diverted. Turning."

"Turning *where*?" demanded MacAllister.

"Too soon to tell."

Valya looked frustrated. "I wish we were a little closer."

Eric stared at the images, at the constant red pulse inside the depression. At the sheer size of the asteroid. "It doesn't look possible." He turned toward Valya. "It's too small to move something that big, isn't it?"

"I would have thought so. But it looks as if it's doing it."

"Could *we* move it?" asked MacAllister.

"A little bit," she said. "If we had a lot of time. And a way to lock on to it. But not like this."

"Monitor reports the asteroid is accelerating."

Valya looked puzzled. "Maybe it has a project of some sort. The wire weave at Origins was made from asteroids in this system."

"Maybe that's what it is," said MacAllister. "That *must* be one of our ships."

"Take my word for it, Mac. It isn't—"

"Uh-oh," said Amy.

The moonrider had let go. It lifted from the surface. Began to move away from the rock.

"The moonrider is also accelerating," said Bill.

"Bill," said Valya, "will you be able to find it when we get there?"

"The moonrider? Or the asteroid?"

"The asteroid."

"Sure," he said. *"If it doesn't change course again."*

Amy looked entranced. The visitors, whoever they were, had actually shown up. Mac had not believed for a minute that anything like this could happen. It was all he could do not to cheer.

He watched the moonrider fade out among the stars. Listened to Bill's report: *"The asteroid remains in a solar orbit. It's moving toward the sun, but I can't see that it's going anywhere in particular."*

"You're sure?"

"Keep in mind this is a preliminary analysis. But yes, they've adjusted the orbit somewhat, but to what purpose I have no idea."

* * *

THE ACTION APPEARED to be over for the night. MacAllister treated himself to a snack, went to bed, and slept peacefully. In the morning he woke with a fresh perspective. For decades, experts had been predicting that advanced aliens would be hard to understand. And they'd used the creators of the omega clouds as a case in point. The clouds had rolled through the galaxy, or at least the Orion Arm of it, causing mindless destruction with mathematical precision. Nobody knew why. Hutch had a harebrained theory about creating art, but MacAllister had drawn a different explanation. The aliens were game-playing. They sent out the clouds, sat back, and kept score. Whoever got the most explosions won.

Maybe the same sort of thing was happening with the moonriders. Or maybe they were conducting an exercise of some sort. Testing, for example, their capability to move asteroids around.

The hypothesis we would have serious problems communicating with alien civilizations was likely to prove true. But not necessarily because the aliens were subtle and sophisticated and simply products of a radically different culture. Rather it might be that the aliens, by any reasonable standard, were deranged. Dummies with big toys invented by somebody back home. Somebody who was too smart to get out and ride around between the stars himself. The idiots always rose to the top and made policy.

It explained a lot of things.

WHEN HE WANDERED into the common room, nothing had changed. There'd been no more moonriders, no visitations with other asteroids, no indication of anything out of the ordinary.

The asteroid had receded, and was now only a dim reflection at high mag.

The monitor, meantime, reported that the asteroid's heading had been changed seventeen degrees laterally. And there'd been a very slight horizontal alteration. It was moving below the plane of its original orbit.

They also had a response from Hutch: *"We won't be able to get a ship out there for several days,"* she said. *"Take a look at the asteroid. There's a possibility it's a base. And I know how that sounds. Nevertheless, see what you can find out but approach with caution."*

A base. MacAllister had been ahead of the curve on that one.

Hutch continued: *"Try to determine what they were doing. Again, keep your eyes open. Especially if the moonriders show up again. Do not assume they aren't hostile. Avoid any close encounter."*

MacAllister laughed. "We're the defense against a vanguard of alien invaders. If they actually *are* hostile, Valya, what sort of weapons have we to defend ourselves? Does this thing have any kind of gun? Or missile launcher?"

"We could throw stuff at them," she said. "I think the assumption when the first interstellars left home, in the last century, was that we wouldn't run into hostiles. Even after our experience with the clouds, nobody takes the possibility seriously. I think this is the first time I've ever heard the word used in an official directive."

"You know," Eric said, "Hutch tells us to maintain a safe distance. We've just watched that thing change the course of an asteroid that's two kilometers long. You say we couldn't do anything like that?"

"Not to that degree, and certainly not in that short a time."

"Okay. That leads us to the next question."

" 'What's a safe distance?' " said Amy. She seemed restless. "I hate it that it takes so long to get there. I wouldn't be surprised if, right after we arrived, we got a report of a sighting back at Origins."

VALYA SPENT MUCH of the time teaching Amy how to play chess while MacAllister kibitzed. Eventually, Eric got into the chess game, and Valya sat down with MacAllister. At his urging, she talked about life in the Peloponnesus.

"It was a long time ago," she said. "My folks had money. They sent me to the best schools. My father wanted me to be a physician, like him."

"What happened?"

"I don't like the sight of blood."

"You're kidding."

"No, really. And anyhow, I wasn't interested. I was an only child, so I became something of a major disappointment to them."

"I can't believe that."

Her eyes lit up. "That's kind of you, Mac."

"How'd you come by *Valentina*? That isn't Greek, is it?"

"I was named for my grandmother. She was Russian." Her eyes sparkled with the recollection.

"So you can relate to Amy."

"Amy and law school? Oh, yes. I know the drill."

"Your parents' attitude must have changed when you became a pilot."

"They pretended it had. But you know how it is. My father used to go on about how much good I might have done as a doctor. He doesn't do that anymore. Just walks around looking as if he's burdened with sorrow." She glanced back toward the hatch. "How many siblings does Amy have?"

"I think she's an only child, too."

"Same situation. All the eggs in one basket." She laughed. It was a sweet sound, but there was sadness in it. "I wish we could have brought her father along. He might have learned something about her. And about himself."

"Do you get to see them much? Your parents?"

"Not as much as I should. Visits can be painful." She looked at him. "How about you?"

"I see my mother once in a while. My father's dead."

"I'm sorry."

He shrugged. "He and I were never close. My folks used to pray for me all the time."

"I don't blame them." The smile spread across her features.

"Amy gets to be a lawyer. You're a doctor. My folks wanted *me* to be a preacher."

"Really? What happened?"

He shrugged. "I got lucky."

"You wandered pretty far from home."

"Sometimes you have to. I can sympathize with Beemer."

"Who?"

"Oh, he's caught up in a court case in North Carolina. He objected to the church school he went to."

"Is he the guy who bopped the preacher?"

"Yes. Nice to know that occasionally someone rebels."

"How about your mother?"

"I shouldn't sell her short. She encouraged me to read. She didn't always like the books I brought home. But she looked the other way when she had to."

"So you didn't keep the faith."

"No. I didn't last long."

She got involved in a short conversation with Bill. Something about fuel correlations, but MacAllister knew she was stalling while she decided how to react. "It can be a major loss, Mac," she said, finally. "There are times when you need to be able to believe in a higher power, or you can't make it through."

"So far," said MacAllister, "I've managed."

"The day'll come."

"Maybe. But the notion that we need a higher power, that's more a human failing than a reflection of reality. The universe pays no attention to what we need. Truth is what it is, and the inconveniences it might cause us don't change anything."

"How did it happen? When did you walk away? Do you remember?"

"Oh, yes. I was about seventeen. Trying to hang on, because I was still afraid of the penalty for getting things wrong. Lose your soul. That's pretty serious stuff."

"So what exactly happened?"

"I don't know. Read too much Dostoevski maybe. Saw the aftereffects of one tidal wave too many. Saw too many kids die in the Carodyne epidemic."

"They had the medications available, didn't they?"

"Yes. But there were bureaucratic problems. Delays of all kinds. So people died by the tens of thousands."

"Things like that happen," she said.

"Then there was Milly."

"Milly?"

"A kitten. A stray. Abandoned by her mother. We brought her into the house when I was a kid. But she had Brinkmann's. A disease. Too far along so they anesthetized her."

"I can see that would be traumatic for a kid. How old were you?"

"Nine. And I remember thinking what was the point of having a deity looking after the planet if he doesn't take care of kittens? He gets credit for the handful of survivors when a ship goes down; but nobody ever seems to notice that, for those who died, he didn't carry his weight."

She was silent for a time. "You must have been a severe disappointment to him. To your father."

"He never made the adjustment. Never forgave me. He wasn't big on forgiveness. Talked about it a lot but didn't practice it."

"How's your mother now?"

"Still prays for me."

Bill broke in: *"Valya, I'm sorry to interrupt."*

"What is it, Bill?"

"The monitor's gone silent."

THEY GOT LUCKY. The *Salvator* emerged into normal space barely an hour away from the monitor. MacAllister's first act was to rotate the view on the display to satisfy himself no moonriders were in the vicinity.

"Put the monitor on the scope," Valya said, from the bridge.

It looked untouched.

"Everybody stay strapped down. Let's go take a look."

MacAllister had never lacked for courage to confront the assorted power mongers with whom he had to deal. He had, on one occasion, even faced down the president of the North American Union. But he didn't like taking physical risks, and the knowledge that an unknown, and unpredictable, force was running around out there left him wondering whether they should take the hint and leave. The moonriders had probably disabled the monitor. And they might well be prepared to disable anyone who showed up in the area. But with two women present and apparently heedless of the risks, it was difficult to say anything.

Eric and Amy, on the other hand, were enjoying the experience. Amy, of course, wasn't smart enough to recognize the danger. She had that same sense of indestructibility that everybody has at fifteen. Moreover, she wanted to be at the center of everything. One day, he knew, she would drive some poor guy crazy.

Eric's problem was that he had seen too many action vids. He visualized himself as the free-swinging sim hero, Jack What's-His-Name. And, of course, there was no point reminding him that, whatever the odds Jack faced, he always had the writers on his side.

Valya put them on course toward the monitor and began to accelerate. MacAllister sank back into his chair. "Do we see anything moving anywhere?" he asked.

"Nothing that's not in a standard orbit, Mac. If we spot anything, I'll let you know."

Amy looked at him and grinned. "Glad you came, Mr. MacAllister?"

"Oh," he said, "you bet, Amy. Wouldn't have missed it." He tried to deliver the line straight, but she picked something up and looked at him oddly.

"It'll be okay," she said. "We can run pretty fast if we have to."

"No, no," he said, as if personal safety were of no concern. "It's not that." He tried to think what it might be. "I was just anxious to get a look at the asteroid."

NONE OF THE monitor's status lamps worked. "General power failure, looks like," said Valya.

"Could that happen naturally?" asked Eric, as they pulled alongside.

"Oh, sure." Valya suited up and headed aft. Eric asked whether she wanted company.

"No," she said. "Thanks anyhow. Nothing you can do."

She disappeared below. Hatches opened and closed. They heard the whooshing sounds of decompression. The ship moved slightly and aligned itself more closely to the monitor, which floated just outside the cargo doors.

MacAllister remembered a favored theme in popular sims and cheap novels, in which a monster is brought aboard a ship inadvertently. Usually, a settlement had been wiped out, cause unknown. The rescue ship gathers evidence and starts home. And the *thing* creeps out of a canteen and, within twenty-four hours or so, is terrorizing the ship. While he thought about that, the cargo doors opened. Bill switched to zero gee, moved the *Salvator* slightly to starboard, and the instrument floated inside. Valya disconnected the monitor's telescopes and sensors. He watched her work over the unit, poking and prodding and running tests.

"Nothing jumps out at me," she said at last. *"It has no power. But we pretty much knew that."* She began opening panels in the device.

"Can you tell why not?" asked Amy.

"Hang on a sec."

"You think the moonriders did it?" Eric asked.

The future pilot shook her head. "I don't think so. Wouldn't the monitor have seen them coming?"

"Yes," said MacAllister. "We would have had pictures."

"It's the calibrator." She'd plugged a gauge into one of the slots. *"It failed, we got a surge, and everything blew out."*

"Could the moonriders have done it?" persisted Eric.

"No. I'd say it's just a routine breakdown." Then she was talking to the monitor: *"Let's see now. . . . Should be one here somewhere. . . . There we go."* And to her passengers: *"I'm going to install a replacement. It'll only take a few minutes. Then we'll relaunch and be on our way."*

Eric looked disappointed.

WHEN VALYA WAS finished, she ran more tests, reattached the monitor's parts, put it back outside, and came back up to the common room. "All right," she said, "let's go take a look at the asteroid."

Yes, thought MacAllister, *there* was the mystery. Why were the moonriders interested in a piece of iron? He tried to keep his imagination on a leash. But he found himself considering the possibility that it might contain an inner chamber, perhaps with a ghastly secret. Or maybe Amy was right, and the thing was a fuel depot. Or maybe it was a rest stop of some sort. On the other hand, if any of those explanations was valid, why adjust its orbit? "How long to catch it?" he asked Valya.

She finished climbing out of the e-suit harness and headed for the bridge. *"A few hours."*

"And it's still not going anywhere particular?"

"Not as far as I can see. It's more or less inbound, toward the sun."

MacAllister sat back and shook his head. How about that? I was right all the time. There are aliens, and they're as incomprehensible as the folks in DC.

HE HADN'T APPRECIATED the size of the asteroid until the *Salvator* drew alongside. His perspective changed, and the long, battered wall outside the ship shifted and went underneath and became a rockscape. They were only a few meters above the surface, close enough that MacAllister could have reached down and touched the thing. Then the rockscape gave way, and they were looking into a gorge. "There's the depression," Valya said. Where the moonrider had gone.

She turned on the navigation lights and aimed them into the gorge. It was a long way down, maybe several hundred meters. "We're not actually going down there, are we?" asked Eric.

"No need to," she said. "We can see fine from here."

MacAllister's imagination was galloping. He half expected to find an airlock. Or, as Amy had suggested, fuel lines. But there was nothing unusual. Below them, the sides of the gorge drew gradually together. The moonrider must simply have wedged itself in, applied power, and proceeded to change the asteroid's course. It just didn't look possible. The asteroid was immense.

He looked across to the horizon. The asteroid was so small that all directions seemed sharply downhill.

Valya was still looking into the gorge. "How about that?"

"What do you see?" asked Eric.

"Not a thing."

MacAllister nodded. "The dog in the night."

Amy grinned. "It didn't bark," she said.

"Very good. I didn't think kids today read Sherlock Holmes."

"I saw the sim."

"What are we talking about?" asked Eric.

"There aren't any marks," said Amy. "There should be marks if something wedged itself in here and shifted the asteroid onto a new course."

"Ah," said Eric. "You're right. It *does* look pretty smooth out there."

"So what do we do now?" asked Amy.

Valya pushed back her red hair with her fingertips. "Damned if I know. I don't think there's anything else to be done here. Unless we want to wait around a bit and see whether they come back."

"Hide-and-seek," said MacAllister. "We pull out, they show up. Maybe Amy's right. Maybe they're delinquents."

Amy cleared her throat. Looked mock-offended. "I didn't say that, Mac," she said.

Valya sat with her head back, eyes closed. "Bill," she said. "Where's the asteroid headed?"

"Sunward, Valya."

"We know that. Go beyond that. Several orbits if you have to."

"Working."

"It's starting to look," said Eric, "as if we'll be going back with more questions than answers."

"It will in time intersect with Terranova."

Everyone stopped breathing. "When?"

"In seventeen years, five months. On its third orbit."

"By 'intersect,'" said MacAllister, "you mean *collide*?"

"That is correct, Gregory."

Eric paled. "My God," he said, "a rock this size—"

Amy nodded. "Would cause mass extinctions."

"Makes no sense," said MacAllister. "There's nothing down there except the wildlife. Why would anybody want to wipe them out?"

"Maybe they want to terraform the place," said Amy.

Valya sat up straight. "Whatever they're about, it looks as if we can assume they're not friendly. Bill?"

"Yes, Valya?"

"I want to talk to Union."

MACALLISTER'S DIARY

The plan is to hang around Ophiuchi for another day or so, on the off chance the moonriders will come back. I'm not entirely sure that's such a good idea since we have nothing with which to defend ourselves. But Valya suggested it, and of course Amy was all for it. Amy's for everything. I'm pretty sure Eric had reservations, but he kept them to himself. I think it's crazy.

Since we now know the moonriders are a potential threat, it's the courageous thing to do. Right and noble and all that. Still, that doesn't make it a good idea. The odd thing is I'd bet Valya, left to her own devices, would also not stick around. But nobody wants to look bad. Probably, if the *Salvator* were carrying four males, or four women, it would be sayonara, baby, we're out of here.

—Friday, April 10

chapter 23

Solitude is only a good idea if you have the right people along to share it.

—Gregory MacAllister, "The World in the Sky"

Neither Eric nor Amy wanted to leave. "This is where the action is," Amy said, after they'd watched a grim-faced Peter Arnold tell them to get well clear of 36 Ophiuchi. Put as much distance as you can between yourselves and the moonriders. Don't talk to them. Don't answer if they say hello. "How do we ever find out about them if we run?"

Valya put an arm around her shoulder. "No choice, *glyka mou*. We have to do what they tell us."

When he was able to speak to MacAllister alone, Eric explained that the Academy was protecting Amy. "If she wasn't on board," he said, "nobody would really care about you and me." He tried to make it into a joke, but MacAllister could see he believed it. The three adults were expendable.

That sort of perspective would never have occurred to MacAllister. And he readily dismissed it. Of course the Academy didn't want to take any chances with Amy, but they also knew *he* was on board.

Valya kept her feelings to herself. She simply shrugged when the message ended and told them to buckle down. "Vega's next," she said. "We've backtracked a bit, so the jump will take longer than it would have from Origins." A bit under two days, she added. Minutes later they were accelerating away from the asteroid.

Seventeen years.

How did these creatures think? Were they going to come back to watch the fireworks?

MacAllister disliked bullies. And people who were cruel to animals. Here were these malevolent sons of bitches, with all that technology, and they were like kids stomping on an anthill. Pathetic. He wondered whether they were related to the idiots who'd devised the omega clouds.

Whatever, he wasn't unhappy to get away. The prospect of sitting around waiting for the moonriders to come back was not appealing. Who knew what they might be crazy enough to do? Still, with Valya on the scene, he tried to look dismayed that they were leaving. It was safe because he knew Valya, like a good captain, would listen seriously to the protests of her passengers but follow her instructions.

"What's particularly annoying," Eric said, "is that we came so close. If we'd stayed here the first time, we might have been able to wave them down. Say hello. Or tell them to go to hell. Something."

Go to hell, MacAllister thought, would have made a great opening in a dialogue with another species. That would look inspirational in the schoolbooks. He immediately began thinking of other moving first lines. *Stick it in your ear, you nitwits.*

Get your sorry asses on the next train out of town.

Sorry, boys, but we don't cotton to strangers here.

He sighed. Imagined himself as a sheriff in the long ago, standing quietly in the dusk with a six-gun on his hip, watching three horsemen slink away.

ERIC WAS GENUINELY frustrated. All his life he'd been watching other people come back on the Academy's ships after scoring triumphs. We found an ancient city here. And a new type of bioform there. We rescued the Goompahs. We did this and we did that. And there'd always been a world of acclaim waiting. Eric had led the cheers. Now first contact with a technological species was, finally, within reach, the golden apple, the ultimate prize, and he was being pushed aside.

He thought about getting on the circuit to Hutch and demanding she change the directive. But he knew she would not. She wouldn't risk the girl under any circumstances.

At this moment, they were scrambling at the Academy to staff another mission and get it out here. Somebody else, a bunch of overweight academics who had spent their lives in classrooms, would get the assignment, and they'd be the ones to say hello. And they'd come back afterward and everyone would shake their hands.

And once again, it would be left to Eric to ladle on the praise.

VEGA IS LOCATED in the Lyra constellation, twenty-five light-years from Earth. It's a main sequence blue-white dwarf star, roughly three times Sol's diameter, and almost sixty times as luminous. It's much younger, only 350 million years old. But because of its size, and the rate at which it's burning hydrogen, it will exhaust its supply in another 650 million years.

It has a pair of Jovians in distant orbits, both more remote than Pluto. There are several terrestrial worlds, including one in the biozone, which is seven times farther out than Sol's, but it harbors no life.

Vega was a popular stop on the Blue Tour because of the presence of Romulus and Remus, a pair of terrestrials of almost identical dimensions, both with atmospheres, locked in a tight gravitational embrace. Technically, they, too, were in the biozone, but they barely qualified, out on the farther edge, where the winter never really went away.

Also lifeless, they were nevertheless beautiful worlds, only 160,000 kilometers apart, half the distance between Earth and the moon. Both had oceans and continents. Snow covered most of the land; the oceans were a concoction of ice and water, prevented by tidal action from freezing completely. The system had an ethereal, crystal quality, like a cosmic Christmas ornament.

The tour ships, in their souvenir shops, carried graphic displays, vids, and models of the system. It easily outsold everything else on the shelves.

Valya waited until she was close enough to get the full effect before putting the twin worlds on the displays. They *were* a compelling sight. Predictably, Amy squealed with delight, and MacAllister admitted she had a point.

"You know," Eric said, "having Amy along has really added something to the trip."

MacAllister smiled wearily. "Indeed it has."

THEY WENT INTO orbit around Romulus. "The planets in this system," Valya said, "are quite young. Like their sun. They're still undergoing the formation process."

"What does that actually entail?" asked MacAllister.

"Mostly, they get plunked by a lot of debris, Mac. There are no giants close in to clear out the rocks and pebbles, so it'll go on for a long time."

MacAllister saw one or two streaks in the atmosphere below.

"Anybody want to go down and look?" she asked.

That brought another burst of enthusiasm from Amy. Eric said yes, of course he would go.

"How about you, Mac?"

"You say there's nothing alive down there?"

"Nope. Nothing at all. Not so much as a microbe."

He wondered about earthquakes and volcanoes. The worlds were so close to each other, he suspected there were all kinds of disruptions. He was more cautious since his experience at Maleiva III. But he couldn't back off again. "Okay," he said. "Sure. Why not?"

Valya reviewed e-suit procedures, and they all put on the harnesses. They did a checkout routine, went below, and climbed into the lander.

Minutes later the launch doors rolled back and they looked out at the night sky. It was studded with stars and dominated by the two planets, both half in daylight. "You want to say the word, Mac?" she asked.

Amy nodded encouragement.

"I doubt I'm a very reliable pilot, Valya."

"Bill will take care of the heavy lifting. Just tell him to go."

"Okay," he said. "Sure. Take us to the surface, Bill."

"*As you wish, Mac,*" said the AI.

The vehicle lifted off and drifted gently through the doors. A million stars looked down on them. The center of the Milky Way lay off to their left, and the silver and blue planets floated, one below, one overhead. It was, for MacAllister, a good moment. He was glad he'd come.

THE LANDER SLIPPED into lower orbit and Remus dropped below the horizon. They crossed the terminator onto the night side, kept going for a long time, and finally eased into the atmosphere. Bill took them down through scattered clouds. The ground was dark. Mac couldn't even tell whether they were over land until Valya switched on a display that relayed sensor images. Probably infrared. It was ocean, with scattered islands, and a storm to the south.

Valya took control from Bill and set down on one of the islands. She handed out oxygen tanks, and they ran another drill. How to breathe, for God's sake. And be careful: Gravity is only 0.8.

MacAllister was seated in the rear, with Eric. He looked out across a stretch of sand. The surf was high, and the ocean moved gently beneath the starlight. The interior of the island was composed mostly of frozen mud. There were a few scattered hills.

"Okay," Valya said, "activate the suit."

MacAllister punched the big blue button on his belt and the Flickinger field formed around him. Air began to flow.

"*Everybody okay?*" Her voice was coming in over the commlink now.

They all checked in. Valya turned on a couple of the navigation lights so they'd be able to see. "*Mac,*" she said, "*tell Bill to decompress the cabin.*"

Feeling silly, but not wanting to make a fuss, he complied. "Bill," he said, sounding as bored as he could, "decompress."

He heard the hiss of air. Then the hatch opened and, with Amy in the lead, they climbed out and stood on the sand. It was hard as rock.

There was always something surreal in people wearing casual clothes standing around on the frozen surface of another world. He had gray slacks and a blue-and-gold Mariners hockey shirt with number seventeen and the name LEVINS on the back. The shirt had been a Christmas present from a cousin, intended as a joke because of his public stance that hockey was a game for idiots. Levins apparently played for the Mariners, who were one of the Canadian teams. He wasn't sure which one. But it was comfortable and seemed to fit the mood of the evening's jaunt.

Valya was in a *Salvator* jumpsuit. Eric wore workout clothes, with a top that read PROXMIRE ACCOUNTING. It was Amy who set the trend. She had a blue pullover, blue shorts, and loafers. The wind howled around her, and the temperature must have been thirty below. MacAllister felt cold just looking at her.

He increased the heat in his suit and wondered how long it would take to freeze if the electronics went down. The e-suits themselves were not visible, save for a brief shimmer around the wearer when the light hit them just right.

They started toward the water. The waves, probably energized by the mass and proximity of Remus, came pounding in. It was, in a bleak way, an extraordinarily beautiful place. This was his first visit to a sterile world. It was unsettling to look out at the ocean, which could have been the Atlantic, and know there was no shell along any of its beaches, no seaweed, not so much as a living cell anywhere.

The frozen sand crunched beneath his feet. They walked out into the surf, and MacAllister felt it break against his shins and try to suck him out. It was a pleasant sensation.

Valya pointed to a glow on the horizon, out over the water. *"We timed it pretty well,"* she said.

Eric went out until the waves were breaking past his hips. Remus was rising.

They stood for several minutes, talking about nothing in particular, watching the golden arc push out of the sea. It was magnificent.

"It is *beautiful, isn't it?"* said Amy.

This was no small, barren moon rising above the ocean. It was a brilliant shimmering yellow *world,* with oceans and continents and rivers, surrounded by the soft haze of an atmosphere. *"It looks different than it did from the ship,"* Eric said.

Valya pushed out and stood beside him. *"It's all expectations. You're on the ground, like back home, and you expect to see a* moon. *Instead, you get that."*

"You know," said Amy, *"my father thinks he's seen this. He's watched the sims. But you really have to* be *here."*

Eric nodded. The light caught his protective field, and it shimmered, providing a spectral effect. *"Maybe,"* he said, *"you could bring him here eventually."*

"No. He wouldn't want to get this far from Washington." She shook her head. *"I wonder how life on Earth might have been different if we'd had a moon like that, and if it had had cities that we could see."*

MacAllister made a mental note to keep an eye on the kid. If she didn't become a pilot, he'd offer her a job with *The National*. Maybe—

"Look!" Eric was pointing in the opposite direction, back across the hills. A streak of light raced down the sky.

"More moonriders," said Amy.

Valya put a hand on her shoulder as the object exploded into a shower of sparks. *"I don't think so,* hryso mou. *It's just a meteor. They get a lot of them here."*

LIBRARY ENTRY

Government sources revealed today that an Academy ship experienced an encounter with a moonrider in the Ophiuchi system, about twenty light-years from Earth. A light-year is the distance light travels in one year, at a velocity of approximately 300,000 kilometers per second. The moonrider is reported to have diverted an asteroid onto a course that would bring it down on Terranova, the first living world found outside the solar system.* The intersection, however, is not expected to happen for almost two decades. Scientists close to the Academy say that a similar event on Earth would probably end civilization and would, in any case, cause mass extinctions. No one seems able to offer an explanation why the aliens would want to do this. Jasmine Allen, a prominent physicist attached to the Air and Space Museum, says that it sounds to her like pure vindictiveness. "If these things are really there," she said, "and they

*This is incorrect, of course. The first life discovered outside the solar system was on Genesis, a world orbiting Alpha Cephei. Because life there however is microscopic, it tends to get overlooked.

actually did this, then I'd say we'll want to stay as far from them as we can."

—The Black Cat Network, Saturday, April 11

ARNSWORTH: BEEMER HAS REASON TO FEAR HELL

Announces Prayer Crusade in Assailant's Behalf

Pullman Helps Kick Off "Reclamation Effort"

chapter 24

Why is it that people want so desperately to shake hands with otherworldly beings? That people will even insist they have seen visitors from Spica hovering above their backyards? In other times it was ghosts and fairies and goblins, and voices in the night. Is the company of our own species so dull that we need to invent the Other? On the other hand, maybe that explains it.

—Gregory MacAllister, "The Galactic Coffee Shop"

The National consisted primarily of political and social commentary. It also carried book reviews, an occasional piece of short fiction, a science column, a column by a professional skeptic, and a few cartoons. At the present time, it was home to a family of correspondents, and a substantial number of periodic contributors. It bore the imprint of its editor. It didn't trust government, didn't trust people in authority generally, and carried as its maxim Ben Franklin's warning: ". . . we have given you a republic—if you can keep it."

The National's causes were all over the place. It favored a health-care system for everybody on the planet. It championed efforts to strengthen the World Council. It wanted programs to see that nobody went hungry and everybody had a place to sleep. It also favored balanced budgets, reduction in the size of government, and the return of the death penalty. People across the political landscape insisted that there was no way to do all those things. MacAllister proudly responded that, once you make that decision, you're necessarily right.

They did not come close to having the widest circulation in the field, but they liked to feel—and loudly proclaimed—that the people who made things happen, or those who might have but stalled around until the dam broke, all read *The National*. By and large they found a lot in it not to like. MacAllister and his legion routinely called into question the integrity of politicians, the good sense of academics, the single-mindedness of the religious establishment, and the taste of the general public.

Because *The National* limited itself to commentary, it wasn't concerned with day-to-day topicality. Wolfie Esterhaus got the news about the moonriders at Ophiuchi from Mac bare minutes before it broke for the rest of the world. But he had an eyewitness account that had arrived just in time to plug into the upcoming issue. He'd want more than what the boss could give him. The real issue, aside from the nature of the moonriders themselves, was the reaction at high levels.

The question surfaced at several press conferences in the Americas and around the world. But everybody was brushing the story off. It sounded too much like previous sensationalist reports. Moonriders kidnap two people on remote Manitoba highway. Moonriders buzz private aircraft. Moonrider crashes into ocean.

Wolfie had a source at the White House. Roger Schubert was deputy assistant to the nation's security advisor. It took two hours to get through.

"Wolfie, I was wondering when I'd hear from you." Followed by a hearty laugh. Schubert was a little guy, with narrow shoulders and a pinched, nervous expression. But he sounded *big*. He had the voice of a professional wrestler. *"You want to know about the moonriders?"*

"Please. Do you guys have anything that hasn't been made public?"

"Not a thing."

"How is the president reacting?"

"The same way the rest of us are, Wolfie. He's waiting for details. Right now it doesn't sound like much."

"You don't think the asteroid thing sounds crazy?"

"That's the whole point: It's too crazy to believe. Let's wait and see what the facts are. I'll tell you this *much: If there really are aliens out there, and* if *they've decided to drop a rock on a bunch of whales, or whatever they've got on Terranova, they're going to have to deal with the Humane Society. And no, of course the president won't like it. He'd probably condemn it. But that sort of thing is a long way from constituting a threat."*

Schubert was sitting on his desk, arms folded. *"Look, Wolfie, I know it sounds spooky. But we don't even know yet how accurate the projection is. Seventeen years is a long time. Maybe the numbers are wrong. Maybe it's a coincidence. Maybe they were just practicing landing procedures. But I can tell you this: If moonriders land on the White House lawn, the president will be ready to welcome them."*

WOLFIE WAS AN ideal number two for MacAllister. He bought into his boss's philosophy, but was diplomatic and soft-spoken. Everybody liked him, and they saw him as a mollifying influence at *The National,* a voice of reason and restraint. Many questioned his motives in working for MacAllister, but they were glad for his presence on the editorial page. God knew what the magazine would have been like if it weren't for him.

In fact Wolfie admired his editor. MacAllister wasn't always right, but he was smart enough to know that. He was willing to change his mind when the evidence pointed in a different direction. That fact alone put MacAllister very nearly in a class by himself.

Wolfie had started life as a Coast Guard officer. He'd served eight years, had participated in any number of rescues of people not smart enough to stay out of the way of storms. A reporter from *The Baltimore Sun* had done a feature story on him. The story had been expanded into a book, on which Wolfie assisted. He discovered a talent for writing, did a series of stories on Coast Guard operations, and finally moved full-time into journalism, first with the *Sun,* and later with *The Washington Post* and *DC After Dark,* for which he still did occasional assignments.

But his heart and soul lay with *The National.* It was the publication the decision-makers read, and feared. You didn't want to get caught in MacAllister's sights.

Wolfie had just started blocking out the next issue when another transmission from the *Salvator* came in. The boss was in short sleeves, and he looked irritated. He had a few more details about the Ophiuchi sighting. A monitor had shut down at one point and had to be repaired. The *Salvator* had been *ordered* away from Ophiuchi. The original briefing provided by the Academy had left the impression the *Salvator* had simply moved on after inspecting the asteroid. But obviously the high-level folks at the Academy were taking things seriously.

He added something else: *"Wolfie, we landed on the asteroid. It's a* mountain. *I can't imagine how anything as small as that moonrider looked could have moved that thing. If it did, their technology is way ahead of ours. Think about that, then consider the fact that they behave like kids who want to pull legs off grasshoppers. I don't want to start a panic, so don't quote me, but I'm not comfortable."*

Later that afternoon, the World Society for the Protection of Animals issued a statement, condemning the diversion of the asteroid by "whoever is responsible," and demanding that the Academy be directed to intervene.

Wolfie called the Academy, identified himself, and asked to speak to Priscilla Hutchins. An AI told him, *"Sorry, she's not available."*

"I'm a friend of Gregory MacAllister," he said. "I think she'd consent to talk to me."

He was directed to wait. Seven or eight minutes later her voice came over the circuit. No picture. *"What can I do for you, Mr. Esterhaus?"* She sounded detached. Almost annoyed. Better things to do than talk to journalists.

"Ms. Hutchins, I'm sorry to bother you. I'm sure you're busy at the moment."

"Pretty much. What's your question?"

Did he only get one? "How confident are you about the information that came out of Ophiuchi today?"

"How do you mean?"

"Are there aliens?"

"Mr. Esterhaus, Wolfgang, your guess is as good as mine. I'm sure the data passed to us by the Salvator *is accurate. We haven't drawn conclusions yet."*

"Ms. Hutchins, if the data are accurate, it seems clear that the aliens are deranged. Psychopathic. Is any other conclusion even possible?"

She thought about it. *"I think we need to wait a bit before we'll have a good read on what's happening."*

"So the Academy thinks—"

"Let's give it a little time, Wolfgang."

"All right, may I ask another question?"

"Sure."

"What are you going to do about Terranova?"

"You mean are we going to divert the asteroid? Turn it off course?"

"That's exactly what I mean."

"That's not my call, Wolfgang. I don't know what's been decided."

"You're saying there's a possibility we might just stand aside and let the thing go down?"

"I'm saying I haven't received my instructions yet. You want to know more, you'll have to go higher in the organization."

WITHIN A FEW hours, the world's attention had become focused on the object the media had begun calling the Terranova Rock. It was at the top of the news everywhere. Wolfie switched around and sampled several shows. The correspondents and their guests were alarmed. That was standard, of course. In an age of complete global media penetration, competition was fierce, and if you fell from a roof in Shanghai, people in Little Rock got the details. Shocking news from Shanghai, the anchors would proclaim. Life and death in the shadow of the Great Wall. Yes, it was not journalism's finest hour. But, MacAllister often argued, it never had been. It was, however, the reason people appreciated *Paris Watch* and *The Atlantic* and *The National*. They were calm, analytical, serious.

Odd objects in the sky had been around for ages. Some enthusiasts claimed they'd been seen in biblical times, pointing to the first chapter of Ezechiel. There'd been other manifestations, but sightings became widespread during the Second World War when pilots in several air forces claimed to see objects they called foo fighters. In the mid twentieth century they became flying saucers, or UFOs. A hundred years later they were ghost lights. Now they were moonriders. The assumption always was that only delusional people encountered them, so it was easy enough to dismiss the reports. Anyone who claimed to have seen one could expect not to be taken seriously again during his or her lifetime.

When humans went to the stars, they continued to report strange objects. There were still occasional Earthbound sightings, for which no compelling evidence was ever brought forth. But when superluminals picked them up, it became a different story because there was usually a record. So the assumption became that the images reproduced by the AIs were gremlins in the software, manifestations of misaligned equations, or careless programming rather than actual objects. Or they might be reflections, or possibly even quantum fluctuations. But the Terranova Rock was changing all that. It was an intriguing story. The rock was there, and it was headed eventually for a living world.

LIBRARY ARCHIVE

. . . The rush to accept the notion that we have visitors, and that they constitute a threat to humanity, is not as premature as some would have us think. We should consider what our status will be if a technologically superior species arrives and begins making demands. Or worse yet, if they are overtly hostile. In the Terranova Incident, the evidence indicates a level of malice one would hope would have been bred out of beings with a high level of technological capability. If that is actually so, then what will our position be if they decide to amuse themselves at our expense as well? What defense have we? At the moment, no navy exists. An engagement would be a trifle one-sided. Let us hope either the World Council moves quickly to alleviate the risk, or that these neighbors, if they're really there, don't come this way.

—*Jerusalem Post*, Saturday, April 11

BEEMER: "I'D DO IT AGAIN"

Accused Assailant Unrepentant in Interview

chapter 25

> A surprising number of terrestrial worlds are in warm locations, with plenty of water, but no life. They are perceived as places where something went wrong. They are "sterile." Maybe so. I tend to think of them as "clean." If we're at all honest with ourselves, we'll recognize that life in fact is an infection. Cephei III has a pleasant climate and trillions of microscopic living things. Cephei IV also has a pleasant climate, and there's nothing crawling around. Where would you rather spend your vacation?
>
> –Gregory MacAllister, "On the Move"

Alpha Cephei. Forty-nine light-years from Sol. Most distant point on the Blue Tour.

When the robot flights went out from Earth during the twentieth and twenty-first centuries, they were looking for signs of life. Researchers, and indeed the general public, hoped *something* would be found on Mars. The imagined creatures of H. G. Wells and Ray Bradbury were, of course, long off the table, but there was hope of finding fossilized bacteria. Or some other evidence that living things had once existed on the Red Planet.

But Mars was every bit as sterile as it had looked on July 20, 1976, when the Viking I lander set down in Chryse Planitia. It was dry, dusty, and a bitter disappointment to millions of people around the world who had hoped, and probably expected, to see at the very least a few shrubs.

The next best hope was Europa.

It had long been thought that life might be found in its ocean, which was sheltered beneath ice packs as much as twenty kilometers thick. There *was* liquid water, kept relatively warm by tidal effects.

An automated mission was dispatched during the third decade of the twenty-first century. It drilled through the ice but found no life or any indication it had ever existed.

There was talk for a while of life-seeding materials on comets, but that never provided a payoff either. So, as the century wore on, it became evident the solar system, save for Earth, was barren. Spectrographic analyses of planetary atmospheres in nearby star systems provided no evidence of an oxygen–carbon dioxide cycle. At that time, no one seriously believed humans would ever leave the solar system. So when, shortly after its eightieth anniversary, SETI shut down and was declared a failure, it looked as if the book had closed on the question of life elsewhere.

Then, on New Year's Day 2079, a probe took pictures of a carved figure on the jagged surface of Saturn's moon, Iapetus. At first, researchers thought it was, like the Martian face and the zigzag wall on Miranda, an illusion. But a manned mission brought the electrifying confirmation that *someone* had visited the Saturnian system. The figure was chilling, a nightmare creation of claws, surreal eyes, and muscular fluidity. Simultaneously humanoid and reptilian, it was a thing out of a horror show, and yet there was a kind of quiet placidity in its expression. Its age was established at about ten thousand years.

A set of prints in the dust suggested that the image was a self-portrait.

Its origin remained a mystery for the better part of a century. Until Ginny Hazeltine showed that FTL travel, despite the common wisdom, *was* possible. And went on to demonstrate how it could be done. Within two years, the first lightships, as they were then called, headed out to Alpha Centauri and Lalande 8760 and Epsilon Eridani and Procyon. These voyages were magnificent achievements, but again the celebratory mood was dampened when word came back that no life had been found.

Most disappointing, at Lalande and Procyon, they saw terrestrial-style worlds, with broad water oceans and warm sunlight. And not so much as a blade of grass. For a time, the belief that humans had been the beneficiaries of a special creation made a comeback. The Iapetus figure became, in the minds of many, a hoax. Others thought it had been left by diabolical forces. And the idea that humans were alone in the universe gained credence.

The fifth expedition went to Alpha Cephei, where they found *two* terrestrial planets within the biozone. When seen from orbit, both looked sterile. And indeed, Cephei IV *was* without life. But its sister world was the gold card.

It was teeming with living creatures. They were single-celled, but they were there! Today, a half century later, scientists are still debating how it happens you can have two worlds in a biozone, with similar conditions on both. And life starts on one but not on the other.

When the *Salvator* arrived in that historic system, MacAllister was thinking about that first expedition and wondering precisely what drove the human effort to find life elsewhere. He had long ago dismissed this yearning for other life as infantile. His position was completely rational: We are better off if whatever neighbors there are stay at a distance. God had done things the right way, he'd once written, when He put such vast distances between technological civilizations. In both time and space.

"There it is," said Valya, putting Alpha Cephei III on the display. It had the requisite big moon, which is apparently needed to produce tides and prevent a planetary wobble, plus two smaller ones. Oceans covered about 80 percent of the planet. It had a sixteen-degree tilt, and ice caps at both poles. The telescope zoomed in, and Mac saw rolling plains and rivers. But the place *looked* bleak. No forests. No grasslands. He could imagine the feelings of the crew in that first lightship.

What was its name?

"The *Galileo,*" said Amy, who was less impressed than MacAllister had expected. "It sure looks dead." And with that she dismissed the discovery that, in its time, had been hailed as the greatest of all time. Well, kids are never much on history. Nor for that matter was anybody else. It had been MacAllister's experience that most people think anything that happened before they were born didn't count for a whole lot.

Happily, there was no sign of moonriders. It was curious how drastically MacAllister's perspective had changed. When they'd started out, almost three weeks ago, he would have been delighted to see black globes in the sky. But not now. The critters were too unpredictable. He was anxious for it to be over. It meant he would go home with no answers, hardly a healthy attitude for a journalist. But at least he would go home.

Valya launched the monitor and, a few hours later, put them in orbit around Cephei III.

SHORTLY AFTER THE *Galileo*'s discovery, the World Space Authority had established a base on the western coastline of one of the continents. Biologists, delighted with the opportunity to study off-world life, had lined up for assignment, and Cephei III had continued to receive researchers ever since. The base was still there, expanded over the years into a major facility, home to teams of specialists who, MacAllister suspected, couldn't find anything better to do with their time than freeload on government funds and university grants.

"Did you want to go down and say hello?" asked Valya. "I understand they do a tour."

Amy announced that she'd rather stay with the ship and keep an eye open for moonriders. Eric agreed. MacAllister had no interest in single-celled creatures, nor in the people who studied them. "Have they ever reported anything out of the ordinary?" he asked.

"You mean biologically?"

"I mean moonriders."

She checked her notebook. "A few times," she said. "Most recent was last year. One of the researchers said she saw a formation pass overhead."

"Is she still here?"

"Back in Rome."

MacAllister had been looking at a history of sightings. There'd been none that couldn't be explained as runaway imaginations or hoaxes until about twenty years ago, when they first started showing up on the superluminal routes.

The earliest deep-space sighting had occurred at Triassic II. A cargo ship, bringing supplies to a ground station, had spotted strange objects moving in formation through the clouds. The pictures, when relayed home, had created a sensation.

During those first few years, such sightings had been rare. But their frequency had begun to increase. In '54 there'd been eleven, the most ever reported in a single year. They'd been distributed among the Blue Tour stars, as well as Sirius and Procyon. There were no sightings farther out, none from Betelgeuse or Achernar or Spica or Bellatrix. Of course those stars weren't on any of the tours. So, were the moonriders only interested in the worlds close to Earth? Or were they everywhere?

THEY'D AGREED THAT each stop deserved some time. That if they just went in and unloaded the monitor and cleared out, they'd be neglecting an important aspect of their assignment: to conduct an active search. MacAllister wasn't sure exactly when the mission changed, when it had gone from laying monitors and maybe if we got really lucky we'd see something, to prosecuting an aggressive hunt and dropping off the monitor more or less as a sideshow.

Valya reported their presence to the people at the ground station. When, at Amy's urging, she asked whether they'd seen anything unusual in the skies, they laughed.

Meantime a transmission came in from Wolfie. He was going to expand the moonrider story in the coming issue, publishing not only MacAllister's report, but covering the reaction at home as well. *"People are getting stirred up,"* he said. *"I think it would be interesting to look at the political ramifications of this. The White House is trying to suggest everything's business as usual, but I understand there are some behind-the-scenes concerns."* Did MacAllister concur? He included a bundle of news reports.

Hutchins had forwarded a digest of the media reaction, so he already knew the Terranova Rock had ignited a firestorm. Now the talking heads were wondering why the aliens would keep their presence secret if they did not have malicious intent. MacAllister dismissed that reasoning. The moonriders were certainly not keeping their presence secret. They were flying right out there for anyone to see. What he sensed on their part was contempt. They didn't much care whether we saw them or not.

He told Wolfie to go ahead. "You've got it right," he said. "The real story here isn't the moonriders, but the overreaction of the media. Which means let's show the public what they're doing. Put it on the cover and play it for all it's worth."

He made the mistake of relaying the conversation to Amy and Eric. Eric looked doubtful. "It's true," MacAllister insisted. "The media are out of control. And it's time somebody called them on it. All they want to do is sell advertising space. So they go with whatever that day's big story is and push it until it's exhausted or something else comes along. We've become an oversized tabloid. Scandal, murder, and moonriders. It's all we care about."

"Does that *we* include *The National*?" asked Eric. "I mean you're complaining about media overreaction, but you put it on the cover."

MacAllister laughed. "We'll be talking about the state of the media, not moonriders. And *that* is serious business."

"Don't you think," said Amy, "the media are broadcasting what people want to hear?"

MacAllister nodded. "Sure they are," he said.

It wasn't the response she'd expected. "Isn't that what they're supposed to do?"

"No." Don't they teach anything in school anymore? "The media should be telling people what they *need* to hear. Not sex and scandal. But what their representatives are up to."

THEY ORBITED ALPHA Cephei III for a full day, which was the minimum time they'd agreed to invest at each site. The most exciting thing that happened was a chess game between Eric and one of the researchers at the ground station. (The researcher won, as MacAllister would have predicted.)

Then they were on their way to Arcturus. He settled down to enjoy a biography that mercilessly attacked the previous president.

NEWSDESK

MOONRIDER SIGHTINGS UP

In the seventy-two hours since the Terranova Rock story broke, reports of flying objects across the NAU and around the world have risen dramatically. . . .

BANNISTER WARNS ATTACK IMMINENT

Retired Col. Frank R. Bannister, founder and president of the Glimmerings Society, which investigates moonrider sightings and other paranormal events, warned yesterday that we were running out of time. Bannister maintains that the government has been hiding the truth for years. He will lead a demonstration outside the capitol building tomorrow.

MOONRIDERS ARRIVE IN LEISURE WEAR

Popper Industries will offer a line of moonrider T-shirts for sale, beginning Monday. The shirts depict a squadron of lights and mottos like WATCH YOUR ROCKS and INVASION TUESDAY.

ANIMAL RIGHTS GROUPS DEMAND ACTION ON TERRANOVA

A consortium of animal rights groups issued a series of wide-ranging protests yesterday demanding that the World Council intervene to turn aside the Terranova Rock. Friends of Animals, headquartered in Jamaica, said that standing by and doing nothing is "every bit as barbaric . . ."

TAYLOR CAUTIONS AGAINST RASH JUDGMENT

Senator Hiram Taylor (G-GA) stated today that "we're a long way from knowing what really happened at Ophiuchi," and that the government should wait until the facts are in before deciding what action to take. "If any."

REINHOLD THINKS TERRANOVA ROCK SHOULD REMAIN ON COURSE

"We don't know what they're trying to accomplish," the former German president said today after a press luncheon. "If there really are aliens involved, they may be conducting an experiment of some sort. We just don't know, and I would be cautious about interfering until we have more information. Whoever did this seems to be at least at our level of technology, and possibly considerably higher. We have everything to gain and nothing to lose by waiting until we are sure what's happening. Certainly, with a lead time of seventeen years, there is ample opportunity for consideration."

SIKONIS WILL BE JUDGE IN HELLFIRE CASE

"Maximum George" Has History of Handing Out Stiff Penalties

chapter 26

> The development of faster-than-light technology expanded humanity's psychological as well as physical boundaries. During the early years of the twenty-first century, human security could be challenged only by lunatics, fanatics, and crazed politicians. That is, by other humans. Beyond Pluto lay only unbroken silence. Nobody even thought about it, let alone worried about any deep-space threat. Even the occasional deranged author who wrote about such things took none of it seriously. But when the *Centaurus* tossed off its restraints in March of 2171 and engaged Ginjer Hazeltine's new engine, the world changed more than anyone could have imagined.
>
> —Gregory MacAllister, "Aliens in the Attic"

Saturday evening, April 25.

Hutch was lounging at home when Peter's call came in from Union. He was in his office. Papers were scattered around, displays lit up, data chips piled in a candy box. *"We picked up a transmission from Origins. I thought you'd want to hear it."* Origins operated under the auspices of the International Science Agency, headquartered in Paris.

"The message was sent to their ops center. Union sent a copy to us a few minutes ago."

All incoming messages passed through a central communications center at Union, where they were relayed to the appropriate addressees. And also were frequently lifted as "information copies" to other agencies that might be interested. The practice was officially denied, but it happened nonetheless. And because everybody benefited, no one complained or tried seriously to get it stopped.

"Okay, Peter," she said. "Thank you."

It was flat-screen traffic. First the Origins Project seal, God's arm stretched out toward Adam's as in the Michelangelo, followed by the director, Mahmoud Stein. Stein was reputed to be brilliant, but in Hutch's view he was stiff, formal, self-important, scripted. Everything he said sounded rehearsed.

He was average size, in his sixties, with dark hair and deep-set eyes. He wore a permanent squint. *"David,"* he said, *"we've got another sighting."* A banner at the base of the screen indicated the AI was interpreting from the French.

She didn't know who David was, but suspected he might be David Clyde, one of the assistant directors at ISA in Paris. *"We didn't get this one on record, either. We're just not equipped for that sort of thing. But three of our people saw it. They were working on the tracks, outside, when it showed up. Big black sphere. No lights."* He was seated, upright in his chair, looking grave. *"When it got close, within a kilometer, it stopped. Hovered. Just sat out there for almost five minutes. Our people called in and we tried to get something on it, but it was well down the tube and we just didn't have time."* His eyes revealed a touch of annoyance. He didn't like having to deal with moonriders. They were an intrusion, something not provided for in the job specifications. *"I've talked to everyone involved. Separately, as you suggested. They all tell the same story. David, there's no question they saw* something. *It took off finally like a bat out of hell, unquote.*

"The incident took place near Ring 66. If it happens again, I'll get back to you."

WHAT WAS GOING on? Hutch let the transmission run a second time. Whatever was happening, it was beginning to scare her. An hour later, Senator Taylor called. *"Sorry to bother you at home, Hutch. I couldn't reach the commissioner. Truth is, I'd rather talk to you anyhow."* He looked unhappy. *"I keep hearing all these stories about moonriders. I'm worried about Amy."*

So was she, although there seemed no basis for it. "There shouldn't be a problem, Senator. There's no report of any hostile action being taken by these things. Ever."

"Except throwing asteroids around."

"We don't really have a sense yet what that was about."

"It sounds crazy."

"I know."

"And malicious."

"Senator, Valentina's one of the best people in the business. Nothing's going to happen to them."

He hunched down, as if to avoid being overheard. *"Can you guarantee it?"*

Hutch shook her head. "You know I can't," she said, finally. "I couldn't guarantee Amy's safety if she were sitting in my living room. But I don't think there's any need to worry."

His eyes got a faraway look. *"I'm sorry I let her go."*

"Senator, do you want me to bring the *Salvator* back? I can do it." It probably didn't matter at this point. The mission had become almost redundant.

That disconnected gaze turned inward. *"If you did that, she'd know I was responsible."*

"I wouldn't tell her."

"It wouldn't matter. She'd know."

"Your call, Senator. We'll handle it as you wish."

"How much longer will they be out there?"

"They're scheduled to go to three more places: Arcturus, Capella, and Berenices."

"Okay," he said. *"Try to keep them out of harm's way."*

TEN MINUTES LATER, Asquith called. *"We're putting together an impromptu conference,"* he said. *"I thought you might want to be part of it."* He was seated in an armchair in his living room, holding a glass of wine in one hand. A notebook rested against his knee.

Tor was watching a ballgame. She excused herself, retreated to her office, closed the door, and brought the commissioner and his armchair up on her desktop. Charlie Dryden appeared, seated behind a table. And two women and a man, none of whom she knew.

Asquith made the introductions. The strangers were Shandra Kolchevska from Kosmik, Arnold Prescott from Monogram Industries, and Miriam Klymer from MicroTech. *"Hutch,"* he said, *"you should be aware that we've gotten clearance to divert the Terranova Rock."*

"Good." Politically, it was a move that couldn't lose. "Have we decided how we're going to do it?"

He turned to Kolchevska. *"Shandra, do you want to explain?"*

She appeared to be an energetic, forceful woman. Middle-aged and blond, she'd have been reasonably attractive except for her eyes, which were unreservedly competitive. *"Ms. Hutchins,"* she said, *"it'll be a team operation. Kosmik will be diverting two freighters from salvage."* Nod to Prescott. *"They'll install drive units. MicroTech is doing the systems design for us, and they'll provide the AIs."*

Klymer picked up the explanation. *"The freighters will be taken out to Terranova—"*

"Piloted by the AIs?"

"Oh, yes. Of course. The ships wouldn't be safe. But we're pretty sure we can get them there. Once they arrive, we'll put them in front of the asteroid. Same course and velocity."

"And," said Prescott, *"gravity will do the rest. The ships have sufficient mass to accelerate the asteroid. It'll miss Terranova by a substantial margin."*

"Very good," Hutch said. "I'm impressed."

"Ms. Hutchins," said Prescott, *"when a contribution needs to be made, we can come together."*

She looked over at Dryden, wondering what role Orion Tours was playing.

Asquith delivered a broad, satisfied smile. *"Hutch,"* he said, *"we want to announce the project at a joint press conference in the morning. Can you set it up?"*

"Sure, Michael. I can do that."

He looked at the others. *"Is nine o'clock okay?"* Nobody had a problem. *"We'll want you there, too, Hutch,"* he said.

She turned to Dryden. "Charlie, can I assume Orion will also be part of the effort?"

"Yes, indeed." He gave her a broad smile. *"We're contributing an engineering team to restore the freighters so they can make the flight."*

Asquith beamed and went on about how it was a shining moment for all of them. *"A lot of people, and I'm thinking here especially of professional cynics like your friend MacAllister, would deny that major corporations can collaborate in a public-spirited enterprise."* He smiled at each of them in turn. *"Ladies and gentlemen,"* he said, *"I think we can all take a bow."*

SO MUCH FOR a quiet evening at home. She had one of Eric's staff members send out notifications for the press conference, explaining that it was concerned with the "recent events at Ophiuchi." It prompted a quick flood of inquiries, which he duly passed to her. Had there been additional developments? More sightings? *Online Express* wanted to know if it was true that aliens had landed in Arizona.

Her workload had declined considerably as the missions dropped off. She had time now to wander the corridors, stroll through the grounds, listen to the fountains. She wondered where she'd be in another year. Sitting on the front porch, maybe, writing her memoirs.

She missed piloting. The universe had gotten smaller, had narrowed down to a strip of Virginia and the DC area. Her big thrill consisted of going with Tor and Maureen to the seashore.

Occasionally, she wondered whether marrying had been a mistake. She loved her husband, and she adored Maureen, liked nothing better than playing tag with her, than running upstairs with the girl giggling behind her. She looked forward to the arrival of her second child. Still, her life had acquired a blandness that she could have endured easily enough had she been assured that one day it would end, and she could go back to the deep spaces between the stars.

She'd been more alive in those years. Or maybe alive in a different way. Her passions had been stronger, the sense of accomplishment greater. Soaring out across a world no one had ever seen before carried with it an exhilaration that life in a bureaucracy—or, if she dared admit it to herself, in a marriage—could never match.

She'd already bailed out of an administrative job once. A year or so after they'd discovered the *chindi*, she'd accepted a staff position, a promotion, partly because it was what you were supposed to do. They'd asked her if she wanted to spend the rest of her life in the fleet. The decision had been easy enough because she'd fallen in love with Tor, and no future with him seemed possible without a groundside job.

She'd lasted fourteen months, had tried to find something else that would interest her, had given up and—with his blessing—gone back to piloting for a year or so. Finally, she settled in as assistant to the director of operations. Not long after that she'd gotten the top job.

It paid well. It was challenging. Sometimes, like now, it was even exciting. But she would have given a great deal to have been out on the *Salvator* with Mac and the others. That was where she belonged.

"Hutch." The AI's voice. *"Dr. Asquith is calling again."*

Twice in one night. She wondered if he was bored. "Everything okay?" she asked.

"Hutch, I want you to see something." He told the AI to run a clip. *"Rita sent this over. They just received it."* Rita was the duty officer at Union Control.

A man she'd never seen before blinked on. Standing by a viewport, through which she could see a star-strewn sky and a planetary rim. *"Shanna,"* he said. His voice was strained. *"We've got a problem. There's an asteroid coming this way. A big one."* He and the viewport blinked off and were replaced by the object itself. *"It's six hundred kilometers across."*

Asquith froze the image. *"This is from the Galactic,"* he said. The hotel that Orion was building at Capella. *"My God, Hutch, it's an attack."*

It wasn't just another big rock. Think Boston to DC. It was a small planet this time. "Let's not jump to conclusions," she said. "When's it going to get there?"

"Don't know."

"Okay, look. It's not what you think."

"Why not?" He didn't sound as if he was in a mood to dispute details.

"The hotel's being built in orbit at Capella V?"

"Yes."

"It's a sterile world. Nobody's going to bother bombing it."

He shook his head. *"I wish I understood what's going on."*

The man at the viewport was back. *"Got more,"* he said. He was heavyset, black skin and beard, about forty, with features that suggested he enjoyed a good time. At the moment he looked scared. *"It's going to take out the hotel."* He was having a hard time keeping his voice calm. *"The goddam thing is coming right at us. Dead on. They're telling me it will miss the planet. But nail us. The bastards are shooting at us."* He stopped a moment. Tried to calm down. *"We have a ship on-station, but it's not anywhere near big enough to get everyone off. Shanna, you need to get us out of here. Quick. Please advise."*

The Orion Tours logo replaced the image.

"My God," said Hutch. "When's it going to happen?"

Asquith shrugged. *"You know as much as I do. Judging from the way he sounds—"*

"How many people do they have out there? At the construction site?"

"I've no idea."

"Okay. I assume Dryden's asked for help."

"I haven't heard from him yet." He was on his feet, treading back and forth. *"That asteroid that passed us a few weeks ago. I wonder if they were behind that, too?"*

"It missed, Michael."

He shrugged again. *"So they screwed up that one."*

"Michael, we get Earth-crossers all the time. We just happened not to see it coming. But something with a six-hundred-klick diameter? If the moonriders could move something that massive, could aim it at a moving target as small as a hotel—" What were they up against?

"What are you thinking?" he asked.

"If they have the capability to push around a rock the size of Arizona, why would they bother?"

"What do you mean?"

"If they have that kind of technology, and they wanted to get rid of the hotel, surely they'd have a more sophisticated way of doing it than tossing a small moon at it. Why not just pull up and bomb it? Or use a particle beam? Why on Earth would you throw rocks?"

"I don't know," he said. There was a touch of hysteria in his voice. *"Maybe when we get closer to them, you can ask."*

ASQUITH GOT DRYDEN on the circuit. Charlie just sat shaking his head. *"I can't believe it. Why would they do something like this? What's wrong with these creatures?"* His voice hardened, and he looked ready to kill.

The commissioner leaned forward. *"When's it going to get there?"*

"We don't know yet. Hartigan forgot to tell us when. We're waiting to hear now."

"How many people you have out there?" asked Hutch.

He consulted a display. *"Thirty-three. We can put eleven of them on the* Lin-Kao. *But that's all we have."* He looked away. *"Wait a minute. We're getting something now."*

Charlie relayed it for them. It was the man by the viewport again. Presumably Hartigan. *"I'm going to start moving people over to the* Surveyor," he said. *"The* Lin-Kao *will have time to make two flights. So I can get most of them off that way."*

The *Surveyor* was an historic ship, now maintained at Arcturus as a museum. It was, with luck, a day and a half away from the Galactic. "So we've got at least three days," said Hutch.

Capella V struck her as an odd location for a vacation site. It would be about five days' travel time from Earth, a bit far, she thought. She recalled that there'd originally been talk of constructing it at Romulus/Remus in the Vega system.

In any case the *Salvator* was in position to help. *"Good thing,"* Peter said when she contacted him. *"Union doesn't have anything ready to go."*

"That can't be right," said Hutch.

"It's true. The place is empty. Usually we have seven or eight ships in port. I've called around. There are a couple coming in, but nothing close enough that they can help."

"And nothing that can be diverted?"

"Negative."

VALYA WAS FORTUITOUSLY on her way to the same *Surveyor* museum at Arcturus. She might even be there already. Hutch punched the ship's name and location into her databank and transmitted to Asquith's screen. He saw it, and nodded. *"Charlie,"* he said, *"the* Salvator *is in range. You want us to send it over?"*

"How many can they take on board?" asked Dryden.

Asquith looked toward Hutch. Silently, she said *seven*.

"Seven," he said.

"Okay. Yes. Please do. I appreciate this, Michael."

Asquith's demeanor had changed. He'd begun to enjoy himself, playing the man of action. *"Okay, Hutch,"* he said. *"Get in touch with Valya and get them started."*

An hour later, toward the end of the evening, she got still another call from the commissioner. *"It'll hit Thursday morning,"* he said. *"We've got almost five days."*

More like four and a half. "*When* Thursday morning?"

"*Around ten, our time.*"

The *Salvator* would have to make two flights. There'd be time, but not much to spare.

LIBRARY ARCHIVE

Do we have an obligation to protect a living world from arbitrary attacks? Probably not. What moral or legal code is applicable? Certainly none that I know of. Do we risk embroiling ourselves in a confrontation with a species whose capabilities may be far greater than our own? It would seem so. It forces us to the conclusion that the prudent action is to stand aside. Let the gremlins do what they want, while we collect as much information about them as we can.

But another question remains to be asked: If we allow these intruders to inflict heavy damage on a biosystem for no definable reason, to kill off whole species, will that not say a great deal about who we really are? And what matters to us? How would that match up with our image of ourselves? Would we be prepared to live with it?

—Charles Dryden, interviewed on the Black Cat Network, Saturday, April 25

MOTION TO MOVE HELLFIRE TRIAL QUASHED

Sikonis: Defendant Can Get Fair Trial in Derby

chapter 27

> The invention of the printing press probably marks the beginning of the decline of civilization. Once you have it, science follows close behind. Next thing you know the idiots have better weaponry. Then atom bombs. Meantime, social organization becomes increasingly dependent on technology, which becomes increasingly vulnerable to error or sabotage. If we can judge by our own experience, it looks as if you get the printing press, then about a thousand years. After that it's back to the trees.
>
> —Gregory MacAllister, "Fire in the Night"

Arcturus. Saturday, April 25.

Three brilliant stars illuminate Earth's northern skies: Vega, Capella, and the brightest, Arcturus. It is the most distant of the three, thirty-seven light-years from Sol, an orange class K giant. It became famous when its light was used to open the 1933 Chicago World's Fair. That light had left the star only a few years after the time of the previous Chicago World's Fair in 1893. It is bright and it is big: 113 times as luminous as the sun. Twenty-six times as wide. It has exhausted its supply of hydrogen and is burning helium.

Its name comes from the Greek word *arktos,* for *bear*. Surface temperature is just under 43,000 degrees Kelvin. Evidence suggests that Arcturus originated in a small galaxy that merged with the Milky Way approximately seven billion years ago. Its planetary system consists of two gas giants and a terrestrial. The terrestrial lies in the center of the biozone. It has oceans and all the ingredients for life, but like so many other places, it remains barren.

That there are only three worlds lends credence to the galactic exchange theory. Also present in the system, and popular with Blue Tour travelers, was the *Surveyor* Historical Site.

More than a half century earlier, Emil Hightower, captain of the *Surveyor,* his three-person crew, and a team of researchers, had been in the act of departing the area when an engine blew. The ship quickly lost life support. Hightower ordered everyone off while he sent out a distress call to the *Chan Ho Park,* with whom they were working in tandem. (At that time, the policy was that ships always operated in pairs in case of just such an emergency.) All except Hightower survived.

The *Surveyor* was heavily damaged and could not be salvaged. It had drifted through the system more than thirty years, until the Hightower Commission formed and arranged to have it moved into a stable solar orbit, where it was restored and converted into a museum. It served as one of the highlights of the Blue Tour.

MacAllister would just as soon have skipped the museum and proceeded directly to Capella, where they were scheduled to spend a night at the Galactic. He had grown bored and was anxious to get home.

But Amy wanted to see the *Surveyor*. So, of course, that's what they would do. The ship was a bona fide piece of history, and he could not justify making a fuss.

Eric was beginning to seem listless also. Maybe he missed the office. Or his rousing social life. "I don't know what it is," he confessed to MacAllister. "When I came, I thought I was going to be able to do something. Maybe help roll out the monitors. Stand watch. Do *something.*" He tried to laugh it away. "But everything's automated. The ship watches for the moonriders. The ship serves the meals. The ship turns out the lights at night. If somebody gets blown through an airlock, I assume the ship will manage the rescue. There's really not much for us to do except ride along.

"You're lucky, Mac. You have stuff to write. The AIs can't help.

You have to do it. Even Amy: She wants to fly one of these things, so she's getting a feel for it. Me, I'm just hanging around."

As are we all, thought MacAllister. He wondered what Eric had hoped for in his life. What had his early dreams been? He doubted they'd had much to do with hawking for the Academy.

But the guy *was* right. MacAllister had been fortunate, and he knew it. He'd wanted to be a reporter, but he'd hoped for much more than that. He'd wanted to influence literature and politics. He'd wanted to become a force for common sense in a society that seemed lost most of the time. He'd also wanted at one point to become a professional football player. But he broke his nose in a high school game and discovered how much football could hurt. After that he concentrated on the journalism. He wondered what it must be like for people to move into their later years and realize that their lives hadn't turned out the way they'd hoped. That the dreams went away. That, maybe worst of all, the lives they'd wanted had never materialized because they hadn't really made the effort.

At home, few days passed during which MacAllister wasn't approached by someone with a book idea. Usually it was a memoir, or maybe a novel, or a book of poetry, and he knew from the individual's expression that it would constitute the capstone of his or her existence. Usually, the book had not yet been completed. There'd be eight or nine chapters, but it was always a project that had been running for years.

Inevitably they wanted MacAllister's encouragement. Preferably his enthusiasm. Often they thought he was a book publisher and might opt for the idea, as if no one had ever before thought of writing a book about growing up in Mississippi, or doing peacekeeping operations in Africa.

Eric sat watching the unchanging stars on the twin displays. On the bridge, they could hear Valya talking to Bill. Then there was another voice. Probably a transmission from Union. When she came back she looked pleased. "They're going to head off the Terranova Rock," she said.

Amy raised a fist. "I knew we wouldn't just sit around and let that happen."

"That's a pretty big rock," said Eric. "How are they going to do it?"

"They'll plant a couple of freighters in front of it. Their gravity will speed it up, and it'll miss Terranova."

"Ships have gravity?" asked Eric.

"Sure," she said. "*You* have gravity, Eric."

"More or less," said MacAllister, keeping his voice low.

"It'll take a long time, but it works."

THE *SURVEYOR* WAS a huge ship by modern standards, more like a cargo carrier than a research vessel. It had big engines, big tubes, and a rounded prow. A few viewports were visible. *EURO-CANADIAN ALLIANCE* appeared in large black letters on the hull. (Hightower had set out one year before the U.S.-Canadian pact had merged the two countries.)

As they approached, lights came on, and the facility said hello. "*Welcome to the* Surveyor *Historical Site.*" The voice was female. Then she appeared, an avatar in the ship's jumpsuit. "*We're delighted you've decided to visit us, and we will do all in our power to ensure a pleasant experience.*" She was attractive, of course. Chestnut hair, blue eyes. "*My name is Meredith,*" she added.

"*I think we'll find an hour or two here worthwhile, Meredith,*" Valya said over the commlink.

MacAllister watched a section of hull open to receive them. "Who pays for this thing?" he asked.

"*Ever the tightwad,*" said Valya, with a smile. "*Orion operates the place, under Academy auspices. They provide the maintenance.*"

"And take the profits," he continued.

"*Are you serious, Mac? There are no profits. The charge is nominal. What they get out of it is public relations. That's all. This is officially a nonprofit operation, but they lose a nice chunk of change out here every year. If they weren't doing it, by the way, the ship would just be adrift and forgotten.*" There was an edge in her voice. MacAllister suspected he'd pushed a bit too far, had known before he said anything that it was a mistake, but something inside him ran on automatic at times like this. He simply couldn't resist the impulse.

They drew alongside the giant ship. Its navigation lights came on, and Valya slipped the *Salvator* into the docking area. Forward motion stopped, something secured them to the dock, and the engines shut down. His harness released.

Valya walked back from the bridge and the airlock hatch swung wide.

Meredith stood just outside in a lighted passageway. *"Glad to have you folks with us,"* she said. *"Please follow me to the welcome center."*

Amy was out and gone before MacAllister could get to his feet. "The *Surveyor* Historical Site is entirely automated," said Valya.

"I'm not surprised," MacAllister said, as he walked out into a receiving room. "It has artificial gravity."

"Installed two years after it became available, Mac." Her voice was still cool.

He tried to explain he meant no offense.

"I know," she said. "It's just—" She shook her head. "Let's just let it go, Mac. It's who you are. No need to apologize."

They followed Meredith up the corridor to the welcome center, which provided hot coffee, donuts, and a map of the museum. Chairs and tables were scattered haphazardly around the room, and a terminal provided a place where you could sign up to become a member of the International Surveyor Society and receive the latest news. A gift shop opened off one end, and a snack bar waited at the other. Double doors led back into the exhibits. *"Restoration of the* Surveyor,*"* she said, *"was, in its inception, funded by the Emil Hightower Foundation. Work began, and was continued, off and on, over a twelve-year period. Today the project is financed by Orion Tours, which offers the most exciting interstellar excursions available to the general public."*

The ship was filled with artifacts from the previous century. Portraits of the captain, the three crew members, and the passengers—there'd been eleven of them—were posted along the walls. The captain's cabin had been furnished so that it appeared "very much as it had been during the flight." The furnishings included pictures of Hightower with his son and daughter, eight and seven years old respectively at the time.

They looked at the ship's laboratory, which felt archaic although MacAllister couldn't have said why. And the common room, four times the size of the one on the *Salvator*. And the workout area, where the avatar invited them to try the equipment. The VR worked, and they saw part of a travelogue tracing the early voyages of the *Surveyor*.

The engineering section had been ripped apart by the explosion. The damaged area had been sealed off with a viewport so visitors could see where the engine had blown, and could look out into the void. A VR presented an animated demonstration of what had gone wrong.

Unlike modern ships, the *Surveyor* had two working positions on its bridge. One belonged to the captain, of course. The other was occupied by a navigator/communications officer, who also served as a backup for the captain in the event of a mishap. Valya's backup, of course, was Bill. AIs had come a long way since 2179.

The museum wasn't exactly bright and cheerful but it was light-years ahead of the *Salvator*. MacAllister was delighted to be able to walk around someplace new. He stopped at every display and watched images of the *Surveyor* during test flights, of Hightower and his crew in preparation for the flight, of the various researchers, unable to hide their enthusiasm at traveling to another star. Only one of the eleven, a middle-aged climatologist from the University of Geneva, had made a prior flight. She reminded MacAllister of a high school English teacher who'd taken him under her wing.

He brought up her avatar and spoke with her. He listened to her discussing the extreme age of Arcturus and its family of worlds. *"It's so* old," she said, *"that, had life developed, it would be billions of years older than we are. Imagine what such a civilization might be like."*

Dead, thought MacAllister. That's what it would be like. The fact that no technologically advanced species had been found in all these years made it pretty clear that the damned things have no staying power. You could see it at home, where, starting with the Cold War, there'd already been a few close calls.

It explained the Fermi Paradox. Nobody visits us because they blow themselves up before they get that far.

Except maybe the moonriders.

VALYA WAS LISTENING to her commlink. And looking distressed. She saw him watching and shook her head. Problems somewhere.

He waited until she'd finished. "What's wrong?"

"Our visitors again," she said.

"What is it this time? Another of the monitors?"

"No." She bit her lip. "There's another asteroid."

"What? Headed for the same world? For Terranova?"

"This one's apparently zeroed in on the Galactic."

"The Galactic? You mean the hotel? Where we're going next?"

"That's the one. Ops says it's a monster. Makes the Terranova rock look like a pebble."

"What the hell is it with these critters?"

"Don't know. But they do seem to have maniacal tendencies."

"It's actually going to hit the hotel?" That was unbelievable.

"That's what they're saying."

"When?"

"Thursday morning. At about ten."

It was Saturday evening. Eric frowned. "Are they going to be able to get everybody off?"

"Don't know," she said. "I guess it's going to be close."

"We can help," said Amy. "It's nearby."

Valya nodded. "We're going to. But look, I'm going to have to make two trips. I'm going to bring them back here."

"Is there time to do that?" asked Eric.

"Maybe. If I get going now."

"If *you* get going," said MacAllister. "*We're* staying here?"

"I need the space, Mac."

THERE WAS NO provision at the museum for overnight guests. The original living compartments for passengers and crew had virtual furniture. "We'll get our gear from the ship," said Amy. "We can camp right here." In the welcome center.

"Are we sure," said MacAllister, "there's nobody else who can carry out this rescue?"

"We're getting help. They have a ship at the hotel, which has probably already started over with some people."

"Do they have to bring them here?" asked MacAllister.

"It's the closest place. It'll drop them off and go back for a second group."

"This place is going to get crowded."

"Can't be helped, Mac. Meredith tells me there's plenty of food here, so it should be okay. As soon as it's able, Union will send a ship to pick everybody up." She looked worried.

"Lucky we happened to be on the scene." MacAllister had a difficult time masking a grumble.

"Talk later. We need to get moving. You guys will want to get your stuff off the ship." She spun on her heel and headed for the exit.

Eric fell in line behind her. "I hope they bring their own blankets," he said.

* * *

MACALLISTER BUNDLED HIS toiletries into a bag, grabbed extra clothes and towels, and looked around, trying to think what else he would need. Valya was at the airlock, talking on the commlink while they finished getting their gear. ". . . Leaving here now," she said. "I'll give you a TOA when I get into the area. I can carry nine. That's pushing it a bit, but we'll be okay for a short flight. *Salvator* out."

"Valya," MacAllister said, "they *do* have running water in this place, right?"

"Yes, Mac. That shouldn't be a problem. And there are two washrooms off the welcome center."

He scooped up a pillow and a blanket, his reader, a lamp, the clothes and toiletries, and hauled them out through the hatch. He wondered about hot water, but that was for another time.

Eric was already in the museum passageway with his bags. Amy came out, loaded down, and MacAllister gave her a hand. "You guys got everything?" Valya asked.

They hoped so. Eric remembered that he'd forgotten his notebook and hurried back inside.

"It won't be the most comfortable sleeping in the world, Mac," Valya said, "but look at the story you're getting."

"The story's out at the hotel."

"Okay. Let's see how things stand after the first flight. If I can take you on the second one, I will."

The comment surprised him. He didn't think his feelings were that transparent.

Eric came out with his notebook, and they said good-bye to her.

"You have any questions," Valya said, "just ask the avatar. I've told her to switch over to Eastern time, by the way, so the museum's lights will be in the same zone you are. You can reach me if you have to. Meredith knows how to make the connection." She stepped inside the airlock. "If all goes well, I'll be back Tuesday night. With some people to keep you company." She pulled the hatch shut behind her, and MacAllister felt suddenly alone.

HE JOINED THE others in the welcome center. They had no view of the outside, but felt the walls tremble as the *Salvator* pulled away.

Then everything was quiet again. He listened to air flowing through the ducts.

"What are we going to do for the next few days?" asked Eric.

Amy looked around. "Did anybody bring the chess set?"

They looked at one another. Apparently no one had.

"The gift shop has some vids," said Amy. "And a player."

"That's not a bad idea," said Eric. "Let's find something we can watch."

But all the vids were documentaries about interstellar exploration, or thrillers with deep-space monsters and black holes. They selected one more or less at random, *Attack of the Heliotropes,* dragged chairs into the gift shop, and settled in to watch. MacAllister had never been a fan of that sort of thing, but it seemed sporting to join them.

After twenty minutes he couldn't stand it anymore. It was embarrassing because Amy and Eric were both caught up in the show. But he pretended he was tired, asked whether anyone would object if he dimmed the lights in the main room. Then he retreated from the Heliotropes, arranged his pillows, angled his lamp, and took care of the lighting. He looked through the reader index and picked Arthur Hallinan's *Rum, Rebels, and Red Giants: An Intellectual History of Western Civilization from the Desert Wars to the Beginning of the Interstellar Age.*

MacAllister knew Hallinan personally. He was a cranky son of a bitch, a guy who didn't allow disagreement, who gave no credit for sense to anybody else. It had galled MacAllister to be forced on three separate occasions to give positive reviews to his books. But he *was* good.

In the distance, as if from another world, he could hear the roar of engines and the hum of particle beam weapons as the united fleets of Earth fought it out with the Heliotropes.

AMY KNEW THE vid was childish, that it was over the top, that it was good versus evil and no room for complexity. But it was still fun. It was what she liked, and she hoped there would never come a day when she'd forget how much joy could be found in an alien invasion. Eric was into it, too. And when it was over and the good guys had won, especially the good guy with the brown eyes and the lovely rear end, she sat back with a sense of elation.

They walked out into the main area. It was dark, save for the glowstrips along the overhead and the designations over the exits and the washrooms, and Mac's lamp. But Mac was asleep, snoring softly.

It was getting late. She arranged her own bedding while Eric wandered down to the snack shop. She hadn't noticed earlier, but the place made a lot of echoes.

She found herself thinking about the *Salvator*, and how they were alone in the museum. The news about the second asteroid was unnerving, and she didn't much like being out here with high-tech lunatics running around. She was having trouble sorting out her feelings. She was enjoying herself, would not have wanted to be anywhere else, but the elation had an edge to it.

She called up the museum's AI. "I have a question for you, Meredith."

"Yes, Amy?"

"If an asteroid were coming on a collision course with the museum, would you know about it?"

"The sensors would pick it up," she said.

"How close would it be when they did?"

"That depends how big the asteroid is."

"Two kilometers across."

"We would detect it at a range of about three thousand kilometers."

Eric returned with buns and fruit drinks. "How fast do they travel?" she asked him. "Asteroids?"

He shrugged. "I have no idea. Probably ten or twenty kilometers a second."

"Make it ten," she said. "A slow one. That would give us five minutes warning."

"Not very much," said Eric.

She looked over at Mac. "Nothing bothers him, does it?"

Eric grinned. "No, it doesn't look as if it does."

"You scared, Eric?"

He nodded. "A little."

SHE RETREATED TO one of the restrooms. There was no shower, so she had to use the sink to wash up. When she was finished she slipped into her nightgown, pulled on a robe, and padded back outside. Eric had turned off Mac's lamp.

He'd gone into the other washroom, where she could hear him splashing around. All the bedding they'd brought from the *Salvator* had been placed in the middle of the room. She thought about moving hers into the gift shop to get some privacy, but she wasn't sure she wanted to be that far away from the others. Anyway, they might take offense if she went off by herself.

She climbed onto the pillows, which didn't work very well. She couldn't move without sliding off onto the floor. Finally, she got things arranged, lay back, whispered good night to Mac, and closed her eyes. Moments later Eric arrived. "Not very comfortable," he said, keeping his voice low.

"It's okay."

"You need anything, Amy?"

"I'm good," she said.

"All right. See you in the morning."

It was one of those places where, when the lights were out, you kept hearing whispers. Air running through ducts. Barely audible blips and chirps from the electronics. Squeaks and rustlings from the corridor that opened into the museum's interior. The sound of moving water somewhere far off.

LIBRARY ENTRY

In response to the attack on the Galactic Hotel, Jeremy Wicker (G-OH) yesterday introduced a bill requiring that all interstellar vehicles be armed. In a related development, there is now bipartisan support for the Brockton-Schultz measure, which would demand that the World Council begin construction of a space navy.

—*Oversight*, Saturday, April 25

chapter 28

Courage is perhaps our most admirable trait. The man, or woman, who possesses it is able to plunge ahead, despite dangers, despite warnings, despite hazards of all kinds, to attack the task at hand. Often, it is indistinguishable from stupidity.

—Gregory MacAllister, "The Hero in the Attic"

Amy woke up twice during the night. The second time she thought she heard something in the outer corridor, the one that led back to the exhibition rooms. She lay for some minutes, barely breathing, but there were only the usual sounds of the museum, the creaking, the electronic whispers, the flow of air, the barely audible hum of the cleaning system keeping the dust off the exhibits. She felt the slight pressure toward the outer bulkhead generated by the *Surveyor's* movement around its own axis. Then she heard it again.

A footstep.

In the passageway.

Mac and Eric were both asleep.

"Meredith?" She whispered the name, got no response. Not loud enough. She thought about waking one of the men, but it would turn out to be nothing, and in the end she'd feel foolish.

And there it was again.

She got up, pulled on her robe, and padded across the floor. The passageway was dark, but there was just enough light to see it was empty. "Meredith?" she said, louder this time.

The avatar appeared a few steps down the corridor. *"Yes, Amy? Did you need anything?"*

"Are we alone in here? Is anybody else in the place?"

"No," she said. *"There are just the three of you."*

"Okay," she said. "Thanks."

Meredith winked off. The corridor was clear. She could see all the way back to the airlock and, beyond it, almost to the bridge. In the other direction lay the doors that opened into the main exhibit areas. Beyond that, where the VR chambers were, and some of the specialized displays, the corridor passed into darkness, save for two patches of starlight cast by viewports.

It was scary, but she was too old to be frightened by shadows and odd noises. She could remember hiding under the blankets at night sometimes when her father was gone on those inevitable junkets, and she was alone at home with the AI. He never knew how she'd felt, and would never have understood.

She took a few steps toward the exhibit doors. The AI obligingly turned lights on for her. She looked into the display rooms, and more lights came on. They were silent. She looked out one of the viewports at the stars. Arcturus was not directly visible, but its light illuminated part of a wing and a pair of thrusters. She passed by, checked the crew's quarters, looking into each room. (They were sealed so you could look at them but could not enter.) She peeked into the VR chambers and the engineering spaces. And finally she retraced her steps, passed the welcome center and the airlock, and went up onto the bridge.

Nothing was amiss.

She felt proud of herself. All secure, Captain. She liked to think she would have acted as Emil Hightower did. She imagined herself moving through the crippled ship, seeing that passengers and crew got out, then coming back here, not taking time to put on one of the ungainly pressure suits they had then, no time for that, have to get to the radio.

Chan Ho Park, *this is Taylor aboard the* Surveyor. *Blast in main engines. Code two. Code two.*

She eased herself into the captain's chair and repeated the message, Code two, come at once, position as follows, until the gathering dark began to take her, and she slumped back.

She had never before seen a bridge without viewports. The captain had been dependent on displays. There was probably nothing wrong with that, but it would have made her uncomfortable if she'd been sitting in the command chair.

Something moved behind her, and she jumped a foot, but it was only Eric. "Problems sleeping?" he asked.

"Not really. I thought I heard something."

He glanced around. "Probably mice."

"You're kidding."

"Maybe." He gazed down at the controls. "I noticed you were missing. I just wanted to be sure you were all right."

"I'm fine."

"Okay. I'm going back to sleep." He grinned at her. "You're not going to take us anywhere, are you?"

"I thought maybe Quraqua," she said.

He laughed. "Let's let it go until morning." And he got serious. "Don't stay out here too long, Amy. It's chilly."

He trundled off through the hatch into the dim passageway. She wondered what it felt like to take a ship into a planetary system and put it in orbit around a living world.

When she had her own command, she would never quit the way Hutch had. Would never take an office job. Not as long as she could breathe.

SHE MUST HAVE fallen asleep. The lights had dimmed and momentarily she didn't know where she was. But the controls were spread out in front of her, and she felt the stiff fabric of the captain's chair against the back of her head.

And she heard something behind her.

Eric again.

She swung the chair around. Someone was out in the passageway. The luminous panels were still on, but the figure was nevertheless cloaked in darkness. And gradually she saw that it was a *woman*.

"Hello," Amy said, her voice just above a whisper. "Who's there? Meredith? Is that you?"

The museum's projection system had obviously broken down.

The woman was approaching, moving smoothly, almost floating. She reached the hatch, and stopped. Amy still couldn't see who it was. It was a projection, a problem with the software. Had to be.

"Amy."

A familiar voice. And she realized what had happened. The *Salvator* had come back. But the voice wasn't *Valya's*. Whose was it?

"Amy, listen to me."

The darkness shrouding the figure faded. The woman was tall. Graceful.

It was *Hutch*.

Amy stared at the apparition. It couldn't be. Hutch was light-years away. And the figure was too tall. "Hutch, is that you?"

"There's something you must do." The woman came through the hatch, although she seemed not to walk. She *did* look exactly like Priscilla Hutchins. But she must have been a foot taller. Maybe it was because Amy was sitting.

The woman wore the same white blouse and dark blue slacks that Hutch had been wearing when they'd said good-bye at Union. "Who are you—?" Her voice squeaked.

"You need not be afraid, Child," she said. *"You have a mission to perform."*

Amy wanted to get to her feet, but her legs felt wobbly. "You look like Hutch."

"Yes."

"But you're not her, are you?"

"No."

She wanted to run. To call for help. To get away from this creature, whatever it was. "You're a projection. Something's wrong with the AI."

"Stay calm. I will not harm you."

"What do you want?"

"Blueprint. The Origins Project."

She looked *exactly* like Hutch. Except for the size. And the eyes. They were the same color. But they were different in a way that unnerved her. Not human. "What about it?" she asked.

"We are going to destroy it."

Amy's voice shook. "Who are you?"

"We will allow you time to evacuate everyone who is there. But do it promptly."

"Wait." Amy wondered whether the apparition was crazy. "They won't listen to me. They'll laugh at me."

"Do it promptly, Amy. Don't test our patience." It *was* Hutch's voice.

"Who are you? Did you attack the hotel?"

The woman was becoming harder to see. The darkness seemed to be gathering about her again. *"We've attacked no one. See to Origins."*

Amy was pushing back in her seat, the way you do when you're accelerating. She watched Hutch fade out. Like a hologram.

IT WAS PROBABLY twenty minutes before she found the strength, the nerve, to go into the passageway and return to the welcome center. Mac and Eric were both sprawled comfortably in their sheets.

She knelt trembling beside Mac and pulled on his arm. "Mac," she said, "they've been on board. I talked with one of them. They said we had to warn—"

"What?" he growled. "Amy? Who was on board?"

"The moonriders. I think. One of them. She looked like Hutch."

He smiled in his closest approach to a fatherly manner. "You've been dreaming, Sweetheart."

"No." She knew that wasn't true.

Then they were both talking at once, she trying to explain what the apparition had said about the Origins Project, he trying to tell her to wait a minute, slow down, take it back to the beginning. "You say it was Hutch?"

"Except bigger. Taller. And she said we—"

"Hold it. Wait. Stop a second. Think about it a minute. What does it sound like to you?"

Eric was awake now, staring at them.

"I'm not making it up, Mac. I was on the bridge, and I was wide-awake."

"All right. And what did it say again?"

"She even had Hutch's voice."

Mac reached for her. Tried to embrace her, but she kept her distance. "Amy," he said, "you need to calm down."

"I'm calm."

"Okay." He sat up and pulled his blankets around him. "Tell me again what she said."

"She said they were going to destroy the Origins Project. Something about a blueprint."

"A what?"

"A blueprint. I don't know what that was about."

"Okay."

"What's a blueprint? Do you know, Mac?"

"It's an archaic term. They used to use blueprints to create architectural designs."

"Okay. Maybe I didn't hear it right. But she told me to get everybody off. Before they do it. How am I supposed to do that?"

"Wave a wand, kid," said Eric. "Did she say *why* they were going to destroy it?"

"No. Just that they were going to do it."

"When? When are they going to do this?"

"I don't know." She was close to hysteria. "She didn't say. What she said was I shouldn't test her patience."

Mac was getting frustrated. "Did she explain why they were throwing rocks at things in the first place?"

"No. In fact she said . . ." Amy had to stop and think. "I asked if they'd attacked the hotel. She said they hadn't."

"There you are," said Mac. "It has to be a dream."

"It's probably an AI malfunction," said Eric. "It happens sometimes."

"I asked her about that. She said no."

"That's part of the malfunction, Amy."

"Well, it's simple enough to check," said Mac. "Meredith?"

"*Yes, Mr. MacAllister?*" Just a voice this time.

"You have a security system, I assume?"

"*Yes. We have the Hornet 26. It is top-of-the-line.*"

"Do you have a record of the time Amy spent on the bridge this evening?"

"*No, I do not.*"

"How come?"

"*I only record events of a specific nature. Theft, vandalism. If a fight were to break out, I would record that.*"

"So nothing unusual happened on the bridge?"

"*Nothing that fit within the security parameters.*"

"That helps," said Eric.

Mac looked unhappy. "I don't know what to tell you, Amy."

"We have a transmission," said Meredith. *"From the* Salvator.*"*

"Patch it through, please."

Valya appeared in the middle of the room. *"Mac, the Arcturus monitor has reported moonriders in your area. Probably not a problem, but be aware."*

MACALLISTER'S DIARY

I've seen it before. People in trying circumstances, under pressure, scared. You wind up with hysteria. I guess adolescents are especially susceptible. We need another woman on the premises. I don't know how to deal with it. Amy's angry with both of us.

As I write this, the lights are out, except for the patches and my lamp. But she's made no move to lie down. She's sitting in a chair with her head thrown back. Her eyes are closed, but she's awake. Valya, where are you?

–Sunday, April 26

LIBRARY ARCHIVE

In an overnight poll, 66 percent of people in the Council nations think the moonriders are real. Of those, 78 percent think they constitute a serious threat. A clear majority favor arming against the possibility of an attack. Of course almost half think the Earth is 6,000 years old.

–*Barcelona Times*, Sunday, April 26

FIRST AMENDMENT UNDER FIRE AGAIN?

Hellfire Trial Reminiscent of Cohen vs *NIH*

Landmark Case Limited Parental Right to Allow Hate Indoctrination

chapter 29

> The uplifters are forever running around telling blockheads they would do better if they would believe in themselves. But they already do. That is why they are blockheads.
>
> —Gregory MacAllister, "Illusions at Lunch"

They didn't believe her. Were never going to believe her.

She almost didn't believe it herself, but *damn* it, Hutch had *been* there, *something* had been there. She had been breathing, and she had spoken with Hutch's voice.

You have a mission to perform.

Amy regretted not having reached out and *touched* her. Not having told the woman she had no way to evacuate Origins. Why had she picked on her? How could she think anyone would believe her?

—Going to destroy it.

They'd looked at the bridge. They'd scoured the passageways. Even looked outside to see if there were moonriders. But the sky was placid.

Now they were back in the welcome center. Eric was asleep, and Mac was pretending to be asleep. She'd be okay in the morning, they'd said. It'll be easier to talk about it then.

She did not want ever again to be alone in this place.

* * *

WHEN SHE WOKE, Mac and Eric were already in the snack shop. She could smell bacon and coffee. She grabbed some clothes, made for a washroom, cleaned, and changed. When finally she joined them, they both looked uncomfortable.

"It happened," she said.

They nodded and looked at each other.

Best, she decided, was to leave it alone. "Any news from anybody?"

"Not really," Eric said. "There've been no more reports of moon-riders."

"That's good." They were eating pancakes and bacon. She sat down and ordered some for herself. "Valya said the first load of people from the hotel would be here Tuesday night, right?"

"That's correct," said Mac. His voice echoed faintly.

"They were lucky there were a couple of ships nearby." Her voice trailed away. "You're looking at me funny."

"Sorry," said Mac. "I didn't mean to. I was just wondering if you're okay."

"I'm fine," she said.

"Okay."

"Amy," said Eric, "this has been a strange trip. And the museum, when we're stuck here and the place is empty, can be pretty spooky—"

"Forget it." Her breakfast came, and she took the plate, got up, and walked over to another table. Well away from them.

"Amy," said Mac, "I wish you wouldn't get upset."

"I'm not upset." She dumped maple syrup on the pancakes. "Mac, think how you'd feel if you told me something important, and I wouldn't believe *you*."

WHEN THEY'D FINISHED, Eric and Mac retreated into the welcome center, while Amy stayed in the snack bar. Mac opened his notebook, and Eric dropped into a chair, closed his eyes, and let his head drift back. He didn't know what to do. But sitting there pretending the problem would go away was only going to increase the tension.

He got up wearily and went back into the snack bar. She'd barely touched her food. "Hi," he said.

She looked up. "Hi."

"Can we talk?"

"Sure."

He sat down beside her. "It has nothing to do with you," he said.

"What do you mean?"

"It's not that we believe you'd lie to us. We both know you wouldn't do that. But sometimes people see things that aren't really there. What you're asking us to believe isn't necessarily impossible, but it flies in the face of common sense."

"I know."

"If either of us told you the same story, would *you* believe it?"

She thought about it. "I don't know," she said.

"Be honest."

"Probably not."

"Okay. There's an old saying: Extraordinary assertions require extraordinary proof." She sat quietly watching him. "If you want people to believe you've seen a moonrider, for example, you have to be able to walk it into the room. Let us ask it some questions. Maybe do an inspection to make sure it's not the AI run amok. Even then I probably won't buy the story. You understand what I'm saying?"

"Yes," she said. "I understand."

"It's far more likely that what you saw last night resulted from a bit too much excitement, or from being alone in a strange place, or from too many french fries, or maybe all three, than that there was actually a visitation."

She cut out a piece of the pancakes, looked at it, exhaled, and put it in her mouth.

"It might actually have happened. I'm not saying it didn't. What I *am* saying is that—"

"I know what you're saying, Eric."

"Okay. Good."

"But if I *am* right, and I can't get anyone to believe me, a lot of people are going to die."

"I hear you." He couldn't think of an answer for that one. "Why don't we just take some time and walk around a bit? Go sightseeing. Maybe it'll clear our heads."

He was hoping it would clear *hers*. She was still angry. And scared. No way she could not be. But he didn't want her to sit and just sulk for the rest of the day.

* * *

SHE TRIED TO concentrate on the pictures and exhibits. There was a portrait of Hightower's wife receiving the posthumous commendation awarded her husband by the World Science Foundation. And another depicting the launching of the *Surveyor*, silhouetted against Luna. You could sit and talk with Hightower's avatar, or with other members of the crew or the researchers. You could re-create the launch, complete with contemporary media coverage. Or watch the *Surveyor* cruising in low orbit over Beta Centauri III.

When they returned to the welcome center, shortly before noon, Mac still had his nose in his notebook. He looked up as they entered. "You guys really made a morning of it. I was getting ready to send in the marines."

Eric described what they'd been doing and recommended he take some time himself to look around the place.

Amy positioned herself so she could see over Mac's shoulder. "Doing an article for *The National*?" she asked.

"Not really," he said. "There's nothing newsworthy here. The story's over at the Galactic."

Amy felt a rush of warmth in her cheeks. But she said nothing.

Eric picked his bedding up off the floor and tossed it across a chair. "She'll probably be able to take you on the second flight, Mac," he said.

"Maybe."

Amy was still standing behind him. "Want to know a secret, Mac?"

"Sure, kid."

"I think she likes you."

He laughed. "Everybody likes your uncle Mac."

"Eric's right. She'll want you to go back with her. To the Galactic."

"I'll tell you the truth, Amy: This is looking more and more like *War of the Worlds* stuff. If that's the case, I'm not sure I want to get involved with it."

"You believe me."

"I know you're telling me what you believe is true. Beyond that, I'm keeping an open mind."

"I don't know how to prove it to you."

"Yeah," he said. "It would have made things simpler if she'd given you something. Some kind of proof." He tapped his stylus on the screen. "Anyhow, I'm not so sure now I want to go anywhere near the Galactic."

"I thought that's what reporters did," said Amy. "Go to the places where the action is."

"I'm not a reporter, Love. I'm an editor. Good editors stay out of the line of fire."

"Oh." She let him see she knew he was kidding.

"Not that we're afraid of anything, of course."

"Right," she said. "Mac, what do you think is going on?"

"I don't know," he said. "I honestly can't figure it out. If they have the technology to move asteroids around, I'd think they could find a better way of attacking us than throwing rocks. I mean, all that does is warn us they're there. If they really meant to come after us, they'd use flash weapons, right? Or nukes or something. They'd hit strategic targets. Not a hotel that hasn't even been completed yet. And an empty world." She stood for a long moment, looking down at him. "What do *you* think, Amy?"

"They might be a really *old* race," she said.

"And?"

"Maybe they don't care about whether we're warned. Maybe they're so far ahead of us they don't see us as a threat. Maybe they're playing games with us. Or maybe with each other, using us as pieces. As pawns."

Mac closed the notebook. "See who can hit the monkeys with the rock. Extra points for a *big* rock." He sat back. "You might have something."

She managed a brave smile, but hearing it put that way sent a chill through her.

AMY SPENT THE afternoon doing homework. After dinner, they played a political game that Mac liked in which you chose strategies that would defame opponents while defending yourself as best you could. He was particularly good at it.

There were no recurrences of Amy's vision. But then she didn't go off by herself anymore. They watched a sim, and by eleven, she was exhausted and glad to climb into her sheets.

Eric also retired early. The day had been wearing for him as well. He would be glad when the experience was over. Mac was awake and working, seated in a chair with his lamp set up beside him. The rest of the welcome center was dark.

He remembered waking briefly and seeing Mac turn off his light. Then he drifted off again, waking a second time to Meredith's soft voice. *"Eric, the* Lin-Kao *is calling. Do you wish to take the call, or would you prefer I respond?"*

"I'll take it in the souvenir shop," he said. He climbed to his feet and padded across the cold floor. The lights came on in the shop. He went in and closed the door behind him. "Okay, Meredith," he said.

The *Lin-Kao*'s captain looked well along in years. He had white hair, grizzled features, steely blue eyes. "Surveyor." He straightened himself. *"We have just made our jump into your area. We'll be there in about five hours."*

"Okay, *Lin-Kao,*" he said, feeling very professional. "We'll be waiting." He felt as if he should say something more. "You may have heard that moonriders were reported locally. You'll be glad to know they are gone. As far as we know."

There was a delay of about three minutes while the signal traveled out, and the response came back. *"Good,"* the captain said. *"I am indeed glad."* His tone suggested he was not much impressed by wild stories. *"We're in good shape here,* Surveyor. *Other than running late. I have eleven people with me. All of whom are anxious to get off the ship. See you when we get there."*

He'd just settled into his blankets when Meredith was back. *"Another call,"* she said, keeping her voice low. "Salvator."

"Okay." Eric trooped back to the souvenir room. "Let's hear it."

Valya appeared, seated in the command chair. *"I'll be at the Galactic in a few hours,"* she said. *"I'll pick these folks up and be on my way back as quickly as I can."*

The green lamp came on, inviting him to answer. "We'll be waiting." He should have stopped there, perhaps. "Valya, Amy thinks she saw something in the museum last night. She thinks it might have been one of the moonriders. She claims it looked like Hutchins. And that it told her they, whoever *they* are, are going to destroy Origins. She insists it wasn't a dream. Anyhow I thought you should know."

He signed off, unsure whether it had been a good idea to pass the story along.

NEWSDESK

HARRIET HEADS FOR GULF COAST
Monster Hurricane to Make Landfall Tomorrow
Evacuations Ordered

ASTEROID CLOSES IN ON ORBITING HOTEL
Galactic Would Have Been First of Its Kind
Has Been under Construction Six Months
Rescue Effort Under Way

MOONRIDERS SEEN IN NEBRASKA
Hundreds Near Omaha Watch Lights in Sky

GROUP GATHERS ON MOUNTAINTOP TO AWAIT SALVATION
"Salvation City" Adherents: The Lord Is Coming Tonight
Seventeen Hundred Packed and Ready to Go
Camped atop Mt. Camelback in Poconos

MOONRIDERS MAY BE GROUP HYSTERIA
Study: Sightings Are Delusional
Rock Clusters, Reflections, Imagination Account for Phenomena
"People See What They Want to See"

MOONRIDER COMMITTEE: THEY EXIST
"Too Many Sightings to Dismiss"

MOONRIDER ACTION TOYS GETTING HOT
Aliens Jumping off Shelves

CHURCH GROUP RECOMMENDS REVIEW OF CURRICULA
NAC: Overemphasis on Damnation?

chapter 30

For males, sex is like baseball. Hit-and-run. Or put one out of the park, circle the bases and score, head for the showers, and clear out. That kind of behavior necessarily upsets the ladies. But it's not anyone's fault. It's the way people are wired, and nothing's ever going to change it.

—Gregory MacAllister, "Love and Marriage"

Amy watched on one of the welcome center screens as the *Lin-Kao* docked, and she was at the foot of the exit ramp when the hatches opened, and the workers from the Galactic trooped in. They were a noisy bunch, six women and five men, carrying their belongings. Plus the captain, whose name was Hugo Something. They dropped their bags, Hugo exchanged a few words with his passengers, glad he was able to help, see you at home sometime, took a moment to wave at Amy, and shook hands with Mac and Eric. "Got to get moving," he said. "There's a bunch more to pick up." And that quickly he was gone.

The new arrivals were happy to be off the ship. "It was a bit crowded in there," one of the women told Amy. "The air was getting stale."

They were all hauling supplies. They'd arrived with the impression that food would be scarce at the museum, and had consequently brought a substantial amount from the Galactic. They also had blankets and pillows. A few took up residence in the welcome center; others moved into outlying locations.

The shadow that had hung over Amy dissipated, and the image of Hutch on the bridge suddenly felt far away. It couldn't have happened. Maybe Eric and Mac were right.

Valya called to say she had picked up her contingent and was on the way back. A few minutes later a transmission arrived from the *Cavalier*. Its captain, a young man who looked barely older than Amy, told them he was on his way from Union to provide transportation home. *"We'll be there in four days."* The announcement was greeted by a cheer.

Amy struck up a friendship with one of the women, Vannie Trotter, a design specialist from Toronto. Vannie was amiable and reassuring, a dark-complexioned woman with black hair and a relentlessly upbeat personality. She was pretty old, about thirty, and had a husband and one son at home. She won Amy's affection by questioning her about the moonriders, and about Amy's reaction to them. At first, Amy said nothing about the experience on the bridge. Vannie was taking her seriously, and she didn't want to do anything to jeopardize that. But eventually she could no longer hold back, and she told Vannie everything.

"It *really* happened?" Vannie asked, when she'd finished.

"Yes."

"What did the others say? The two guys who were here with you?"

"They think I was dreaming."

"Were you?"

It seemed remote now. Something that couldn't have happened. But she remembered how she'd felt when she saw the image, and how certain she'd been when she was pleading with Mac and Eric. "No," she said.

Vannie smiled and drew closer to her. They were sitting on one of the padded benches that lined the walls in one of the exhibition rooms. The room was dominated by the *Surveyor*'s lander. "Don't be too hard on them," she said.

"You believe me, Vannie?"

"After what I've seen," she said, "I'm ready to believe anything. Sure. Maybe they'd try to pass a message."

"But why me?"

"Don't know, Babe. Maybe you were the only one here with an open mind."

"I don't know what to do, Vannie. People will think I'm crazy."

She nodded. "Who can you talk to that you can trust?"

She thought about it. "I have a few friends at school."

"Any adults? How about your folks?"

"My father would never believe it."

"Anybody else?"

"Maybe Hutch."

"Hutch? Who's he?"

"Hutch is a *she*. She's the one who arranged for me to come out here."

"Okay. Don't worry about these guys anymore. They have their minds made up. When you get the chance, talk to this Hutch."

"You really think she'll believe me?"

"You persuaded *me*, Amy."

THE MUSEUM WAS much easier to take since the additional people had arrived. That was an unusual reaction for MacAllister. He generally preferred to be left alone. But in that place noise and company were a distinct improvement. A supply of beer and liquor showed up from somewhere. Several played horns and stringed instruments. By midday Monday a serious party was under way.

Valya called late Tuesday evening to announce she was back in Arcturus space.

He was glad to be able to talk with her again. Even though it meant dealing with the delays caused by her distance from the museum. He got on the circuit and said hello. Commented that the people from the Galactic had made themselves at home. Told her that the *Cavalier* was on its way. Everything's good here.

Her image froze while the signal traveled out, and, several minutes later, the response came back. *"Mac, I'm glad everything's well,"* she said. *"Sounds as if you're having a good time."* He was in the souvenir shop with the door closed. The party had died down, and most of the people were off somewhere watching a horror sim. But there was still a fair amount of singing coming through the thin walls. *"No problems of any kind?"*

That was code for Amy. Valya had no way of knowing who'd be with him when the transmission came in.

"No," he said. "She seems to have gotten past it." He found a chair and sat down. "This is a hell of a way to hold a conversation. You say something, go get a coffee, do some reading."

He sent the transmission and went outside, picked up his notebook, brought it in, called up the latest news reports, and looked through them.

Eventually, her image came back to life. *"It's because you don't do it often enough, Mac,"* she said. *"You need to get out more."*

"I'm certainly out now," he said. "Really out. Anyhow, we missed you."

"I'm sure. Nobody to fight with. No sign of the moonriders?"

"No. They never showed up. How many people are still back at the hotel?"

"I don't think Hugo's gotten there yet. After he picks up his load, there'll be four. The asteroid may show up before I can get back. So the plan is that when it gets close, they'll use one of the shuttles and clear out. I'll get them from the shuttle."

"Have you seen the asteroid?"

"Yes. It's pretty big."

"Listen, Valya. You're obviously going to be leaving here as soon as you drop off your passengers. We talked about my going back with you. I want to do that. I'll be ready to go when you dock."

She looked pleased. *"Good. I could use the company."*

THE *SALVATOR* ARRIVED just before midnight. Several of the construction workers stayed up to greet their colleagues. Valya was last to come through the connecting tube. She waved at MacAllister, started in his direction, but saw Amy in the passageway. She signaled MacAllister to be patient, strolled over, and took the girl aside.

The conversation was short. It looked amicable enough, but it had no animation. Valya was asking questions, Amy shook her head yes and no, but the responses seemed abbreviated. Of course it was understandable. It was extremely late, but Amy had insisted on staying up to wait for the *Salvator*. Or maybe just on staying up.

Eventually Valya nodded, gave the girl's shoulder a squeeze, and came away.

"I just don't know what to think about it," she told MacAllister. Then her eyes refocused, and she surprised him with an embrace. "It's good to see you again, Mac."

"You, too. Is she okay?"

"You tell me." She took a deep breath and looked at the time. "Got your toothbrush?"

A few minutes later she hustled him through the airlock into the *Salvator* and onto the bridge. "The air's bad," he said. It didn't so much smell bad, as that it felt oppressive. Stuffy.

"We had too many people crammed in here," she said. "We're supposed to have a seven-passenger capacity. Just give it a little time, and it'll clear." She ran quickly through her checklist, gave some instructions to Bill, and virtually pushed MacAllister into the right-hand seat. She sat down beside him, secured the harnesses, and asked if he was ready to go while simultaneously shutting off the magnets that secured the *Salvator* to the dock. Then they were under way.

"Yes," he said. "Anytime you're ready."

She laughed. It was a sound he enjoyed hearing. Damned women. Nature makes fools of us all. Valya told Bill to set course for Capella, then pushed back and exhaled. "I'll be glad to get this over."

MacAllister nodded as the image of the museum in the navigation monitor shrank. "What did she say when you talked with her?"

"Amy? She pretty much invited me to go away. Did it politely, but that was the message. What did you guys do? Tell her it was her imagination?"

MacAllister decided he would never understand women. "It *was* her imagination."

"Of course," she said. "That doesn't mean you tell her that."

"What would *you* have done?"

"Just listened. Agreed that it was a scary experience. *She's* the one who has to decide it didn't really happen."

"She wanted us to tell her what to do."

"And you did. *Orea takanes*. Now she knows exactly how to handle things." She tried to shake it off. "I'm sorry. It really wasn't your fault."

Right. Men are naturally slow-witted. "You're a sexist," he said quietly.

"Oh, Mac, you just see right through me, don't you?" Her eyes grew serious. "The museum must have been a little scary at night. You shouldn't have let her wander around in there by herself." She shook her head. "No wonder she started seeing things."

"Valya, she's sixteen. I don't think she wanted us following her around."

"She's *fifteen*. And she's still a kid." She patted his arm. "It's all right, Mac. You meant well."

It was the sort of comment he often made about politicians and bishops.

They were both dead tired. They went back to the common room, where Bill provided some cheese and pineapple juice. It tasted okay, but it wasn't exactly elegant. Valya fell asleep in her chair with the snack untouched.

MacAllister was seated opposite her. He dimmed the lights, and she looked almost ethereal, her head resting on the back of the chair, red hair framing finely chiseled features, one arm in her lap, the other resting on a side table beside her juice.

He returned to his quarters, found a quilt, brought it out, and draped it over her.

He went back to his chair, killed the lights altogether, closed his eyes, and sat listening to her breathe.

Yes, my dear, alone with you at last.

SHE WOKE HIM. "Mac, you need to get into your harness. We'll be making our jump in a few minutes."

The daylight illumination was on. He checked the time. It was almost ten.

"It'll be a twenty-two-hour run to the Capella system," she said. "Which puts us in there at about 0800 Thursday."

"When does the asteroid arrive?"

"Just after ten."

"That gives us plenty of time to get them off, doesn't it?"

"It would if the jump took us in close," she said. "But we'll be lucky to get within three hours. No, safest is to stick with Plan A: Assume the rock will get there first. They'll use a shuttle to get out of harm's way."

He followed her onto the bridge, took his seat, and activated the harness. He'd already begun imagining how the story would appear in the media. *Prominent Editor Rides to Rescue.*

MacAllister Saves Four in Race with Asteroid.

MacAllister Wins Americus for First-Person Account of Galactic Ordeal.

"It'd be nice," he said, "if we could get there *before* the asteroid. Take them directly off the gridwork."

She'd started the countdown with Bill. "Why?"

"Makes a better story."

"If we didn't get there in time, which we probably wouldn't, there's a good chance they'd be killed."

MacAllister grinned. "That would be a good story, too."

She leaned over and whacked him, and they both laughed. "But you're not really kidding, are you?"

"Not entirely," he said. "If we were late, they could still get clear, right? I mean, they've got the shuttle."

"Forget it, Mac. The asteroid's as big as a sizable chunk of Arizona."

"*One minute,*" said Bill.

THE *SALVATOR* SLIPPED into the transdimensional mists, and so did the conversation. They retreated to the common room and talked about MacAllister's journalistic passions and why Valya enjoyed piloting interstellars and would consider no other line of work. Why MacAllister liked giving trouble to people who, he argued, needed to be kept in line. Why Valya enjoyed solitude. "Most people only talk about themselves," she said. "Which would be okay if they had some imagination. But I get tired listening to stories about spouses who don't understand, or incomprehensible physics experiments, or what sims they watched recently. It's empty chatter and, if you're not careful, it can crowd you out of your life. Up here it's quiet, and you're alone with yourself."

"Thanks," he said.

"For what?"

"For taking me along."

"Mac," she said, "you have your problems, but you do make for entertaining flights."

He sat quietly, enjoying the moment. "You know, Valya, when we get home, I'd like to take you over to the Seahawk."

"The Seahawk?"

Everybody in Arlington knew the Seahawk. But he played her game. "Nicest club on the Potomac," he said.

"Oh, yes. I have heard of it." She looked out at the mist. "Yes, that would be nice." Her eyes brushed over him, came back, locked. She was making up her mind about something.

"You don't think very highly of men, do you, Valya?"

"They're okay. Some of them."

"What's their primary problem?" MacAllister was quietly amused, but tried not to show it.

"Bottom line?" she said.

"Please."

"Don't take offense, Mac. Most guys aren't very bright."

MacAllister saw no reason to be offended. "Most people generally aren't very bright."

"There's an extra dimension with men."

"Sex."

"It's more complicated than that. But yes."

"What else?"

"Isn't that enough?"

"Maybe. But there's more. You're not good at hiding your feelings."

"Guys are more self-centered. It's why you only hear males talking about What's the meaning of it all?"

"Explain."

"To a woman, it's self-evident. Life is what it is. A brief stroll in the sunlight. A chance to enjoy yourself for a century or so. Love. Be loved. Have a few drinks before the fire goes out. But guys think there has to be something more. That's why all the big religious figures are men. They'll claim it just doesn't make sense that the world could move on without them. Must be an afterlife. Has to be more than this. So they live on, as saints or whatever. The guys never really want to leave the table." Her lips curved into a smile.

MacAllister felt warm. "You *are* lovely, Valya," he said.

The smile widened. "There's my point. Even you, Mac."

"What? Enjoying the company of a beautiful woman? It's just part of the stroll in the sunlight."

She asked how it felt to be feared by so many politically powerful people. MacAllister realized she felt the conversation had wandered into deep water and was trying to get onto safer ground. Which was okay. "I really don't think about it," he said.

She sighed. "Of course you don't. After all, who *would* want to be a guy the power brokers are all afraid of?"

"I think you're overstating things a bit."

She was enjoying herself. She knew the effect of those luminous eyes. Add the high-voltage personality, and you had an extraordinary woman. Yet there was always a part of her that seemed aloof, that stayed outside the conversation, amused, detached. As if she'd done all this before.

"I'm sorry to interrupt," said Bill. *"We have an incoming transmission."*

At home, Tilly could be shut down. He wasn't always present, always lingering in the background as Bill seemed to be. Mac and Valya were not really alone after all.

One of the construction workers appeared in the middle of the room. He was about forty. He had dark skin and a black beard, and he ate too much. He looked both scared and tired. *"Valentina,"* he said, *"I just wanted you to know we're lined up and ready to go. Appreciate it if you could let us know your TOA as soon as you can."* He hesitated, reluctant to break away. *"We'll be glad to see you."*

The image clicked off. "I think you have a fan," said MacAllister.

"Yeah. Next time you ask me why I do this stuff for a living—"

It was MacAllister's turn to smile. "I'm sure you get to rescue people at least once a month."

"Well. Once is enough, *kardoula mou*."

"My Greek's a little rusty."

"It means 'opinionated one.' "

"I don't believe it."

"Would I lie to you?"

"I'm going to look it up."

"You are entitled to do so." She sighed. "Bill."

"Yes, Valya."

"Response for the hotel."

"Ready."

The lighting shifted gently as Bill lined up her image. "Karim, we'll make the jump into your space about eighteen hours after you receive this. As soon as we're there, I'll let you know. Hang in. You'll get off with no problem."

The lights rose and fell again. Went back to normal. "You never married, Mac, did you?"

"I was married," he said. "Years ago. My wife died."

"I'm sorry."

He shrugged. "It happens."

"You have a reputation as a misogynist. Carefully cultivated if I read you correctly. I wouldn't have thought you'd have wanted a woman in your life."

He had no family, no one he could really talk to. He kept everyone at a safe distance. And here was this Greek pilot, standing at the edge of the clearing. "Jenny was special," he said.

Her eyes slid shut, closing off that azure gaze. "She must have been. You want to tell me about it?"

"Nothing to tell," he said. "She died young. Katzmeier's Disease."

"Must have been a painful time."

"Yeah."

She could see he didn't want to go any further, so, after a long pause, she retreated. Talked about the flight back from Capella with a crowded ship. Asked how the reports for *The National* were coming. Was he going to mention Amy's claims?

"No," he said. "They're not really relevant to anything."

"Unless the Origins Project blows up."

"That's not going to happen."

"If it does, *if*, and it happens without warning—"

"Valya, they throw rocks you can see coming for a long time—"

"Eric told me the apparition denied the asteroid stories. If Amy's got it right, more than a hundred people will die out there."

"If something were to happen, there'd be time to get them off."

"Worst-case scenario. If it *did* happen, suddenly, a surprise, how would you feel? All those people dead?"

"I don't deal in hypotheticals, Valya."

"Sure you do. It's bread and butter for the media. What *if* she's right? I mean, the moonriders were there, weren't they? In the vicinity of the museum?"

"We didn't see anything."

"The monitor picked them up."

"We dropped the monitor a long way from the museum."

"Hell, Mac, they could have been at the front door, and you wouldn't have seen them."

"Are you really going to argue she actually talked with an alien?"

"I'm talking like you said: hypotheticals."

He was tired of Amy's story. "Look, assume for a minute the moonriders wanted to talk to us. Warn us they were going to take down a major facility. Why would they pass the message to Amy? Why not me? Or Eric?"

"Maybe they thought she'd be the easiest one there to talk to."

"Ho-ho." He kept his tone soft. Make it clear he was above taking offense. "Although there *is* something ominous about the Origins Project."

"Really? And what's that?"

He told her about the call from Anthony DiLorenzo.

"I'll be damned," she said. "He really said that?"

"Yes, he did."

She thought about it. "I just can't believe it's possible, Mac." They sat looking at each other. "We need to change the mood," she said.

She went back to her quarters. He heard her talking with Bill. Then she returned with a bottle of wine. "With the noted Gregory MacAllister on board, I think the captain is justified in declaring a special occasion."

"Do I get to make a speech?"

"Go ahead."

"You are the loveliest captain this side of Sirius."

She reached for an opener while he examined the bottle. "I'm not sure, Mac, but that may not be much of a compliment."

"Accept it in the spirit intended."

"Indeed I will."

They opened it and filled two glasses. "You're a remarkable guy, you know that?"

"Thank you."

"You can be a bit of a strain sometimes, but God knows, as I think I said earlier, you're always a kick to have around. Anyhow, if we're about to be overrun by moonriders, or sucked down into the universal black hole, we should probably drink up while we can." She filled their glasses. "When we get home, I'll cook a meal for you. If you like."

"Yes," he said. "I'd like that very much."

He began to suspect she was offering herself to him. MacAllister had never been quick on the social subtleties attendant on romantic relations. Still, there was no mistaking the luminous quality of her face, the body language, the growing huskiness in her voice. But something warned him off. He'd managed his share of intimate encounters over the years, so it wasn't that he was a stranger to such things. But something restrained him. It might have been the eternal vigilance of the AI, the sense that any playing around on the *Salvator* was necessarily a *ménage*. Or maybe it seemed improper when they were supposed to be racing to the rescue of four stranded construction workers. Whatever it was, it seemed too soon. Laid her at the first opportunity. What would that say about him? And yet he wondered why he was hesitating. Why on Earth did he care about the proprieties?

Sex with Valentina would mean more than a simple romp with one of the groupies who often sought him out. It would not be a quick roll in the hay, then back out into the workaday world. Even if there was a workaday world beyond the hatches. But there was more than that. Take Valentina into his bed, and he knew he would never again be free. It might already be too late. He found himself thinking of her at odd hours, wondering what she might be doing at any given moment, wondering how she would react if he admitted to being entranced by her.

Hutch had told him once that captains were prohibited by regulation from improper relations with passengers. On consideration, it now seemed a wise, if unrealistic, restriction. So he held back.

They talked politics, books, and vids they'd both liked. (MacAllister didn't like many.) They speculated on the moonriders, circled back to Amy's dream, wondered whether anything intelligible would ever be learned at Origins. MacAllister mentioned how good she looked, and she observed that Mac had a lot of *savoir faire* for a reporter.

Eventually it simply became too much. Probably she'd intended it from the beginning. Or maybe he had. However that might have been, she got too close, or *he* did, it was impossible later to remember which, and suddenly, her lips were pressed against his, and he was helping her out of her blouse. No buttons anywhere. Just sort of pull in the right places and clothes fell away. "We shouldn't be doing this," she whispered.

Mac, for once, was at a loss for words.

She tugged at his belt, but stopped and asked him to wait a minute. She strode topless across the deck and onto the bridge. The lights dimmed and went out, leaving only a few glowing strips. She became a shadowy figure moving toward him, shedding clothes as she came.

"Why didn't you just tell Bill to do that?" he asked.

"Bill's in sleep mode," she said.

He hadn't even known there *was* a sleep mode.

The sofa wasn't lush, but neither were the beds in their compartments. The sofa had the advantage of providing more space. He was thinking how the *Salvator* was not built for romance, but she certainly was. There was a last fleeting notion that he should not let this go any further. Then his good sense kicked in.

LIBRARY ARCHIVE

I don't know whether I have ever felt quite the same degree of exhilaration as on that night, racing across the stars, knowing the whole time the asteroid was bearing down on that group of unfortunates stranded at the Galactic. It was one of those occasions when one ceases to be simply a reporter, and becomes instead a participant.

—The Notebooks of Gregory MacAllister

chapter 31

> The sheer size of the Capella asteroid, and the thought of the kind of technology it must have taken to redirect it and aim it at the Galactic, to arrange that it arrive at the precise time and place to intercept the hotel, carries one overwhelming message: The best way for the human race to handle the moonriders would be to hide under the table.
>
> —Gregory MacAllister, *Journals*

He came out of a deep sleep to find her coming back off the bridge, wrapped in a sheet. "Anything wrong?" he asked.

"Just waking Bill." She stopped for a moment, pretending innocence, to let him get a better look.

" 'Naked Singularity,' " said MacAllister.

"Mac, you're shameless."

"Or maybe 'Unclad at Capella.' "

"Are you trying out titles?"

"How'd you guess?"

"For a *National* story? Or your autobiography?" She pulled the sheet tighter, revealing more. "How about 'Orgy at Ophiuchi'?"

More than ever, he felt the restrictions imposed by the bulkheads. He would have liked to take her out somewhere, to a park, or a restaurant, or simply for a walk downtown. He wanted to show her off.

"Last night was very nice, Mac," she said. "I think you do not believe all the things you say."

"What do I say?"

"That there's a legitimate point of view for celibacy."

"I never said that."

"You imply it."

"That's because families are such a hassle."

"Do you have any? Children?"

"No."

"Then what do you know about it?"

"Bizet never went to a bullfight."

"That sounds like a myth. How could anybody possibly know whether he did or not?"

"All you have to do is listen to people who've been through the experience. Do *you* have any kids?"

"No."

"Okay. Most people who've been parents will tell you that when they first started thinking about marriage they would have been smart to head for a mountaintop and go into philosophy."

"Mac," she said, "you deliver these generalizations, and they are both funny and wicked. But we both know life is much more complicated. The country is fortunate to have you. Although I would ask where you'd be if your father had behaved as you suggest?"

MacAllister showered and dressed. Then she showed him pictures of the hotel. Some walls and panels were in place, and even a few viewports, but the Galactic was still, for the most part, no more than a large gridwork. When completed, it would have resembled the Crystal Palace.

Watching the images seemed to have a depressing effect on Valya. "You okay?" he asked.

"I'm fine."

"Something's wrong."

She didn't reply.

"The hotel?"

"No," she said. "It's okay."

"They can build a new hotel, Valya. And everybody's getting out."

"Damn it, Mac, I don't care about the hotel."

Oh. "We're talking about last night."

She shrugged.

"There's no commitment," he said.

"I know."

"Then what?"

He could see her debating whether to answer. "Call it sleeping with the enemy."

"I'm not an enemy," he said.

She nodded. "I know, Mac. I know."

CAPELLA FEATURES FOUR suns. Two were immediately visible when they arrived in-system. They were yellow-white class Gs, one slightly brighter than the other. *"These two,"* said Bill, *"are both much larger than Sol. Each has a diameter of about fourteen million kilometers."*

MacAllister tried to recall the size of the sun.

"Ten times greater," said Bill, apparently reading his mind. *"And much brighter. Capella A is eighty times as luminous. B is about fifty times brighter."*

"That sounds as if they burn a lot of fuel," he said.

"That is correct. Each of these two has completed its hydrogen-burning phase." He paused. *"They're dying giants, Mac."*

"Bill," Valya said, "open a channel to the shuttle." The AI complied, and she sent a message to Karim, informing him of their position and arrival time. Half hour or so after the asteroid was going to arrive.

Ten minutes later they had a response. *"We're fine,"* Karim said. *"We're well clear of the asteroid."*

"Okay, sit tight. We'll be by to pick you up." She switched back to the AI. "Bill, give me some vectors and fuel consumption."

AS THEY ACCELERATED toward the shuttle, MacAllister asked about the other two suns.

Two dim red stars showed up on the navigation screen. *"They're both class Ms, Mac. Red stars. Quite dim, as you can see. They're a double star themselves, but they're almost a light-year away."*

The yellow suns seemed quite close to each other.

"They are," said Bill. *"They're only one hundred million kilometers apart. Roughly the distance from Venus to the sun."*

"It's one of the reasons they wanted to build the hotel here," Valya said. "It's a spectacular sky."

Bill replaced the red stars with a close-up image of a blue world. *"You don't usually get planets orbiting a close binary,"* he said. *"Usually, they're ejected. If they survive, they will normally orbit one star or the other. When the stars are as close together as these are, that's not going to happen, and you just don't find planets. Capella is the exception. Here we have not one world, but* two, *orbiting the gravitational center between the two suns. The hotel is located at Alpha Capella II."*

"As I understand it," said MacAllister, "Alpha II is not a living world. Right?"

"That's right. But it's supposed to have great skiing. And in fact they claim there's a lot to see. Towering mountain ranges, long island chains, rugged coasts."

"Does it have a breathable atmosphere?"

"Unfortunately not. I think I read somewhere it's loaded with methane."

"I don't know," said MacAllister. "I'd expect people planning to vacation on another world would want dinosaurs. And I know they'd prefer oxygen."

She laughed. "Oxygen, maybe. But lizards? I've seen some big ones up close. You can have them."

Bill was putting groundside images on screen. Canyons. Mountain peaks. River valleys. Waterfalls.

MacAllister frowned. "I wasn't talking about *me*. But most people like animals."

She was watching the display. Never took her eyes from it. "It's a lovely world, Mac. Slightly larger than Earth. And there's a magnificent river system that puts the Mississippi to shame. It's perfect for rafting."

"That sounds like Eric. You might consider a career in public relations."

"No, thanks," she said. "I've got what I want. I'm going to stay out here until they come to get me."

KARIM CALLED. *"WE left an imager at the hotel to watch the thing come in. Would you like us to relay the visuals to you?"*

"Please," said Valya.

The asteroid looked more like a *planet* than a rock. Otherwise, it was run-of-the-mill: misshapen, scarred, cratered, ridges here, smooth once-molten rock there. It was just visible over the rim of the world. It might have been coming off the ocean. "How big is it again?" asked MacAllister.

"The diameter's roughly six hundred kilometers at its widest point." She showed him. She put up an image of the *Surveyor* museum. The asteroid and the *Surveyor* appeared about the same size. She moved the museum closer to the asteroid. His perspective changed and he watched it dwindle. Shrink to the size of an insect. And ultimately vanish. "It won't collide with the hotel," she said. "It'll be more like a swat."

"And it won't hit the planet?"

"No. It'll skim past, right at the top of the atmosphere. It'll obliterate the hotel and go back out."

"Perfect shot," said MacAllister. "I wonder if these guys play pool."

The asteroid was turning slowly. You had to stay with it a few minutes to see the movement. As he watched, a chain of craters came over the horizon.

Below, on the planetary surface, storms drifted through the atmosphere. And towers of cumulus. There was snow at the caps and on some of the mountaintops. But there was no green. Alpha II had a sandstone appearance. It was a beautiful woman with no soft lines.

Valya switched to a view of the Galactic. "That's taken from the shuttle," Valya said.

The hotel glittered in the light from the two suns, a sprawling, mostly open framework. "How long have they been working out here?" he asked.

"I think about nine months."

"Doesn't look as if they got very far."

"Don't know," she said. "I'm not up on construction projects."

From the perspective of the imager at the hotel, the asteroid was rising, climbing higher above the curve of the world. Getting bigger. Overwhelming the sky.

Bill appeared in his captain's uniform. *"One minute to impact,"* he said. *"It's closing at thirteen kilometers per second."*

It blocked off the sun.

MacAllister held his breath.

"Twenty seconds," said Bill.

Somebody on the shuttle let go with a string of profanity.

The perspective changed. He was looking at a moonscape, and it was as if they were in a plunging ship. Going down.

Then the screen blanked.

THEY PICKED UP Karim and his three companions without incident. MacAllister accepted thanks from everyone for the rescue, even though he'd just been along for the ride. Valya broke out more wine, and they converted the return flight into a celebration. They talked about how big the asteroid had been, and how good it was to get on board the *Salvator*. How nice to be able to snuggle inside a set of bulkheads again.

MacAllister had never before considered the human propensity to put up walls everywhere. He'd always thought of it as a need for privacy from other people. But he decided that even more important, walls were a way of setting aside a portion of space from the rest of creation, of blocking out the vastness that, seen too vividly, wounds the soul.

It was exactly the kind of line that, uttered by someone else, he would have ridiculed. What the hell did it mean?

As much as he'd enjoyed having Valya to himself, something had changed, and MacAllister was grateful for fresh company.

"I'll tell you," Karim said, "we were never really sure we were out of the thing's path. I kept thinking suppose the numbers were wrong. Or the sensors had screwed up? That son of a bitch kept getting bigger. We were supposed to be clear, but you couldn't tell that sitting out there watching it. And there was a lot of debris running with it."

Two of the other three were women. "Closed my eyes," one of them said. "I thought we were dead."

Later, as they enjoyed a rowdy meal, Karim commented that management must have known what it was doing after all.

"How do you mean?" asked MacAllister.

The other male laughed and helped himself to some grapes.

"We were three or four months behind," said Karim. "They had us out here, but we were always short of resources. Never had the people to do the job right."

"The way things turned out," the guy with the grapes said, "it's just as well."

They spent much of the return voyage singing. One of their favorites was "I Been Workin' on the Platform."

LIBRARY ARCHIVE

Famed editor Gregory MacAllister helped rescue a group of construction workers stranded in the path of a giant asteroid today. MacAllister was onboard the *Salvator* when it arrived in the Capella system to snatch four people who'd escaped from a construction site in a shuttle. . . .

—*London Daily Telegraph*, Thursday, April 30

chapter 32

> Plato is correct about democracy. It is essentially mob rule. And once the mob gets an idea into its collective head, it's almost impossible to get it out, or modify it in any way. In an era of mass communication and irresponsible media, it can be a deadly characteristic.
>
> —Gregory MacAllister, "Women and Children Last"

The news from the *Salvator* and the museum was uniformly good. They'd gotten the engineers and construction workers out of the Galactic without a hitch; the *Cavalier* would arrive shortly to pick them up and bring them home; and the media were already circulating MacAllister's first-person account of the rescue. From the museum, Eric mentioned something about Amy and a bad dream, but that hardly seemed consequential. *"She'll be fine when she gets home,"* he added. *"This place gets pretty spooky at night."*

Senator Taylor, watching reports while the asteroid closed in on the hotel, told Hutch that he and Amy would not go through anything like this again. Hutch knew that would ultimately be Amy's decision, but she kept her opinion to herself.

She saw a report that Orion was filing an insurance claim for the hotel. The risk, of course, had been apportioned among a half dozen companies, and there were already rumors they would refuse to pay because the policy didn't cover acts of war.

Charlie Dryden called to ask where Asquith was. *"I can never reach him when I need him,"* he complained.

The commissioner was at a conference in Des Moines. He had a talent for being out of town when crises loomed. It was his philosophy, he claimed, that his people should be able to make decisions without him, so he frequently turned off his commlink. That would have been okay, except that he didn't back his staff if they made calls with which he didn't agree, or that didn't go well. It was one thing to take a subordinate aside and explain the preferred course of action; it was quite another to back away publicly and imply to the media that someone in the organization had acted without authority. He always claimed he named no names, and thereby protected his people, but everybody knew. Hutch had been through it a few times, had taken him to task, and had even threatened to resign. When driven to the wall, Asquith always apologized, privately, and promised it wouldn't happen again; but he seemed unable to help himself.

Dryden was seated by a window overlooking a body of water. He wore a light blue jacket and a string tie. *"I wanted to say thanks for getting our people out of the Galactic,"* he said. *"If not for the* Salvator, *I hate to think what would have happened."*

Hutch returned his smile. "It was our pleasure, Charlie. I'm glad we were in a position to help."

"I understand there were no injuries."

"They've reported everybody's okay. This time tomorrow, they should all be on their way home."

"Good." He sat back, relaxed. Over his shoulder, she could see a sailboat tacking in a brisk wind. *"On another subject, what's your sense about these moonriders?"*

"I honestly don't know what to think, Charlie. I don't know what they are, and I can't imagine what they're trying to do. It doesn't look as if the world is prepared to deal with them."

"We became complacent."

"I guess we did." Certainly, she had. A widespread assumption had developed that everything we could see in the surrounding cosmos belonged to us. And there was nobody out there to dispute any of it.

"I think we need a navy," he said.

"A battle fleet?"

"Yes."

"It would cost a fortune."

A flock of ducks or geese, something, fluttered down onto the water. *"Hutch, it's the price of security. In uncertain times."*

TWENTY MINUTES LATER, one of her staff sent over a segment of the *Blanche Hardaway Hour* that she thought might be of interest.

Blanche was a tall, fragile-looking but utterly ruthless blonde. She did a daily tabloid show, lots of scandal, lots of moralizing, lots of the cheapest sort of politics, regular attacks on the Academy as a waste of money.

She had a guest, but he was just sitting there while she went on a tirade. *"—To wait around any longer and take chances with lunatic aliens,"* she was saying. *"Congress should get on the stick and take action. We don't want to wait for the World Council to get in gear. This is not one of those things they can talk to death and pass a bill on sometime in the next century. I've been saying for years now that we cannot assume we're alone, as we have been doing. And we cannot assume that anybody we meet out there is going to be friendly. We need armed ships. Guns, Frederick. A* navy. *An armed* fleet *that will demonstrate to these creatures, whatever they are, that they better not mess with us. Now, am I right? Or have I missed something?"*

Frederick was oversized. About seventy, he had dark hair and the look of a guy who'd wandered into the wrong studio. He shifted his position and assumed what he must have thought a professorial attitude. *"No question,"* he said. *"As I see it, what we need to do . . ."*

She killed the volume. Watched the big man waggling his finger and lecturing the audience. There'd been a lot of that lately. "Marla," she said, "do a sweep for me, please. Last six hours. I'd like to see any commentaries taking the same position: The moonriders are a threat, and we need to build a fleet to deal with them."

"Very good," said Marla. *"It'll take a minute."*

"Meanwhile, you can shut down Blanche and Frederick."

The picture went off.

She got two calls on administrative issues, then Marla was back. *"Ready to go."*

First up was Red Dowding warning the viewers in his flat, matter-of-fact style that time might be running out "for the human race." Judith Henry, a regular on *The Capital Crowd*, advised that we may not have the luxury of guessing wrong. And Omar Rollinger, on *Sunrise with Omar*, commented that there will be weak-kneed people who say we shouldn't rush into anything, but it might already be too late. A dozen more shows were queued up.

There were plenty of pictures. The asteroid sweeping the hotel aside, the *Salvator* collecting survivors from the shuttle, preparations going forward to send a pair of cargo ships to turn aside the Terranova Rock. Several commentators thought the mission shouldn't be launched until an armed escort could be provided.

ASQUITH WAS BACK that afternoon, looking flustered. "Don't have time to talk," he told her.

"What's going on, Michael?"

"Another hearing."

"The appropriations committee again?"

"No."

"Who?"

He was dragging a change of clothes out of his closet. "Defense. They're trying to decide whether the moonriders are a threat. The truth is it's probably politics. People are excited, so they have to do something. They called a committee meeting with no advance warning." He disappeared into his inner sanctum, then popped right out again. "People are worried about what they're hearing."

"The media have gone berserk."

"The media always go berserk. A kid falls off a bike in Montana, they're all over it. Until something else happens. This time, though, the fears may be real."

"Michael," she said, "don't you think this is all a bit over the top?"

"Who knows?" His expression seemed frozen. "Whatever the moonriders are, they're obviously not friendly. If we get attacked, what do we fight with? We'd be helpless."

"If they have the capability to divert anything as massive as the Galactic asteroid, and aim it dead on at the hotel, we're going to be helpless no matter what."

Asquith smiled. "I can just see the Congress saying something like that to the voters."

"I'm not concerned about the voters. I'm not a politician."

"You better be concerned, Hutch. The voters pay your salary."

"That's not significant at the moment. I was trying to make a point."

"As was I. If it gets around that we can't compete with these lunatics after all the money that's been put into the program over more than sixty years, longer than that really, then when this is over, you and I will be out on the street. And deservedly so."

It was a beautiful spring day. A bit on the warm side, maybe. Bright sun in a cloudless sky. "What are you going to tell the committee, Michael?"

"I'll ask that they increase our funding so we can beef up the surveillance program we've just initiated. Track these things down. Find out what they are. What they want."

"We'll need ships. New ones."

"Right. That's what I'm going to request. And I'm going to ask for some armament. We have to confront the problem head-on." He actually looked pained. "We need to get the Council on board. If they're not willing, then the NAU should go it alone with our allies. Whatever it takes. It's what they want to hear. So they'll buy into it."

"Okay."

"We need to think about what kind of armament should be placed on Academy ships. I'll want a proposal on my desk in the morning."

"Michael, I don't know anything about weaponry."

"Ask somebody. Particle beams, lasers, and nukes. That's what we'll want. And anything else you can think of."

NEWSDESK

ATTACK IMMINENT FROM OUTER SPACE?

Amid Laughter, World Council to Debate Options

LANBERG TAKES AMERICUS

Black Hole Physics Wins for Winnipeg Native

CHILD ABDUCTIONS UP ACROSS COUNTRY

Experts Advocate Tracking Devices

CAVALIER NEARS *SURVEYOR* MUSEUM
Galactic Engineers to Start Home Tomorrow
Orion Will Rebuild
"Won't Be Scared Off by Crazies," Says CEO

SUPERLUMINALS TO DIVERT TERRANOVA ROCK
Corporate Giants Cooperate to Save First Living World
Kosmik, MicroTech, Orion, Monogram Combine Resources

HURRICANE SEASON: MORE STORMS, MORE INTENSE
Population Decline in Hurricane Alley Continues
Dakotas, Saskatchewan, Manitoba Booming

CONGRESS: TERM LIMITS WILL NOT GET OUT OF COMMITTEE

PROPOSAL TO BAN SMOKING IN HOMES WHEN CHILDREN PRESENT
Iowa Bill Promises Major Clash
What Are the Limits of Government?

TREATMENT OF LIVESTOCK BECOMES ISSUE IN WYOMING
Do Steers Have Rights?

BLACKOUT IN PHOENIX
Energy Relay Collapses
City in Dark for Six Hours

LOOKING BACK: LAST NUCLEAR PLANT CLOSED 100 YEARS AGO TODAY

HELLFIRE TRIAL TO GET NATIONAL COVERAGE
Starts Thursday

chapter 33

Truth, beaten down, may well rise again. But there's a reason it gets beaten down. Usually, we don't like it very much.

—Gregory MacAllister, "Why We All Love Sweden"

When the *Salvator* docked at Union, officials, journalists, and well-wishers were waiting. Valya and her passengers strode out of the exit tube and were greeted by shouts and applause. Amy spotted her father in the crowd. With Hutch beside him. He waved and pushed through. "Good to see you, Hon," he said, wrapping his arms around her. Everybody was taking pictures. "Glad you're home. I was worried."

"I'm fine, Dad," she said. "It was a good flight." That sounded dumb, but she didn't know what else to say.

People began tossing questions at her. There was confusion; some of them thought she'd been with Valya during the rescue at the Galactic. When they discovered she'd stayed behind in the museum, they went elsewhere.

Eventually Hutch worked her way to her side. "Hey, Champ," she said, "welcome home. You guys had quite a time out there."

She moved to embrace the girl, but Amy stiffened. Allowed it to happen but didn't respond. Hutch was too much like the woman on the bridge.

Hutch got the message and let go. "Anything wrong, Amy?"

Amy needed to talk to her alone, but that would be difficult to manage. She wondered whether the others had told her what had happened. Kid's gone funny in the head. Talking to people who aren't there. Talking to *you*, Hutch.

"I'm fine." She knew. Amy could tell.

The event morphed into a press conference. How had MacAllister felt when he saw the asteroid hit the hotel? Had he been worried the moonriders might go after *him*? Would he be likely to support—?

MacAllister cut the last question short. He'd grown quickly impatient with the questions, and pointed everybody at Valya. "Here's the young lady who did the rescue," he said. "She's the one you want to talk to." And Amy caught his whispered aside to the pilot: "Good luck."

Valya answered a few questions and quickly turned the proceedings over to Eric, who was experienced at these things. Who was nearly delirious at being the center of attention.

Was it true moonriders were detected near the museum? Had they *seen* them? (Disappointment that no one had.) "Did you at any time feel your life was in danger?"

"No," Eric said. "We kept the doors locked." He expected the comment to get a laugh. But none came. "I don't think any of us ever felt directly threatened." He looked around for confirmation, and got it from MacAllister and Valya. It wasn't what the media wanted to hear.

A short, bearded man, dressed as if he represented the underground press, asked whether they thought we should arm the ships.

"Yes," said Eric. "Absolutely." They'd seen the people trooping in from the Galactic, especially that last bunch, the ones who'd been thrown into space for several hours. "Whatever these things are, they have no regard for human life."

Jessica Dailey from the Black Cat wanted to know whether Eric spoke for everybody.

"He does for me," said Valya.

"What about you, Mr. MacAllister?"

"I guess so," MacAllister said grudgingly. He looked uncertain.

Nobody asked Amy.

* * *

THE JOURNALISTS FOLLOWED them onto the shuttle, where there were more questions and more pictures. Amy finally got her turn in the spotlight. How would it feel going back to school now that she was a national celebrity? That surprised her so thoroughly that she could only smile and ask when she'd become a celebrity.

More people were waiting in the terminal at Reagan. A beautiful chestnut-haired woman threw herself into MacAllister's arms. (Amy saw a strange look in Valya's eyes, but it passed quickly, and the pilot turned away.) One of the journalists drew her father aside, and she saw her chance. Hutch was standing only a few feet away, talking with Eric.

The conversation broke off when she approached. Hutch offered to give her a hand with her bag.

"It's okay," Amy said. "I need to talk to you." Eric discovered he had something else to do and left them.

A news team was headed their way. Hutch nodded. "I know. But this is not a good time. Call me tonight."

"Okay."

"And, Amy—?"

"Yes."

"Whatever it's about, we'll take care of it."

AMY WAS NOT close to her father, even though he always tried to do the right thing. When she performed in the school theater, he was there. He came faithfully to watch her play softball. He talked to her about homework and her future and did everything he could to replace the mother who'd abandoned them both so many years before. But he'd never learned to *listen*. Their conversations were always one-way. So when she came home from the *Surveyor* museum with a story no one would believe, she did not sit down with him and tell him what had happened.

Other than Hutch, there was no one to whom she could turn. She had a couple of indifferent boyfriends, but neither would be able to understand what she was talking about. They'd both think she'd taken something. And there was a math teacher who was reasonable and sympathetic, but who was far too rational to believe a story like hers.

She had shed whatever doubts she might have had about the reality of the experience. The image of the ultratall Hutch walking out of the darkness, issuing that deadly warning, was simply too vivid. It *had* happened.

Damn moonriders.

Why had they picked on her in the first place? They had the Academy's public information officer available, and the editor of *The National*. But the blockheads came to *her*. What was she supposed to do? Pass it on to the principal?

She rode home alone. Her father claimed important Senate business and put her in a taxi. Fifteen minutes later she was in her Georgetown town house replaying the experience over and over.

She became gradually aware of the silence, accented somehow by voices outside. And a barking dog.

She switched on the VR. Brought up *Tangle*, her favorite show. Find your way through the maze. Don't get distracted by boys, clothing displays, misnomers, false trails. But she couldn't keep her mind on it, and finally realized she might be on the news. She switched over and saw trouble in Central Africa. A serial killer loose in Oregon, imitating the murders done in *Relentless*, a popular vid from the year before. There seemed to be no end to homicidal kooks. A Senate committee was conducting hearings on whether to support the creation of an armed interstellar fleet. It would be the world's first space navy. Then, yes! There she was. Standing off to one side at Union while Eric answered questions.

Well, tonight she'd talk to Hutch and pass the whole thing over to her. She was the big hero. Let her worry about it.

ERIC WAS HAPPY to be home. And pleased with himself. During the taxi ride from Reagan, he'd also watched himself on the news shows and decided he'd looked pretty good. Self-effacing, heroic, and always ready with a punch line. The real Eric Samuels had arrived at last.

One of his neighbors, Cleo Fitzpatrick, had been walking past as he unloaded the cab. She'd smiled brightly, told him she'd missed him, said how she'd been reading about him. Cleo was a physician. She was also a knockout who had never before paid any more than minimal attention to him. "It's good to have you back, Eric," she'd said, with an inviting smile.

It was good to *be* back. Once inside, he dropped his luggage and said hello to his AI. She whispered a throaty greeting. *"It's nice to see you again, Big Boy."* He wondered what it said for his life that the thing he had most missed was his AI. He eased down into a chair, closed his eyes, and savored the moment.

He had achieved what he set out for. He'd been part of something significant. Beyond his wildest dreams. They'd confirmed the existence of the moonriders and rescued the personnel from the Galactic. Not bad for a guy whose biggest exploit until now had been winning a commendation for perfect attendance in the fifth grade.

But he couldn't get his mind off Amy.

Kids are flexible, though. She'd get over it. He was suddenly, unaccountably, tired. It was so good to be home. Lounging on a comfortable sofa again. Stretched out in a private place, with the shades drawn against the midday sun.

It was a good life.

MACALLISTER HAD SEEN the look on Valya's face when Tara Nesbitt showed up at Reagan. Tara was an occasional friend and sometimes a bit more. Perfect for inciting a little jealousy.

He directed Tilly to call Valya and felt his pulse pick up a notch when she appeared in the room. *"Hello, Mac,"* she said. She'd gotten rid of the jumpsuit and the work clothes, exchanging them for shorts and a University of Kansas pullover. The woman always looked good. Didn't matter what she wore.

"Hello, Valentina. I just wanted to be sure you'd gotten home okay."

"Yes, I'm fine, thank you." The Greek lilt in her voice was somehow more pronounced than it had been on shipboard.

They went on in that vein for a few minutes. She was seated on a sofa, crosshatched by sunlight. Her red hair glistened, and she looked genuinely pleased to see him. The chemistry was running both ways.

Not necessarily good, he thought. He had avoided emotional attachments all his life. Except once. And he'd paid a substantial price for that. "How long are you going to be home?"

"I haven't received my next assignment yet. They have more pilots than ships at the moment, so I expect I'll be unemployed for a while." She leaned back against a cushion. *"Might have to find a job over at Broadbent's."* Broadbent's was a furniture chain.

"You don't seriously think they'd cut back, do you?"

"They've already done it. Hard to see what else they could have done the way things are going. But"—she shrugged—*"there's always work for people like me."*

"I was wondering," he said, "if you'd care to have dinner with me. We promised ourselves an evening at the Seahawk."

"Wish I could, Mac. But I'm wiped out. I'm going in and collapse for the rest of the day."

"How about tomorrow?"

"I've got relatives in tomorrow. How about Thursday?"

"Sure," he said. "That sounds pretty good."

AMY CALLED PROMPTLY at seven.

"I understand something happened at the museum," said Hutch.

"Yes, ma'am. I think I talked with one of them." Amy was in her bedroom. Pictures of Academy ships hung on the walls.

"With one of the moonriders?"

"I had no way to know for sure. But something that wasn't human."

"You say you *think* this happened."

"It happened, *Hutch,"*

"You're sure."

"Yes."

"Okay. Describe it for me. Tell me everything. What you saw. What you heard. Don't leave anything out."

"All right."

"I'm going to record it."

Hutch had heard that the apparition had more or less taken her form. Now she listened intently while Amy told her story. How she'd been unable to sleep. Sitting on the bridge. How the figure wrapped in darkness had come down the passageway.

How it had been Priscilla Hutchins. But a taller version.

And its message. *Blueprint. The Origins Project.*

"We are going to destroy it."

"Did she say why?"

"No. When I asked why she just said for me to get everybody off. That they wouldn't wait forever. Or words to that effect."

"Okay. Let's go back a minute. What's 'blueprint' all about?"

"It's an old term for a building plan."

"No. I'm aware of that. I'm just wondering what it means in this context."

"I don't know. I asked her what she wanted, and she said 'blueprint.'"

"Was there anything else?"

"No. Yes. She denied they'd attacked anyone."

WHAT WAS *BLUEPRINT*?

"George." The household AI.

"Yes, Hutch."

"Do a search on 'blueprint.' I want to know—"

"Yes—?"

What *was* she looking for? "If there's any connection with unknown aerial or space phenomena?"

There were several action vids by Blueprint Entertainment that pitted various heroes against outer space monsters.

And a 250-year-old blueprint of a moonrider—they called them UFOs then—obtained originally by a married couple who claimed to have been riding all over the solar system in the vehicle.

And *Blueprint for Armageddon*, published in the twenty-first century, a book predicting an attack by aliens. It even had pictures of the creatures, but none of them looked anything like Hutch.

There was also the Madison, Wisconsin, urban legend about a *thing* running loose that left monstrous footprints and bled blue. The whole affair was supposedly hushed up by the authorities. For reasons not given.

And an oil painting, *Cosmic Blueprint*, by somebody she had never heard of, depicting two ships, one obviously alien, watching each other in the foreground of a ringed planet.

She gazed thoughtfully at the alien vessel and realized she'd missed the obvious. "George."

"Yes, Hutch."

"Let's try it again. Make it 'blueprint' and the 'Origins Project.' " She rubbed her eyes. It had been a long day, and she was tired.

"I have more than seventeen thousand hits," said the AI. *"Do you wish to narrow it down?"*

Bingo. "Yes. Eliminate all that have to do with the design of the facility itself. How many are left?"

"Four thousand three hundred seven."

"Pick one at random. Let me see what they're talking about."

"The vast majority are simply technical documents."

"Pick one."

George put up a title page: *Blueprint,* credited to two names with which she was unfamiliar, and filled with text and equations that meant nothing to her, references to hybrid tangles and monolith reversals.

She looked at a few more documents, all similar, all incomprehensible, and called Amy back. "Answer a question for me, Love."

"Yes, ma'am."

"What do you know about Origins?"

"Just what I learned on the flight. Why?"

"Were you aware of any of the initiatives they're involved in? Any of the things they're doing?"

"I know they bounce particles off one another. That's all."

"*Blueprint* appears to be the name of one of their projects." Amy bit her lip. "My question is, could you have learned about it somewhere else? Before you got to the museum?"

"No," she said. *"I never heard of it."*

"You're sure?"

"I'm positive."

SHE CALLED ERIC. "They have a *Blueprint,*" she said.

"Whoa. Who has a blueprint? What are we talking about?"

"Origins."

"Are you sure?"

"Yes."

"I wasn't aware of that. She probably saw it somewhere and remembered it."

"That was my first thought. Eric, she insists that didn't happen."

"That's very strange."

"You guys checked with the AI, right? We have no record of this visitation other than Amy's word."

"That's correct." Eric took a deep breath. Closed his eyes. *"Hutch, they have a lot of people out there. At Origins. If there's even a chance she might be right . . . "*

"Okay. We'd better look into it. I'm going to talk to the commissioner. *You* make some calls. Use your contacts. See if you can find out what Blueprint is about. And ask them when they're doing it."

"The public information office is in Paris. It's closed at this hour. I can try to track down some of the people who are involved."

"Do it. Get back to me as soon as you have something. But Eric—?"

"Yes?"

"Don't say anything to them about moonriders. Okay?"

SHE USED HER time to inform herself about the Origins facility. How many people were currently there. Whether they routinely kept a ship on station. (They didn't.) What kind of person the groundside administrator, Hans Allard, was.

Eric called back. *"I talked with Donald Gaspard,"* he said. *"He's part of the consulting team for Blueprint."*

"Okay. So what's it about?"

"How's your physics?"

"Try me."

"It has something to do with using the collider to make small black holes."

"Black holes?"

"Small ones. Micros. Apparently they've been doing it all along. For years, according to Gaspard. Blueprint will be an extension of the effort. But he says there's no danger to the facility. The holes dissipate quickly. Almost right away. I think he said within microseconds."

"Why are they doing it? What's the point?"

"It helps them figure out the parameters of the other dimensions. He said there are eight or nine of them. Other dimensions."

"Nine," she said.

"The point is that they're trying to push back past the Big Bang. To find out how it happened. What's on the other side. And how we arrived at the settings for our *universe."*

"That's why they call it Blueprint."

"I guess. I'm not sure what it means."

"But they haven't started it yet?"

"Not Blueprint, no."

"When are they going to begin?"

"Gaspard didn't know. He's not sure they've set a date yet."

"Okay, thanks, Eric. I'll take it from here."

GASPARD WAS IN New York. She jotted down his code and asked George to connect with him.

He was a physicist acting as liaison between Manhattan Labs and a consortium based in Marseilles. She was surprised by his appearance. He looked not much older than a high school kid. He had a bright smile and a lot of energy. Cinnamon-colored hair, matching eyes, and a long nose. She immediately thought of a young Sherlock Holmes. But he dispelled that quickly with a decided French accent. *"Yes,"* he said, after she'd introduced herself, *"I spoke with your Mr. Samuels."*

"We're fascinated by what you're doing, Professor." It seemed an odd title for one so young. "Do you really expect to be able to penetrate beyond the Big Bang?"

He lit up. His favorite subject. *"Yes,"* he said. *"There is no doubt."*

"Can you explain it to me? Tell me what you plan to do?"

It would be his pleasure, *madame.* He launched into a description of particles, equations, evaporating holes, collider capabilities. She tried to follow but quickly got lost. It didn't matter. She asked innocuous questions: How long do you think it will take to get that result? How much energy is employed? And, eventually, one that intrigued her: "What kind of results do you expect? What will you find?"

"That's impossible to answer, Madame *Hutchins. We are only at the beginning of transuniversal physics. At the moment, we know almost nothing."*

She wondered why anyone would want to destroy the effort. It seemed harmless enough. "Do you foresee the possibility that we will acquire weapons capabilities from this?"

"Weapons?" He let her see the question was absurd. *"I can't imagine how. But who knows? Why do you ask?"*

"Idle curiosity, Professor. I'm impressed that you can manipulate black holes. I would have thought that would entail a level of risk."

"At no time," he said. *"It was never an issue. The black holes we have always worked with. They are quite small. Microscopic. They are by nature unstable."* He shrugged and smiled. Voilà.

"You told Eric you weren't sure when they would run Blueprint?"

"That is correct. They haven't set a date yet, but I suspect it's imminent. Most of their support personnel left last week."

"You're not going?"

"Oh, yes. I'm leaving Tuesday. But I'll be there purely as an observer."

"I see."

"If everything goes according to plan, it will be an historic occasion."

"That makes it sound as if they're going to be working with a more massive hole."

"Ah," he said, *"holes do not have mass. But for practical purposes, that's true. We need more energy than we've been able to produce previously. Blueprint will be bigger than anything we've done before. That is the advantage of having the hypercollider. And this is only the beginning. We are entering a whole new era,* madame. *I would very much like to be here when the project is finished."*

"You're referring to the construction of Origins."

"Yes. When it is finally done, I think everything will lie open to us."

"Is the larger hole safe?"

"Oh, yes. There's no question about that. We wouldn't do it if it wasn't safe."

"It'll dissipate on its own."

"Absolutely."

"You look doubtful, Professor." Actually, he looked supremely confident.

Gaspard waggled his head back and forth. Grinned. *"Well, of course, when you're dealing with a completely new area of research, you can never be one hundred percent certain. Of anything."*

"What could go wrong?"

"Nothing, really."

She smiled at him. Come on, Gaspard, we're all friends here. "Worst-case scenario."

He considered it. *"There's a remote chance, extremely remote, the experiment could cause a tear."*

"In—?"

"The time-space fabric. But the chance of that happening is so slight that it is essentially zero."

"If that *did* occur, Professor, a tear in the time-space fabric, what would be the result?"

He looked uncomfortable. Tried to wave it away. *"It would disrupt things."*

"What things?"

"Pretty much everything."

"Are we talking about losing the facility?"

"Well, yes. Along with—"

"Everything else."

"Yes. But it's not going to happen."

"It would proceed how? Instantaneous lights out for all of us?"

"Oh, no. It would be limited to cee."

"Light speed."

"Yes."

"We're talking about the possibility of destroying, what, the entire cosmos?"

"I keep trying to explain, that is not really a consideration—"

"Maybe it should be."

THE TRUTH WAS, Hutch didn't *want* to believe Amy's experience had actually happened. Not only because the prospect of a shoot-out with a species that appeared to have advanced technology was not a happy thought, but also because the whole idea of an apparition in a lonely museum just begged to be written off as someone's imagination.

She had to decide whether she believed the story or not. If she did, she was going to need the commissioner's support. There could be no cautious statements with him, no observation that we have reason to believe. Either it was so, or it wasn't.

She found him in a downtown restaurant. He had company and wasn't happy about being disturbed. *"Yes, Hutch,"* he said wearily. *"What is it?"* She could hear the murmur of conversation in the background and the occasional clink of dishes or silverware.

"Sorry to bother you, Michael. I thought you should know what's happening." They were audio only, but there was no mistaking the resignation in his voice. "There was a direct encounter, a conversation, with the moonriders."

"We talked to them?" His voice became simultaneously hushed and high-pitched. *"Wait a minute."* She heard his chair scrape the floor. He

assured someone he'd be right back. Then: *"We talked to them by radio? Are you sure?"*

"Not radio. At the museum."

"They stopped by the museum?"

"Yes. In a manner of speaking."

"Hutch, what are you talking about?"

She described the incident, holding back only that the moonrider had resembled her. "If she's right, they're all in danger out there."

"Amy?" He sounded despondent.

"Yes."

"Well, that's just great. Does the senator know?"

"I don't think so."

"I'll have to tell him." He sounded like a man in pain. *"Why on Earth are they doing these things?"*

She hated to mention her suspicions about Blueprint. He'd want to dismiss it. And might use it to dismiss everything. But it would come out eventually. So she told him everything. To her surprise, he listened quietly. When she had finished, she could hear him breathing. Then: *"God help us. You really think there's something to it?"*

"Yes."

"All right. Let me talk to Taylor. Then—"

"Michael, don't say anything to him until tomorrow. Give me a chance to get back to Amy. Warn her, so she can tell him herself."

"You say they're going to run this Blueprint soon?"

"It sounds as if they'll do it within a week or two."

These things don't happen. *"It's a kid with an overactive imagination,"* he said. *"It has to be."*

"She told the others about Blueprint right after it happened. It's too much of a coincidence, Michael. How much clout do we have with the Europeans?"

"Not much. Look, even if I pass this along, I can't swear to it. Nobody's going to believe it." He was talking to himself under his breath. *"Okay. I'll head home. Keep a channel open. We'll talk to Allard from there."*

We?

SHE ALERTED AMY, who got annoyed. *"I wish he wouldn't involve my father."*

"We don't really have a choice."

She was silent for a time. *"Okay, I'll tell him."*

"Something else you should be aware of. We'll try to keep your name out of it, but I doubt we'll be able to. You'll probably have to deal with the media again. This time they might be a bit more aggressive."

ASQUITH WAS IN a dinner jacket when he appeared in Hutch's home office. He was also in a foul mood. Maybe it didn't help that it was raining, and he looked wet. *"Why didn't you tell me about this when it first happened?"* he demanded.

"I didn't think there was anything to the story. That's beside the point now. We need to call the Europeans. Warn them."

He dropped into a chair, looked away, played with his cuffs. *"How?"* he said. *"How do I tell them to evacuate two hundred people, but the only evidence we have is a kid's dream? How are we going to look?"*

"You'll also want to tell them to cancel Blueprint."

"Hutch, this is crazy. My career is on the line here. So is yours."

"There's a lot more on the line than our careers, Michael."

"That's easy to say. You know, this probably is nothing more than the kid's imagination."

Hutch was tired. It had been a horribly long day. "Let's grant that. So we give them a warning, nothing happens, and you and I look dumb. But suppose it's the other way round and we sit on this and two hundred people die?"

"I know. It's not an easy call."

Don't say what you're thinking, Babe. "We have no choice, Michael. If you want, you can disappear, and I'll make the call. If it goes wrong, you can deny all knowledge."

"No." He climbed gallantly out of his chair. Squared his shoulders. *"It's my job."* It was right out of a vid. You go ahead, get clear, I'll take the heat on this one. He told the AI to get Dr. Allard. Then he turned back to Hutch. *"Make yourself comfortable. This might take a while."*

It took only seconds. Allard's official title was Director of the European Deep Space Commission. Hutch had met him at a formal dinner several years earlier, but had never really had a chance to talk with him. It was four or five A.M. in Paris, but he nevertheless seemed to be in his office. *"Hello, Michael,"* he said cheerfully. *"To what do I owe the pleasure?"*

Hutch was safely out of Allard's view, apparently there for the sole purpose of lending moral support.

Asquith led off by describing the *Salvator*'s visit to the Origins Project. Marvelous concept, and all that. Very good.

"Thank you." A modest bow. *"But I know you didn't call me at this hour to extol the virtues of the initiative."* Allard was in his sixties, with sharp features softened by a sense of absolute calm. This was not a guy who got excited. He had intelligent eyes, a wide brow, a goatee. *"Isn't the* Salvator *the same ship that performed the rescue at the Galactic?"*

The commissioner nodded, yes, and took his opening. *"Hans, your organization is involved with a project called Blueprint."*

"That is so. We'll be running it in a few days."

"We had a curious experience while our people were at the Surveyor *museum. We think we may have made contact with aliens."*

Allard's eyes widened slightly. *"Aliens?"*

"Yes. We're pretty sure."

Hutch shook her head no. You have to be absolute about this. It happened. We don't *think* it did. But he waved her off.

"If I may ask, in what way was this contact made?"

"The details aren't important, Hans—"

"The details aren't important? How can you say that, Michael?"

Asquith pressed ahead. *"The aliens are concerned about Blueprint. They've indicated they are going to destroy Origins."*

"My God, Michael. That's the wildest story I've ever heard."

"Nevertheless, it's so." He kept his voice firm, and she was proud of him.

"How did it happen?"

"It happened at the museum . . . " He described the visitation. Mentioned the warning that moonriders were in the area. That they'd specifically mentioned Blueprint. That Amy'd had no idea what Blueprint was.

Allard resisted for a while. Rolled his eyes. Clamped jaw muscles. *"When?"* he said. *"When are they going to do this?"*

The two men stared at each other. *"We don't know when. But it seems logical they will not permit you to initiate the experiment."*

"So they are going to destroy the project within the next week or so."

"Yes."

"What did these aliens look like? Did they have faces?"

"There was only one of them. She looked like a young woman."

"And this young woman said they are going to destroy Origins? No question about it?"

"Yes."

"I take it no one else witnessed any of this?"

"No."

"Is there any independent evidence it happened?"

"None other than what I've mentioned."

"Michael, you're aware Blueprint is not exactly a secret. It's been in the media. This person might easily have seen it and forgotten about it. And you've nothing else?"

"Not at the moment, no."

"Very good. Thank you for warning me. I shall certainly take it under advisement."

When he was gone, Asquith sat looking dejected. *"I told you."*

"Maybe," said Hutch, "we can get him the evidence he wants."

"You're suggesting we send a ship out there ourselves to, what, look for rocks?"

"Yes. That's exactly what we need to do."

"Hutch, I really hate all this."

"Doesn't matter. We can't just stand by and hope we've misread things."

"Do we have a ship?"

"Not really. The *Salvator* is scheduled for the Moscow Affiliates Group."

"Okay." He shrugged. What the hell. *"Cancel them."*

"This'll be the second time, Michael. They won't be happy."

"Then don't. Let it go."

"I'll make the calls."

"Do it. And, Hutch? Let's try to keep a lid on this, okay?"

SHE CALLED VALYA at home and explained.

"You need a volunteer?"

"Yes. You're the obvious person for the assignment."

"You want me to go to Origins and do a sweep and make sure there are no incoming."

"Yes."

She was in a blue robe, sipping a drink. *"Okay."*

"I don't like asking you to go out again so soon. I could get somebody else."

"No. I'll do it. It's just that it seems like a waste of effort."

"You don't believe Amy's story?"

She was seated behind a coffee table, on which a book lay open. *"No,"* she said. *"Not really. I think she got hysterical. But what do I know? I wasn't there. I'm pretty sure Eric believes her."*

"What about Mac?"

"Mac didn't want to talk about it. I think he was afraid of hurting the kid's feelings. Which tells me the answer to your question." She put the glass down and leaned back. *"When do I leave?"*

"Can you be ready to go by Thursday?"

"You're giving me a day off?"

"Maintenance needs time with the ship."

"Okay. I'll be there."

"One other thing, Valya. I'm trying to raid Union's supply of air tanks. I'm going to put as many of them on board as I can get my hands on."

"Why?"

"Worst-case scenario. In case there's a rock inbound, and it's too close to mount a rescue. You won't have enough to save everybody, but you'll be able to get a few."

"Hutch, aren't you overreacting a little bit?"

"Sure. And I won't mind listening to the jokes if they're not needed."

SCIENCE IN THE NEWS

The Blueprint experiment holds out hope that we may for the first time be able to start piecing together the events that led to the Big Bang. Until the construction of the Origins Project, scientists had been unable to accelerate sufficiently massive particles to achieve the desired results. Now, however, we can create black holes of an adequate size to produce, as they dissipate, sufficient levels of energy to reveal the character of the dimensions that our senses do not perceive, but which account for quantum action. In plain English, we may finally break through the ultimate singularity and discover how it all happened.

—Tuesday, May 5

VATICAN ISSUES STATEMENT REAFFIRMING
REALITY OF HELL
Pope: "Forewarned Is Forearmed."
—*Los Angeles Times,* May 5

chapter 34

> People tend to think well of their fellow humans. We see them as, for the most part, generous, noble, brave. We admire their tenacity in desperate times, their willingness to sacrifice themselves for the common good, their kindness to those in need. These perceptions generally result from another human trait: our failure to pay attention.
>
> —Gregory MacAllister, "Down the Slippery Slope"

Wednesday was MacAllister's first full day home. He planned to do little except lie around. He'd held a brief morning conference with Wolfie and left him to get the current issue of *The National* up and running. There were several calls requesting interviews and asking him to make guest appearances. He accepted a few, agreed to do the interviews that evening, and was about to climb onto his sofa when Tilly announced a call from Jason Glock.

He'd forgotten about the Beemer trial.

"Starts tomorrow," said Glock. He was extremely tall, a head higher than MacAllister, who checked in at over six feet. Blond hair, impeccably dressed, eyes that looked right through you.

"How do we stand, Jason?"

Glock always gave the impression everything was under control.

"I'm not optimistic," he said. *"The issue clearly flies in the face of the First Amendment. People have a right to tell kids whatever they want about religion."*

"Do they have a right to push human sacrifice?"

"Of course not, Mac. But this isn't human sacrifice. It's just a church school."

"I'm not sure the effect isn't similar."

"Whatever, we'll never persuade a judge."

"What are we claiming? Temporary insanity?"

"We're going to argue that the damage done to Henry's psyche was so severe that when he encountered the preacher he lost his judgment."

"Why not insanity?"

"The judge wouldn't buy it, take my word. I've done the research. But he is open to the argument that a justifiable anger drove our client to take matters into his own hands. He'll still be guilty, but I think we can get clear with a minimum penalty. Probably a fine."

"Do that, and the church schools will continue to poison kids' minds."

"Mac, my responsibility is to take care of my client. Not put the churches out of business."

"What actually happened, Jason? How'd the assault take place?"

Glock was seated behind a table littered with papers. *"Henry was in the store. He was waiting in line to pay for several novels, one of which was* Connecticut Yankee. *The Reverend Pullman came in. Beemer saw him and, after a few moments, left the line and followed the preacher to the back. There, in the self-help section, they engaged in a loud dispute that rapidly devolved into pushing and shoving. When Pullman tried to walk away, Henry took one of the books, put the others down, and went after him. The preacher heard him coming and turned just in time to get whacked with the Mark Twain."* He couldn't restrain a laugh.

"Fortunately, there were no serious injuries. The store manager and his security officer pulled Henry away from Pullman. Pullman was visibly bruised, but he declined medical assistance. Police arrived and arrested Henry. As they dragged him out of the store he was screaming that Pullman had ruined his life.

"The guy will never be sure," said Glock, *"that he's not going to hell."*

"What kind of person is he?" asked MacAllister. "I mean, is he violating the Commandments on a regular basis?"

The lawyer smiled. *"Not as far as I can tell. Probably no more than the rest of us. But he's lost the conviction that the Bible is literally true. And Pullman made it pretty clear during the classes what the penalty was for that."*

The trial would start at nine. A seat had been reserved for MacAllister.

HE DECIDED HE'D skip the trial, at least on the first day. If he went, he wouldn't get back in time to have dinner with Valya.

He switched on the news. The Black Cat was running a clip of Charlie Dryden, who was saying that, by God, Orion Tours wasn't going to be scared off. *"You can bet there'll be another Galactic. We've decided, though, that Capella may not have been the best place for it."*

"It's going to be somewhere else?" asked the interviewer.

"We were always divided about the site. There was a lot to recommend Capella, but we've come to feel that people would prefer a world where they can see some animals. So we're going to build at Terranova."

That fitted exactly with MacAllister's notion. He personally preferred a quiet world. But he'd always known most people would want animals. Something they could throw bread crumbs to.

So they would build another Galactic. Something stirred in his memory. The comments of Karim and the others after the *Salvator* had rescued them. *Three or four months behind.*

Never had the people to do the job right.

The way things turned out, it was just as well.

MacAllister didn't think of himself as cynical. *Realistic* was closer to an accurate description. It was remarkable, though, a tribute to his character, that he *wasn't* a cynic. As a working journalist, he'd seen constant abuse of power and authority, too much greed, too much hypocrisy. The current surge of interest in building an armed fleet, in expanding the interstellar presence, would be of enormous benefit to Orion, which owned and operated three of the six deep-space stations. Other giants would benefit, as well. Monogram would get prime contracts for building warships. Half a dozen companies would profit from designing weapons systems. Much of the software would be created and installed by MicroTech. And then there were outfits like Kosmik, that had been forced out of the terraforming business when the desire to colonize never really materialized. Kosmik would love an opportunity to help establish naval bases around the Orion Arm.

Trillions would be involved if the World Council took the moonrider threat seriously.

Trillions.

The sun was a red splotch in his curtains.

He called Hutch and got right through.

"On the run, Mac," she told him. *"What can I do for you?"*

"Got a question. From what I've heard, the Galactic asteroid was too big to have been diverted and aimed at the hotel by anything we have. Is that correct?"

"Yes."

"You're sure?"

She looked at him suspiciously. *"Do you know something I don't?"*

"No, not really. I just wanted to know whether it would have been possible for, say, a couple of cargo ships to redirect that thing?"

"No."

"No chance?"

"No more than you'd have of pushing the state building off its foundation. You could maybe nudge it in one direction or another if you installed a bunch of thrusters. But to manage a pinpoint strike. Without leaving a trace? No." She waved it away. *"It's not possible. With no technology we can imagine."*

"Okay," he said. "Thanks."

"By the way, Mac, we'd like to have you over for dinner. Are you free tomorrow?"

Hutch would say yes if he asked to bring Valya, but it might put her in a spot. Bosses and subordinates and all that. That was another problem with relationships. They complicated everything. "Have to pass, Hutch. I've got commitments. Maybe next week sometime?"

HE CALLED WOLFIE. "Did you ever hear any stories about construction of the Galactic running behind schedule?"

"The hotel?"

"Yes."

Wolfie was in his apartment. Someone else was there, out of view. A woman, undoubtedly. Wolfie mixed women and alcohol with enthusiasm. But he was a good journalist. *"Not that I can recall,"* he said. *"Want me to look into it?"*

"Yeah. Don't make a project of it. But try to find out if there's anything to it. And if so, why?"

He disconnected, poured himself a glass of brandy, went back to the sofa, and slept until Tilly woke him. *"Valya is on the circuit, sir."* His breathing changed again. Maybe her relatives had gone home early.

The moment she reappeared, though, he knew that wasn't it. *"Mac,"* she said, *"I have to bail on the dinner tomorrow night. Sorry."*

"Me, too," he said. "Anything wrong?"

"No. I'm fine. I'm going to be gone for a while. They're sending me out again."

"Already?"

"Looks like."

"When?"

"Tomorrow morning."

"On the *Salvator*? I mean, you've got an assignment?"

"Yes."

"It's short notice, isn't it? Where are you headed?"

"Can you keep a secret?"

"Are you serious?"

"I mean it, Mac."

"Sure."

"They're sending me hunting for asteroids."

"You want me to talk to Hutch? I can probably get it canceled."

"No. It's my job."

Damn. "Okay." He sighed. "Are we talking about Origins?"

"Yes."

"They're taking Amy seriously."

"Yes."

"The Europeans have their own resources. Why don't *they* send somebody?"

"I guess they don't believe the story. Hutch was pretty vague about it. I suspect she's not sure how to proceed. They probably don't want to push too hard because it's so crazy."

"They have anything more to go on than Amy's dream?"

"What more could they have? I think it's a fool's run, but Hutch asked, and I didn't see how I could say no."

"I guess not."

"You want to come?"

It was tempting. But it would mean another week or two in that tin can. He had a lot of work to do. And there was the trial. "I have to pass, Valya. Is anyone going with you?"

"No. But that's not the issue."

"I understand. And I appreciate the offer. I'm just not able to manage it right now."

"Okay."

"See you when you get back?"

"Absolutely. Talk to you, Mac."

DECIDING THAT AMY'S dream might have some substance in reality had unsettled Eric. He didn't want to spend time alone in his modest two-story home outside Falls Church. The commissioner had left a message directing him to attend a staff meeting at the Academy that afternoon. A few weeks ago he'd have been right there. But it was a nice day, and he'd never been to a staff meeting at which anything was accomplished. So he decided to pass. He'd come up with a story later. Instead, he changed and went out for a stroll. Until about two years ago he had jogged regularly, but his knees had stiffened. Now he walked instead. He usually maintained a brisk pace, but today he decided he'd take his time.

He always had an audio book with him. On this occasion, he was starting *Command and Control*, an analysis of military and political leadership during the last sixty years. The book led off with the economic competition that had developed between Canada and the United States during the last century, and how it had led ultimately to their union. He was listening to an account of the cod wars when his link vibrated. It was Hutch.

He stopped on the edge of a grassy field and thought about letting the AI pick up, but Hutch wouldn't give him away. "Yes, ma'am?"

"Eric, we're sending Valya back to Origins to take a look around. Something about the mission will probably leak. Which means you may hear from the media later today or tonight."

"Okay."

"Officially, it's a routine flight. After the incidents at Terranova and Capella, we're just being cautious. Okay? It's no big deal."

"Unofficially, you think she's going to find another rock?"

"Maybe two of them. For all we know, maybe the moonriders are thinking of hitting both ends of the accelerator."

"Who's going with her?"

"Nobody. She'll be fine."

"And if she sees an incoming?"

"Then we can sound the alarm."

"When's she leaving?"

"Tomorrow morning."

"You know, she doesn't believe it's going to happen. Last time I talked to her, she thought Amy had imagined everything."

"That hasn't changed. She thinks I'm pushing the panic button."

"Okay."

"It doesn't make any difference. She'll do the job."

Eric hesitated. Destiny was waiting.

"Did you have something else?"

Valya was going to go out there, spot a pair of incoming asteroids, give the alarm, and save one or two hundred lives. "Yes. I'd like to go along."

ORIGINS WAS TWENTY-FOUR light-years away. Fifty-five hours flight time to get into the area, plus whatever it would take to get to the facility.

It was time for Hutch to decide whether she was willing to go the whole route with Amy. There was no safe way to play it.

She called Operations and got Peter. "We may want to get some resources over to Origins in a hurry. Do we have anything at all available if the need arises?"

"Nothing close by."

"What about the *Rehling*?" It would be carrying two VIPs home from Nok. But it would be within range of Origins. It could only accommodate eight or nine people, but it would be something.

"It hasn't left Nok yet."

She stared at Peter's image. He was annoyed, trying not to show it. He thinks I'm going off the deep end, too. "Tell them to head out now. I want them to get to Origins as quickly as they can."

"You're sure about this? They're supposed to bring Autry and Cullen home. Those guys will not be happy."

"Do it anyhow. We have anything else?"

"Nothing closer than a couple weeks."

"Okay. Take care of it, Peter. And let me know what the TOA looks like."

"Will do."

"Something else. I'm going to want a summary of everything that's going to be at Union during the next twenty-four hours. I don't suppose one of the *Stars* is in port?"

"Negative. They wouldn't send one of those anyhow. Wouldn't matter what sort of emergency was going on."

"Sure they would. It all depends how you ask."

He laughed. *"Okay. You'll have the summary in a few minutes."*

SHE CALLED ASQUITH. "Michael, I'm diverting the *Rehling*. Sending it to Origins."

"What?" He looked baffled. *"Why? Haven't you already sent the* Salvator *out there? Isn't that enough?"*

"It's a precaution. If there's an event at Origins, we wouldn't be in a position to do much for them."

"For God's sake, Priscilla, it's none of our business. Origins isn't our operation. Let Allard worry about it. We've warned him. We're covered."

"It's done, Michael."

"Who's on it? Anybody who's going to give us trouble?"

"Cullen and Autry."

"That's just great. They'll scream to high heaven."

"Michael, if an attack happens, we don't want to be in a position where we know we might have done something about it but just sat here."

"Have it your own way, Priscilla. But I think it's crazy." He was at the capitol, supposedly conferring with a congressional work group. He looked a bit rumpled.

"I want you to do something for me, Michael."

"What is it now?"

"Call Dryden. Explain what we've got, and ask him if Orion can send a couple ships to Origins."

He pressed his fingertips against his temples, a man with a headache. *"I can't do that."*

"Why not?"

"Look." Father to daughter. *"You want to put your reputation on the*

line because this kid has wet dreams, go ahead. But I'm not going any further with this. You're that hot about it, you *take care of it. You can tell him you're speaking for me, if you want."*

"Okay."

"Let's not make it sound like an emergency, though. Right? This is something that isn't going to happen. We know that. He'll know it. It's just a precaution. Or maybe a public relations move. But if something goes wrong, you're out there by yourself. Understand?" He was about to disconnect when he remembered something. *"By the way, I'll be traveling on Academy business tomorrow. Attending a conference in Copenhagen. You've got the helm until I get back."*

Hutch knew the symptoms. Asquith thought the whole thing would blow up, and he was getting as far from the fallout as he could.

"*WHY?*" DRYDEN ASKED. *"What's the problem?"*

"There's a chance there might be an attack at Origins."

"You can't be serious."

"That sounds a trifle odd, considering what Orion's just been through."

"Is there another asteroid coming in?"

"Not that we know of, but we have reason to believe a strike may be imminent."

"Hutch, look, I can't just grab some liners and send them off on a wild goose chase. What's your evidence?"

"I'm not free to say."

"Then I really can't help. I'm sure you understand. We'd be happy to do what we can, but you'll have to take us into your confidence."

"Let it go," she said.

She also needed to warn Origins. There was no indication Allard was likely to pass the Academy's concerns on. She knew a few people at the facility. But if she communicated directly with them, it would constitute defying the director. If nothing happened, the Academy would be seriously embarrassed, and she would be making profuse apologies. Maybe there was a better way. She asked Marla to get Mac back on the circuit.

"Hi, Beautiful," he said. *"What do you need?"*

"You have any contacts at Origins?"

"I know a few people there. What did you need?"

"Can you get a warning to them? Without involving the Academy?"

"What did you want them to hear?"

PETER SENT A schedule listing everything that was currently at Union, or that was expected within the next twenty-four hours.

A lot of people on the orbiter owed Hutch favors. Over the years, the Academy had supplied ships and information to virtually every off-world corporate entity. They'd provided training, and even occasionally gone to their rescue. She'd included their VIPs on survey runs, when it was feasible, and had encouraged Academy technicians to help where they could.

She looked over the list of ships, their current status, and their capacities. Then she made her first call to Franz Hoffer, at Thor Transport, which specialized in servicing the deep-space stations. "Probably not going to be a problem," she said, "but if you can arrange things so a ship is available in the event we need it, I'd be grateful."

"We can let you have the Carolyn Ray," Franz said. *"It'll only hold twenty people. But it's all we've got."*

"We'll take it, Franz. And thanks."

Franz was a small, thin man. Blond hair. Mustache. Always perfectly pressed and combed. *"We'll have to do some preps."*

"Okay."

"Bring in a pilot. It can be out of here Friday."

Two days. "Okay," she said. "Thanks."

Nova Industries moved capital equipment to interstellar construction sites. Lately business had been slow, and they'd officially mothballed the *Rikart Bloomberg*. But it could be made ready to go in a couple of days. *"It will accommodate thirteen,"* they said.

Maracaibo would send an executive yacht, the *Alice Bergen*. They apologized. It could only carry five, but it was all they had. They'd bring in a pilot immediately. Get it under way late Thursday.

Beijing FTL agreed to send the *Zheng Shaiming* as soon as they could refuel and run systems checks. Probably Friday night. No later than Saturday morning. It had a capacity of twenty-six. Mitsubishi donated the *Aiko Tanaka*, an experimental craft that had been undergoing testing. That gave her sixteen more.

WhiteStar, which operated the big cruise liners, could have settled the issue had any of its three mainline ships been available. But they weren't. They could however provide two service vehicles. "*Not comfortable,*" Meaty Hogan, their maintenance boss told her, "*but they'll each hold four passengers, and they can leave as soon as we get the pilots over to them.*"

"How many in an emergency?"

Meaty thought about it. "*Five. But not for an extended period.*"

The French government had a vehicle in transit. The *Christophe Granville*. "*It can accommodate twenty-two, and be at the site in a few days, Priscilla,*" said their operations chief. "*You wish us to divert?*"

"Please."

"*It is done.*"

The Norwegians contributed the *Connor Haaverstad*, capacity fourteen. It was undergoing maintenance, however, and would not be able to leave for three days. "Send it when you can," said Hutch.

"*We'll try to hurry things along.*"

When she got home that evening and told Tor what she'd done, he was as supportive as he could manage, considering he believed she'd committed a major-league blunder. Thrown away her reputation and her career. As she lay beside him on that darkest of nights, she suspected in her heart he was right.

LIBRARY ARCHIVE

Our preliminary review of the global defense posture indicates that arming vehicles operated by the Academy, the Alliance for Interstellar Development, and the European Deep Space Commission will constitute, at best, a temporary fix. The hard truth is that we cannot ensure security against an enemy whose capabilities are unknown, and may far exceed our own. However that may be, a fleet of ships whose armament is jury-rigged will not provide a long-term answer. We need to start thinking seriously about a battle fleet whose capabilities will be of the highest possible order our technologies can support.

—Joint House/Senate Report, Wednesday, May 6

The rush to arms is just one more glorious boondoggle. We've been on this planet for a million years or so, and nobody's bothered us yet. The last thing we need is battle cruisers in space. If there are really intelligent aliens out there, surely we can talk to them. We haven't even tried. In any case, there are plenty of empty worlds. Why would they bother us?

—*Epiphany*, May 6

PART THREE

valya

chapter 35

> Most people, other than politicians and CEOs, mean well. The problem is seldom with their intentions. It is rather with their tendency to sign on with a superorganism, a political party, a creed, a nation, a local action committee, and in its name to support deeds they would never undertake as individuals.
>
> —Gregory MacAllister, "The Hellfire Trial"

Eric caught the eight o'clock flight from Reagan to Union. Valya was already there. She'd gone up on the *Dawn Rider*. He felt good about himself. Vaguely heroic. "Are we ready to go?"

Yes indeed. She gave him a hand with his bags, and he walked up the boarding tube and back into the ship. "It feels as if I'm coming home."

"I guess it does," she said. "We had two days on the ground, and here we are again." She hesitated. "I don't want you to take this the wrong way, but I couldn't figure out why you went the first time. Sightseeing, maybe. Whatever, I surely have no idea why you're here now, Eric. I asked Hutch, and she just said you wanted to go."

"I enjoy taking flights with beautiful women."

"Seriously."

"I'm serious." He let her see he meant every word. A few weeks ago he'd have been reluctant to say such things to her. "It also occurred to me there might be an attack. If there is, you could probably use some help."

"To do what? Fight them off?"

He laughed. "The truth is, I just wanted to be there. In case something happens."

"You're going to be disappointed," she said. "We'll go out there and ride in circles for a week or so and see nothing. Then we'll come home."

"Maybe."

"Come on, Eric, we both know the girl was scared. She was scared, and you and Mac were asleep."

"Maybe."

"I just think it's a waste of time. But I'm glad to have you along."

"Valya—"

"Yes?"

"If you feel that way, why are you making the flight?"

"It's my job, Eric. Hutch says go, and I go." She went up onto the bridge, and he heard her flicking switches and talking to the AI and to the operations people. He went back to his old cabin and unpacked.

After about twenty minutes she warned him to belt down. He thought about joining her up front, but decided she'd be happier alone for the moment. He knew Hutch planned to keep the *Salvator* on station until Blueprint had been completed. Probably two weeks. He had heard the rumors about the possibility of a cosmic catastrophe. If it happened, he'd be right there to see it.

He spoke into the commlink. "Valya?"

"*Yes, Eric?*"

They'd begun to move. "If there's a time-space rip—"

"*A* what?"

"A time-space rip. Do you know what that is?"

"*It doesn't sound good.*"

"If it were to happen, could we outrun it?"

DOWNTOWN DERBY, NORTH Carolina, was awash with demonstrators carrying signs reading HELLFIRE HURTS and SAVE YOUR SOUL WHILE YOU CAN and FIRST AMENDMENT ON TRIAL. Others waved banners declaring NO MORE CHILD ABUSE and PEOPLE INVENTED HELL; NOT GOD. Police did what they could to keep them apart. They lined the streets for several blocks in all directions. Vendors sold T-shirts carrying slogans on both sides of the argument. Others hustled Bibles out of trucks. Organ music drifted through the morning air, and local and network journalists were everywhere.

Glock had sent MacAllister a pass he had to show three or four times to get *to* the courthouse. At the door, weary-looking officers inspected it again, compared it with his ID, and let him in. The courtroom was small and jammed. Imagers were set up so the proceedings could be sent around the world. He had lost his day with Valya, but it was almost worth it.

Glock, stationed up front, waved and pointed him to an empty seat near the defense table. Henry Beemer, the defendant, sat nervously beside his much taller lawyer. He was pale and thin, an introvert by appearance. Not married. MacAllister, appraising the man, decided it was not by choice. He looked like the kind of guy who takes authority seriously. And therein, Henry, he thought, lies your problem.

He pushed through the crowd and sat down. Glock leaned back and shook his hand. "Good to see you, Mac," he said.

Every time the courtroom doors opened, the noise in the street, people yelling and ringing bells and singing hymns, spilled in. "The idiots are out in force," MacAllister said. "What kind of judge do we have?"

"Maximum George. Despite the name, he's okay. As I said yesterday, he won't overturn the First Amendment, but he's not unreasonable."

The Reverend Pullman sat on the opposite side of the bench, wearing clerical garb and one of those unctuous smiles that proclaims a monopoly on truth.

There was no jury. Glock had opted to leave it to the judge, who was, he said, less likely to be influenced by the religious goings-on than a crowd of citizens, however carefully chosen.

At precisely nine A.M., Maximum George entered. The bailiff called everyone to attention, the judge took his place behind the bench and rapped his gavel twice. The crowd quieted, and the trial was under way.

After a few preliminaries, the prosecutor got up to make his opening statement. He was long and lean as a stick, with mid-Atlantic diction laid on over a Southern accent. He described the unprovoked assault on the unsuspecting Reverend Pullman. Mr. Beemer had approached the preacher in the Booklore bookstore, right across the street from the courthouse, Your Honor. He had accused the preacher of promoting the gospel. Not satisfied with the preacher's response, he had begun pushing and shoving. And, finally, he had assaulted the puzzled victim with a book.

The book was lying on the prosecution table. MacAllister was unable to read the title but he knew it was *Connecticut Yankee*. He couldn't restrain a grin. If you were going to go after one of these hellfire guys with anybody, Mark Twain was your man.

The prosecutor expressed his sincere hope that the street demonstrations would not detract from the essential, and relatively clear, facts of the case. And so on.

Finally, he sat down. Glock stood, explained that the defense would show that the attack was *not* unprovoked, and that the aggrieved party was in fact Mr. Beemer. "I think," he concluded, "that will become very quickly evident, Your Honor."

MacAllister's attention drifted back to the book.

To Sir Boss.

To his attempts to bring nineteenth-century technology and capitalism to Camelot.

To the sequence he remembered most vividly: the Yankee, who has been sentenced to the stake, recalls a coming solar eclipse, which knowledge he uses to terrify Merlin, the king, and everybody else by announcing he would darken the sun, and then apparently *doing* it. An unlikely piece of fiction, of course. Still, it made for a riveting sequence.

"The prosecution calls its first witness."

It was a leather-bound copy, red-brown with a red ribbon, the title in gold.

"Ms. Pierson, is it true you were on duty at the Booklore when the defendant wantonly and deliberately attacked the Reverend Pullman?"

"Objection, Your Honor. The prosecution has presented no evidence—"

The pages were gold-gilded.

"Sustained. Rephrase, Counselor."

"*Attacked*, Your Honor."

It was all about gold.

* * *

THERE WASN'T MUCH to the prosecution side of the case. Four witnesses took the stand to describe how Beemer had been standing with a stack of books, about to check out, when he'd abruptly turned around and walked into the back of the store. One witness testified that he had clearly been following the Reverend Pullman. Two of them saw him come up behind the preacher, still carrying his books, and demand to know whether Pullman knew who he was. When Pullman demurred and tried to edge away, Beemer kept after him. "In a threatening manner." Finally, the defendant had laid the books on the floor—one witness insisted he'd simply dropped them—seized the biggest book in the pile, and tried to hit the preacher in the head with it. The Reverend Pullman had warded off the blows with his hands, begging the defendant to stop. And had finally gone down. Several bystanders had dragged a still volatile Beemer away.

Glock made no serious effort to cross-examine the witnesses. He told the judge that the defense did not dispute that the attack had happened as described.

They broke for lunch. In the afternoon, Pullman took the stand. The prosecutor asked if he understood why he'd been attacked.

Pullman said no. "Mr. Beemer claimed to have been a student of mine years ago at the church school and said I'd ruined his life. He kept screaming at me."

"Were you injured during the attack?"

"I was severely bruised. When the police came, they wanted to take me to the hospital."

"But you didn't go."

"I don't like hospitals. Anyway, I didn't feel I'd been injured seriously. Although that was no fault of his. Not that I haven't forgiven him."

Glock stepped forward to cross-examine. "Reverend, you say that, at the time of the incident, you did not know what provoked the attack."

"That's correct."

"Are you now aware why Mr. Beemer was upset?"

"I've been informed of what he said. And I should add that hundreds of children have attended our school, and this is the first incident of this kind."

"No one has ever complained before, Reverend?"

"No. What is there to complain of? We teach the word of the Lord."

"May I ask how old the students are who attend the school?"

"They are grades one through six." He considered the question. "About seven to thirteen."

"Reverend, what is the word of the Lord regarding hellfire?"

"That it is eternal. That it is reserved for those who do not accept the Lord and His teaching."

The prosecutor objected, on the grounds that none of this had anything to do with the charges.

"We are trying to establish a rationale, Your Honor. The Reverend Pullman doesn't understand why Mr. Beemer was upset with him. It's essential that we all know what provoked a man with no history of lawbreaking, no history of violence, to attack a former teacher."

"Very well, Mr. Glock," said the judge. "I'll allow it. But let's get to the point."

"Specifically, Reverend Pullman, hellfire sounds like a dire punishment, does it not?"

"It certainly does. Yes."

"How hot is it, would you say?"

"The Bible does not say."

"What would *you* say?"

"I don't know."

"Enough to scorch your hand?"

"Oh, yes."

"Enough to sear the flesh?"

"I would think so."

"And it goes on for a thousand years?"

"It goes on *forever*."

"Without stopping."

"There is no lunch break." Pullman turned a broad smile to the onlookers.

"Very good, Reverend. Now, if I am, say, twelve years old, what might I do that would incur this sort of *punishment*?"

"You mean hell?"

"Yes."

"There are various sins."

"Could you give us some examples?"

"Murder. Adultery."

"A twelve-year-old, Reverend. Let me put it to you this way. Is it possible for a twelve-year-old boy to warrant hell?"

"Yes."

MacAllister found himself again fixating on *Connecticut Yankee*.

"What can he do that would deserve that kind of punishment? Aside, perhaps, from murder?"

"He might miss Sunday service."

He saw the Yankee in the courtyard while the light drained from the day.

"That in itself would be sufficient?"

"Yes. Of course."

"What else?"

"Dancing."

And he thought of the Galactic.

"Dancing?"

"Yes. It is strictly forbidden. I know that, for godless people in a godless society, the reasoning can be difficult to grasp."

MacAllister lost the drift of the proceedings. The courtyard at Camelot floated before his eyes, and gradually dissolved into the skeletal gridwork of the Galactic. He saw it as he had from the *Salvator*, turning slowly, reflecting light from nearby Capella.

He watched the asteroid, growing larger on one of the screens. Recalled how difficult it had been to gauge its size until it got close to the hotel, which, at the end, had been only a brief glimmer of light going out.

And he knew how it had been done.

But as he thought about it, and realized the implications, his heart sank.

GLOCK BROUGHT IN a psychiatrist who had examined Beemer. "No, not clinically insane," the psychiatrist said, "but disturbed. Mr. Beemer suffers from a radical strain of paranoia, induced by the religious environment imposed on him when he was a child. At the heart of that environment were the teachings of the church and its school regarding divine punishment."

When the session ended, MacAllister spoke briefly with Glock. "The truth is," said the lawyer, "the wrong man's on trial."

Outside, some in the crowd recognized MacAllister. "Try going to church once in a while," someone called. And: "You're damned, MacAllister. Repent while you can." Sunflower seeds were thrown toward him. The seeds represented the argument that one should look toward the light and eschew the darkness. Some of the believers had bought into the notion there was a conspiracy to override the First Amendment and shut down the churches. That idea had gotten around, and though there was no chance of its happening, and in fact no likelihood MacAllister could see of Beemer's not being found guilty, there were nevertheless some who were stoking precisely those fears.

The organ, which had been silenced by police during the trial, was operating again. It was playing an inspirational tune while the crowd sang "Going to Meet My Lord." They picked up the volume as MacAllister strode past.

Beemer and Glock exited by a side door and were whisked away by police.

It was like traveling in time, like watching the 2216 supernova explode again. This must have been what it was like in Tennessee three centuries earlier during the Scopes trial. He retreated to his hotel and listened to the crowd thumping and banging in the streets. The counterdemonstrators, unfortunately, were just as fanatical. They probably would have closed the churches, had they been able. They were at the moment trying to shout down the organist and his choir. MacAllister looked around hopelessly. His supporters were every bit as deranged as those arrayed on the other side.

The real enemy, he thought, was fanaticism.

THE MEDIA REPORTED that state police were coming in to bolster the local force. And the hellfire trial was for them the story *du jour*. Even the moonriders were crowded out.

He closed the blinds against the crowds and wished he could have shut out the noise. Getting a hotel in town had turned out not to be a prudent course of action. He'd expected some disarray, but nothing like this. The trial would probably end tomorrow. He suspected things would get worse.

He called Wolfie.

"They were running behind on construction," he said. *"But I haven't*

been able to find out why. The official claim was that there was a supply bottleneck. But it was trumped up."

"Okay," he said. "I don't need details."

Wolfie grinned. *"What's all the racket? They still trying to save your soul down there?"*

"The crowd's getting a little testy." He heard glass shattering somewhere. And a scream.

"You've been all over the news reports, Mac. You look pretty good. One guy challenging a mob. I bet you didn't know what you were starting with this one."

"Are you paying attention, Wolfie?"

"Sure."

"I want you to find out when the papers were filed to authorize construction of the Galactic."

"That should be simple enough."

"Then I want you to track back from that date, say, over a seven-year period. During that time span, somebody will have done survey work in the Capellan system. Check ships' manifests, movement logs, whatever."

"All right."

"You might also want to take a look at scientific papers published during the period. Somewhere, you'll find somebody, a planetary physicist of some sort, most likely, who was out there on a project."

"What was the nature of the project?"

"Don't know. Doesn't matter. We want this person's name."

"Okay."

"If we're lucky, we'll also discover a link with Orion Tours. Particularly Charles Dryden."

"Who's Dryden?"

"An executive over there. Wolfie, I want you to get on this right away."

"Will do, Boss."

"Let me know as soon as you have something."

HUTCH WAS DRAINED. Sitting in for Asquith was never a pleasure. There were always political meetings, public relations issues, and a host of administrative details. Most of the decisions could have been put on automatic by establishing policy, or, better, relegating them to lower-level executives. Like personnel matters, or which scientific entities should be given seats in the front at the next conference on star formation. But Asquith had never been good at delegating, so the people under him weren't accustomed to taking action on their own. When Hutch kicked decisions in their direction, they tended to scramble and panic.

Peter kept in touch and gave her the latest positions of the *Carolyn Ray*, the *Bergen*, and the WhiteStar ships. The *Rehling* had left Nok and was on its way. The others would all be en route within a day or so.

When time allowed she watched the hellfire trial. She sympathized with Beemer, but couldn't see that he had a chance. She was proud that Mac had taken his side. A few minutes after the judge had recessed the trial for the day, she got a transmission from Marcus Cullen, one of the passengers on the *Rehling*. It was for *her* personally, not for the commissioner. The transmission was only a minute or so long, the AI informed her. She could have ignored it until later, but she hated to put unpleasantries off. Cullen was a crank. He wielded a lot of influence, although his fellow physicists did not have a high regard for him. He seemed to be disappointed in his life, a guy who'd never really accomplished anything, had never even gotten into the race for any of the big prizes. So he'd concentrated instead on accumulating power. He was president of Duke University, and a close friend of the president.

"Hutchins," he said, *"I am not happy with your action. You've added several days to a flight that was already tedious enough. Every day I have to spend out here costs my university heavily. I understand we are going to rescue, whatever that's supposed to mean, the staff at Origins. From, as best I can tell, a nonexistent threat. You better damn well know what you're talking about or your job is gone."*

NEWSDESK

COMMON SENSE COMMITTEE PLANS CONTACT EFFORT

Will Look for Chance to Say Hello to Rock-Throwing Aliens

Harper: "Our Opportunity for Major Advances"

"May Be a Million Years Ahead of Humanity"

CONGRESS CONSIDERS EMERGENCY MEASURES
Arms Bill Will Pass Easily
Global Effort to Mount Defenses
Gallen: "If They Come for Us, We Will Be Ready"

MARINES IN ORBIT
Special Forces to Get Training in Space Operations

FUNDAMENTALISTS DENY ALIENS EXIST
"Another Effort to Undercut Biblical Teaching"

WORLD COUNCIL OF CHURCHES SAYS BIBLE TRUTH INTACT
"Nothing in the Bible Prohibits Others"
"We're All God's Children"

MOONRIDER GLOBES LATEST ACTION TOYS HIT
What Do Moonriders Look Like? Toy Manufacturers Stand By

REPORTS OF SIGHTINGS UP AROUND WORLD
Globes Seen Everywhere
Authorities Insist No Moonriders near Earth

MOONRIDER "ABDUCTEES" GIVE WARNING
"They've Been Watching Us for Years"
"Nobody Would Listen"

INTERSTELLAR BLUES OPENS ON BROADWAY
Perfect Timing for Musical about Lost Alien

MOONRIDERS STILL PRIMITIVE, SAYS BROWNSTEIN
"If They Have to Throw Rocks, We Have Nothing to Fear"

MOONRIDER REACTION RANKS WITH 20TH-CENTURY UFO HYSTERIA

WE'VE BEEN WARGAMING THIS FOR YEARS
Military Says It's Ready

chapter 36

> Human beings, by and large, are a cowardly and despicable lot. They snuggle up to bosses. They support personalities rather than principles. They don't pay attention when serious malfeasance is in the saddle.
>
> –Gregory MacAllister, *Life and Times*

On the second day of the trial, Glock introduced a series of psychiatrists who testified they had treated persons with various disorders that could be ascribed to overzealous religious instruction when they were young. A psychologist argued that he had looked through the curriculum for the schools conducted by the Universal Church of the Creator and declared that students reared in that tradition, when they attended college, consistently lagged behind others in both the humanities and the sciences. "Their minds were closed," he said. "It was not simply that they were indoctrinated with information that was demonstrably false, for example that evolutionary processes occur only on microscopic levels, but also that they were trained to resist competing ideas. No consideration whatever was to be given to any notion that did not comply with accepted doctrine."

Glock placed a copy of the curriculum and several studies in evidence.

The prosecution introduced experts who testified that religious training helped people adjust to a disorderly and often frightening world. Religious people live longer. They are less likely to acquire police records. They are, by most measurable standards, happier with their lives. The Reverend Pullman was merely providing the training in morals and decency that parents everywhere desired for their children.

It went back and forth while the crowds outside grew larger and noisier. Glock asked for simple fairness, for an understanding that the defendant was haunted by the visions of his youth and should not be punished for striking out at a person who had so abused him during those early years.

Objection, Your Honor. *Abuse* is a stretch.

The prosecution had the final word. "The defense has tried to put the Reverend Pullman, and indeed Christianity, on trial. The Reverend Pullman has done nothing that is not sanctioned by the U.S. Constitution. Indeed, he did nothing other than meet his obligation to the Church and to the greater society he serves. Mr. Beemer, on the other hand, has committed simple assault. There is no question about it. There are witnesses. The defense does not deny it."

When the prosecutor had concluded, the judge thanked both counsels and adjourned.

"What do you think?" MacAllister asked Glock.

The lawyer gave Beemer an encouraging smile. "It's okay, Henry. Try to relax. I think we'll be all right." He turned back to MacAllister: "We're asking him to find against the Constitution. That's not going to happen. It *can't* happen. But Henry will very likely get a minimum sentence. And I think we've started a national debate."

MACALLISTER HAD CHECKED out of his hotel before going to the courtroom. He went back to pick up his bags and grabbed a taxi. An hour later he was on a glide train to Alexandria.

In some respects he had never grown up. He'd had a model train when he was a kid and still loved riding through the countryside. He sat back and gazed out at the rolling hills and fields. Mostly farmland. Orange-growing country.

He got up after a while and walked to the dining car. He hadn't had lunch and was looking at the menu when Wolfie called. *"There's an Elenora Delesandro,"* he said, *"who did a study of asteroids in the Capella system six years ago. She published her results in* The Planetary Field Journal, *May, 2230."*

"Good. Is there any mention of a giant asteroid? I'm trying to remember the size of the thing."

"Six hundred kilometers. But it doesn't show up in her report."

"Where is she now? Delesandro?"

"She teaches physics at Broken Brook."

"Which is where?"

"Fargo."

He wandered over to the service bar, ordered a tomato-and-cheese salad, and carried it back to his table. Then he opened his notebook and called up Delesandro's article. It was titled "Capella: Stellar Winds and the Shell-Burning Phase."

It was too technical for MacAllister's tastes. He went through it several times before he was able to follow the argument. Capella A is a giant star, and consequently went through a period in which it blew off the outer layers of its atmosphere. Delesandro seemed to be trying to determine the nature of this supersolar wind, whether it had come off uniformly or streamed out in jets.

Had the wind come off uniformly, the asteroid orbits would have tended to become circular. If the gas erupted in jets, eccentricity would have been pronounced.

If a dominant gas giant exists in the system, asteroids will orbit the star in half the time that the gas giant requires. The situation at Capella is complicated by the fact that there are two stars forming a single gravitational center. But it was possible to adjust for the complexities, and it was apparently this challenge that had drawn Delesandro's interest initially.

There *is* a Jovian world at Capella. It completes an orbit every fifteen years. The average asteroid then, under normal circumstances, and after applying Delesandro's formula, would have needed seven and a half years to circle the sun. Wind interaction would have altered that. And smaller asteroids would be more disturbed than larger ones. So looking at the difference between small and large provides a researcher with considerable data.

The arrival of the superstellar wind phase signals the start of shell-burning. At this point, hydrogen fusion has begun in the shell instead of in the core itself, which, of course, is made up of helium. (Of course it is, thought MacAllister.)

This is the stage during which the star begins to evolve away from the main sequence and expand into a red giant.

Delesandro had included a table of asteroids, listing their dimensions and their orbital periods. One fit the dimensions of the Galactic asteroid quite closely.

He finished his salad, looked up the astrophysics section at the American Museum of Natural History, picked an astrophysicist at random, and made a call. An AI informed him the individual was not available, so he asked who was, and got through to an Edward Moore. *"How can I help you?"* Moore asked, in a gravelly voice. He was a broad-shouldered athletic-looking guy. Obviously worked out a lot. Gray hair, thick mustache, casual demeanor. He was wearing a white lab jacket.

MacAllister introduced himself. "We're looking at the asteroid that hit the Galactic construction."

"Yes," he said. *"I saw that. Strange stuff."*

"I have an article in front of me from *The Planetary Field Journal*, of May 2231. It's about asteroids near Capella, by Elenora Delesandro. Are you by any chance familiar with it?"

"No," he said. *"I'm sorry to say I'm not."*

"We're trying to determine what really happened."

"Good," he said. *"Somebody needs to look into it."* He asked his AI to retrieve the *Journal*. *"What exactly did you want to know?"*

"There's a table of asteroids on page 446."

"One moment." His brow furrowed. *"Okay. I see it."*

"Down near the bottom there's one, 4477, that has a diameter of 613 kilometers."

"Yes. That seems to be correct. Is that the one that hit the hotel?"

"That's what I wanted to ask you."

"Hold on a second." He looked through the pages. *"There's a data file attached. Give me a few minutes to look at the numbers."*

"Okay."

"Where can I reach you?"

WOLFIE GOT BACK to him as he was returning to his seat. *"I've got a link between Delesandro and Dryden."*

"Excellent," MacAllister said. "When and where?"

"At something called the Bannerman Award dinner. Given annually in Fargo on the university campus. In 2229, Dryden was one of the speakers. Delesandro was on the guest list."

"That's two years before the construction license was issued."

"That's correct. I can also tell you that, at the time, they were planning to put the hotel at Terranova."

"When did they change their minds?"

"Not sure. The first mention I can find of Capella is in an interview given by an Orion executive six months after the award dinner."

"Does he say why they were making the switch?"

"He doesn't mention Terranova at all. And something else: Delesandro changed her address during the next semester."

"Don't tell me. From poorer to richer."

"I couldn't get the specifics, Boss, but I got a look at the properties. The new one's definitely upscale."

Wolfie said he'd let him know if he got anything more. MacAllister rode the train into Alexandria, got off, and was on his way up to the street when Moore called again. *"I checked the data file,"* he said. *"And the pictures."*

"And—?"

"It's not the same object."

"You mean the asteroid that hit the hotel is not in the file."

"That's correct."

"But it was one of the larger objects in the system, Dr. Moore. Doesn't it seem strange that she didn't include it in the general catalogue?"

"Not necessarily. A planetary system is a big place. She might simply have missed it."

HE GOT HOME, glad to be away from the noise and general tumult in Derby. He dropped his bags inside the front door, collapsed onto the sofa, and called Hutch. She was in a meeting, but she got back to him a few minutes later. *"What's going on, Mac?"*

"How well do you know Charlie Dryden?"

"Not that well. Why?"

"Don't trust him."

"I don't. What brings the subject up?"

"I'm pretty sure the attack on the Galactic was faked."

Her eyes slid momentarily shut, and her lips tightened. *"What makes you think so?"*

"I'm still working on the details. I'll give you everything I have when I can."

"I don't see how it's possible, Mac."

He explained how it might have been managed.

"That implies," she said, *"Terranova, too."*

"Yes."

"How sure are you, Mac?"

"I don't think there's much question."

Hutch's dark eyes smoldered. *"If you're right, you know what it means about Valya."*

He knew. God help him, he knew. "But I don't see how she could have managed it."

"Damn," she said. *"It never did feel right."*

"I thought the same thing."

"I'm sorry. I know this isn't going to be easy on you."

"In what way?"

"Come on, Mac. I'm not blind."

"It's not a problem."

"Okay." She played with a pen. Dropped it on her desktop. The silence stretched out. *"All right. Let me get out of your way."*

"What are you going to do now?"

"Nothing for the moment. Until I find out what's going on at Origins. Maybe that's faked, too. We're going to want to take a look at the Ophiuchi monitor."

"Why?"

"To nail things down."

"How do you figure she did it? Did she rig the monitor in some way?"

"That's the way I'd have done it."

"Tell me how."

"All Valya had to do was load a doctored chip into it. If she did that, what we saw at Terranova, the sighting, everything, would have been pure showbiz."

"But we saw the rock. We saw it from the ship. We all but landed on it. It was really there."

"Sure. But you didn't see the moonriders. You didn't see what put it on course for Terranova."

"You're saying it could have been an ordinary ship."

"Yes."

"One of ours?"

"Sure. The asteroid wasn't that big. Not like the one at Capella. Any of the major corporates could have managed it."

"That might explain why we had to go back to the monitor to do repairs."

"I wasn't aware of that. You had to repair the monitor?"

"Yes. It was in *The National*'s account."

"I missed it. And I guess I didn't look as closely as I should have at the trip report."

"She was removing the chip," said MacAllister.

"Sure." Hutch took a deep breath. *"How do you explain what happened to Amy?"*

"Bought and paid for? Like Valya?"

"No," she said. *"I don't believe that."*

AN HOUR LATER he got through to Delesandro. She recognized his name. *"It's quite an honor, Mr. MacAllister,"* she said. *"Is there something I can do for you?"*

She was a middle-aged woman. Light brown hair, dark blue sweater thrown over her shoulders, fireplace visible off to one side. A bookcase behind her. She looked scared.

"Yes, Dr. Delesandro. I think there is. I wanted to talk to you about your work in *The Planetary Field Journal*. From Capella."

She tugged at the sweater. *"That's a few years back."*

"Doctor, you're aware of the incident at Capella last week."

"Of course."

"The asteroid in question was of a significant size. Apparently, judging by your work, there were only a handful in the entire system that were larger."

"That's correct." Her voice was soft. He had to strain to hear her.

"The asteroid that hit the Galactic doesn't appear anywhere in your report."

"Yes, I know. I obviously missed it. When I did the survey."

"How would that happen?"

She held up one braceleted arm in a who-knows gesture. *"Planetary systems are very big, Mr. MacAllister. A lot of empty space."*

"I keep hearing that."

"I'd be surprised if I hadn't missed others."

"Really?"

"Any general survey like mine is necessarily a hit-or-miss proposition. We look at the overall structure of a system; we don't try to categorize everything."

"But the asteroid would have been somewhere in the inner system."

"Who knows? If these moonrider creatures have the capability they seem to possess, it might have come from anywhere."

"I see."

"Was there anything else I can help you with?" She was trying hard to look at ease.

"Yes. My information is that a survey of this type, by its nature, does try to perform a comprehensive sweep."

" 'Comprehensive' is a relative term, Mr. MacAllister."

"Doctor, doesn't it strike you as odd that the asteroid—the *very* large asteroid—that you didn't notice happened to be the one that struck the Galactic?"

She swallowed. *"Not at all. I—"*

"Do you think there might be any others of that size you missed?"

"I don't know. I really do not know. It's certainly possible. Likely, in fact."

"I understand you're acquainted with Charlie Dryden." He made it a simple statement of fact.

She had to think it over. *"Not well,"* she said.

"You understand, Doctor, that Dryden and his people conspired to put lives at risk. That you were party to that conspiracy."

"I beg your pardon, Mr. MacAllister. But I have no idea what you're talking about."

She looked like a cornered rabbit. The woman wasn't used to lying. "Let me tell you what happened," he said. "During the survey mission you discovered that one of the asteroids, a *big* one, was going to have a close encounter with Alpha II. Literally skim the top of the atmosphere.

"You came home and started putting your results together. During that period, you met Dryden at the Bannerman Award ceremony at Broken Brook. Maybe you knew him earlier. I don't know. But during the course of the event, you mentioned the asteroid. He got interested, and either then or later, he asked you to omit it from your report. And paid a considerable sum in exchange for your forgetting about it altogether."

"Mr. MacAllister, you have a wild imagination. For God's sake, I wouldn't tamper with the results of a study like that. Ask any of my colleagues. They know I wouldn't."

"Anybody can make a mistake, Doctor."

"I don't have to listen to this."

"You can listen now, or you can read about it in *The National.*"

"This is crazy," she said, and broke the connection.

DECISIONS FOR THE upcoming issue were only two days away. MacAllister went back to reading copy, analyses by Arleigh Grant ("The Wolf in the Garden: Why the Greenhouse War Is Going Nowhere") and Chia Talbott ("Looking Back from the Parthenon"). There was also a clutch of book reviews, including one that was going to generate an angry reaction from the author, a prize-winning historian who had apparently lost his ability to think straight. He was interrupted periodically by calls, mostly from his writers.

One was from Delesandro.

"Okay," she said. She was sitting straight up.

"Okay what, Doctor?"

"You're right. But I didn't have any idea what it was about. I didn't know what he intended to do until I heard the reports that it would hit the hotel."

He was thinking about Mark Twain again. "They deliberately built the hotel in its path."

"Apparently so."

"Apparently?"

"Yes. That's what they did."

"It was a nice piece of engineering. They needed perfect timing."

"Yes. Yes, they did."

"When you realized what they'd done, did you talk to him about it?"

"Yes."

"What reason did he give you?"

"He said something about wanting to provide a surprise for a group of tourists."

"And that made sense to you?"

"No. Of course not."

"But you didn't ask too many questions."

"No."

"Was it a generous payment?"

"Not for what I'm going through now, no."

"Okay."

"Can you keep my name out of it?"

"No. I'm sorry, but that won't be possible."

"I didn't think so."

"Give me the details, and I promise the story will not be unsympathetic. I doubt you'll need to worry about formal charges."

"You don't understand. My reputation will be ruined, Mr. MacAllister. It'll be the end of my career." She looked desperate.

"I'm sorry," MacAllister said. "I have no control over that."

He'd already written the story. When he got off the circuit, he brought it up again on-screen, made a few minor changes, and wrote in the title: "The Capella Hoax: Orion Tours Invents a Few Moonriders."

He had no doubt that, by the time the investigation ended, there'd be conspiracy indictments against half a dozen major corporations. He read through it one more time. Satisfied, he forwarded a copy to Dryden, inviting him to comment.

Then he called Hutch. She was in another meeting, so he left the information with her AI.

MACALLISTER ALWAYS READ himself to sleep. That evening he was starting an exposé of government waste and corruption titled *The Last Honest Man*. He had not yet finished the introduction when Tilly informed him he had a call. "Dryden?" he asked.

"Yes, sir."

MacAllister put on a robe and went into his study. Dryden's image was standing waiting for him. The man was absolutely white. *"What do you mean by this, MacAllister?"* he demanded, struggling to keep his temper. He waved a few sheets of paper in the air. But his hand trembled. *"If you print any of this, I'll sue. I'll end up owning* The National.*"*

"Is that your comment?" MacAllister asked in a level voice.

"So help me—"

"Okay. We'll be locking it down tomorrow. You want to respond, you have until six P.M. to get it to me. Good night."

MacAllister signaled Tilly to close the circuit. "He'll call back," he said. "Tell him to put it in writing. I don't want to be bothered."

LIBRARY ENTRY

The Origins Project is simultaneously the most ambitious scientific and engineering operation in history. The discoveries that await can, at this time, only be the subject of speculation. It's painful to realize that no one in my generation will live to see its completion.

—Paul Allard, *The New York Times*, Friday, May 8

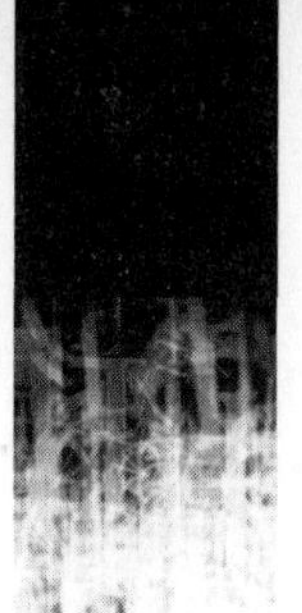

chapter 37

> Lies hold civilization together. If people ever seriously begin telling each other what they really think, there'd be no peace. Good-bye to tact. Good-bye to being polite. Good-bye to showing tolerance for other people's buffooneries. The fact that we claim to admire Truth is probably the biggest lie of all. But that's part of the charade, part of what makes us human, and we do not even think about it. In effect, we lie to ourselves. Lies are only despicable when they betray a trust.
>
> —Gregory MacAllister, *Life and Times*

Hutch watched the transmission from MacAllister with mounting anger. Valya had betrayed them all. Delesandro's admission clinched it.

It explained why Asquith had been so insistent that Valya pilot the mission. "Marla," she said, "get the commissioner for me."

How much was true and how much concocted? Was *any* of it true?

"Hutch, the commissioner's office reports he's away on personal business. Unavailable until Monday. Myers is acting." The personnel officer.

It was of course just like him. Anything blows up, somebody else takes the fall. The rescue fleet Hutch had cobbled together was on the way. Nine ships in all, plus the *Salvator*. If she'd been misled also about the projected attack on Origins, as her instincts told her she surely was, she was going to look extraordinarily foolish, as would the Academy. The media would have a field day with her. Furthermore, her actions would play directly into the hands of Taylor and the others who were trying to squeeze the organization. She'd been less rattled when she'd been blundering through the clouds over Maleiva III.

It put her in the curious position of hoping for a catastrophe. It was not something she was quite ready to admit to herself, let alone anybody else. But there it was. And with it came an overwhelming sense of guilt. That she was prepared to see people put at risk to be proven right.

Marla broke into her thoughts. *"There's an incoming transmission from the* Salvator."

She was trembling with rage. "Put it up, Marla," she said. "Let's see what the bitch has to say."

Valentina's image appeared, seated on the bridge. She was wearing the light and dark blue Academy jumpsuit. Not for much longer, though.

"We've made the transition into Origins space," Valya said. *"Preliminary long-range scan indicates negative results, but we're still a long way out. Anticipate arrival at the facility in six hours."*

A few minutes later she was back with more: *"I've talked with the East and West Towers, and they report nothing unusual."*

Hutch froze the image. Valentina had been a trusted Academy pilot for fifteen years. She wondered how it had happened. Had she been bought? Or had she done this out of some misplaced idealism? Not that it mattered.

She wondered briefly if she would herself have been tempted to rig the game to save the Academy. It was a thought she quickly thrust aside.

"I'll keep you updated. Salvator *out."*

Out was the operative word.

Valya and Hutch had never been close, had never been on an extended operation together. But Hutch had come to respect her. She'd fire the woman, of course. The only question was whether she should also prosecute. She'd have preferred to let everything ride until the *Salvator* returned. Then deal with it face-to-face. But

MacAllister knew, and Dryden knew, so it was going to be getting around, and she had no doubt one or the other would be in touch with her, Dryden to tell her to look out, MacAllister to vent his rage at being lied to.

"Marla," she said, "message for the *Salvator*."

"*When ready.*"

"Routine precedence. Captain's eyes only."

"*Very good.*"

She sat for several moments, collecting her thoughts. It wasn't the first time she'd had to terminate someone, but it had never before felt so personal. "Valya," she said. "I would have preferred to do this here. You'll probably be getting a message from the people at Orion, and I thought you should hear it first from me. We know what happened at Terranova, and at the Galactic.

"We haven't accounted for Amy's experience. If you can shed light on that, if you know beyond question that's another hoax, then let's just forget this pony ride. Turn around and come home.

"If you don't have an explanation for what happened to her, stay on-station at Origins until we can relieve you. You're of course aware that, if an attack *is* coming, we have no idea what form it may take."

She wanted to say more, to express her sense of betrayal and outrage, but putting it into a transmission where she couldn't see a reaction just didn't give her the satisfaction she wanted.

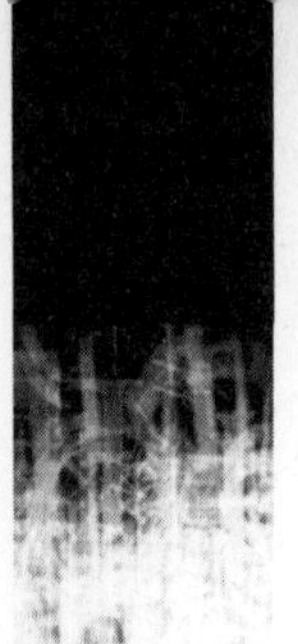

chapter 38

> Truth is slippery, not because it is difficult to grasp, but because we prefer our preconceptions, our beliefs, our myths. It's why nations are so often surprised by people like Napoleon and Hitler and Guagameil. Why individuals still buy natural cures for arteriosclerosis. Why we hire door-to-door guys to fix the roof.
>
> —Gregory MacAllister, "Show Me the Money"

Mission Operations kept Valya informed who was coming behind her. And when they were expected to arrive at Origins. All TOAs of course, depending on how good the jumps were. What a donkey drill.

But she played along, shaking her head at the commotion caused by one hysterical teenager. She was surprised Hutch had bought the story. The woman was usually too clear-eyed to be taken in like this.

She was uncomfortable with the situation. She didn't like deceiving friends, didn't like withholding information. She'd thought she was doing the right thing, providing the Academy with a badly needed boost. But events had ballooned out of control. Who could have believed when she agreed to help Dryden that Amy would get some kind of night sweats case, claim to have held a conversation with moonriders, and throw everything into chaos? She'd seemed like such a sensible kid.

Eric was in the right-hand seat. He enjoyed being on the bridge, probably imagining how it would feel to take the *Salvator* into his own hands and guide her into the East Tower dock.

"Transmission from Hutch," said Bill. *"Eyes only."*

Uh-oh.

With no one else on board save Eric, she could imagine only one reason for that designation.

She took a deep breath and became more aware of the acceleration. She was in the middle of a course correction, pushing her into her seat, squeezing her chest, and reminding her of the immense power of the machine in which she sat. Not unlike a good male, she thought. A lot of power, and just barely under control.

She'd suspected all along, despite Dryden's assurances, that eventually they'd be caught. But it shouldn't have come so soon. She'd told herself that when it did come out, it would happen only after the plan had failed and the Academy went back to closing down its operations, or after a success, when the big starships were heading out again in a new age of exploration. In either case, it wouldn't have mattered all that much. Certainly, in the latter event she'd have been more than willing to accept personal disgrace, secure that in the long view her contribution would be appreciated.

But this was just too soon.

"I'll take it in my cabin," she told Bill, trying to suggest to Eric that such matters were routine. "In a few minutes."

"They're not going to tell us the moonriders have already hit the place, are they?" Eric asked.

"No," she said. "It's probably a personnel thing. Those always come in like this. Next assignment, probably."

"You look pale."

She summoned a smile. From way back. "I'm fine." If they dismissed her, what would her chances be of catching on with one of the carriers?

Nil.

The drive shut down, and she released the harnesses. "I'll be back," she told Eric.

"Okay," he said. "I'll be here."

He was an innocent. Despite the reputation that public relations people have for conniving, Eric actually believed everybody played by the rules. She wondered how good he was at his job.

She retreated to her cabin, closed the door, and took a deep breath. She should have told Hutch the truth when she started talking about sending the *Salvator* out here.

Too late now.

"Okay, Bill," she said, "let's see what Her Highness has to say."

Hutch appeared in the center of the room. She was propped against the back of her desk. White blouse, blue neckerchief. Hair perfect. Eyes intense. The woman's expression was enough to deliver the message.

"I would have preferred to do this here."

Her heart quickened.

"You'll probably be getting a message from the people at Orion."

Anathema to it all. Didn't the idiot realize she'd done it for *her*? Hutchins, if we leave the future to people like you, we'll wind up sitting on the back side of the moon.

" . . . haven't accounted for Amy's experience. If you can shed light on that, if you know beyond question that's another hoax, then let's just forget this pony ride. Turn around and come home."

Hutch, at least try to understand.

"If you don't . . . stay on-station at Origins . . . "

At the end, Hutch seemed about to say something else, but abruptly she was gone, replaced by the Academy symbol. A scroll and lamp framing the blue Earth of the United World.

Well, you couldn't blame the woman. Hutch was what she was. She'd have been willing to sit there and preside over the end of the Academy, and for that matter over the end of mankind's future in space, and go down bravely with the ship.

Valentina Kouros, on the other hand, wasn't one to stand idly by and accept disaster. She understood that Dryden and his corporate friends had used her, but she had used *them*, too. The space program was on the move again, and if it had taken some *katafero*, then so be it.

She wondered whether there'd be criminal charges.

Whatever happened, she could expect to live the rest of her life on the ground.

Well, okay. If that was the price she had to pay. "Bill, I have a response to the message. Director's eyes only."

"Ready."

"Hutch," she said, "I don't know anything about Amy. We'll proceed as directed to Origins, survey the area, and await relief." She stared straight ahead, thinking what else to say. "At your pleasure."

When the message had been transmitted, she wrote her resignation. Kept it short. Made it effective on her return to Union. And sent it off.

She returned to the bridge. Eric was sitting comfortably with his legs thrust out in front of him and his hands clasped behind his head. "Everything okay?" he asked.

"Sure," she said.

THEY WERE STILL several hours away from Origins.

Eric was a talker, but Valya was in no mood to keep up her end of a conversation about trifles. She suggested they retreat to the common room and watch a vid. He thought that was a good idea—Eric always liked entertainment—so they made themselves comfortable. It was his turn to make the selection and, probably in deference to her, he went with *Thermopolae*, an historical drama about the celebrated stand of the Spartans. "Do we want to do substitutions?" he asked.

"Sure," she said. "Whatever you like."

Eric became Demetrios, a captain in the small Spartan force. "You look good in a horsehair helmet," she told him, as he stood surveying the famous pass. He smiled modestly.

The female lead, now Valya, was an Athenian dancing girl who'd fallen in love with Demetrios. They watched it through to the end, including a ridiculous scene in which the two lovers—she has refused to leave his side—hold off a small army of Persians before finally succumbing.

While it played out, she decided there was no point hiding the truth from Eric. He was going to find out eventually. So the credits rolled and the vid makers informed them that the sacrifice of the Spartans had bought valuable time and thereby saved western civilization, and she steeled herself for the ordeal.

When the lights came on, Eric commented that it was a strong show, and how painful it had been to see her killed off at the end. "Eric," she said, "I have a confession to make."

There was no spoiling his mood. He was a man on a mission. Making his life count for something. Maybe not Demetrios. But a spear-carrier. Or maybe just somebody bringing the water. And she was about to tell him it had all been a hoax. "You've fallen desperately in love with me," he said.

She took his wrist in her hands. "I wish that were it."

His voice changed: "What's wrong?"

"Eric, I've been lying to you. All along."

"About what?"

It went with a rush. The bogus transmission from the Ophiuchi monitor. How the Terranova asteroid had been aimed months ago by a pair of Orion cargo haulers. How the other asteroid, the one at Capella, was also a fabrication. Orion had known about it well in advance, she said, and they'd put the hotel precisely at the impact point. "I didn't realize they'd play it so close," she said. "They had the timing for the rescue down, but it was a near thing. If I'd known . . ."

He listened, at first merely frowning, but gradually she watched his features darken. Had it been Mac, who often looked irritated, it would not have meant so much. Mac was accustomed to dealing with liars. But Eric, easygoing, amiable Eric, was different. He was not simply angry; he was hurt.

He struggled to respond. And she wondered what there was for him to say after she'd played them all for idiots. It's okay, Valya. No hard feelings. I understand.

"I'm sorry," she said. Then just sat there.

He looked past her. At the bulkhead. At the open hatch to the bridge. At the spot where the Athenian dancing girl and her Spartan captain had stood against the Persians. "Thanks for telling me," he said.

He seemed frozen to his seat.

"If you want, Eric, I'll let you off at the station. Hutch knows. She's sending another ship as soon as she can find one. To relieve us. If you don't mind waiting around, you'd be able to go home with them."

"Okay," he said. "Yeah. Maybe that wouldn't be a bad idea."

"I'm sorry," she said.

He stared down at her. "I'm not the one you're going to have to answer to."

The air in the room felt warm and close. "I've written my resignation. I'll be lucky if Hutch doesn't press charges."

He got up and started for the passageway. "I wasn't talking about Hutch," he said.

VALYA HAD NEVER seen a moonrider. She'd seen pictures, supposedly taken live, but she knew how easily those could be generated. She simply didn't believe the moonriders existed. Call it denial. Call it provincialism. To her, it was a question of accepting her instincts. She no more expected to see aliens in superluminals than the eighteenth-century explorers expected to find Pacific island natives in capital ships.

The current mission—presumably her last—was an exercise in futility, but it had been assigned, so she'd do what was required, as she always had. Almost always. In any case, she was in no hurry to go back.

They rode through the void in strained silence. Eric had remained only a few minutes in his cabin before apparently thinking better of his reaction. He returned to the common room and tried to behave as if he hadn't walked off on her. But there was no getting around the abysmal cloud that occupied the middle of the room. "I take it," he said finally, "there's no threat. Was Amy bought, too?"

That scored a direct hit. "I never took a cent," she said. "I did it because I thought it was something that needed to be done."

His features were rigid. "Tell me about Amy."

"I don't know anything about Amy. I wasn't there. For all I know, it really happened."

"Can I believe you now?"

"I don't lie," she said.

"Of course not." He picked up his reader and began paging through it, trying to behave as though she wasn't there.

"Eric," she said, "I'm sorry about all this. I'm sorry you got involved. There was nothing personal in it."

"I know," he said. "It doesn't matter much one way or the other."

When he pretended to bury himself in his reading, she went up onto the bridge.

WHEN THE *SALVATOR* got within range of Origins, she reactivated the sweep. "Look for asteroids," she told Bill.

"There will be no asteroids here, Valya," he said. *"It is no small matter*

to find even a dust particle. This area was chosen for the Origins Project for that very reason."

"Do the sweep anyhow, Bill," she said. "Let me know if you see anything."

She felt like a damned fool. Eric never looked up. She walked past him and went below to conduct an inventory of the breathers Hutch had sent along. She counted eight, some with a two-hour air supply, most with four.

What had Hutch expected her to do with eight units? There were almost two hundred people at Origins.

She stayed below more than an hour. When she was finished with the inventory, she opened the hatch to the lander and slipped into the pilot's seat. The cargo bay was dark and quiet. She sat staring at the launch doors. Finally, the tears came, and the emotions she'd been holding back overwhelmed her. My God, she thought, what have I done?

The launch doors beckoned. She could instruct Bill to take Eric to Origins. She pictured herself adrift in the lander, air running out, waiting for the end. Hutch would shake her head and comment how she'd had it coming.

She tried to steel herself to do it. Get it over with. It was a way to show that, despite everything they thought about her, she was an honorable woman.

Mac also probably knew the truth by now. There was a guy who would know how to forgive. She could imagine him looking at her with those belligerent eyes and shaking his head. And walking away from her.

Never darken my door.

She was close to doing it. At least she thought she was. She actually closed the hatch and sat trying to find the words to tell Bill to depressurize the launch section.

But she'd promised she'd check for asteroids.

What a laugh.

Was there a chance, any chance at all, that monsters would come out of nowhere on a vector for one of the towers?

Still, she'd said she would do a sweep.

She desperately wanted a reason to prolong her life. And it was all she had.

When you depressurize, you can hear it at first. Hear the air getting sucked out. After a couple of minutes the sound goes away because there's not enough air to carry it. She wiped her eyes and wished there were a way to make everything right.

People like to say they're not afraid of dying. Valya was. The time in daylight is so short, so *marvelous*. She hated the thought of plunging into the night. Of taking that final deep dive into annihilation.

It would have been easier if she were leaving behind an admirable record. If she could believe Mac would stand at night and look at the stars and remember that she had been part of his life. If Hutch would regret the loss, even a little, and the Academy, or maybe a small group of friends, would hold a service for her, where someone would cry.

SHE WAS STILL hours away when she braked, connected with the facility's approach beam, and made final course adjustments. From this point she would not use her engines.

The preliminary sweeps, as she knew they would, revealed only empty space in all directions. Eventually the *Salvator* drew within visual range of the East Tower. Abiding by procedure, she sent an audio-only report to Mission Ops: "We read negative 6.5 million kilometers out. Assuming maximum approach velocity of twenty-five kps, predict no threat can materialize within next three days."

The chance of finding a rock coming in faster than that was pretty much nil.

She could imagine Hutchins sitting in her office, amused at Valya's being forced to turn her last mission into a wild goose chase.

AHEAD, THE EAST Tower floated in the dark. It was visible only as a circle of starless space. A transmission was coming in. *"Welcome to the Origins Project, East Tower."*

"Hello, East Tower. *Salvator* requests clearance to dock."

"Very good, Salvator. *We'll bring you in."*

"Buckle in, Eric," she said.

He had made an effort to lighten the mood. Told her he wished her luck and changed the subject. But the atmosphere remained tense, and there wasn't much anyone could do about it.

Controlled by the complex of gravity fields. they eased into the dock, and a familiar voice came over the link. *"Hi, Valya. I heard you were coming."* It was Lou Cassell. *"We didn't expect to see you back here so soon. Still chasing moonriders, are we?"*

It was nice to hear an unstrained human voice again. Eric had completely lost the ability to talk with her. He sounded by turns sad, apologetic, accusing, deferential. But good old Lou was just the tonic she needed. "Actually, there's some concern they might be coming here," she said.

"That's what we heard. I'll believe it when I see it."

"I don't think there's anything to it, Lou."

"I'll tell you, Val, if they were to show up here and start dropping rocks on us, I'm not sure what we'd be able to do about it."

She laughed. "Relax, Lou. We've all gone a little bit crazy."

Airlocks opened. She climbed out of her harness and walked back to the common room. Eric was back in his cabin, getting his gear.

Lou came through the hatch, and she told him how glad she was to see him. He looked surprised at the intensity of the embrace he got. His smile brightened the place and made her feel human again. "Good to see you both," he said. At which point she realized Eric was back. "Anybody else on board? No? Well, come on in and make yourselves comfortable. Are you going to stay over?"

"For a day or two," she said. "If you have room for us."

They went out the hatch and strolled through the exit tube. "There really is talk about moonriders," she said.

"I know." Lou obviously thought the subject laughable. "Apparently, your people got in touch with Allard, and he let us know. We got a message from a reporter, too. Saying the same thing. Telling us to look out."

"MacAllister?"

"Yeah. That might have been the name."

That caused a twinge. "I assume everybody had a good laugh."

He shrugged. "Tell you the truth, it shook us up a little. I mean, it sounds crazy, but if the Academy was taking it seriously, we were, too. I mean, that business at Capella was really strange." He looked at her, then at Eric. "You want to tell me what all this is about? I understand you saw moonriders at the *Surveyor* site, but I don't see how that would translate into an attack against us."

"We didn't really see them, Lou," she said. "The monitor reported some dark objects moving around. That's all we know." That had surprised her when it happened. But she suspected there was a natural explanation.

Eric gave her a nod of approval. Yes, keep Amy out of it. "Anyhow," he said, "they just wanted us to come by and make sure everything's okay."

This time they got to meet Mahmoud Stein, the East Terminal director. Stein appeared to be well past retirement age. He had black hair and brown eyes that never seemed to come quite into focus. He was smaller than she was, solemn, with perfect diction, enunciating each word as if it were being recorded for posterity. He shook their hands and said how pleased he was to meet them. But he also laughed about the moonriders. "Do you people really think we're going to get attacked by little green men?"

"No," she said. "I think the Academy is just being cautious."

Stein had better things to do, and he let her see it. "It's just like Allard, though," he said. "He warns us of something like this and doesn't bother to send anyone to help if it were to materialize. We have seventy-two people here, with no way to move any of them off in a hurry if we had to. I guess that tells you how seriously he was taking it."

Valya shrugged. "You don't have a ship here anywhere, I guess?"

"We have two shuttles."

"Well," she said, "I wouldn't worry about it. And we have ships on the way. To stand by. Just in case."

He shook his head, a man in the employ of morons. Something in the gesture reminded her of Mac. "I suspect it is a waste of resources, young lady. But nevertheless I appreciate your concern. It's nice to know *somebody* cares."

"I have a question for *you*, Professor," said Eric. "Valya says rockets and maneuvering jets aren't allowed anywhere near the collider."

"That's correct."

"But you have shuttles."

"Two of them at each tower, yes."

"How are they powered?"

"Some of our people would tell you by hot air."

"I'm serious."

Stein laughed. "They operate within magnetic and gravitational fields projected from stations along the tube. They orient with clutched gyros. It's quite effective."

"Suppose there's an emergency?"

"If necessary, they can maneuver by ejecting tennis balls."

"Tennis balls."

Valya smiled. "The director is pulling your leg, Eric."

"Well," said Stein, "actually they're trackable missiles. But they *look* like tennis balls."

THEY WERE REINTRODUCED to a few of the people they'd met on the first flight. To Jerry Bonham, a quiet, nervous guy from Seattle. His specialty, Lou explained, was flow dynamics. "He's been here six months. I think he hopes to make this his home." And Lisa Kao Ti, an engineer, part of the team seeing to the expansion of the collider.

"It's been, what, a month since you were here?" Lisa asked. "We're about three hundred kilometers longer than we were then."

"And this is Felix Eastman," he said, introducing them to a copper-skinned man in a bright yellow shirt. "From North Dakota. Felix is working on Blueprint."

They were in a lounge. There were probably a half dozen others present, and all conversations stopped when Eric asked whether there was any general danger attached to the project. "There is a slight risk," Eastman conceded. He was young, not yet out of his twenties. "But the odds are heavily against any kind of major mishap." He smiled. Nothing to worry about.

"But it *is* possible there could be a problem?"

"Mr. Samuels, anything not prohibited is possible. Yes, of course there's a possibility. But so small that we really need not concern ourselves with it."

"If this mishap were to occur, worst-case scenario, what would it entail? What would happen?"

"Worst-case?" He looked around and they all grinned. "Lights out, I guess." He actually sounded enthusiastic at the prospect. Valya watched quietly. Talent did not always make people bright.

Another young man stepped forward. Again, not much more than a kid. But she could see he had a high opinion of himself.

"Maybe I can help," he said. "My name is Rolly Clemens. I'm the project director for Blueprint."

Eric nodded. "Glad to meet you, Professor." He shook hands, but looked uncomfortable. Calling a kid "professor" must have seemed out of order. "Tell me about the possibility of catastrophe."

"Eric," he said, "there isn't much that is *not* possible." He adopted a tolerant expression. "But I don't think you need worry."

"You're sure."

"Of course."

"If the 'lights out' thing were to happen—"

"It won't—"

"Indulge me. If it were to occur, it would also involve Earth, right?"

Clemens was trying to be patient. They were talking nonsense. "Yes," he conceded. "It would involve everything."

"How long would it take before the effects were felt? At home?"

"A little more than twenty years."

"Why so long?"

"Because," he said, shifting to lecture mode for slow students, "it would cause a rift, and the rift would travel at light speed." He looked bored. Been through all this before.

What the hell, you can't live forever.

"If you're really worried about it," he continued, "you needn't be. The chances of something like that occurring are so remote they defy imagination."

A woman stepped out of the crowd. Plain-looking, black hair, also in her twenties. "I wouldn't be so sure," she said. The comment earned her a glare. But she plunged on. "Who's to say it can't happen. Who's calculating the odds? We're in unknown territory here."

"Oh, come on, Barb," said Clemens. "How many times are we going to have this conversation?"

"In the end," said Eastman, "you can't be certain of anything. But what's life worth if we don't take an occasional chance?" He was trying to make a joke of it.

She threw up her hands. "You people know it all. No need for me to be concerned."

"Doesn't it strike you," said Eric, "that if there's any chance at all of a catastrophe on this order, we shouldn't be doing the experiment?"

"It's the nature of experimentation," said Clemens. Whatever that meant.

LOU GOT DINNER for them. Afterward, Eric settled in with several others to listen to projections about the things mankind was going to learn from Origins when it was completed, in another century and a half. Did they think the construction effort would actually continue that long?

They were all convinced it would. Valya suspected it would become a casualty of belt-tightening before the year was over.

The facility was on Greenwich Mean Time, several hours ahead of the clock Eric and Valya had been living by. Consequently their hosts eventually peeled off and left them in an otherwise empty room.

She wished she could sit down at a radio and carry on a conversation with Hutchins. And Mac. She would have liked to be able to explain why she'd done what she had. Both of them probably believed she'd been bought. God knew what they thought of her.

She sat quietly while Eric talked about the downside of public relations, how people acted as if he were only a flack, how they refused to take him seriously. "They think I'm always trying to sell the product," he was saying. Through a viewport, she could see the soft reflection given off by the collider, fading into infinity.

Yet, if she had it to do again, she would change nothing.

IN THE MORNING, she told Eric she was going to the West Terminal. Did he want to come?

She knew he was glad to be out of the ship's confined quarters, and would probably have liked to put some distance between himself and her. But he was a gallant sort. Dull, but his heart was in the right place. "I'll go along if you don't mind," he said.

They had breakfast in the cafeteria, said good-bye to Lou and a cluster of Eric's newfound friends, climbed aboard the *Salvator*, and let the facility's gravity controls launch them. The tubular weave of the accelerator glowed in their lights. They moved out along it, drifting past automated machines unwinding wire from spools and knitting it into the structure.

They passed one of the support rings every few seconds. Eventually, an hour or so away from the East Terminal, a couple thousand kilometers out, they approached the midsection of the accelerator, where particles were slammed into each other at the speed of light.

Eric seemed to be feeling better than he had. He'd made a peace of sorts with what she'd done, and they were even able to talk about it. He told her he understood her motivation, and he'd do what he could to help her keep her job.

That wasn't going to happen. She knew that, but she appreciated his kindness. She was trying to think of a reply when Lou called them from the terminal. *"Valya,"* he said, *"I think we have moonriders."*

ERIC SAMUELS'S OCCASIONAL JOURNAL

I'm starting this because there's a possibility that a record of events may be helpful later.

Valentina admitted to me yesterday that she was part of a conspiracy to perpetrate a hoax that would entice the government to spend large sums of money on interstellar exploration and on defense. "The truth is," she told me, "we don't really know what's out there." However that may be, she has proven herself untrustworthy. I regret her actions, because she didn't think things out before allowing herself to get caught up in all this.

She says she cannot account, however, for Amy's experience at the *Surveyor* museum. It's possible the corporate entities behind this were able to arrange that as well. But I can't see how, and I can't bring myself to believe Amy would have been a participant. God help me, I hope not.

–Sunday, May 10

chapter 39

> Decisions are always made with insufficient information. If you really knew what was going on, the decision would make itself.
>
> –Gregory MacAllister,
> "Advice for Politicians," *Down from the Mountain*

Valya ignited her engines—she wasn't supposed to do that in the vicinity of the accelerator—and started a long turn. She relayed Lou's message to Union Ops, with the comment she was on her way back to the East Tower.

While the *Salvator* shed velocity and swung wide of the tube, Lou kept her apprised of the situation: *"They're just floating out there. Two of them. About twenty kilometers away. Black globes."*

"No lights anywhere?"

"Negative."

"You try to talk to them?"

"They don't respond, Valya."

"Lou," she said, "you might want to think about evacuating."

"We have no way to do that."

"Can you put me through to Stein?"

"As a matter of fact, he wants to speak with you. Hold on."

Stein appeared. The self-contained vaguely superior mode was gone. *"Do you two know something you haven't been telling me?"*

"No," said Valya. Damned if she was going to drag Amy into this. Anyhow, what difference would it make?

"You have no idea what those things are?"

"No."

"Why do you think they're a threat?"

"It's a long story."

"I'm listening."

"One of our people may have talked to them."

"And what did they say?"

"She says they told her to arrange the evacuation of the Origins Project. Because they were going to destroy it. That's why the Academy contacted Allard."

"Why? What's it about?"

"They mentioned Blueprint."

"It might have helped if you'd told me all this last night."

"Professor, I didn't think you'd have believed me."

"I'm not sure I believe you now."

"We're wasting time. What are you going to do about evacuating?"

"Not much. I have seventy-one people here. Seventy-two counting me. I've got two shuttles. What am I supposed to do with everybody else?"

"Get as many off as you can."

"You really think they're going to shoot at us? If that's the case, we're safer in here. The shuttles are too exposed."

She didn't know what to tell him. Didn't know what she believed. "Maybe we should just take them at their word."

"What do you mean, 'their word'? Could you please describe the nature of the conversation? How'd it happen?"

"We thought the person imagined it. It's beginning to look as if there's more to it than that."

"Son of a bitch."

"Have you informed the other tower yet?"

"We're doing that now. Damn. I don't believe this is happening."

"Neither do I, Professor."

He scattered a stack of pens and chips across his desktop. *"Okay. I'll get as many people off as possible. But when this is over, somebody's head is going to roll."*

"We'll be there as quickly as we can. We can take some of your people."

He switched off, and an uncomfortable silence settled on the bridge. *"Ta kaname thalassa."*

"What's that again?" asked Eric.

"We screwed up."

"You can't really take a dream seriously," he said. "How long will the air supply last in the shuttles?"

"Don't know. They'll cram them to capacity, which won't help." She took a deep breath. "Bill, outgoing to Hutchins."

"Ready."

"Hutch, we've got moonriders. Two of them so far. Stein is evacuating the East Tower. As much as he's able. Let the incoming ships know. I'll keep you informed."

Lou came back. *"Nobody knows what to think. It's pretty hard to believe."*

"I know."

"The moonriders are still keeping their distance." He stopped to say something to someone out of the picture. She could hear laughter in the background. And someone saying he was in the middle of a job, find somebody else. Then a hand passed him a note. *"They tell me I'm wrong. They're coming closer."*

"Are you loading the shuttles yet?"

"No. They were both down the line. One of them's coming in now."

They had finally completed their turn and were starting back toward the East Tower. Off to port, the thin wire strands of the collider flashed occasionally as they raced past. Valya looked ahead, could see only stars.

"Okay, they are *getting closer. No question about it. How far out are you, Vulyu?"*

"Not far. Twenty minutes or so."

"You think we're really in trouble?"

She felt helpless. "I just don't know, Lou. How are they deciding who goes on board the shuttles?"

"Volunteers."

Volunteers? To stay or go?

"Okay, the white shuttle's pulled in. They're running the boarding tube out now."

"Can't we move faster?" asked Eric.

"We're at optimal. Have to be able to stop when we get there."

"Opening up."

Valya was uncertain what she should do when she arrived. Try to drive off the globes? Or dock and take more people on board?

"Okay. There we go. We're starting to load."

"How many can you put into a shuttle?"

"Eight. Counting the pilot."

"What kind of shuttles are they?"

"TG12s. Both of them."

She looked toward the AI's status lamp. "Specs, Bill?"

"The TG12 is designed to hold a total of six. They can accommodate eight, but it won't be comfortable."

"I doubt they care about comfort," said Eric. "How far away is the fleet?"

"The closest is seven or eight hours," she said.

"Not going to be much help."

"The globes have closed to within about a kilometer."

"Bill, try to raise the damned things *tou diaolou*. See if we can get a response. And while you're at it, get me the West Tower."

"Complying."

"Shuttle's full," said Lou. *"Closing up. The other one's in sight now."*

"West," said a male voice.

"This is the *Salvator*. You know the situation at the East Tower?"

"Not really, Salvator. *We can't figure out what's going on."*

"Is anything unusual happening at your end?"

"Everything's quiet. No moonriders."

"There's a possibility you will come under attack shortly."

"Attack? Why? What sort of attack?"

"Don't know."

"You don't know much, do you?"

"Save the humor. You might need it later."

"Valya," said Lou, *"the white shuttle's away. Blue shuttle coming in now."*

"Are the globes still coming closer?"

"Negative. They're holding steady."

"Okay. Let me know if anything changes. West, tell whoever's in charge over there he may have to evacuate on short notice."

"I'll tell her, Salvator, *but she isn't going to be happy."*

Right. Her feelings are significant at the moment. "Bill, show me a picture."

The navigation screen, which had been providing images of the collider tube immediately ahead, abruptly shifted. The terminal and the globes came into view. Infrared images. The globes were side by side.

"Distance between them," said Bill, *"is one two zero meters. They're manipulating gravity fields. The objects are identical. I can pick up devices on the hull. Sensors, antennas. Cones that might be communications gear or possibly weapons."*

"Are they responding to query?"

"Negative. They are silent."

"Okay. Keep trying."

"The objects are seventy-seven meters in diameter. Perfect spheres, save for a series of ribs or ridgelines."

"Loading the blue shuttle," said Lou.

She had a bad feeling. "Are *you* getting on this one, Lou?"

"No. I feel safer here."

Something about the way the two vehicles were lined up chilled her. "You might get on if you can."

"We'll be okay."

"West Tower calling," said Bill. *"Dr. Estevan. She is the deputy director."*

Terri Estevan was a tense woman who looked as if she never smiled. Brown hair starting to go gray. Thin lips. Not somebody who'd liven up a party. *"What's going on?"* she demanded.

Valya went through a conversation similar to the one she'd had with Stein. Was this a serious threat? What was she supposed to believe? Through it all, there seemed to be the implication that it was Valya's fault.

Somebody was going to answer some serious questions when this ended. Then she was gone, and Lou was back. *"Blue shuttle away,"* he said.

"Okay, Lou." She watched it move out from the dock, headed along the tube in her direction.

"Something's happening," said Lou.

The globes were beginning to glow. Bill switched over to the telescopes, and they could see the objects, now bathed in orange auras.

They began to move. Drew closer together, until they were almost touching.

The *Salvator* was coming up fast. Valya began to brake.

The globes reddened.

A pair of scarlet beams winked on. Like lasers. One from each globe. They crossed each other and both went wide of the facility. Then they intersected, combined into a single luminous coruscating shaft. It struck the tower, which also began to glow.

"Look out, Lou," Valya called.

"*What's happening?*" demanded Lou.

The tower erupted in a fireball.

NEWSDESK

The notion that anyone intelligent enough to build a star drive would not be capable of malevolent behavior now ranks with other discarded ideas, like the conviction that a state capable of producing world-class symphonies would not invade its neighbors, or that serial killers are always half-wits.

–Rose Beetem, the Black Cat Network,
Sunday, May 10

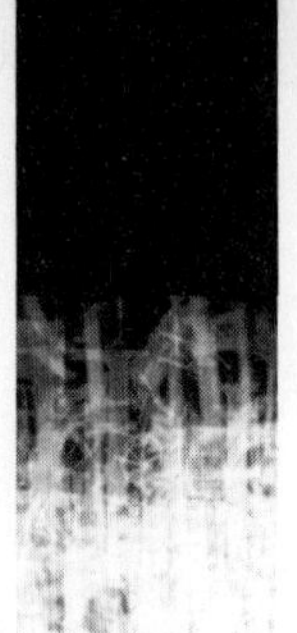

chapter 40

> The beginning of wisdom is to admit to being inept. We're all a bit slow. We have our moments, but in the end, we have to resort to bumbling through. It is what makes conviction so egregious.
>
> —Gregory MacAllister, "Plato and the Comedians"

"—smoking ruin—"

Valya's transmission described the destruction of the East Tower in a flat voice, her emotions barely under control.

"—tower is gone—"

It was a Sunday. Hutch relayed the message to the homes of the other department heads and of her staff.

"The shuttles are clear, and the moonriders seem willing to let them go."

"George," she said, "do we have any way of getting to the commissioner?"

"No, ma'am. He's still listed as unavailable."

She lowered herself into a chair and just watched. Valya's image blinked off and was replaced by pictures from the *Salvator*'s scopes. Smoke and debris and two black globes.

"—Still trying to reach them," said Valya. *"Maybe find a way to talk to*

them. If they talked to Amy, they must understand English, but I get no response."

The head of personnel called. Doug Eberling. An excitable guy who'd found a home with the Academy and had no ambition other than to stay out of trouble. *"Is that really happening, Hutch? My God, I can't believe it."*

"—To notify the West Tower. I've been talking to the shuttles. They're okay. A little bit shocked."

"Hutch," said Eberling, *"what can we do?"*

"The shuttles are telling me power's off in the tube. They aren't getting their boost from the rings."

"What's that mean?" asked Eberling.

"It means," said Hutch, "they don't have much in the way of propulsion. Just a few missiles they can fire off and that's it."

Peter showed up on the circuit. *"Looks like you were right, Hutch."*

"They're moving," said Valya. *"The moonriders are moving again."* Her voice rose several decibels. *"They're following the tube. Hutch, they're headed for the other tower."*

The *Salvator*'s scopes stayed with them. They'd lined up on either side of the collider and were beginning to pick up speed. Chasing the shuttles?

They moved frantically aside, trying to evade. But the globes cruised serenely past, making no effort to pursue. Thank God for that at least.

SHE INFORMED THEIR government liaison, so he could pass it up the chain of command. The World Council probably didn't have the news yet. But it sounded as if a war had started.

Valya had sent information copies of the transmission to the ten ships of the rescue squadron. Hutch added a warning of her own: *"They are hostile. Do not put yourself at unnecessary risk. We'll send updates as soon as we get them."*

Another message went to Valya: *"Do what you can, but don't lose the* Salvator. *As the situation changes, please keep us informed. Continue information copies to the incoming vessels. Good luck."*

Then a call came in from Allard. *"Goddam you,"* he said. The man was literally sputtering. *"We have at least fifty dead."* He stared at her across a vast gulf, struggling to contain his rage. *"Where is Asquith?"*

"He's not available at the moment, Professor. I have a call in to him, and I'll relay your concern when I'm able."

"You may relay more than my concern. What did you people know that you neglected to tell me? How could you possibly let this happen?"

His voice trembled, and she thought he was close to cardiac arrest. "We gave you everything we had, Professor."

"Nonsense! You told me something about a dream. An apparition."

"We gave you what we had. It was your decision to sit on it." Although she understood why he had chosen to ignore their warning. They had not, after all, been convinced themselves.

Abruptly, tears welled up in Allard's eyes. *"God help us,"* he said.

THE NEWS WAS getting out. Hutch had several calls in succession from the media. She admitted that yes, an attack had occurred, but at the moment that was all she had. *"I don't know any more than you do."*

Then there was Charlie Dryden. She'd been too busy to tell him what she thought of him. When he called, though, it was obvious he knew Mac had spoken to her. He was tentative rather than his usual charge-the-battlements self. *"Hutch,"* he said, *"I hate to bother you. But is it true?"*

"Yes. We have a lot of people dead."

"I don't believe it." He looked genuinely shocked.

"Is that by any chance because you thought the moonriders were your own invention?"

"Well, that's not exactly true. Look, Hutch, we meant no harm."

Interesting how the first-person pronoun he normally used had gone plural. "Cut the act, Charlie. Anyway, the details, at the moment, don't matter. I'm busy. What do you need?"

"I was hoping I could do something to help."

"You could have helped three days ago when we needed two carriers."

"Look, Hutch," he said, *"what we did, I know that doesn't sit well with you—"*

"It's okay, Charlie. I enjoy being lied to."

"You wouldn't have come in willingly. We knew that. But we were trying to save the program—"

"I don't have time for this."

"We had a ship standing by near the Galactic. In case there was a problem. Nobody was ever in danger."

"If you don't have anything else, I have to go."

"No," he said. *"I don't have anything else. I just wanted you to know this was something we felt we had to do. We wanted to protect the Academy."*

"Give me a break, Charlie. You and your pals don't really care about the Academy, except as a wedge to get government contracts for your own outfit. Was the commissioner part of it?"

"No," he said. *"He didn't know anything about it."*

"Well, at least you're not a snitch, Charlie."

"Hutch, I'd really be grateful if you could bring yourself to overlook this. I meant well."

She smiled at him. "I take it you're headed for court."

"No. I don't think so."

"I'll try to arrange it. Good-bye, Charlie."

GEORGE WAS USUALLY pretty unflappable. He was, after all, an AI. But when he whispered Hutch's name a minute or two after she'd disconnected Dryden, he sounded impressed. *"Call from the president,"* he said.

Hutch thought she'd better sit down for this one. "Put him through, George."

A young woman blinked on. Black hair, well dressed, artificial smile. *"Please hold for President Crandall,"* she said.

Hutch tried to arrange herself. Try to look cool. As if presidents call every day.

The woman was replaced by the man himself. Patrick O'Keefe Crandall, the first Canadian president, now in his third year. He was seated in an armchair, looking at a document—somehow it was a document and not simply a piece of paper—but when he saw her, he stood. *"Ms. Hutchins. I've been meaning to have you over to the White House."* The New White House, actually. The old one, now an island, was a museum. He glowed with the charm that had helped him carry fifty-two states in the last election.

She stood, too. "It's a pleasure to meet you, Mr. President."

"May I call you Hutch?*"*

"Yes, sir. Of course. Whatever you like." Dumb.

He laughed. It was okay. *"Hutch, I understand the facility at Origins is under attack."*

"Yes, Mr. President. That is so. They've destroyed the East Tower."

"I'm also informed you have direct contact with a ship on the scene."

"That's correct, Mr. President."

"Good. I want you to stay on top of this. Anything that comes in should be forwarded directly to me. Your AI has the code."

"Yes, sir."

"I've been informed you have a small squadron of ships on the way."

"That's correct, Mr. President."

"That they left a couple days ago."

"Yes."

"You knew in advance an attack was coming." He studied her carefully, trying to make up his mind about her. *"I wonder if you'd explain how that happened."*

Her reluctance must have shown.

"It's okay," he said. *"We're on a secure circuit."*

So she told him everything. He listened, his expression composed, nodding occasionally, explaining he understood when she described her reaction to the story. She added they'd made an effort to keep Amy's name out of it. If that story made the rounds, the kids at her school would never let her rest. And the media would be all over her.

"And you say the thing looked like you?"

"Yes."

His eyes widened perceptibly. It was a reaction everybody in the country was familiar with. *"Well,"* he said, *"they certainly have exquisite taste."*

She smiled at the compliment. "I don't know where it came from."

"We'll give it some thought. Hutch, thank you for your efforts. And we're grateful you didn't wait to send out those ships."

SHE SENT A warning to Valya to let her know her messages were being relayed directly to the White House. It would be two hours before she received it, probably too late to be of any practical value, but it was all she could do.

She'd just finished when another transmission came in from the *Salvator*. *"We've checked with both shuttles. They're okay for now. I'm going to leave them to get over to the West Tower on their own. There are sixteen souls on board. No sign anybody else made it."*

Hutch forwarded the message to the New White House and her other consumers. Then she called Amy.

"I've been watching it on the news," Amy said, looking stricken. *"How many dead?"*

"Looks like upward of fifty."

"I told *you. Nobody would listen."*

"I'm sorry, Amy. You were right, and the rest of us were wrong. We should have trusted you from the first moment. But in the end we *did* listen. Because of you there's a rescue fleet moving in. At the other terminal. A lot of lives will be saved."

She shook her head. *"Fifty dead. How could you let it happen?"*

NEWSDESK

ORIGINS ATTACKED
Fifty-Six Feared Dead at Science Outpost

WORLD COUNCIL IN EMERGENCY SESSION
Pasturi to Issue Statement

DID ALIENS DO IT?
Random Attacks Baffle Experts

HAND OF GOD SERVES WARNING, SAYS TRAPLEY
"Some Things We Are Not Meant to Know"
Project Was Examining Creation

CRANDALL WILL ASSURE NATION
President to Speak Tonight

DEFENSE COMMITTEE CALLS FOR MORE SPENDING

HURRICANE HARRY TO MAKE LANDFALL TOMORROW
Evacuation in Carolinas, Georgia

LIBRARY ENTRY

During the late twenty-first century, when the Lysistrata movement was at the height of its power, and the world's major powers were being forced to disband their militaries, there were those who warned that we would eventually regret the action. The assumption was that a rogue state would surreptitiously arm itself and create havoc in its region and possibly around the world. Eldrige Westin led the assault on Lysistrata. "Those who seek peace, but who are not willing to fight for it, will have no peace, and will quickly lose the ability to seek anything." American women thanked him by voting him out of office.

It looks now as if the hour of retribution may be upon us. We have been attacked, not by our own kind but by something outside our experience. The politicians will not admit it but, whatever this force may be, we stand naked before it. If it comes here, we will have no defense other than to throw ripe fruit in its direction.

God help us.

—Marianthy Golazko, *Parthenon*, Sunday, May 10

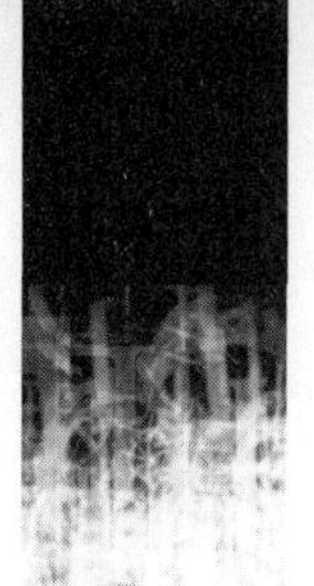

chapter 41

> The creative act requires both will and intelligence. Breaking things is easy. You only need a hammer.
>
> —Gregory MacAllister, "On the Road"

Where the East Tower had been, there were only a few scorched struts and beams, somehow still connected to the collider tube. Black smoke and debris drifted away in all directions.

"Incoming transmission," said Bill. *"From one of the shuttles."*

It was audio only, three or four panicked voices. *"Who the hell are they?"*

"Salvator, *is anybody coming?"*

"They killed them all . . . "

And Bill again: *"The other shuttle wants to talk to you, too. As does West."*

Ahead, something lit up the sky. And subsided.

"What was that?" asked Eric.

"I've no idea." She told both shuttles she'd be with them in a minute and directed Bill to link with West. It was Estevan. If she'd been tense before, she looked on the verge of a breakdown now. *"What's happening out there?"* she demanded. *"We've been cut off from the Tower."*

"It's been destroyed, Doctor. By alien hostiles. It looks as if they're on their way over to see you."

"My God. What do they want?"

"I think they disapprove of something you're doing."

"What are you talking about, Valya?"

"Let's discuss it later. Stein managed to evacuate a few of his people. They weren't attacked. So whatever's driving these things, they want the structure gone. Not *you*. I suggest you get as many people off the platform as you can."

"How am I supposed to do that? We have two shuttles and that's it." She paused, trying to collect herself. *"When will they get here?"*

"They're just past the second ring." She did the math. The rings were 150 kilometers apart. The globes had needed about ten minutes to get from the first ring to the second one. "If they maintain current velocity, you've got about five and a half hours."

Why were they moving so slowly?

"Maybe that's their top speed," said Eric.

"I doubt it," she said. "Bill, let's go back to the shuttles."

"Very good," said Bill. *"They're panicked."*

He switched over. Screams and yells erupted from the speaker. "You're safe," said Valya. "They're gone."

A woman's voice spilled out. Margo Somebody. *"I'm the pilot.* Salvator, *do you see the bastards?"*

"They're well up the line. Headed away from you."

"Toward West?"

"Looks like. Listen, stay put. Help's coming. I'll make sure somebody gets over here to pick you up. They're still probably six or seven hours away. But just sit tight."

She did a final search of the area, on the off chance she might have missed something. But there was no one on the commlink, and the scanners revealed no intact bodies anywhere. "Okay," she told Eric, finally. "Let's get out of here." She swung back alongside the tube and began to accelerate.

Minutes later, they passed the first of the rings that supported the collider. It was charred. Now they knew what had flared up. A second ring was in the same condition.

Dead ahead, she made out the globes. They were dark, proceeding at a leisurely pace. On impulse, she slowed and blinked her navigation lights. The globes blinked back.

She tried a second time, but the phenomenon did not repeat.

"They're taking the entire thing down," said Eric.

"Apparently." She brought Bill back up. "What's the latest on the rescue fleet?"

"Valya, everything is currently on the way, but they're all still in hyper. The Rehling *is supposed to make its jump into local space in about an hour."* After which they'd need some time to get to the Tower. *"The* Rehling *can carry nine passengers. The* Granville *should be running a couple hours behind that. But if they get a good jump, they'll still beat the moonriders to the Tower. The* Granville *can carry twenty-two. The others have next to no chance to get here before that happens."*

She reconnected with Estevan and gave her an update.

Estevan listened, rage and frustration barely controlled. *"All these years of work,"* she said. Her voice trembled.

AN HOUR LATER, as they approached the West Tower, Bill announced a message from the *Rehling.*

"Valya." The voice belonged to Mark Stevens, a veteran pilot with whom she'd worked on several occasions. *"We've just completed our jump. Got a good one. We'll be at the West Tower in about three hours."*

"Make it as quick as you can, Mark."

A frightened crowd awaited them as they debarked. "What are these things?" they demanded. "What's happening? Is it as bad as we're hearing?"

"Help's coming," Valya said.

"And these things are coming here, is that right?" demanded a tall, gangly young man with red-blond hair and a Denver Hawks jacket. "Why are they doing this?"

"Nobody knows," she said. When they get here, you can ask them.

"We're all going to die." A frightened voice, somewhere. Somebody else whimpered.

"We can take some of you off on the *Salvator,*" Valya said. "More ships are on their way."

It didn't help much.

The interior was a mirror image of East Tower. The dining room that had been on the right was on the left. Conference rooms were reversed, as were the library and a gym. They pushed through, picked up an escort, and hurried down passageways and climbed into the upper levels until they reached Estevan's office.

The deputy director looked as if the world had ended. She sat in a chair with a notebook open on her lap, staring at the opposite wall. She glanced up, said hello, thanked the person who'd accompanied them, and signaled for her to close the door on her way out.

Design charts of Origins at various stages of construction covered the walls. There was also a picture of two toddlers. Probably the director's grandchildren. Estevan was smaller than she'd appeared on the commlink. Her face was ashen, and a vein throbbed in her neck. "For God's sake," she said, "what are we supposed to do? You tell me to evacuate. Where? How? I have no ships—"

"They're coming," said Valya.

"When?"

"The *Rehling*'s three hours out. The others haven't jumped yet, so it's impossible to be sure. But the *Granville* should also be here before the moonriders. And if we get lucky, maybe one or two others."

"How many can they carry?"

"Thirty-one between them."

Estevan closed her eyes and fought back tears. "It's maddening," she said. "The potential for this facility . . ." She tried to shake off the mood.

"How many are on the station?"

"Seventy-eight, counting me." She almost sounded resentful. "You look surprised." It *was* more than Valya had expected. "So what do we do, Valya?"

Na pari o diaolos. How did Valya wind up in charge? This was a bit above her pay grade.

The *Salvator* could squeeze nine on board, not counting herself and Eric. That was well over capacity. But she could manage it for a limited time. Assuming the *Granville* and the *Rehling* got here before the moonriders, that would leave thirty-eight still on the station. "You said you had shuttles?"

"Two."

"Are they the same as the ones at the other end? The TG12s?"

"Yes. I believe so."

"That's sixteen more."

"They only hold six. Including the pilot."

"They'll hold eight in an emergency."

Estevan didn't believe her. "They'll suffocate."

"The air'll get a bit close. But it's only until more ships arrive. And we've got a lander on the *Salvator*. That'll take another four." That left what? Eighteen. "How many breathers does the Tower have?"

Estevan made a call to get the answer. Whoever was on the other end had to check. Valya lowered herself into a seat. Estevan exhaled. Looked around the room. Then spoke into her link again. She listened, nodded, frowned. "We have six," she told Valya. "They're telling me there are usually two more, but they went to the East Tower a week ago."

"And your shuttles each have two?"

"Yes."

Each breather had a two-hour air supply. "Have them make sure the air tanks are filled and ready to go," she said.

"Why?" she asked. "What's the point?"

"You put as many people on the ships as the life support will maintain. Then you give the rest breathers and put *them* on board, too. It'll be uncomfortable, but they'll survive until the other ships get here."

Valya had the eight from Union, and the two that were routinely kept on board. That was twenty. If the *Rehling* and the *Granville* got there before the moonriders, they could get everyone off.

ESTEVAN BROUGHT IN her senior staff, three men and two women, and introduced everybody. Larry Kleigmann, head of the science department, took the lead in thanking Valya and Eric for coming. "Glad somebody cares about us," he said, exchanging glances with the deputy director. He was from Ohio State, a physicist, probably unmarried. "After all we went through trying to get the sons of bitches to fund the collider," he said. "It took us twenty years to persuade them to say yes, and look what happens."

Angie Sudara was the acting construction chief. Her boss had been at the other tower. She was barely five feet tall, middle-aged, light brown hair, good-looking in an unkempt, windblown way. "Good to see you guys," she said.

Julie Halper headed the West Tower medical department. Julie was a Nigerian, obviously a woman who worked out, with a good smile, but, at the moment, an intense, scared expression.

And Santos Kerr, tall and lean, in a white jumpsuit. A mathematician who had, Kleigmann explained, been with Origins from its inception.

And finally, the deputy's chief of staff, Ho Smith. It sounded like the name of an action hero, but he looked scared. Ho had Asian features, but spoke Oxford English.

Without wasting time, Estevan got down to business. "Right now, it looks as if these savages will be here in about three and a half hours. The *Salvator* is here to evacuate some of us, and Valya tells us it's ready to go.

"As things now stand, we should be okay. I wish we could do something to stop these idiots from blowing up the rest of the facility. Ho has been trying to contact them, but they're not talking to us." She glanced over at Ho. He nodded. Yes, he had been trying, and no, there was still no response.

Did any one have a suggestion?

No one did.

"Okay. Then let's go talk to the troops."

ESTEVAN MARCHED THROUGH the somber crowds in the passageways, trying to be reassuring as she went, wearing a smile as if everything was under control.

She strolled into the dining area flanked by her staff and followed by, Valya thought, everyone in the facility.

She signaled for Valya and Eric to stand with her. Then she waited for silence. When it didn't immediately come, Kleigmann bawled for everybody to "shut it down."

She climbed onto a chair. It was a bit wobbly, and Santos took her hand to steady her. She started by giving her assurance that everyone was going to get off the station before the aliens showed up. Then she introduced Valya and Eric, who had arrived "in the first of several evacuation vessels." That brought cheers. "Ladies and gentlemen, you already have a pretty good idea what's going on. But let me lay it out for you."

She was good. There'd been a transformation of sorts between the quivering wreck in the office and the woman who now dominated a frightened audience. In a tense but matter-of-fact tone, she explained what had happened and what was being done to rescue them. "I'll be honest," she said. "This whole thing is as scary for me as it is for you. But we have every reason to be optimistic. Help is on the way. And the good news is these creatures don't seem intent on killing *us*. Apparently, they simply want to destroy the facility."

"Why?" asked a thick-waisted man standing against the wall.

"We don't really know, Harry. It may have something to do with Blueprint." That brought sighs, protests, and a few I-told-you-so's. "I know there's been some discussion among us as to whether we should have been proceeding with it. That's all moot now. All we care about at the moment is getting away from here.

"The way things are proceeding, the aliens are still roughly three hours away. I can't guarantee that, but so far they've been moving at a constant rate. Valya tells me she thinks they want to give us time to get clear. I hope she's right. We have at our immediate disposal one ship, two shuttles, and a lander. We expect two more ships to be here before these creatures, whatever they are.

"Fortunately, it'll be enough to accommodate everybody. Some of us may have to wear a breathing apparatus for a couple of hours, but that's a small enough price to pay.

"We're going to put twenty-nine people on the two shuttles, the *Salvator*, and the *Salvator*'s lander. In addition, we have twenty breathers. That means we can put an additional twenty people on the *Salvator*, or whatever other ship shows up."

"Is there room?" someone asked.

Estevan looked down at Valya. "It'll be a bit snug," Valya said. "But we can live with it."

"We could wait for the *Granville*," said Estevan, "but we think it's smarter to get as many people off as early as we can. Just in case."

"You think the *Granville* won't get here?" someone asked. A voice in back.

"We'd rather be safe than sorry. The *Rehling* can take out nine. It also has two breathers, which we'll collect. Whoever's left will be picked up by the *Granville*. If you look around at the main door, you'll notice Ho and Angie back there with a box. There are folded slips of paper in the box, numbered one to seventy-two. Take one as you go out. Show it to them, and they'll record your number. Those numbers will be the sequence of departure. Number one will be out the door first. Seventy-two will leave when the senior staff does.

"Any questions?"

"Yes, Terri. When do we expect the *Granville*?"

"We don't know. Actually, there are several ships en route. We're waiting for them to complete their jumps, which should come at any time.

"We're going to wait until the last minute to launch the *Salvator*. That way we conserve oxygen. The senior staff and I will be riding out on the *Granville*. Along with the highest numbers."

She answered a few more questions, mostly repetitious, and decided to close it out. "You've been a good team to work with," she said. "I know some of you had friends on the East Tower. You're aware only sixteen people survived over there. But they didn't have the advance warning we do." She got down off the table and moved confidently through the room. Everything was going to be fine.

WITH TWO HOURS remaining, good news came in. *"This is WhiteStar II,"* said a woman's voice. *"Just made our jump, and we are on target. We're about two and a half hours out. Maybe a bit more."*

Wonderful. "Thank you, *WhiteStar II*," said Valya. "We'll put the beer on ice. Be advised it looks close whether you get here first, or the crazies do. Recommend you lose no time. How many breathers do you have on board?"

There was a delay while the signal crossed. *"Hotfoot,"* said the pilot. *"Will be there soonest. Have two breathers."*

She passed the news to Estevan, who nodded as if she'd known all along. "No sweat," she said.

They collected four breathers from the two shuttles, loaded eight people on each, and launched them.

THE MOONRIDERS WERE still an hour and a half away when the *Rehling* arrived. It already, unfortunately, carried two passengers. Mark Stevens was first off the ship, striding into the reception area where about twenty people waited with a scattering of luggage. He was a good-looking guy, dark hair, quiet. You could see the concern in his eyes. There were comments from the crowd. Good to see you. Thank God you got here.

Valya met him at the airlock. He reacted with a pained smile, and they embraced. "You okay?" he whispered.

"It's been scary."

"I know. Hang in there. Everything'll be all right."

One of Stevens's passengers emerged. His expression suggested he should be treated with deference. He had white hair, thin lips, narrow eyes under enormous brows, and what appeared to be a permanent frown. This was Charles Autry from Seaside University in Sydney. Valya had transported him to Nok some years earlier. He'd been obnoxious throughout the voyage. Immediately behind him came Marcus Cullen, tall and lean, an aristocrat by inclination, born into money and influence and never recovered. He was the president of Duke University. "It's just been one thing after another," grumbled Autry. "Let's get this show on the road."

Stevens smiled at Valya. "We're not happy at being delayed," he said.

"Typical screwup," Autry said. "Bureaucracy at work."

Cullen looked directly through Valya as though she did not exist. His gaze swept around the room without reaction and came back to Stevens. He sighed and made a point of checking the time.

Valya resisted the temptation to ask whether either of them would volunteer to stay for the *Granville*. "Mark," she said, "do you have some breathers on board?"

"We have two."

"How much oxygen?"

"A two-hour supply for each. Why?"

"We're going to steal them."

"Okay," he said. "You're welcome to them."

"Could we *please* move this along?" said Cullen.

Estevan appeared. "One through nine," she said. Nine people picked up their bags and began to move forward. She stepped back to make room for them. "Enjoy your flight," she said. "I'll see you at Union."

There was some shuffling in the crowd. A few sighs. Some guilty looks. Somebody in back said she had a child at home. Someone else explained he hadn't intended to come out here in the first place. He'd been pressured.

There were handshakes and embraces.

Autry wondered aloud whether they were ready to leave yet.

Valya glared at him, but he never noticed. "*Stazoun meli,*" she said.

Stevens put a hand on her shoulder. "They're okay. They're not used to this. They got detoured, and now they have to ride home in a crowded ship."

"I'm sympathetic."

"I can see that." His jaw muscles worked. "You going to be all right?"

"I'll be fine."

"Don't wait too long to get clear yourself." His new passengers filed through the airlock. Then Cullen and Autry, and finally Stevens. Minutes later, as the *Rehling* was pulling away from the dock, they heard that the *WhiteStar* had not gained any time. If nothing changed, it would be several minutes behind the the moonriders.

Bill broke in. "Transmission from the *Tanaka*."

"Salvator, *jump is complete. We estimate TOA three hours ten minutes."*

Bare minutes later, the *Carolyn Ray* checked in. *"Four-plus hours out."*

"Ray," she said, "we have two shuttles with sixteen survivors in the vicinity of the East Tower. Those will be your responsibility."

EVERYONE IN THE place was making it a point to approach Valya and Eric and shake their hands. Don't know what we'd have done, they said.

They were, on the whole, a young crowd. Most of those who identified themselves as physicists were in their twenties or thirties. Administrative staff tended to be older, as were the engineers.

Darryl Murillo, a consultant to the construction crew, was able to rig a display that showed precisely where the moonriders were by tracking the destruction of the rings. Murillo was from Barcelona, a tall, well-built guy in his midthirties who spoke English with a Castilian accent. "When we get home," he told Valya, "I would be honored if you would be my guest for dinner."

The long tradition in physics, of course, was that you did your breakthrough work, if there was going to be any, during your first ten years. Otherwise, you could forget it. And there was no place more on the cutting edge than the Origins Project. Kleigmann looked proud when they talked about it. "The top people on the planet are out here," he said. Then his eyes grew distant. "I hate to think what we've already lost in the other tower. There were a lot of good kids over there."

Estevan made it a point to stay out of her office. She patrolled the corridors, took over a table in one of the larger conference rooms, stayed where she could be seen. She laughed and talked as if nothing unusual were happening. Meantime, crowds stayed close to Murillo's displays.

Eric was also showing a side Valya hadn't seen before. "I've spent too many Saturday nights at home," he said. "Did you know I'm almost forty?" It seemed an odd comment until she thought about it.

Actually, she'd have guessed he was a few years older. "Is there a woman in your life, Eric?"

"Not really," he said. "Maybe one. Jeri Makaiya. But I've never been out with her. Never asked her out."

"Why not?"

"She works for me. It's not smart. Romantic entanglements in the office. In fact, they've got a rule against anything like that between supervisors and subordinates."

They were down under an hour, sitting at a table in the cafeteria, next door to the conference room where Estevan was holding court. "That can be a problem," Valya said. "There *are* other women. I'd think you would make a pretty nice catch, Eric."

He smiled shyly. "Thanks." Then: "She's the one I really like."

"Then break the rule."

He shook his head. Can't do that.

"You have to decide what's important. If she matters, you can't just walk away. If you do, twenty years from now you'll still regret it." Being at leisure in a place you know is about to be blown apart has a curious effect. Valya found herself reviewing her own life, thinking about the good times, old friends who had gotten lost along the way, moments when she might have chosen another path. There wasn't much she regretted, almost nothing she'd have done differently. Maybe Terranova. (Her feeling about that kept changing.) Maybe Jamie Clemens, whom she'd once loved. Still loved. But she'd walked out of his life and later changed her mind, but by then he was angry or taken. She was never sure which.

And now there was Mac.

What a rollicking, hard-nosed, unpredictable son of a bitch he was. She'd never known anyone remotely like him. Were all journalists like that? She knew he'd be resentful, would make her pay a price for her deceit. But she thought she could repair the damage, could hang on to him. When she got back she'd go see him. And she'd do what she had to.

Meantime, it was getting late. "Time to load our passengers, Eric."

Her commlink vibrated. It was Bill.

"*We have a transmission from the* Granville," he said.

"Let's hear it, Bill." Pray for good news.

"Salvator." The voice sounded French. "*We have just made our jump. Did not get as close as we'd hoped. But we are on our way and will be there in three hours.*"

Her heart sank. Eric stared at her. "What?"

"Two hours late." *Granville* was their *bus*. She acknowledged, and did the numbers again: *WhiteStar II* could take five. Seven with the air tanks they should have on board.

That would leave what?

Eleven.

ERIC SAMUELS'S OCCASIONAL JOURNAL

Valya has been magnificent. She helped Estevan pull herself together, and has managed to convince everyone by her quiet, cool confidence that they're all going to get home okay.

But she informed me just minutes ago that the *Granville* won't be here in time. She's in now giving Estevan the bad news. I don't envy her, going through all this. And the ironic part of it is that she knows she's been terminated.

—Sunday, May 10

chapter 42

> We are at heart a cowardly species. But that's good. Fear is a reflex installed to keep us alive. But sometimes the fittings come loose. When that happens, and the victims routinely defy their instincts to clear out, they often do not live to reproduce. Considering the probabilities, it's hard to understand why courage has not been bred completely out of us.
>
> —Gregory MacAllister, *Life and Times*

Terri Estevan was crushed by the news. "Is there no chance?" she asked in a trembling voice. "None at all? Maybe one of the ships will get lucky, and jump into a favorable position. Like the *WhiteStar*."

"It's possible," said Valya. "But it's unlikely."

"All right." They were alone. Valya had emptied the room before telling her.

For a long minute neither spoke. Estevan collapsed into a chair and fought to stifle a sob.

Valya did not know what to say. It was, after all, Estevan and ten of her associates who were going to be stuck there when the moon-riders arrived. Valya would be well on her way out of town. There was no way she could offer consolation. "We'll take everyone who has a breather," she said. "Better not wait for the *WhiteStar*."

"Can you do that? Is there room?"

"We'll make room."

SHE RECALLED HER staff.

Kleigmann. Angie. Julie Halper. Santos. And Ho Smith.

They knew as soon as they came back into the room that something was terribly wrong. Estevan stared past them. "The *Granville*'s not going to make it," she said.

Kleigmann's expression turned stony. Angie bowed her head and her lips began to quiver. Julie sagged against a table. Santos murmured a prayer. Ho found a bottle somewhere and poured himself a drink, tossed it back, then offered the bottle around.

Estevan braced herself. Took a deep breath. "I will stay, of course. I'm sorry, but I must ask you, each of you, to join me."

"Maybe they won't attack right away," said Julie.

"It's possible," said Valya. "They took their time at the East Tower."

"I'll stay with you," said Angie.

Kleigmann nodded. Yes.

"What happens," said Santos, "if I say no?"

"I don't know." Estevan wiped tears out of her eyes. "I honestly don't know what to do."

"Me, too," said Julie. "I'll stay."

"I don't want to do this," said Santos. "I didn't sign on for anything like this."

"I know," she said. "But we're department heads." She said it the way she might have said *warriors*. Or, thought Valya, *Spartans*. "We can't ask others to stay behind if we clear out."

"We ought to be able to squeeze a few more people into the *Salvator*."

"Life support is already overloaded," said Valya. "It won't take any more."

"I'll stay," said Ho. He looked as if he were in pain.

Santos shook his head. "I'm not going to do it."

"You don't really have a choice," said Kleigmann. "What are you going to do? Go out there and take a breather from one of your subordinates?"

Santos's eyes slid shut. His lips were pressed tight together, and his face was a study in agony.

Unless the *WhiteStar* arrived quickly, seven more would have to stay.

Estevan caught Valya's eye. "Better get the *Salvator* loaded and moving." She got to her feet. "I better go tell everybody."

Valya had been looking for an opportunity to exit, and that was it. "You're right," she said. "I better get going."

They all looked at her. How weak had that sounded?

Estevan got up. Shook her hand. Embraced her. "Thanks for everything you've done."

"I wish we could have done more." She said good-bye to the others, wished them luck, and with an overwhelming sense of relief, or guilt, got out of there.

THE CORRIDORS WERE almost empty. Eric had loaded the *Salvator*. Valya collected everyone else with a breather and told them to board. After they'd gone through the airlock, eighteen remained in the tower.

Two women stopped her to ask if she'd heard anything new from the *WhiteStar*. "It's about twenty minutes out," she said.

So were the globes.

One of the two explained she was scheduled to leave on the *Granville*. She was an attractive woman, about twenty-five, black hair, dark eyes. With a scared smile. Trying to be brave. "It's getting late," she said.

"I know," Valya told her. "I don't have details." She broke away and felt their eyes on her back as she hurried into the ship. Behind her, Estevan was calling everyone to the dining area.

SHE WAS RELIEVED to get back to the *Salvator*, to get on board, and close the hatch behind her. Put a barrier between herself and the Tower.

The interior was jammed. Thirty-plus people on a ship built for seven. Bill, aware that the airlock had shut, made his announcement: *"Everyone with a breather, please put it on and commence to use it. Thank you. If you need assistance, let us know."*

Eric appeared to help with compliance. Several of her passengers were crowded into the common room. Others, she knew, were down in cargo. She exchanged smiles with them, squeezed past, and went onto the bridge.

"Everybody on board?" she asked Eric.

"I hope so," he said. They were stacked on top of one another.

"How about the lander?"

"Lander's full." Thirty-five altogether. Plus Eric and herself.

"Moonriders are sixteen minutes away," said Bill.

"Where's the *WhiteStar*?"

"Estimate twenty-four minutes."

Well, there was nothing she could do about it. It was time to get clear. Get as far away as she could.

She activated the allcom. "Ladies and gentlemen, we'll be getting under way in about sixty seconds. We're going to take it slowly, but anyone who's not in a seat please find something to hold on to. I'll tell you when you can move around freely."

"What's wrong?" Eric asked.

She shook her head. Nothing.

Behind them, a female passenger sat on the deck in the hatchway. She was using a breather.

The ship's scopes had picked up the black globes. They approached side by side, straddling and slightly above the tube.

"Where's the *Granville*?"

"They made up some time," said Bill. *"They're one hour fifty-three minutes out."*

An hour and a half behind the moonriders.

"Bill, I assume you haven't been able to contact them?"

"Yes," he said. *"I've been in constant contact."*

"With the moonriders?"

"With the Granville. *I apologize. I misunderstood. No, I have been transmitting constantly to the moonriders. They do not respond."*

"We'd better get started, don't you think?" Eric's voice. Somehow far away.

"Yeah."

He activated his harness. He wasn't going to need it, and he knew that. He was sending a message.

Nobody subtler than Eric.

"Valya."

"No," she said.

"No what?"

"I can't do this."

Outside, the long narrow dock pointed toward the stars.

"Can't do what?"

"You're captain, Eric."

"What?"

"I'm going back."

"What do you mean, going back? There isn't time."

She got up. The woman on the deck watched them curiously. Eric grabbed her arm. Held on. "You'll be okay," she said. "You don't need me."

"You'll get yourself killed."

"I'll take an e-suit with me."

"What will you do with an e-suit?"

"If I have to, I'll jump off the platform." She shook her head angrily. No time to argue. "Bill?"

"Yes, Valya."

"When Eric tells you to, I want you to pull away to a range of three hundred kilometers."

"Okay."

"Do whatever Eric says. He'll be my alternate until you hear otherwise."

"Yes, Valya."

"Eric, the *Granville* will be here in about an hour and a half. The *Bloomberg* and the *Tanaka* are running right behind it. Set up a rendezvous plan with the incoming ships—"

"I can't manage this," he said.

"Sure you can. All you have to do is tell Bill what you want him to do, and he'll take care of it. Transfer everybody with a breather to one of the other ships. There isn't *plenty* of time to do it, but there *is* time."

"All right."

"After you've done that, get the people out of the shuttles. The shuttles *here*."

"Goddam it, Valya, I wish you wouldn't do this. I don't see what you can do for them."

"Eric, please—"

"Just tell me *why*."

She had no answer. Maybe she could help. Maybe she just couldn't bear the thought that Estevan was a better woman than she was. Or Angie. Or a bunch of other people.

She collected an e-suit harness from the maintenance locker. But it had no oxygen. The tank had been given to one of the passengers. She looked down at the young woman on the deck. "May I have the breather?" she said.

The woman stared back at her, frightened. "Why?" She had a Russian accent.

"It's okay. You won't need it. There'll be one less rider."

SHE DIRECTED BILL to reopen the airlock. Eric watched her leave the bridge. Listened to her reassure her passengers—*his* passengers now—as she passed through the common room. Then she was gone and the airlock hatch closed.

Dumb.

He changed seats. Felt his authority increase. He was the captain.

The young woman who'd given her breather to Valya still looked confused. He indicated the chair he'd just vacated. "Climb in," he said.

OTHER THAN VALYA, eighteen people were left in the tower, most of them gathered in the dining area with whatever they planned to take with them. Estevan sat up front with Julie, Angie, and Ho. They were talking softly, two conversations going at once. Estevan looked up, startled to see her. "What are you doing here?" she asked.

"Same as you. Trying to figure a way to get everybody off."

"Can't be done," said Ho.

"You've lost your mind, Valya," said Estevan. "Has your ship left yet?"

"Probably."

"Call it back."

"You need help."

"What can you do?"

"I'm still thinking about it."

"You've got a suit," said Angie. "You can jump for it, if you have to."

"I could do that." That was what she intended to do if necessary.

Estevan studied her. "I'm tempted to crowd everyone on board the *WhiteStar*."

"The cabin's way too small. No way you could do it even if you had an air supply, which you don't. You're lucky it can fit seven. They'll be on top of one another as it is."

"Well," said Julie, "welcome to the Short Timers Club."

ON THE DISPLAY, the moonriders were burning another set of accelerator rings. "That's the last," said Angie. "They'll be here in ten minutes."

The *Bergen* called in. "*We had a good jump, Origins. Will see you in two hours.*"

And the *Zheng Shaiming*. "*Two and a half hours,* Salvator. *We will be able to take twenty-six of your people.*"

They drank coffee, and nobody said much. Estevan sighed, put her cup down, and got up. "How far away's the *WhiteStar*?"

"Fifteen minutes," said Angie.

"Not going to make it."

"Don't be so quick to give up," said Valya. "The moonriders won't open fire right away."

Estevan seemed exhausted. "Good," she said, pushing herself out of her chair. "Glad you have things under control, Valya." Her tone had an edge. She got up, walked over to one of the other tables, and asked how they were doing. There was a whispered exchange between Angie and Julie, and it wasn't hard to interpret. Say good-bye.

All heads turned in her direction. People hoping she had news and immediately seeing she did not. Estevan managed a smile. "I want the people who are going on the *WhiteStar* standing by the airlock. When it gets here, we'll open up, get on, and clear out. Okay?"

They weren't going to be hard to persuade.

A telescopic window opened on the displays. They saw lights.

The *WhiteStar*.

TOA: thirteen minutes.

Estevan gently tugged Valya out of her seat and looked at the breather. "You, too," she said. "Go with them."

Valya wanted to say yes, please, get me out of here. Kleigmann nodded, smiled, gave her a thumbs-up. Angie mouthed the words *good luck.* Someone had mentioned that Angie had a family. Three kids.

And Julie and Santos, about whom she knew nothing.

And Ho Smith.

"We see you," said the *WhiteStar* pilot. *"Valya, we can see the moonriders, too."*

Estevan answered: "*WhiteStar,* I don't think you can beat them in here."

"Have your people ready to go. This will have to be in and out."

"We'll be ready."

"How many of you are there?"

"More than you can carry. We need you to take seven, plus two wearing your breathers. And one more who already has a breather."

"Seven exceeds our life-support capacity."

"It'll only be for an hour or so. You can exchange when the other ships get here."

"You're making me liable."

"It's an emergency, *WhiteStar*. Please."

"Okay. Do it."

Valya hated the moonriders. Absolutely and unequivocally. She would happily have killed whatever rode the globes had she been able to reach them.

Estevan was jabbing a finger at her. "Get going," she said.

Valya shook her head. "Not on the *WhiteStar*. I need somebody to get me a go-pack."

"Why?" demanded Estevan.

"Maybe I can buy some time."

"What? How?"

"I need a lamp. Brightest one you have."

SHE STRAPPED ON the go-pack and went out through the main airlock, past the people waiting for the *WhiteStar*. There were a couple of remarks, how come she gets to leave? Wish I had one of those.

Then she was outside. The gravity unit was located in the central deck. It projected in both directions, so there was a distinct up and down along the hull. It was tricky. Had she lacked the go-pack, she could not have maneuvered, and in fact might easily have fallen off the tower and drifted away.

She used the thrusters to climb the tower, which was mildly flattened at both poles. In the distance she could see the *WhiteStar*, a single point of light, growing steadily brighter. The stars seemed very far, and the collider tube was lost in darkness.

So were the moonriders. She didn't see them until they were on top of her. Two polished black spheres, dwarfed by the tower. She watched them approach, still side by side. She switched on the lamp and raised it above her head.

Eric picked that moment to call. Was she planning on getting aboard the *WhiteStar*? What was happening?

"No time now, Eric," she said. "Talk to you later."

"You are going to get clear, right?"

"Yes," she said. "Later." She moved the lamp back and forth, pointing its beam toward the globes.

They kept coming.

"Come on," she said. "React."

Gradually, they changed their angle of approach and rose higher in the sky. They were slowing down, keying on her. Maybe.

They moved into position above her, directly in front of where she stood. One on either side.

And stopped.

A good sign. She hoped.

She opened a sweep channel. If they had a receiver, they couldn't miss the message. "Hutch sent me." She tried to visualize Hutch in case there was a telepathic element to the communication. And Amy. "We are trying to evacuate. But we need more time."

No answer came back.

"Please do not fire on the Tower until we get everybody out. It's going to take a couple of hours." Did they know what an hour was? She visualized the *WhiteStar*. And somewhere behind it, the *Granville*.

It was hard to keep her voice steady and her knees from trembling.

Estevan got on the circuit: *"What are they doing?"*

"Just sitting there."

"Okay, Valya. You've done all you can. Get off. Get away while you can."

"If I get off, they might open fire."

"Let us worry about that."

She wanted to go. God help her, she wanted to get as far away as she could. But she thought she knew what would happen. "Give it a few more minutes."

"You're impossible."

"It would help," she told the moonriders, "if you would say something. We know you understand English."

Eric broke in again to plead with her to do what Estevan wished. *"Get away from there, Valya. Please."*

"Everything's going to be okay, Eric," she said. "Relax."

THE *WHITESTAR* BROKE into a cluster of navigation lights. Red and green to port and starboard. White light aft.

Lamps glowed on her commlink. The *WhiteStar* was talking to Estevan.

Valya took a step toward the globes. Looked directly at them. They held their position.

She listened to the air flow inside the e-suit.

The *WhiteStar* cruised in, slowed, slowed more, and disappeared below the curve of the hull. She felt the vibration as it connected with the dock.

The globes watched. She could literally feel eyes on her.

Don't shoot.

Below, they'd be waiting for the airlock to open. She counted the seconds. Noted how solemn the stars were. How far they seemed from this particular place.

She tried not to think what the globes had done at the other end of the hypercollider. What they had come here to do. How many they had already killed.

Below, the hatches would be opening. And Terri's people would be crowding into the ship.

The globes were waiting. Giving them time.

She could feel her heart beat. "Terri?"

"Hello, Valentina. Where are you?"

"Still on the roof. What's taking so long?"

"We're moving as fast as we can. Just another minute or two."

"Okay."

"You can get out of there now."

"Okay."

"Gotta go. Busy."

She wondered what would happen if she went directly for the globes? Took them head-on? Might they open a hatch? Offer wine and an evening's conversation? Or start shooting?

Lights appeared below the rim. The *WhiteStar*. It was pulling away.

"Terri."

"Yes? Have you gotten clear?"

"I'm still here. You get them all off?"

"All nine. Now please go away."

She looked up at the globes. If you were exactly at the right angle, you could see starlight reflected from the one on her right. "Where's the *Granville*?"

"Eighty-three minutes."

"Maybe they'll wait."

"Valentina—" There was no missing the exasperation in the voice.

The globes were moving again. Drawing closer together.

"Whoever you are," she said, "thanks for waiting. We need you to hold off for one more ship. It'll be a while."

It was beginning to feel cold inside the suit.

"I know you can understand me. I know why you want to destroy the project."

She saw movement out of the corner of her eye. And heard Terri's voice. *"Valya, get clear."*

A plate had begun to lift off the surface of the tower. It was disk-shaped, set in a cradle, and the cradle was attached by extensors to a base.

"You can have the place," Valya said. "We won't try anything like this again. Just please give us a little more time to get everybody off."

"Valya, get out of there."

On the far side, a second plate was rising. Angling itself toward one of the moonriders.

Each had targeted a globe.

They were gravity generators, part of the system used to manipulate local traffic. "Terri, this is not a good idea."

"For God's sake, Valentina, we're not going to sit here and let them kill us. Are you clear yet?"

The devices locked on to their targets.

"Wait!"

"Do it!"

"No, Terri. They—"

The tower trembled beneath her as power flowed into the generators. Lamps along the bases began to glow. The globes started to descend. To *fall.* Red lights blinked on, the same ones she'd seen at the East Tower, and those deadly beams flared out and swept the sky. Touched one of the generators. It exploded. Simultaneously, one of the globes plowed into the hull. Valya dived for cover, scrambling behind a dish antenna.

The metal shuddered beneath her.

When she looked again, one moonrider was *gone*. The other remained where it had been, while coral lightning played across the sky and sliced gaping holes in the tower. She jumped clear, igniting the go-pack. It pushed her up and out, away from the conflagration. For a moment, she thought she was going to make it.

chapter 43

I can't imagine what life would be like without the knowledge that death is inevitable. It is because of that single, overwhelming reality that we have the arts, religion, the illusion of love, and probably even architecture. It is doubtful whether, did we not see ourselves as helpless transients, we would appreciate life for what it is. On the other hand, being grateful is not that big a deal.

—Gregory MacAllister, "Death at Manny's Grill"

Eric recoiled as the sky lit up. His passengers, watching images on the ship's display screens, gasped obscenities and sobbed and held on, to the ship or to one another. They cursed the moonriders with unbridled fury and swore vengeance. They demanded explanations from God. And they wanted to know whether the *Salvator* could move faster.

He had heard Valya's transmissions, and he had no hope for her. Nevertheless: "Bill, get Valya."

"No carrier wave, Eric."

"I'll try it." He leaned over his commlink. "Valya, answer up."

Nothing.

"Valentina. Where are you?"

Where the tower had been, there was only darkness.

The woman with the Russian accent sat frozen, unable to believe what she'd just seen. Eric switched over to the deputy director's circuit. "Terri. Are you there?"

The globes had become lost in the carnage. He couldn't tell whether they were still there.

"Terri? Larry?"

Thick black smoke drifted away.

"Anybody? Anybody at all?"

My God.

He sat back, told himself not to panic. It didn't feel *real.* Close your eyes, count to ten, and it will go away.

The Russian woman's name was Alena. Somehow, their positions had reversed, and she was doing what she could to calm *him*. "Okay," she told him. "Everything okay."

There were voices on the link.

He ran a check with the four shuttles. One of the West Tower shuttles reported an apparent heart attack. One of Angie's engineers. They were doing what they could for the victim.

He asked Alena to walk back and check the passengers. She nodded, released herself from her harness, and left the bridge.

Mark Stevens informed him the *Rehling* was okay. The *WhiteStar* pilot said that she'd been hit by debris *"—got my tail feathers singed—"* and had lost thrust. A few minor injuries, but the ship was otherwise okay.

"Eric," said Bill. *"The moonriders are gone."*

"You sure?"

"Yes. I lost them during the attack. They are no longer there."

"Okay, Bill. Thanks." He used the allcom to inform his passengers. Moonriders had left. No immediate danger. There were a few rabid comments. And some cheers. Then he got on the circuit with the incoming ships and described what had happened.

He recorded a message for Mission Operations: "West Tower destroyed. We got almost everyone out. Ten probable dead. Including Valya." He hesitated before transmitting, as if the reality of the loss wouldn't take hold until the report was on its way. Then he let it go.

* * *

WITHIN A FEW hours, the survivors were safe and secure, though not without some adroit juggling and sharing of air tanks, some exquisite maneuvering by the *Granville* and the timely arrivals of the *Carolyn Ray* and the *Zheng Shaiming*. And, Eric thought, not without the deployment of his own organizational skills.

He had unloaded his passengers onto the *Ray* and was still in the area hoping for a miracle when a message came in from Hutch: *"Eric, I'm sorry to hear about Valya and the others. The Academy is proud of her, and of you. Unless you've already started back, transfer your passengers to one of the relief ships. When that's been accomplished, conduct a final search for victims. You probably won't find any, but look anyway.*

"When you're satisfied there's no one, nothing, to be found, come home. Bill tells me he's been instructed to do as you direct, so just tell him to go home, and he'll take care of it. The World Council is sending a couple of ships to investigate, but don't wait for them."

He watched it several times. Despite what she said, he knew the Academy wasn't going to be proud of him.

BILL BROKE THE silence. *"I'm sorry about Valya, too, Eric."*

"I know, Bill." He knew of no relatives. Not that it mattered. Hutch would see to contacting next of kin. He hoped she would tell them how Valya had died. "Let's go in and do a sweep, Bill. We're looking for bodies."

The tower was gutted, as the other one had been. The hull on which Valya had stood was ripped away. The smoke was dissipating; he looked out at charred struts and beams and a few battered decks.

He stayed two days. The other ships came and redivided the passengers. They asked if they could help. And they left.

When they were gone he did one last scan of the area and told Bill to take him home.

ERIC SAMUELS'S OCCASIONAL JOURNAL

AIs have a range of modes. They can be cheerful or morose, they can be sports enthusiasts or literary snobs, they can play chess at a range of levels, they can be irreverent or pious. Whatever the moment requires. It is what persuades us they have no reality in and of themselves. They are software and nothing more. No soul informs the electronic synapses, no mind looks out of its assorted sensors and lenses. When you are alone with an AI, you are alone.

The flight home will take three and a half days. For the most part, I'll probably stay up front, on the bridge. Where Valya's presence still lingers. And I can still take comfort in Bill's respectful silence.

—Wednesday, May 13

chapter 44

Fiction is unlike reality because it has an end, a conclusion, which allows the characters to stroll happily, or perhaps simply more wisely, out through the climax into the epilogue. But life is a tapestry. It has no satisfactory end. There are simply periods of acceleration and delay, victory and frustration, seasoned with periodic jolts of reality.

—Gregory MacAllister, "Valentina"

The news came first from the *Rehling*, relaying reports it received from the *Salvator*, the *WhiteStar II*, and the West Tower. They described Valya standing atop the sphere, confronting the globes. Trying to talk the moonriders away while the *WhiteStar* docked and took people on board. And the desperate run of the *Aiko Tanaka*, which blew its drive unit trying to get there in time.

Those who had witnessed the event, most of them watching through telescopes on the *Salvator*, or from the shuttles, had to have been struck by the sheer courage of the woman. She was wearing a go-pack and could easily have gotten clear. But she stayed. Even when the globes closed in, were obviously preparing to attack, when she had to know they were getting ready to fire on the Tower, she had stayed. She'd refused to leave Terri Estevan and the others.

But Hutch saw something else. She replayed the message she'd sent to Valya. *"I would have preferred to do this here. But you'll undoubtedly be getting a message from the people at Orion—"*

Damn. Why hadn't she waited? Send something like this to a woman alone in a ship. Alone except for Eric, which was the same thing.

"We haven't accounted for Amy's experience. If you can shed light on that, if you know beyond question that's another hoax, then let's just forget this pony ride. Turn around and come home."

She suspected, no matter what had happened at the West Tower, Valya would have been lost.

Her resignation had arrived, effective at the end of the current mission. But Hutch had tabled it. Hadn't intended to allow her to resign. Valya was to be terminated.

And so she had been.

Hutch sighed. My God. What had she done?

She relayed the incoming Origins traffic, without comment, to Asquith's office. The commissioner was still missing, although he'd left a message to the effect that he would arrive later that day "to see that everything was running properly."

Hutch directed Marla to connect her with MacAllister. She knew the media might already have the story, and she didn't want him finding out that way. But his AI told her he was unavailable. *"In conference,"* Tilly said. *"I'll inform him you called."*

"Please ask him to get right back to me."

"Of course, Priscilla."

Thirty seconds later Mac was on the circuit. Dark blue jacket, an ID tag hanging from his top pocket, a notebook in his hand. Looking worried. *"I just heard. They hit the other Tower."*

"Yes," she said.

"How many casualties?"

"Looks like ten. The report I saw says they got most of their people out."

"Well, thank God for that. Is Valya okay?"

Hutch looked away, and he knew immediately. *"What happened? She was in the ship, wasn't she?"*

"Apparently she tried to challenge the damned things. Stood on top of the Tower and delayed the attack while they got people loaded and out." She was struggling to control her voice.

"She was standing *on the* roof *when they attacked?"*

"Yes."

He lowered himself into a chair and stared at something she couldn't see. It was the first time she had seen him at a loss for something to say. Finally: *"You're sure?"*

"Yes."

His eyes slid shut. *"Okay."*

"I'm sorry."

"So am I." He shook his head. Fought back tears. *"We were planning on running the Galactic story in this issue. But it would get lost now. I think we'll wait."*

They stared at each other across light-years.

"Something else," he said. He had to stop to regain control of his voice. *"A couple of my people have been talking with some heavyweight physicists. You remember the notion that the hyperaccelerator might rip a hole in the time-space continuum? Whatever that is?"*

"You're going to tell me—"

"It's apparently not that far-fetched. We can't find anybody who thinks it's likely, but a lot of them say it could have happened."

"Moonriders to the rescue."

"That's what it sounds like. There was so much involved in this project, nobody wanted to speak up. Say something about Origins, and it was your career."

When he was gone, she got up and walked over to the window and looked down on the cobblestone paths and fountains. There were always visitors down there. They came to see the Retreat, which had been brought in from the Twins and reconstructed just north of the Academy. And the Library, with its wing dedicated to George Hackett, whom she still loved so many years after his death on Beta Pac III. She'd never told Tor about him because she'd never entirely succeeded in putting him behind her. There had been times she'd made love to her husband while visualizing George.

It was a Friday afternoon. End of the week. And she watched two kids with a dog running past the Library. She knew that Valya also would never go away.

THE FIRST INDICATION she got that Asquith was back came in the form of a memo. *"See me."*

You bet.

She walked into his office and found him on the circuit with someone. Audio only. He looked up and pointed toward a seat. She stayed on her feet. "Have to go, Charlie," he said. "I'll get back to you." Then she got his full attention. "You did the right thing. Getting that rescue fleet in place."

"Thanks."

"Congratulations. I'm sorry we lost Valya, but the Academy is going to come out of this looking pretty good."

She waved it away. "A lot of people are dead. Maybe we should have taken Amy more seriously."

"Listen. Hutch, we can't blame ourselves for that. We tried to warn them." He came around the desk, stood in front of it, leaned back against it.

"Was that Dryden you were talking to?"

"Yes. Why?"

She let the question hang. "You knew all along, didn't you?"

"Knew what?"

"About Valya. About the setup. You knew what was going on, and you let it happen. You lied to me. And you let me lie to the media."

"That's not so."

"Dryden denied you were part of it, but they couldn't have managed it without you. You might not have known the details of what they were doing, but you knew something was happening. You insisted on my assigning Valya to pilot the original mission. You set it up."

He hesitated. Saw it was no use. "Okay, I knew. And if you'd had any guts, Priscilla, I wouldn't have had to lie to you. This was something we needed. You and me professionally. The Academy needed it. And by God, unless you were willing to stand by and watch us close up the interstellar program and shut down everything we've worked for, you should be glad *somebody* was willing to put his neck on the line."

"We could have done it without the lies."

"Really? How? If you knew a way, I wish you'd have clued me in. And please don't stand there with that holier-than-thou expression. I didn't do this for myself.

"And to set the record straight: Nobody was ever in danger. Orion had a ship near the Galactic ready to go in and take everybody off had the need arisen."

She stared at him for a long moment. "You know, Michael, you're pathetic."

He was above such things. "I was thinking the same thing about you, Priscilla. You're good at running an established operation. But you don't have the courage to make the tough calls. You don't have any guts."

"Right. And how do you think the Academy's going to look when this story comes out?"

"Nobody can prove anything."

"The woman who first spotted the Galactic asteroid has given MacAllister a statement."

"I know that," he said. "I mean, nobody can prove *I* was involved." He stared at her, daring her to show he was wrong.

"Maybe not. Dryden might protect your back while he gets dragged through the courts. However that goes, *I* want you to resign."

The look of smug superiority went away. "If you try to blow the whistle on me, Priscilla, I'll implicate *you*. And you'll also destroy Valentina's reputation. Although I don't suppose you care about that."

It had been a long time since Hutch had wanted literally to throttle someone. "You're a political appointee, Michael. Nobody has to prove anything. A whiff of scandal, and you're gone. Hiram Taylor already doesn't like you very much. Doesn't like me either, but that's of no consequence. If he were to find out you were involved, your career would be over. And there'd be no need to bring in the media."

He had gone pale. "That's blackmail."

"Why don't you resign while you can still do so with your record intact?"

"You're a bitch, Hutchins."

She turned and headed for the door. "Cite personal reasons. Family concerns. That's always a good one."

VALYA'S MOTHER LIVED in Athens, a brother in Russia's St. Petersburg, and cousins in New York City and Albany. She took a deep breath and called the brother first.

He took the news about as well as she could expect, and stayed on the line while she informed the mother. When it was done, Hutch was emotionally drained.

Amy was next. She caught her on the way home from school. And couldn't miss the chill. *"What did you want, Hutch?"* she asked.

"You'll be seeing news reports soon, Amy. The moonriders hit the West Tower."

"I saw they were headed that way."

"We managed to save most of the people who were there. Seventy of them. And sixteen more from the East."

"Good." She sounded relieved. *"I'm glad to hear it."*

"I'll see that you get credit for it."

"I don't want *credit."*

"I know that, Amy. Nevertheless, you're responsible for so many surviving the attack." She smiled. "The media will want to know how it happened. You should think about what you're going to tell them."

"People will think I'm crazy."

"No, they won't. Not after we back you up. After what's happened."

"Thanks, Hutch." She was softening a bit.

"There's something else."

She tensed. *"What?"*

"We lost Valya."

"What do you mean, lost?"

Hutch described what had happened. When she'd finished, Amy asked whether she was sure, whether there was any chance. *"I'm sorry,"* Amy said. *"I knew she'd gone back out on the* Salvator. *It's hard to believe."*

"I know."

"She was a lot like you, wasn't she?"

"I'd like to think so."

NEWSDESK

MARKET RALLIES ON NEWS OF INCREASED EARNINGS REPORTS

Biolog Quarterly Up 36%

THREE DEAD IN BOATING ACCIDENT ON LAKE SUPERIOR
Collision in Clear Weather a Mystery

MANHATTAN VAMPIRE OPENS TO RECORD CROWDS
Latest Cole Thriller Sucks Up Millions on First Weekend

CARMEN, QUIGLEY TO MARRY
Couple Reveals Betrothal at Press Conference
Caribbean Honeymoon Planned

LOTTERY WINNER WILL NOT QUIT JOB
Highway Artist Feels Need to Create

CORRUPTION CHARGES IN SAN DIEGO
Hackel, Coleman Indicted
Judges, Police Also Believed Under Investigation

TEEN KILLS GIRLFRIEND'S PARENTS WITH AX
"Quiet Boy," Say Neighbors
"Hard to Believe It Could Happen Here"

TORNADOES WIN SEVENTH STRAIGHT
Kim Huang Homers in Tenth

chapter 45

It is not faith per se that creates the problem; it is conviction, the notion that one cannot be wrong, that opposing views are necessarily invalid and may even be intolerable.

—Gregory MacAllister, "Downhill All the Way"

The judge in the hellfire trial had not struck MacAllister as the kind of person who would have been prepared to take a stand against the popular will. He also had not looked particularly imaginative. Glock had reported that he was a Presbyterian, an occasional churchgoer, a family man with three kids. His actual religious beliefs were not on record.

Maximum George was a small, round man, balding, with black hair and enormous eyebrows. His expression had revealed nothing during the course of the trial.

MacAllister watched from his study while he entered the crowded courtroom, which immediately went dead quiet. He needlessly rapped the gavel a couple of times, did some preliminary business, then announced he was ready to deliver a verdict in the case of the City of Derby vs. Henry Beemer. *"The accused,"* he said, *"will rise and face the bench."*

Beemer and Glock stood together.

"Mr. Beemer," he continued, *"you have, it seems to me, just cause to be resentful about your early schooling. Young minds are open during those years, imaginations are especially fertile, and we trust adults to tell us what is demonstrably true. What is put into our minds at that period is not easily removed or modified. I hope that the Reverend Pullman will, despite the obvious strength of his religious convictions, take these matters into account when he enters his classroom in the future.*

"That said, I cannot find that the Reverend Pullman has violated any law, and even if he had, the attack on him would have been itself unlawful. Therefore, Mr. Beemer, I pronounce you guilty, and sentence you to three days in the county jail. I hope, sir, not to see you before me again."

GLOCK CALLED LATER.

"You didn't appeal," said MacAllister.

"It's a minimum sentence, Mac. That's as good as we're going to get."

MacAllister sighed. "It's a pity. The attack was justified."

"Maybe," said Glock. *"But you can't write the laws that way."*

LIBRARY ARCHIVE

So long as men and women are free, no one is safe. People will be in danger because others can't operate vehicles responsibly or shoot straight. Because physicians are sometimes incompetent and lawyers dishonest. But most of all they will be in danger from ideas. It is the price we willingly pay to be free. Nor would we have it any other way.

—Maria DiSalvo, *Lost in Paradise*, 2214

epilogue

> There is no justice. There are occasional acts of vengeance, or regret, but there's no real justice. In the natural scheme of things, it is not possible.
>
> —Gregory MacAllister, "Valentina"

Dryden and six others, from Orion, Kosmik, MicroTech, and Monogram, were convicted of conspiracy to defraud the government. They received substantial fines and were restricted indefinitely to their homes, with limited use of telecommunications equipment. Shandra Kolchevska and Miriam Klymer, both of whom had been at the corporate meeting in Asquith's office, were among them. Monogram's Arnold Prescott escaped conviction through a technicality.

Asquith resigned. Hutch was wrong in her assumption that rumors of a scandal would ruin him. He was, after all, a politician. As this is written, he is serving as the president's senior science advisor. Dryden never mentioned his name in the courtroom, leading to her suspicion there'd been a payoff somewhere. MacAllister declined to tell what he knew about the Terranova incident, as did Hutch. So Valya came out of it with her reputation intact. The world, MacAllister has written somewhere, needs all the heroes it can get.

The various corporations involved in the hoax are all prospering.

The World Council learned a lesson, although there are some who say it was the wrong one. They are in the process of arming government vessels. For the first time in more than a century, research into advanced weaponry is moving ahead. The first warships will be coming online by the time this is published.

Moonrider sightings have declined precipitously, and none that could be substantiated have occurred in recent months. Sources high in the World Council promise that, when the aliens return, we'll be ready for them.

Today, Valentina Kouros stands with George Hackett and Preacher Brawley and the other heroes of the Great Expansion, the people who have given their lives in the cause of furthering human knowledge. High schools and libraries in a dozen countries have been named for her, including one in Athens. Hutch, MacAllister, and Amy attended the dedication. As did four of the persons who'd escaped on the *WhiteStar*.

Another one for Amy to model herself after.

And maybe there should be some recognition as well for Vannie Trotter. Vannie is the woman who provided support for Amy at the museum. The two have since become close friends.

A FEW DAYS after the ceremony, Hutch resigned from the Academy. Have to take care of my daughter, she told the acting commissioner. And there's a son on the way. When Tor asked about the real reasons, she couldn't tell him. Didn't really know herself. Except that she couldn't go back to the office she'd occupied when she sent that last message to Valya. Anyhow, maybe being a mother *was* the real reason.

Eric Samuels remains at his post as public relations director. Those who work for him say he's a different man from the one they knew. One of them told Hutch he's learned how to be a good boss.

Senator Taylor has given up trying to cut off Academy funds. With the appearance of the moonriders, he lost his enthusiasm for the effort. "The world out there," he told *The New York Times*, "just doesn't seem as safe as it used to."

No one has yet been able to explain the phenomenon that has come to be known as Amy's Vision. No known method will project holographic images through a steel hull. That seems to imply some sort of telepathic capability. That possibility is reinforced by the fact that the moonriders were able to trigger memories of Priscilla Hutchins. But again, no method of thought transference is known, either.

Equally puzzling: Why did the aliens choose an adolescent to carry the warning when they had a major journalist and a ranking Academy official available? The best answer must be that their methodology would not have worked with the other two. Some experts have suggested that a young person would have a more open, and hence accessible, mind. MacAllister has reacted on several occasions by branding the idea preposterous.

The senator still hopes his daughter will come to her senses and develop an interest in law school. At the moment, it looks unlikely.

Regarding the attack at Origins, it does seem that somebody, somewhere, got the point. There was at first an outcry to begin rebuilding the hypercollider, at an increased pace. To show the moonriders they couldn't bully us. But there's been no concerted effort by the world's physicists to get it done. Some have even been quoted to the effect that we might have had a narrow escape.

MacAllister remains at the helm of *The National*. He still has dinner periodically with Hutch and her family.

The struggle against the Greenhouse Effect goes on. Democratic leaders everywhere are reluctant to raise taxes to pay for what needs to be done. MacAllister commented recently that Plato was right, that democracy is mob rule, that the voters can be counted on consistently to find the candidate with the fewest scruples and put him in office. Friends and acquaintances have noticed he makes more Greek references than he used to.